A Fictitious Reality

by Sean Donovan

First published by CreateSpace in January 2013

ISBN-13:
978-1482370928

ISBN-10:
1482370921

Printed in the USA

Table of Contents

Endurance

The last few days have been the most tumultuous time of my life. This six month trip has turned into both a blessing and a curse. In what seems like the blink of an eye, the world has turned completely upside down. Events have transpired out of my comprehension and control that changed the course of history and the world as I've always known it. Our trip to the remote island of Rahiti in the South Pacific has seemingly saved our lives, but also alienated my brother and me from the life we've always known. On the upside, we're living in paradise; on the downside, we may never see the rest of our family, friends or our home ever again. My brother and I simply wanted to escape the pressures of business and society and take a six month sabbatical to surf, relax and enjoy island life. We got way more than we bargained for.

Days of sorrow and frustration passed as I went through the motions of life. I prayed to the Universe and to God to help me through my grief and uncertainty. And just as I asked, I also received.

I received a gift in the form of an epiphany during my morning yoga session today. I had managed to let my mind go into deep meditation in spite of the fact I was surrounded by overwhelming beauty; the island itself as well as the 3 naked Rahitian girls whose lithe bodies were displayed in unbelievable positions all around me.

I somehow managed to let it all go – and when I did, thoughts of profound significance were downloaded straight into my soul.

These thoughts overcame me and filled me with a new appreciation of life. I surrendered to nature, my environment and the Universe itself. It was a liberating feeling. Brilliant ideas flowed into my open mind like waves onto the beach. One such idea was to make a list of everything that I was grateful for. This thought stuck in my mind amidst all of the other wisdom of the Universe. It was a great idea. It would help tremendously. I could hardly wait to do it.

I broke my meditative state and finished out the yoga session, but today I curtailed my usual bathing ritual with the girls and instead of taking a walk while air-drying, I hurried back to the Stan-dunk and towel dried my body. I popped open the laptop and began to type faster than I had ever done before.

My appreciation list went like this. "Today and now I am more grateful than ever for… My mind and body, my health, my brother, the safety the islands have afforded us, the bounty of food that nature provides for us, the perfect wave that Mata shares with us, the love and hospitality that Maruia and the tribe convey to us, the sunrise that starts the day, the stars that dot the sky and bring dreams to light at night, the dolphins that entertain, the fire that provides heat, the sand that cushions my feet, the water that we drink, and the fond memories that we think. I thank God for the gifts that we receive each day and my ability to still work and play. I am grateful for the shelter provided by the Stan-dunk and the hard

1

work, planning, money and love that went into building it. I am grateful for every experience that I have ever had in my life – both good and bad - because I realize that I am a culmination of my past experiences – and I am grateful for them and who I have become. I am grateful that I woke up and put two feet on the ground today."

As I wrote and read and then wrote and read my list some more, I truly realized that I am the way I am for a reason. It became crystal clear to me that everything I had done in the past made me who I am today. Today I truly am a culmination of my past, my being, my habits, my likes, and my dislikes. This was my essence. I realize that my entire life had been purpose driven and the purpose was to drive me to survive this hardship. It was my drive and my purpose that is supposed to help me through the most trying time in my life.

My daily workouts and yoga regimens have kept my body healthy and my mind stress free up until this point. It was clear that I had become accustomed to this for a reason. The purpose now was to continue the very things that had kept me stress free and healthy in the past and use that focus to take my mind off of the catastrophe of "The Day."

My affection for water has kept me well hydrated and toxin free and has helped me stay in great shape and peak performance in spite of my stress. I needed to remain focused on my water intake and the collection of rain water on the island.

My vegetarianism has made it easy for me to survive where only fruits and vegetables are readily available. My routine detoxification, fasting and cleanses have made it easier for me to go long periods of time without food and has helped keep my digestive system balanced and in line. Now I needed it more than ever to end the constant butterflies and subsequent nausea that had taken over my insides.

My past interactions and differences with my brother prepared me to deal with the emotional turmoil we were going through and the entirely different ways we were individually dealing with it. My planning, meticulousness and OCD nature made it possible for me to plan this trip in the first place. And, ironically, it was this trip that removed my brother and me from harm's way.

My plans, gifts, generosity and kind heart helped the Rahitians improve their lives on the island. Now it will be their turn to help comfort Lance and me through this painful time. My love for other people will now bring love in return to help the emotional pain of my losses.

My determination and my drive will make it possible to persevere through this unbelievable situation. This purpose driven life has made my focus clear and my reason for living more evident. I am supposed to be here. I am supposed to live and not perish back home. I am supposed to support my brother and help him through this crisis. I am supposed to be me.

I became in tune with the now and the fortunes I have had. My former life became detached and more of a dream. My daily rituals, chores and interactions on the island became my new life and reality.

Lance, however, had become engrossed in the past and more detached from the present and the beauty around him. My mission became to focus on what I could control and I prayed that other things would come into my control as a result. I hoped I could lead by example for Lance and be strong for him so that he may follow my lead and get through this time.

My mind shifted - and it felt great. I made up my mind that I would no longer live in the past. Since "The Day," my body was in the South Pacific, but my mind was back home in the States. This dual life that I had been living the last couple of weeks was tearing me in half. I realized that the secret to finding peace was to let go of the past and live my life in the present. I knew that I now had to focus on the now. It was the only thing that mattered – it was the only thing that I could control. I realized that if I could focus on what I could control that other things may come into my circle of influence as well. I told myself that my past was a former life and that I had been reborn here right now. The slate was clean. My past was over. I was a culmination of my past and that is what the past amounted to – and nothing more.

It was this mind-shift that completely changed my attitude about my life and the events of "The Day." It was this mind-shift that brought back good feelings and appreciation of life. It was this mind-shift that made me realize that there were more important things than dwelling in the past and living in sorrow. I would do the best I could do. I would do as much good for others as possible. I would help those in need as I had done with my contributions on the island. Right now I realized that Lance needed me more than anyone else. I must convey my mind-shift to Lance and I must take his pain away and put enjoyment back into his life. I became intent on helping my brother through his emotional crisis.

Lance was resistant and distant, but I was persistent. I made chores fun as I turned them into games. I tried to interest him in these games/chores to occupy his mind and body. I tried to persuade him to join us for yoga. I gave him the best looking fruits that I grew and harvested. I always kept some herbs on hand for a quick "smoke-n-smile." In spite of all of my efforts, Lance seemed to only be interested in surfing. Even eating and sleeping took a backseat to surfing. I was glad that there was something that he was still passionate about, so I made a big deal about it and made an adventure out of surfing each day with him. I told him of my epiphany and my appreciation and gratitude list every time we surfed. I explained that he had been passionate about surfing all of his life because the culmination of that was now the realization that surfing was to be his savior and release. He dismissed my thoughts as "some crazy voodoo shit", but we didn't stop surfing. We visited Mata Utu daily for our daily dose of surf. I treated it as a pilgrimage. This pilgrimage was not only great exercise and a mental release, but quality time spent with my brother. Some days were better than others and I came up with the mantra that there were no such things as bad days – only better ones. Some days Lance spoke, some days he didn't. It didn't matter though – at least we were together.

Today in Mata Lance broke down emotionally as we sat on the point waiting to take the plunge. We had stopped earlier on the hike for a minute to pick a couple of mangoes. Lance had been quiet all morning holding true to his stoic tone and somber attitude. The kayak trip to Mata this morning consisted of me singing a little and discussing some plans to finish up some small additions and details on the Stan-dunk. His responses had been minimal. Instead of talking, he focused on stroking. Right, left, right, left. I

3

watched the muscles in his back and shoulders tense and relax from the right side to the left side. I recognized that one positive thing about this trip was that Lance had lost over 40 pounds and gotten into peak physical shape. It is amazing how depression can melt the pounds off of your body when you choose not to eat and when your focus becomes surfing. I really believed that the one thing that kept Lance going was our daily surf rituals – especially the trek to Mata Utu. The daily three to four hour round trip occupied our minds and bodies with something positive. It was just the two of us and nature. It was our escape from the escape of the trip. It was a time of physical exertion and mental relaxation which brought a euphoric high in spite of his ominous low. I knew Mata was the best therapy for both of us; however, I feared Lance was losing his grip and even his will to surf. Today that became evident.

I sat on the beach watching the waves build at the point on and then peel and break on the outer reef the entire length of the island. Today was a typical Mata right break. The waves were clean and glassy and almost double-overhead. I peeled and sliced my mango as I was mesmerized by the sea. I reached out to hand Lance the knife, but he didn't grab it. I turned to look at him and saw the saddest sight. He sat there on the rocky point in silence. His eyes fixed, yet gazing at nothing as tears rolled down his cheeks. He held his uncut mango in his hand tightly – in fact so tightly that I could see the pressure in the peel from the force of his fingers. I sat there with my arm extended, knife in hand. He did not even acknowledge me.

I turned my gaze away from him and retracted the offer of the knife for the time being. I returned my focus to the ocean. I wanted to say something, but couldn't find the right words. What could I say? I had felt the same way too before my epiphany, but I was now dealing with my emotions in a much different way. From the corner of my eye I could clearly see the tears streaming down his cheeks.

I remembered a beautiful July night back in Virginia Beach last year when Lance, Jasmin and I biked down the boardwalk to Tortuga's Restaurant. It was a gorgeous evening with low humidity and temperature in the mid 70s. I was out in front with Jasmin behind me and Lance bringing up the rear on his Townie bicycle. The pedals on my bike squeaked and groaned with every stroke and thrust of my leg. The symphony of sounds my bike made was music to my ears. I remember the night vividly. We rode past the pier and the smell of cotton candy and popcorn filled my nose and made my mouth water. Those common things were taken for granted - until now that they were gone. The thought and memory of that night was so vivid that I closed my eyes and returned to that exact moment in time – at least in my mind. I felt the breeze on my face and heard the sound of my bike in my ears. My mouth watered as I recalled the smell of the cotton candy and popcorn again. My face smiled wide from the good feelings invoked knowing that Lance and Jasmin were behind me biking. I really didn't have a care in the world then. It was a great feeling – a memory that I would hold onto forever. Nothing could spoil that or ever take that away from me. That memory was positive and engrained in my mind forever.

The mental replay of memories can have a profound effect on the mind and body. I chose to make them positive, but Lance remained stuck on the negative. The mental and emotional pain of the traumatic experience of "The Day" and the loss of our loved ones had really began to wreak havoc on the physical side and mental side of Lance's being. I learned through him that a broken heart and an anguished mind

4

can cause massive changes in your physiology. Particularly, there is a direct correlation between mental stress and intestinal health. This became evident in Lance's loss of appetite and subsequent massive weight loss.

Your attitude really can affect your appetite, hormone release, posture, and overall health. Even Lance's face had changed entirely. Lance became a hollow shell of his former self. I wanted so bad to help him, but I realized I had to also protect myself from his negative energy and emotional drain. I tried to find a comfortable distance, balance and energy exchange with him. Ironically, it was his demise that added to my appreciation of the health, life, environment and attitude changing and mind-shifting epiphany that I had experienced.

Sometimes truths in life are not clear and answers are not available by conventional means. Sometimes the only answer is to trust in the Universe and know that everything happens for a reason. I really believe that everything does happen for a reason. I had no idea what the reason was for this crazy world-changing event, so I gave up on trying to understand it and simply focused on what I still had – here in the now. I made the conscious decision to live in the now and appreciate it. There was absolutely nothing anyone could do to change the past. And the events in the world proved that the future is not guaranteed.

Music always invoked positives vibes for me, so I began to recall a favorite song that began to play in my head. I had listened to this song numerous times in the past – while driving in my truck in the city back home, practicing yoga at my house, waiting for Lance to meet me for a surf session, and many other occasions. This was one of my favorite songs and had remained in my playlist rotation for years, but it never had quite the same meaning as it did right now. The song is "Beach in Hawaii" by Ziggy Marley.

There was no song more perfect to describe my exact feelings at this moment in time. I could hear the music begin to play so vividly in my mind it was as if I had headphones on and was hearing the musical vibration directly in my ears. It was as if it was being played by a recording device. The sound of maracas shaking and the plucking of mandolin strings began the song and gave way to the lyrics from Ziggy's voice.

"On the beach in Hawaii. Hey - I wish you were here with me – walking on the beach in Hawaii. Playing on the golden sand - looking at the ocean now I understand. Love is like the poor man see - and I wish you were here with me – on the beach in Hawaii."

The mandolin strings intensified and increased in tone and pace as my pulse followed suit. The crash of a cymbal and the sound of drums began to play and build a crescendo as the lyrics came back.

"Since you've been gone away - I think about you every day. Don't you know I miss you much - and you know I need your touch. I'm on a rocky cliff. Oh, I wish you were here with me."

The drums got louder and the mandolin more profound. The female chorus kicked into my ears.

"I wish you were here with me…" Then Ziggy answered "On the beach in Hawaii."

I felt the groove and began to sing out loud myself – changing only a word or two to fit our exact situation and location.

"A little paka-lolo - and I say Mahalo. Ujjayi breathing - to get the real feeling. Stanley gonna let you know - that I wish you were here with me."

Then I changed the tone in my voice to match the female chorus as I sang more loudly and energetically "I wish you were here with me - On the beach in Rahiti… Oh I wish you were here with me… In Rahiti."

I then swayed my body and moved my head in accordance with the mandolin, drums and maracas as they played in my head. I thought of my mom and family, Claire, Jasmin and all of my friends back home and I pretended they were dancing and having fun right on the beach in front of me.

"Oh I wish you were here with me – on the beach in Rahiti." I sang and repeated the final verse over and over again until Lance finally cracked a fake smile, stood up, hurled his uneaten mango into the sea, grabbed his surfboard and jumped off of the rocky cliff in front of me.

Connie

The adventure started six months ago. I stood in the parking lot of the Richmond Deep Water Terminal and gazed with amazement at the culmination of 9 months of hard work, deep thought and a lot of money. The prize was a tractor trailer sized Conex box full of a rather unorthodox cargo load I lovingly nicknamed "Connie". Clyde stood next to me in disbelief and commented that it was "the most precious cargo he had ever had the pleasure of checking into his dock." Probably not, but after seeing my face almost every day or so for the last nine months, he made the comment out of appreciation for all of the effort that he saw go into packing this box. I also think he was buttering me up so that he might get some recognition or preferential treatment at the party tomorrow night.

Clyde was a mild mannered man of color in his early fifties. He worked the security gate at the Richmond deep water terminal. Most of his job included watching soap operas and talk shows (which he vehemently denied to defend his masculinity), but occasionally he would sign a truck driver in or out and direct them to their cargo box. Rarely did he leave the comfort of his 8x8 climate controlled box of an office unless it was to walk down to chat with me during one of my supply runs. He was perfectly content in his office watching the tube, watching the cargo yard or watching traffic pass by on the interstate from his small sliding window. He loved his job and always seemed cheerful despite the monotony.

I, on the other hand, would have gone stir-crazy if I spent more than an hour in his office. I may have been the only real breath of fresh air he got on a regular basis as he made it a habit of leaving his "box" for a few minutes to walk over to visit me while I unloaded. But after a few briefs minutes of visiting he would promptly return to his post. Today he stayed with me a little longer since it was a Friday afternoon and departures and arrivals at the gate were scarce. He also wanted to get more details about the setup for the party tomorrow.

Security on the terminal seemed like an easy gig – who was going to walk away with a 20 ton cargo box? There was only one entrance in and out of the terminal and it was past him – unless the box was leaving by ship – and in that case, it would require the use of the crane which Jim operated. Jim's view from atop the 60 foot crane was much more appealing to me than Clyde's window or TV.

The deep water terminal was a picturesque place despite the industrial setting and the hundreds of metal cargo boxes strewn, but stacked neatly all over the acres of the outdoor terminal. The landscaping and cleanliness of the terminal was also quite impressive considering it was not really a public place. I may have been the only one who ever appreciated the perfectly mowed and edged grass and the litter free asphalt that ran from interstate 95 all the way to the dock on the bank of the James River. I had the pleasure of not only visiting Jim's crane, but also driving it under his direct supervision on several occasions. It was a fun job for him and an exciting extra for me.

The guys at the terminal loved me. I brought a different element to their day whenever I visited. The only real contact they had with the public or "customers" were the ship's crews which brought the cargo boxes in by ship and the truckers who left with them on the back of their 18 wheeler tractor trailers. I don't think they ever had a customer like me before.

While the truckers and sailors bitched and complained about waiting during loading and unloading, I cheerfully unloaded my pickup truck into Connie at the end of my work day almost every day. I always stopped to take the time to say hi to the guys and quite frequently I brought them a snack or a beer at quittin' time. This type of behavior was in my nature and it conveniently afforded me such benefits as driving the crane, staying slightly after gate closure, and most importantly, Connie got a sweet spot to herself on the far side of the lot away from the incoming and outgoing congestion. She resided in a less used area of the terminal which made her easy for me to access on a daily basis. Apparently it was common to rent boxes and terminal space, but no one else visited and packed theirs every day. The other boxes would come in already loaded on truck or boat. Some would come and go the same day while others would sit and wait for their ship or truck to come in.

Connie had waited for nine months for her load to be complete and her ship was due to come in tomorrow. In celebration of that, I convinced Jim and Clyde to talk to the "powers that be" and authorize a party at the terminal.

According to the port manager, it was the first ever request to have a party at the terminal. The last party they had was when a former employee retired after 30 years of service. Sixteen employees attended by mandate (and for cake and soft drinks) and the party was over at quittin' time.

The party I was planning was quite different. My guest list was around 1200 deep. There was going to be live music, a beer truck or two, catered food and at least two of my friends were bringing their boats and mooring up to the dock. This party would not start until well after quittin' time and may not end until starting time the next day!

The terminal was an unexpected place for a party, which aside from its seclusion from anything residential made it even more appealing in my book. It would take a lot of ruckus to disturb anyone out here. Other attributes to the party place included nearly unlimited parking, a proximity of less than 5 miles from downtown Richmond and a gorgeous view of the river.

My Evite was testimony to the surefire success of the party. Out of 2400 Facebook friends and invited guests, 446 had RSVP'd yes on the 1st day alone and the list had steadily grown each day. Virtually no one had RSVP'd no. I anticipated that we would have almost 1000 RSVP's and if everyone brought a date, we would have about 2000 people at the party.

When I threw a party, word usually spread quickly as I had developed a reputation for being an excellent party planner and host. Not to be cocky, but when I threw a party, people came and always had a great time - often times it would be the talk of the town long after it was over.

This party was particularly interesting because of its venue and the secrecy that I had maintained about my project over the last nine months. I could not take all of the credit this time and I had a lot of help from friends and business contacts. John at the waste disposal dumpster company was providing dumpsters, trash receptacles and port-o-potties for the event. My friend Keith drove a beer truck for a local distribution company and his boss was more than happy to serve the event and even pull some strings to have the Virginia ABC board conveniently not know about the invitation-only event. A sailing buddy Dabney owned a limo company and he dedicated his fleet to this event on a Saturday night to make sure that everyone got home safe or sober. A friend of a friend knew someone who had a wedding party rental company and I negotiated a great deal on 500 chairs, a tent and tables. The catering was handled by the deli at Ellwood Thompson, a local health conscious grocery store, which I visited every day for all of my vegetarian food needs. Almost the entire staff of Ellwood gladly accepted my invitation to serve at the party (at no cost) and the owner appreciated my past business so much that he gave up the food at half price.

Music would be a real treat for the night too. I used my connections to score two very diverse and interesting music groups for the night. The opening act was to be performed by a guy known as "Mista Beat". He was a friend of a friend and gladly accepted the invitation to show off his talents and woe the crowd with his beat-boxing ability. I heard this guy perform once at a small local club, and let me say, he can make more sounds with his mouth than a full orchestra, a marching band and an electric synthesizer combined.

The main act would be the band "Earthtones", an environmentally friendly band whose members were former tenants of mine. As their landlord, I had "turned a deaf ear" to dozens and dozens of complaints about their rehearsals and late night jam sessions – now it was their chance to make it up to me. Even for free they were ecstatic to play all night at the party. Both performances were sure to please the ears of my party people.

I learned a long time ago that it is not what you know, but rather who you know that gets things done in life. The collaboration of these individuals plus some avid partygoers would make tomorrow night a huge success. The only thing I didn't have control over was the weather, but the forecast looked great for a nice September night outside. The party was budgeted at $7500 which was $1500 less than the cost of Connie's trip half way around the world, but the party figure paled in comparison to the $186,000 value of her contents. This party was exciting to me in every aspect – especially the announcement of my plan and purpose. I even made sure that the editor of Style weekly magazine, a writer and a photographer were there to chronicle the whole event which was sure to get some press in the next issue of their local magazine.

I was determined to make this party extra special because it would be the last one I would throw (in the US) for at least the next six months. I wanted everyone to talk about it and remember me while I was gone. Clyde assured me that he would miss me as he lit up a smoke and made his way back to the gate. I took advantage of my solitude and made my way down to my favorite "secret spot" on the bank of the river. It was a gorgeous view on a secluded, grassy section of the river bank. I couldn't imagine any other city that had a terminal in such a serene and scenic location, yet so close to the city and adjacent to the most major interstate on the east coast. I was high on life. This was no ordinary Friday. I could feel the energy in the air. I couldn't wait until tomorrow. I stood on the bank and reflected a bit. I knew I would miss this place, but I took solace in the fact that I would see some new places just as beautiful - and I could always come back here.

I said goodbye to Clyde at the gate and waved to Jim as I left the terminal. As I ascended the ramp onto I-95, I looked over to the right and caught a glimpse of Connie. I smiled with satisfaction of my accomplishment. Tomorrow she would be surrounded by food, booze, limos, family and friends. I knew I wouldn't be able to sleep tonight from anxiety and excitement, but I rolled home to try to get some rest for the full day of setup and partying that would follow.

I was exhausted and excited all at the same time. I broke my daily routine and resisted the urge to go from the terminal to the gym. Instead, I headed home to relax and unwind a little - I would need to be well rested for tomorrow.

When I arrived at my home-based office, I filled the Jacuzzi tub with hot water and poured a glass of wine to relax. While I waited for the tub to fill, I sat down at my desk and woke up my computer by nudging the mouse. As I waited momentarily for the computer to come out of hibernation mode, I stared thru the large glass windows in the front of my office out across Cary St. They were my "windows to the world" as I called them. I got more entertainment and interaction from people-watching all day than I did watching TV.

I clicked my internet browser and directed it to open my Evite account. I almost dropped a load when I saw the total "yes" RSVP's - one thousand one hundred and eleven - 1111. The amount wasn't as astounding as the number itself. Eleven had always been my lucky number. My first apartment number was 611. The garage I rented for my old auto restoration business was numbered M-11-11. It seemed as though every day, without fail, I managed to coincidentally look at either my phone, computer screen, clock, watch or navigation screen in my truck when the time was exactly 11:11 - am or pm - it didn't matter. The number always followed me - for whatever the reason.

I'm not really superstitious, but I assumed it to be good luck - since that always followed me as well. It was a sure sign that the party would be great. I was so enthralled by the number of RSVP's that I sat staring at the screen with a huge smile on my face.

I perused the invitation that my graphic artist friend had creatively produced. The animation on the Evite was original, apropos and priceless. It consisted of an aerial horizontal view of a semicircular cross section of the world from a south of the equator perspective.

To the right on the east coast of North America, an animated skyline of Richmond, Virginia rose from an otherwise flat landscape.

Then to the far left bottom in the middle of the blue animation of the ocean, a volcano and a cluster of palm trees and hibiscus flowers rose from out of the blue - literally.

In the air above the animated earth, there was a curved dashed red line originating from Richmond and ending in an arrow point at the tropical destination - much like you would see showing the path of an airplane from city to city. Midway through the dashed line was a large stork flying in mid-air with a diaper hanging from his mouth. In the diaper was a green cargo box with white lettering "Connie" on the side of it. The stork wore a hat bearing my contracting company's logo - FBI Contracting "Fix-Build-Improve" and he also had a name tag on that said "Stan".

A lot of detail went into the design with little or no direction or instruction from me. My designer explained that even though Connie would be making the voyage by sea on a cargo ship - not by air and certainly not by stork, she wanted to illustrate that Connie had been my "baby" for the last 9 months. It was indeed ironic that this project took as long to develop as the birth of a child. If Connie's trip went as planned from here, she would bring a new life to its destination - much like the birth of a child.

I loved the design. I also loved the text on the Evite, but I may be a little biased since I wrote it. It read: "Come join the departing party with the Duncan brothers as they celebrate Connie's departure to the South Pacific. You've heard the rumors, now come find out the details of our upcoming trip. You may not miss us while we are gone for the next 6 months, but at least don't miss our best party yet. Of course there will be food, booze, friends and fun. Music provided by "Mista Beat" and "The Earthtones". We will even have limos available to get you home drunk. Bring a friend, bring a smile, but most importantly - bring yourself! 1201 Deep Water Drive. Saturday, September 16th - 7 pm until whenever." That pretty much said it all and I think that the Evite worked effectively as it enticed eleven hundred and eleven people to respond "yes". I smiled with satisfaction.

I grabbed my glass of wine and headed to the Jacuzzi for some relaxation. As I sat in the bubbly, warm water of the tub, I tried to let my mind go and daydream about the island life I would be living in a matter of a few weeks.

The intrigue of the island was immediately replaced by thoughts of Connie and my preparation for her and the party too. I wondered if I had forgotten anything, but I knew that was impossible. I was always prepared - I even had checklists for my checklist. A detailed inventory log itemized all contents of the box. Battery operated power tools, generators, solar panels, two tough-book laptops, two satellite phones, lumber, nails and hundreds of building and construction components, weatherproof storage containers, household furnishings, sun block, insect repellent, 240 one liter bottles of FIJI water and even seeds from dozens of organic fruits and vegetables – but most importantly, 4 surf boards.

All 55,000 pounds of cargo was neatly and tightly packed to utilize every square inch of the 3600 cubic feet inside the container. It was the most organized mess you've ever seen. A designer/engineer created the packing plan from our inventory list and even laid out a detailed schematic on CAD to show exactly where everything was located and how it should be packed. The lumber was even packed in a specific pattern to minimize warping and cracking and everything was packed in the order in which we would need to use it.

Nonetheless, I began to inventory Connie's contents in my mind. Forty two sixty pound bags of concrete, twenty four sixteen foot six by six salt treated posts, fifty four two by six joists, 14 boxes of galvanized framing nails, eight 120 watt solar panels, 20 rechargeable batteries, two Bosch complete battery powered tool kits, 2 satellite phones, Toughbook laptops, chalk, string line, levels, hammers.... I needed to stop thinking about it - everything was there including the CAD drawings and plans as well as the CAD packing map of the contents of the box.

Even if I had forgotten something (which was not possible), there wasn't room left for a hair inside the cargo box. I consoled myself and calmed my OCD nature with the fact that I had renovated dozens and dozens of homes and rarely missed a detail. The planning that went into this trip was far superior to any planning that I had ever done in my life. The only problem in my mind was that I would be a long way from a Lowes or Home Depot where I was going.

I always exuded a cool and relaxed persona, but it was inherent in my nature to worry and stress inside about something all of the time. Maybe that was part of the reason I had yearned to take this trip - the South Pacific would be the perfect refuge from stress for me. And on that note, I exited the Jacuzzi, dried off and then went to sleep with peace of mind.

The next morning I awoke at my usual 6:45 am and was already in planning mode again. I ran through my daily to-do list and the party checklist in my head as I ate my bowl of fresh berries and granola. I then put on some reggae music as I commenced my routine morning yoga session. I found yoga with reggae to be the perfect recipe for clarity, calmness and relaxation. It also kept my back limber and my body in great condition for the demanding mental and physical stress that I put on myself each day. Today would not be ordinary, but it would certainly be as equally demanding as my typical day of work, working out, planning and constant interaction. I liked it though. I needed to stay busy to feel fulfilled each day.

As I practiced yoga in the floor of my office, I looked out the windows at the quiet street outside. It looked to be a beautiful day weather-wise. I wrapped up my 20 minute yoga session and strapped on my running shoes. I emerged from the office and was delighted by the crisp, fresh fall air outside. I started my morning run as the fresh air hit my lungs. It was exactly one mile each direction to the Smoothie King shop. The run was fairly easy for me especially since it was broken into two legs as I stopped to take a brief break and shoot down 4 ounces of wheat grass juice. The first mile of the run was a warm up and then the grass juice gave me an extra kick so that I was able to run at almost a full sprint for the second mile. I loved my morning ritual and knew that I was going to miss it very much, but I also knew that breaking routine and experiencing new things occasionally was what life was all about for me.

Today, like every other morning, I ran in my familiar urban setting and saw the same basic scenery and same people. In a matter of a couple of weeks my scenery would change dramatically. My mind flashed through images of the tropical paradise that I would soon visit. Aside from the beautiful beaches, scenic views from high atop volcanoes, crystal clear teal green water, lush tropical flora, crisp clean air and a pollution free environment like no other on the planet – my favorite thing about the island of Rahiti was the people that inhabited the paradise. I could not wait to return to the island, but there was still a lot of work to be done today and a party to host tonight.

After a quick shower, I headed out for my only business appointment for the day. It was an 8:30 am meeting with Mr. Brooks. Mr. Brooks was one of my top contracting and real estate clients. He had purchased more than a dozen houses through me over the last couple of years - all of which my contracting company renovated for him. Once renovations were complete, my real estate company then had the exclusive resale or management rights. I valued my relationship with Mr. Brooks as he "buttered my bread" on both sides with every transaction. He was an older, astute business man who had become one of my close friends as well.

This morning we were to conduct a final walk-thru on a very nice Victorian house we just finished renovating. Although I had a lot to do for the party today, it was imperative that I meet with him early because he was leaving town this afternoon to go to an out of town wedding and he would be unable to attend the party tonight. Plus, I wanted to get final payment from him for the project as well.

I beat him to the appointment in time to open up the house, turn on all of the lights and make sure everything was presentable. He showed up at 8:30 on the dot.

"Well, Mr. Duncan - nice to see you up and about early on such a beautiful Saturday." He said as he walked up the front steps.

"Yes, sir - same to you. I think you are going to like what you are about to see." I said as I extended my hand to greet him.

"Of course I will. I always do. That's why you are my go-to guy. I realize this walk thru is a mere formality, but I am eager to see this masterpiece and get you paid as well."

I shook his hand and was happy to be in his company. It was rare in my business that a client was actually on time, let alone eager to pay me. Other clients seemed to be on my back throughout their projects and then magically disappeared when it was time to make final payment. Mr. Brooks on the other hand, was opposite. This was the first time in over two months that he had been to the property. Last time he saw the property it was a dilapidated mess that had been sitting vacant for over ten years. I negotiated a great acquisition price for him and then immediately started a massive $184k renovation on the day of closing. Everything about the project had run smoothly and we finished almost two weeks ahead of schedule.

"Come on in sir and I'll give you the tour." I said as I invited him into the newly renovated house.

"Ok, let's make it quick. I've got a flight to catch and I still have to pack. And don't you have a party to tend to for tonight?"

"Yes sir, but don't worry about that. I've got everything under control. In fact, my guys should be there setting up as we speak. I just wish that you and your wife could make it to the party too. You may be the only folks in Richmond not there tonight."

"I know Stan, but this wedding... If it wasn't for the two weeks we are staying to sail in the Hamptons afterward, I might not even care to go. It's one of my nieces who I rarely see that's getting married and I'm expected to make an appearance."

We entered the house and I could tell he was impressed as soon as he walked in the front door. The smell of "newness" filled the entire house. The house was built in 1898 and with the exception of the original hardwood floors, mantels and brick exterior walls, everything else was new. I was proud of this project. After several years of building rapport and establishing trust, Mr. Brooks had finally given me carte blanch to design and renovate however I saw fit. He was always pleased; and after all, I was the one who had to sell or rent the final product. It was an excellent arrangement for both of us.

"Got your white glove, Mr. Brooks?" I asked in jest.

"It doesn't look like that will be necessary Stan. I think I could eat caviar off of the floor in here. How do you do it so efficiently? I've worked with dozens of so-called "class A" contractors over the last forty some odd years and every other one of them would always disappoint. I would come to their "final" walk-thru with a note pad and my hand would invariably be cramped from writing and the note pad would be full by the time I left. You son, are very different."

I smiled ear to ear and took his remarks to be a huge compliment. "It's all about the planning and the follow through, sir."

"Have you got pictures of the house?"

"Of course I do. Don't I always give you a DVD showing before and after shots along with progress pictures of the renovation work?"

"Yep, that's why I don't ever have to come to see for myself. But this one I really want to show my wife. She is going to want to move in here herself."

"Come on, sir - I hardly believe she's going to want to leave the mansion on the river and move downtown into this old shack. Isn't your garage bigger than this house?"

"Dunno, how big is the house?"

"3260 square feet exact." I answered immediately.

"Maybe it's bigger. Did you measure this one yourself, Mr. Meticulous?" He poked me in the arm with his comment.

"I filled it to the roof with water and then measured the volume of its contents and then divided that by the overall height to get the exact square footage to the micrometer, sir." I gave him a little elbow nudge to emphasize my sarcasm.

"Huh, that's what I love about you - hard working and still witty."

"Well, I'll be happy to come measure your garage for you in the same fashion. If you will let me borrow your Bentley, I'll come do it right now."

"Son, you keep up this kind of work and I'm going to give you my Bentley." I knew he was joking, but it was a pleasant thought. I could have bought a Bentley, but instead I just invested about the same cost in my Connie project.

We walked through the double parlor in the front two rooms of the house and he stopped to slide the pocket doors from their hiding place in the wall.

"Smooth as silk. Probably better than the day the house was originally built." He said with approval.

"I hope so. We have over 20 man hours invested in track alignment and adjustment alone. There are also new ball-bearing rollers on the doors capable of holding twice the weight of each door."

"Of course." He nodded his head in agreement as we made our way to the kitchen. When we entered the kitchen he stopped dead in his tracks. I saw him cut his eyes from the countertops to the wall cabinets to the exposed brick fireplace, but his gaze ultimately fixated on the chandelier. "Wow, what is that made of?"

"Hammered copper - it's one of my favorite features of the house." I proudly answered.

"It's gorgeous, how much did it cost?"

"Don't worry about it. It was within budget." I answered - assuring him it was ok.

"No way - I've seen a lot of lights and there is no way that one is within budget for a renovation like this."

He was right - it wasn't in the budget. If he knew what it cost, he may have a heart attack. I saw the fixture in the lighting store and fell in love with it. It went perfectly with the Saint Cecelia granite

15

countertops and the natural wood cabinetry. I used my negotiating skills to get the price down to only five times what the allowance was. I had no intention of charging him a penny over allowance though. Call it my gift of appreciation to him.

"Mr. Brooks, let's just call it a "little extra" in appreciation for your business and leave it at that."

"Okay, but there better not be a picture of it on the DVD - my wife is going to want to put it in our house." He winked at me and then returned his stare to the light for a few more minutes. It was thoughtful "little extras" like this that separated me from your typical run-of-the-mill contractors and he knew it.

"Ok, sir there's a lot more house to see. If you stare at the light too long it might break." I wanted to coax him from the kitchen so I could get this meeting wrapped up. I didn't want to rush him, but I had a lot of things to do today. It's funny how he was the one who started the tour in a hurry, but was now enthralled by the work and taking his time. He followed me into the den, but turned to glance at the chandelier one more time. His appreciation of the fixture made it worth every penny I spent on it. He stopped to admire the custom wood entertainment center and built-in shelves in the den and then we made our way upstairs into the bedrooms and baths. His smile grew larger and wider with every room we went into. We ended back in the foyer downstairs and he shook my hand.

"So, do you think it will sell fast for full list price?" He asked.

"Well, I have my best agent ready to put a sign in the yard and put it in the multiple listing data base tomorrow at a price of six-fifty like we initially agreed. Next weekend we will have our first open house. I'm confident it will sell, I just hope it sells before I leave on my trip so I can be here to personally hand you the check at closing."

"Yeah, that concerns me a little, Stan. You got time to catch coffee real fast and chat?"

"Sure. I'll lock up and follow you."

Damn, I was hoping to get the check and go to the bank to make a quick deposit before I headed over to the terminal. I wasn't a coffee drinker and I was afraid Mr. Brooks was upset that I was leaving. I locked the house and jumped into my truck and followed him over to the Starbucks. I grabbed a table on the patio and waited for him to come out with his coffee.

"So, Stan, tell me again why you are leaving for six months." He asked as he slid into the patio chair next to mine and got comfortable.

"Well, since you didn't invite me to go sailing in the Hamptons with you, I figured I would plan my own trip to the South Pacific instead." I cracked a big smile as I nudged him in jest.

16

"Son, you can go sailing with me anytime you like. You just have to ask. I've got a big sailing yacht in the Hamptons and a smaller racing sailboat in Deltaville just an hour or so away. Anytime you want to go, just let me know."

"I appreciate the offer, but the trip I'm about to take isn't going to involve any sailing - only surfing, relaxing, sunning, swimming, gardening and kayaking. And, oh yeah, we are building a community center on the island of Rahiti."

"Really, tell me about it." He sipped his coffee with an interested look on his face.

"Well, the whole idea started a few years ago between me and a few friends. I have traveled to the South Pacific before and actually spent two weeks there a couple of years ago. I totally "roughed it" and went island hopping in an outrigger kayak for 12 days and met some amazing people. I met an island community on the island of Rahiti which is not too far from Tahiti. There were several extended families living on the island and they took me in for a few days. I absolutely fell in love with their culture and way of life. They live very primitively by our standards, but they are so happy, peaceful and natural that they are conveniently oblivious to what the rest of the world has to offer. They live in grass huts, wear homemade clothing made from natural materials, fish for dinner and pick fruits, veggies and herbs from the plants that grow naturally on the island. The island is totally self sufficient and they have everything they need right there and rarely have to leave."

"How do you communicate with them?"

"Well, the younger generation on the island took advantage of an education system in Papeete, Tahiti that extends something like a scholarship to the local natives. Most of my generation and younger are actually well educated and speak somewhat fluent English. The elders speak only Tahitian and the natives your age speak a mix of Tahitian, French and English. Surprisingly, communication was not a problem at all as my younger friends were more than happy to translate between me and the elders. They were all very eager to learn about the rest of the world and our way of life back in the USA."

"Very interesting - and how have you kept in touch?"

"Well, there are no cell phones or computers in Rahiti. In fact, they don't even get mail there. About once a month or so my friends would go to Tahiti for a couple of days and would send me emails and mail from there. We have kept in touch on a monthly basis for the last few years. I promised them when I left last time that I would return - and now I am fulfilling my promise. My last night in Rahiti was one of the most memorable experiences in my life. I sat on the beach and watched the sun set behind me as the moon rose over the water in front of me. I was so enthralled with the island life, the people and the natural beauty that I almost threw my passport into the water and stayed forever. If I didn't have a business and family here to come back to I'm sure I would have stayed. I swore to myself when I left that I would return again when the time was right. I have been preparing to return since the day I departed. Now the time is right. I plan to make a big difference on the island when I return this time."

Mr. Brooks was very interested as he sipped on his coffee. "So what kind of difference are you going to make?"

"My plan is to improve their way of life without compromising their culture. We have so many things here that we take for granted. There, none of the same things matter. I could show up on the island with a suitcase full of cash and they would rejoice - not because they would spend it, but because paper money would burn in their campfire easier than dead palm leaves. Money is insignificant in their culture. The most precious resources to them are water, the earth, family and friends. What matters most is what you can contribute to the society. Their biggest fears are when it's going to rain again so they can get fresh drinking water and water for the plants or when a typhoon is going to come and destroy their village. I plan to contribute to the island in a way that is going to help both of their fears."

"What are you going to do?"

"Well, I have a Conex cargo container at the deep water terminal that will leave by ship tomorrow morning in route to Tahiti. There are enough supplies and tools in the container to build a community center large enough to house every resident of the island in the event a storm comes. I have also developed a canteen system that will utilize the roof and gutter system to collect rain water and store it for times of dry season. Think about this Mr. Brooks - how many times a day do you open a door or look out a window? Well, they have neither on the island. Having a safe, secure structure with hurricane proof glass windows and doors will be a huge improvement to the island. I have gone out of my way in my planning to design and engineer a structure that will withstand the forces of nature, but not taint the natural beauty of the landscape. I have everything planned out to the nth degree. Every nail and screw is inventoried."

"How are you going to supply power to the job site and what tools will you use?" He asked in a somewhat doubtful tone.

"All of the tools are battery powered or use pneumatic air cartridges. The batteries will be recharged by solar panels. We will operate our Toughbook laptops and satellite phones by satellite and solar power as well."

He nodded his head in approval and understanding. "So you will have computers and phones?"

"Yes, ironically I am going there to escape the "electronic leashes" that I rely on every day, but I do want to stay in touch with everyone back home at my leisure and discretion. I will be uploading pictures and updates to Facebook periodically so that my friends back home can follow our progress. Plus, I had to throw in the sat phones or else there was no way my brother would leave his wife for 3 months."

"So who is going? Just you and your brother?"

"Initially, my brother wasn't even in the equation. He is such a "homebody" that I didn't ever imagine that he would go. Several other friends and I came up with the plan, but none of them followed through. Either they couldn't afford to go financially or they couldn't leave their jobs and lives for extended periods of time. That's why I love being self employed and having a staff that I can rely on to handle my business while I'm gone. All of my friends talked a good game, but when it came down to making the final commitment and putting the money on the line, they all bailed out on me. I didn't care because I was determined to go by myself if I had to, but I finally convinced my brother to go with me. I had to entice him with surfing. He is a semi-pro surfer who lives at Virginia Beach and he is addicted to surf. There is no better place in the world to surf than the South Pacific. He is also a self employed Realtor and he agreed to go along with me for the first three months of the trip. Then several of my friends have told me that they are going to come and visit for a few weeks at a time once I get there and get settled."

"Sounds very interesting and it sounds like you have put a lot of effort into the planning - as usual. How much is this whole thing going to cost?"

"I'm glad you are sitting down because I wouldn't want you to pass out and fall when I tell you."

"Give me a shot - I've had more money pass through my hands than some people would earn in ten lifetimes." He said with a grin on his face.

"Ok, the contents of the cargo box "Connie" are worth $186k alone." Mr. Brooks' face lit up and he raised an eyebrow in disbelief.

"How did you pull that off and what the heck have you got in there, son?" He anxiously asked.

"Connie contains everything from lumber to laptops, seeds, water - you name it, it's in there. I have been packing it for the last nine months. Every job I did over the last year or so, I bought a few "little extras" for Connie - an extra 2x4 or tube of caulk here and there - one for the job, one for Connie - it all added up over time. It also made for a nice hidden business write off. I'd rather give my extra profit to my friends in Rahiti than the IRS."

"Now you're a man after my own heart. Good business sense - I like it. Did you say you have seeds in there too?"

"Yes sir. You know I've been a vegetarian for the last 15 years. I started collecting seeds from all of the fruits and veggies I ate over the last year or so. I vacuum sealed them and packed them away. I've always been an avid gardener all of my life - my grandparents instilled that in me. It is my hope to start a garden in the fertile soil of the South Pacific and introduce the natives to some fruits, herbs and plants that don't naturally grow there. The year-round growing season should yield some crops pretty fast. I researched the growing conditions and the existing flora on the island to ensure that I wouldn't introduce anything harmful to their environment."

19

"Of course you did, Stan. Is there anything that you don't take into consideration?"

I smiled and winked back at him "Rarely, sir."

"Well, do it - and do it while you are still young. How old are you and your brother?"

"I'm 35 and my brother is 32. But I learned a long time ago that age is only relative to how you look, feel and act. I hope to be as good looking and energetic as you when I'm your age." I had to butter Mr. Brooks up a little - he was a great looking man in his early sixties.

"I appreciate the compliment son, but you have a little something on your nose." He offered up a napkin as if to wipe my nose and imply that I was "brown-nosing" or kissing his ass. We both laughed out loud. "So when do you and your brother leave?"

"Well, we are having our "departing party" tonight in celebration of Connie's departure tomorrow, but we will remain around for the next couple of weeks until I get the call that she arrived in Tahiti. Once she is there, we will jump the next flight to Tahiti. Finishing your project two weeks early has made it much easier for me to see my way clear to leave without hesitation now."

He nodded in approval, but still had a slight look of concern on his face. "Are you going to worry about your business while you're gone?"

"Yeah, but I'm going to try not to think about it. I feel like I have put 9 years of effort into building this well-oiled machine and I am curious to see if it can survive on its own for a while. I have a great staff that is more than capable of handling everything for you while I'm gone. The business books I have read tell me that the best owner/manager is the one that is not needed - it means I have done my job well and built a company that is viable on its own - without me."

"True, but it's your personal touch that makes your business the best Stan. I will miss that."

"I'll only be gone six months - and if you need me, I'll jump a flight back home just for you." I said in a reassuring tone.

"I know you will." He breathed deeply with a sigh of relief - or submission - I couldn't tell. Then he reached in his pocket and pulled out a check and slid it across the table to me. I know it would normally be rude to study the check in front of the client - even though I have had clients forget to sign the check or make it out wrong, I trusted Mr. Brooks and this was probably the fiftieth check I had gotten from him. None of them had ever been wrong before. But this check caught my attention immediately. The amount was wrong. I had floated the entire job and agreed to one lump-sum payment upon completion - an arrangement I would never make for anyone else other than my parents and Mr. Brooks. The check should have been for $184,000.00 even, but instead it was for $200,000.00. I slid the check back across the table and shook my head.

"I'm sorry, but you gave me the wrong check."

"Nope, I only have one check in my pocket son and it is made out to FBI Contracting - that's still your company right?" He grinned at me as he raised his eyebrows.

"Yes, sir - but it is too much - $16k too much to be exact. I can't accept this."

"You can and you will accept it. Just consider it a "little extra". It might help cover some of the cost of that amazing chandelier - and your trip too!"

I surrendered, smiled and put the check into my wallet. I rose up from the table and hugged Mr. Brooks. I thanked him, said goodbye and then headed for my truck.

"Have a good trip. See you in six months." He said as I walked away.

"Yes sir. Have a good wedding and have fun sailing."

I had a major bounce in my step as I strolled to my truck. I just received a very nice unexpected bonus. That $16k would more than pay for the party tonight as well as my airline tickets to the South Pacific - and some of Connie's trip too. What a cool client. I got to the bank fast before the check burned a hole in my pocket. I was pleased to see my favorite bank teller working the window when I got to the bank. I quickly filled out a deposit slip - I loved all those zero's in the check!

"Good morning, Mr. Duncan!" the teller said.

"Good morning, Maria - how are you today?" I asked as I slid my deposit into the drawer.

"I'm good, but I will be better when I get off in a couple of hours. I can't wait to go to your party tonight." She said with a slightly seductive tone in her voice.

"And I can't wait to see your smiling face there either." I said as she received my deposit check and glanced up at me with an even bigger smile on her face.

"Quite a payday for you on this Saturday, huh Mr. Duncan?" She said with a coy look on her face.

I knew she had always liked me, but I couldn't tell whether it was me she liked or whether it was the figure in my bank account that peaked her interest in me. Either way, she was a cool girl and was always cordial to me and willing to help out with all of my banking needs and special requests.

"Yeah, not bad for a Saturday morning." I said non-chalantly. "I'll see you tonight." I grabbed my deposit slip and pulled out of the drive thru with the satisfaction of having finished another quality job. That transaction also concluded my business for the day. Now it was time to party.

I made a bee line straight from the bank to the interstate and headed south to the deepwater terminal. I cranked the reggae music in my truck to get me in the party mood. When I arrived at the terminal I could see my guys already setting up. Clyde greeted me with a smile and raised the gate and waved me on in. I wheeled through the parking lot past all of the containers and headed over to Connie. The band was setting up stage in front of her and the rental chairs, tent and tables were being set up as well. My project manager Robbie met me at my truck before I could even open the door to get out. I rolled down the window to hear what he had to say.

"Everything is on schedule as planned, Mr. Duncan. The port-o-potties are on their way and will be set up over there. I checked the wind direction to make sure the potties were downwind of the party set-up. We don't want to fumigate everyone with that smell. Oh, yeah Jim cleared the south side of the lot for additional parking, so there shouldn't be any issues there. And the beer truck is gonna park right over there."

"Well done Robbie. You're always on top of things."

I sat in my truck a minute and took in the site. There were over a dozen employees, friends and volunteers here already at 10am on a Saturday morning helping set up - all for free. Good friends are good to have. I hadn't heard from my brother Lance yet, but I was sure he was on his way up from Virginia Beach with his wife and a couple of their friends.

The weather was perfect and the setup was even more perfect. I noticed Jim operating the crane and loading cargo boxes onto the huge ship that was in port. I made my way across the parking lot and walked down to the dock. I stood there in awe at the size of the vessel in dock. There must have been thousands of cargo containers onboard. Connie would join them shortly - her 'ship had arrived' so to speak. Jim noticed me standing on the dock and beckoned for me to come up in the crane and join him. I climbed onto the crane platform and up the ladder to the machine.

"Come on in Mr. Duncan."

"What's up Jim? Working hard today?"

"Not as hard as your guys are down there. You've got a great crew." He responded.

"Yeah, I know. I also have some great friends at the terminal too. Thanks for clearing out the additional parking area."

"No, problem. I wanna make sure we got plenty of room. I heard you got over a thousand people coming tonight."

"That's right - last count was eleven hundred eleven."

"That's amazing - how do you know that many people?"

"Good networking and a history of throwing some great parties will bring people out every time." I said as I patted him on the back.

"Well, I'm happy to finally get to attend one of your parties. I get off at 5 and I will go home and shower and change and me and the wife will head on back over around 6:30. I don't want to miss a minute of it. Oh, by the way - I'm saving a sweet spot for Connie right on top center of the ship. I'll load her up first thing in the morning."

"Really? You're working on a Sunday morning?"

"Yes sir - when the ship's in port I work until she's gone." He proudly answered.

"You're not holding up the ship for the party or Connie are you?"

"Nah, couldn't do that. We got some cargo coming in by semi tomorrow morning anyway. I wanted to leave Connie in place so she could be the centerpiece of the party."

"Good thinking. I appreciate that. I'll see you later on."

I shook Jim's hand and climbed down the crane and headed over to the stage. I could see Todd and the band were busy setting up the speakers, amps, lights and instruments. Todd approached me as soon as he saw me headed his way.

"Hey Stan - it's not gonna bother anyone if we fire up a little tune-up jam session in a bit is it? We want to make sure everything is sounding good. By the way - this place is awesome. I never knew it existed. I must have driven by here a thousand times and never paid any attention to it. What a cool venue."

"Yeah, I picked the spot just for you guys - purposefully far away from all of my other tenants. So jam out all night long as loud as you want until your heart is content. I don't care if you stop traffic on the interstate out here!"

Todd laughed and started to walk away.

"Oh hey, one more thing Stan - where is this Mista Beat guy? We need to know how to set up for him. We've got everything miked up and a monitor set aside for him. Just need to know what kind of other equipment he is working with."

"His mouth and a microphone - that's it Todd." Todd shook his head in disbelief. "Just wait til you hear this guy." I said.

"Ok, mouth and a microphone huh?! We got plenty of microphones. When is he getting here?" Todd asked again.

"I'm not sure - he's coming in from New York today."

"Wow, you pulled an act down from New York for this party?" He said in disbelief.

"Sure, he's from all over. He's a traveling one man show. You're gonna love him."

"Ok, we'll see."

Todd turned back to the stage and barked out some orders to his band and roadies. I got a little vibration in my pocket as my phone began to ring. I pulled it from my pocket and popped my blue tooth headset into my ear. It was Lance.

"Hey, bro - what ya doing and where you at?" He asked in his surfer lingo.

"I'm at the terminal getting ready. Where are you?"

"Driving - passing Williamsburg now. We should be there in about an hour or so. I've got a caravan of about five cars following me. I brought the VB posse. We're ready to get the party started early, but we are all gonna be pretty hungry when we get there."

"No problem, I'm ordering pizza for my crew here in a bit anyway. How many more pies do I need to get?"

"Throw 4 cheese, 2 pepperoni and 2 veggie into the mix for us - I'll pick up the tab on that." Lance said.
"Right on bro. Do you know where you are going and how to get into the terminal from the interstate?"
"Yep, got it locked in my GPS. I can't wait to see the setup. Can I peek inside Connie too?"

"You bet. She's sitting here all packed up and her ship is in port. The beer truck should be arriving in a couple of hours as well. Put the pedal to the floor and drive safe. See ya soon."

I ended the call just as the band cracked their first notes through the sound system. The guitar screamed through the speakers and the drum beat echoed across the parking lot and reverberated off of the cargo boxes far on the other side of the lot. Wow - it sounded good - and loud too! I made my way down to my secret spot on the river bank to relax for a minute.

As I sat there on the bank of the James River I felt a huge sense of accomplishment. From my grassy patch here on the side of the river bank I had a familiar view of the serenity of nature in front of me with dense foliage, birds, and occasional fish breaking the surface of the water. The leaves had just begun to change colors for the arrival of autumn. To my back, a different view 180 degrees from that of the river extended from the bank of the river to the interstate.

The Richmond Deepwater Terminal had been a place that I had driven by hundreds of times in my lifetime, but never paid much attention to. The terminal was clearly visible as it was adjacent to interstate 95, but was hardly an attractive sight from the vantage point of the highway. It was certainly not a place that I ever imagined would consume so much of my time - let alone would be the location of my best party yet.

Acres of asphalt stacked high with steel cargo containers, cranes and 18 wheelers told the story of the world in transit. I got excited thinking about it. I loved to be in transit - even within my own home town. The idea of traveling had gripped me since I was a child. I had been all over the world for brief periods of vacation time, but I had never left home for such an extended length of time as I was about to do. I knew I would miss this place and when I returned and the trip was over I wondered if I would come back here to the terminal to visit. I doubted it as there were even more scenic spots on the river downtown closer to my home.

Richmond was one of the only cities in the country that had class-5 rapids in an urban setting. I loved being on and near the water - whether it was a beach, a lake or the river I had always been drawn to the water. I knew that in a matter of a few weeks I would be on an island surrounded by teal green waters, tropical plants and warm weather. I couldn't wait. I let my mind drift off into paradise for a bit. My daydreams were quickly interrupted by a buzzing and ringing in my pocket. I pulled out my blue tooth headset and popped it in my ear. It was Robbie.

"Beer trucks are here, sir. Keith wants to see you. Where you at?"

I didn't want to give up my secret spot, so I stayed aloof and told him to stand by as I discreetly emerged from the woods near the bank of the river. I hung up the phone and headed over to the truck.

"Miller Lite?" I shouted as I headed toward Keith and the truck bearing the Miller logo. "I thought I ordered Heineken!" I said in jest.

"Bite your tongue, Stan. There's a tap of Heineken on there just for you." We shook hands and he confirmed where I wanted the truck to be located. "Look man, I'm risking my ass and my ABC license for this. Only for you though, Stan." He stated with concern in his voice.

"Keith, I appreciate all of your help with this. I promise you that it won't be a problem. No one is going to drive away drunk and no one is going to know a thing about what you have done. It's just partying as usual for all of my people. All of the ABC agents will be downtown policing the bars. The only people that will be here are people that I personally know and invited."

I reassured him that his efforts were appreciated and he had no legitimate worries. I patted him on the back and he started to set up the taps.

"Look, since I brought the beer, have you got some ladies for me to meet tonight or are you keeping them all for yourself?" He asked with shy curiosity.

"I'm sure there will be plenty of ladies for all of the single guys here. I will make sure to introduce you to some of my friends. You will be pleased."

"So I hear you are quite the ladies' man, Stan. I'm going to just follow you around and ride your coattails all night. Throw a brother a bone if you would!" He said as he made a gesture as if he was a dog begging.

"I don't know where you get your intel, but I have some female friends who would be more than happy to meet the guy who brought the beer!"

We smiled and parted company as I headed back to my truck. I had a few calls to make and needed to do it in the silence of my truck. The terminal sounded like a full-blown party already with the band warming up, the crane going, the beer truck running and everyone shouting out directions during the setup. I decided to leave the noise and retreat to the solitude of my mobile office - my truck. Robbie and the crew had the setup under control and I wanted to watch the action from the peaceful quiet of my truck. I hopped in the truck and closed the door - silence was achieved. There would be plenty of noise and action tonight - right now I just wanted to relax a bit so I put on some soft reggae music on the truck's sound system.

I popped in my Bluetooth earpiece and dialed up the pizza shop. My friend Micah delivered pizza from a local Italian restaurant. I dialed him directly and put in an order for 24 pizzas. My next call was to my florist, but I hung up before the phone rang twice as I saw the flower delivery trucks already entering the gate of the terminal. Clyde checked the two florist delivery trucks into the terminal and pointed them in the direction of the stage. Robbie greeted them and directed them as to where to park. The flower delivery team consisted of three Hispanic males and one beautiful American female. It was my friend Sarah, the owner of the florist. She spoke directly to Robbie for a moment and then he pointed her in my direction. Robbie did a double-take, snapped his head around and his eyes stared a hole in her back as she walked away from him and toward me.

Sarah was a tall, blond, blue-eyed beauty with a perfect figure. She strode across the parking lot in her high-heels, short skirt and tight blouse - hardly an outfit appropriate for flower delivery. She smiled and sauntered across the lot toward me as her crew began to unload some giant palm trees and other tropical plants. I rolled down my driver's side window and directed her to get in the passenger side of the truck.

"Hello, gorgeous." I said as she entered the truck and closed the door behind her to escape the deafening sound of the band and terminal activity.

"Sorry I'm late, it took longer than expected to load up the palms this morning. I didn't want to pre-load the truck last night and have them sit in an un-climate controlled environment overnight. "

I cut off her apology and responded "Better late than pregnant right?" It had been an inside joke between us during the brief times that we had dated.

She leaned over across the arm rest console of the truck and hugged me and kissed my cheek. "I've missed you, Stan. It's good to see you again."

"Same to you, girl." I replied with a little less emotion than she had displayed.

She began giving a detailed explanation of the plants that she brought for the event. I watched her three workers unload each tropical plant as she gave a dissertation about it. My mind wandered off at the sight of the palm trees in their huge pots. I knew that I would be seeing the real deal in a matter of a few weeks. She scanned the terminal and the parking lot as she continued on about the types of palm trees, hibiscus plants and other flowers she chose for the occasion. I watched as the workers struggled to lift the heavy palm trees onto the stage as the band played.

"This is the first time I have ever been to this place. I didn't even know it existed. I must have driven by it a thousand times. What an interesting place for a party, Stan."

"Yeah, I'm glad you like it. The party will be starting in a bit. I've got some pizzas coming for you and your guys. I'm glad you could make it here with them. I see you are already dressed in your party attire, so I assume you will be hanging around to party and not work?"

"I hardly wore this outfit to work in. I admit that I wore it on the off chance that I would see you here this morning. As long as my guys are dressed to work, I can afford to look good and not get my hands dirty. I prefer to work with my brains." She said with a smile and a twinkle in her eyes.

"And so you do - beauty and brains - you have the perfect combination for success." I responded quickly as I winked at her.

"It really has been a long time since I heard from you, Stan. You must not be dating anyone?"

Her comment implied my lack of flower delivery orders that I usually utilized her florist for when I was dating someone. Although Sarah and I had dated on and off a few times, she didn't mind my business and she loved delivering flowers to my other lady friends. She was obviously still interested in me, but did not manifest any jealousy over my other exploits.

"Yeah, I've been laying low and staying out of trouble. No sense in getting involved with anyone since I am leaving for six months very shortly."

My response was met with a laugh "You, Stan Duncan - get involved with a girl? I'm sure you could still squeeze in a date or two on your way to the airport!"

Her commentary was in jest, but not far from the truth. I had remained aloof with her in the past and had dated many women in search for the perfect mate, but perfection had alluded me to this point. I pointed over to Connie.

"See that big green box with Conex written on the side?" I asked her as she followed my finger across the lot with her eyes.

"Yeah, I see it." She said.

"Well, that box is nicknamed Connie and she has been my date and the recipient of all of my affection for the last 9 months. I have stuffed her full of a valuable load and I plan to rendezvous with her for the ultimate vacation." Sarah blushed and flashed me a coy smile as she comprehended my innuendo.

"Got a load for me and any extra room on the honeymoon?" she said with an alluring tone in her voice. "You are certainly welcome to join us in the islands for a bit. I have extended the invite to many of my friends and you are certainly welcome to come too."

"I'd love to, but there is no way I can leave my business right now. It's such a stressful time - with the economy the way it is and all. I don't know how you can do it either Stan."

"Well, from my viewpoint there is no better time to go to the islands and escape when you are under stress."

"Maybe, but I deal with my stress daily with a cigarette and a glass of wine. It's convenient and quick medicine for my woes." She said with a satisfied tone in her voice.

"Sure, but there are other ways to handle your stress besides succumbing to the addiction of tobacco and alcohol. You should try things like yoga, meditation, a long run, surfing or watching the sunset. There won't be any cigarettes or wine where I am going and there will be no need for them either."

"Well, I would have to take a couple of cartons and bottles with me on the trip. I doubt I could even make it on the plane ride there without a smoke. How long is the flight anyway?" She inquisitively asked.

"It's about 4 hours from here to LAX and then another 14 hours from there to Papeete, Tahiti. There is definitely no smoking on the plane either. It is a perfect reason to quit - especially when you reach the islands and breathe that fresh South Pacific air."

Ironically, it had been her constant smoking that had really dissuaded me from pursuing any long term relationship with her. It baffled me how such a beautiful girl could smoke - it completely tainted her image when I saw her light up and puff. The smoking habit was especially puzzling as to why someone who chose to work around the sweet smell of fragrant flowers could enjoy the smell of cigarette smoke.

She answered by saying "I have a better reason to quit smoking."

"What's that?" I responded.

"Kissing you! I never smoked around you because I knew you wouldn't kiss me if my breath reeked of smoke. Guess what - I haven't had a cigarette yet today either." She said as she smiled and placed her hand on my leg and leaned closer to me. "Have you got time to take a drive and catch up on old times for a bit?"

The thought was very tempting and most guys in my position would have jumped on the opportunity - literally. But I had my mind in other places right now so I politely declined her offer. I broke the momentary awkward silence and changed the subject. "So, how much do I owe you for the plants?"

"You don't owe me a thing. They are on loan for the night. If you want to keep them, that's a different story." She replied as she sat upright in her seat again and removed her hand from my leg.

"Let me pay you something. Surely you have to pay your labor today. I don't want to put you out - I know times are tight."

I urged her to accept some payment as I dug into my console and retrieved my checkbook.

She pushed my hand and checkbook back into the console. "Look, I'm happy to help out today. As long as my labor can attend the party tonight, they are happy to work for free today too. Just take me to dinner when you get back off of your trip."

"Deal." I quickly answered.

"You must have already spent a fortune on this party anyway. How do you do it Stan? Why do you do it?" She inquired.

"Well, this party is possible through the generous efforts of other friends just like you. As for why do I do it - there is no reason to be successful if you can't share your success with loved ones around you. Parties like this will create memories and good times for people that will last long after the party favors,

29

food and booze are gone. I want to make a good impression before I leave - I want people to remember me when I get back." My explanation was answered with another question.

"I'm sure you will throw another party when you get back. Any reason to have a party is a good reason for you - right?"

She was right. Any reason to party and celebrate life with friends was a good reason to me. Right now, I had other things to do besides socialize with her. I picked up my Blackberry and scrolled through the screen at some emails and texts I had received in the last few minutes.

"I'm sorry to be rude, but I have some calls to make and emails to return and my brother and a bunch of his friends are on their way. The pizza will be here soon too - please help yourself. Let's chat again in a bit or later tonight at the party - Ok?"

I hoped that my comment and dismissal of her company wouldn't downplay my appreciation of her help. She understood and excused herself from the truck. She sauntered away with a purposeful sway in her hips. She predictably turned back when she was about halfway across the parking lot to see if I was still checking her out. I was, but my gaze was concealed by my sunglasses and my head was turned away as if I was looking in a different direction. I missed that girl too, but not bad enough to commit serious time and emotion to her.

About that time my phone buzzed again. It was my friend Claire. "'Good morning Stan, how are you today? Getting ready for the big night?"

"Yeah, I'm at the terminal right now getting set up. What are you doing?" I didn't really want to chit-chat right now, but I didn't want to be rude either.

"Well, I was wondering if you needed any help. I'm free all day if you need me. I'd love to be there with you guys." She said.

"We've got everything under control, but come on over if you like. Pizza is on the way, the beer trucks are here and the band is warming up. Bring your party clothes for the night and you can change here to save yourself a trip back home."

"Okay, I'm on my way." She responded quickly and eagerly.

Claire was a cool chick and would be no distraction or problem to have around. She could fit in anywhere, anytime. She was the type of person I really loved having around. I hung up the phone and smiled at the thought of her arrival.

I looked in the rear view mirror of my truck and saw my brother and his entourage entering through the terminal gate. His Range Rover was followed by several other cars. Clyde pointed them in my direction and they cruised through the parking lot and headed in my direction. Lance pulled up next to my truck and I directed him as to where to park. Of course, Lance's first request was to park where his truck wouldn't get "messed up". I assured him his truck would be safe where he parked, but I jokingly told him that there was a $10 parking fee plus an extra $50 for the private security guard I hired to stand guard over his precious SUV.

"Take it out of the $25 grand I put into the party and Connie". He replied. The only difference was that he wasn't joking.

"So, did you guys have a good drive up from the beach?" I asked him and his group of friends.

"Yeah no traffic at all, but I left a great surf session early this morning to come here." He responded as if he wished he were still in the water.

"Well, there will be plenty of time to surf once we get to the islands. Who wants a beer?" I asked as I walked his friends over to the beer truck. The music was deafening and we had difficulty hearing each other. Ron was the first to jump on the offer of the beer.

"Dude, I'll take a beer or two. What kind do you have?" Ron inquired.

"Well Ron, I have your favorite kind of beer for this party - Free beer!" I smiled and grabbed a stack of cups from the table in front of the beer truck. I began pouring the beer from the tap until Keith came over and relieved me of the duty. I introduced Keith to Lance, his wife Jasmin, Ron, Andy, Lee, Adam, Mike and Mike, Elizabeth and Kevin. Everyone got served a beer (or two) as they surveyed the scene of the terminal. I could tell it was definitely more than any of them expected.

"So where is she?" Lance asked.

"If you are referring to Connie, she is right there behind the stage." I said as I pointed to the large green box behind the source of the music. I walked over to the stage and gave the band the signal to stop playing.

Todd concurred "We were just about to wrap up the warm-up session anyway. We are going to grab a beer and then head home to change and get ready. We will be back at 6." I introduced the band to my brother and his beach friends as the band packed up. "Oh Stan, is our equipment going to be safe here unattended until we get back later?"

"Actually, why don't you put everything valuable in the green Range Rover over there. I have an armed security guard that is going to stand sentry over the truck today." Jasmin laughed out loud over my comment. "Yeah, all of your stuff will be fine right here on the stage until you get back. There is no chance of rain and no chance of theft either."

"Good enough" Todd answered as he and the band jumped off the stage and headed over to meet Keith at the beer truck.

"Finally a little bit of quiet time." I sighed with relief as we walked around the stage to the cargo container.

"Those guys sounded very good." Adam commented. "But very loud - this is a killer sound system setup. Who owns the equipment?"

"The band owns everything but the stage. They also do recording for other local bands as well. You are gonna love them and the opening act as well." I slid the key into the lock on Connie's door and jiggled the lock free.

"So who is the opening act?" Lee asked as everyone crowded around the cargo container to see what was inside. I stopped short of releasing the lever that kept the doors securely shut.

"Well, the opener is a surprise act that I prefer to keep secret. I don't want to spoil the fun by telling you too much." I preferred to keep all attention on Connie for the moment anyway.

"Isn't the opener a guy named 'Mista Beat'?" Andy asked before he was abruptly cut off by Lance.

"Dude, screw the bands and open the damn container. I want to see what we are taking to the island with us." I purposefully was slow and deliberate in opening the container to keep Lance and his friends in suspense as long as possible. When I finally swung the huge steel cargo door open there was a gasp and excited mumbling among the group.

"Holy shit Stan!" Someone said.

"Wow" Lance added.

"Could you possibly fit anything else in there?" Jasmin asked.

"There isn't room for a roach to take up refuge in there". Ron added.

"There you go guys. Nine months of hard work and a lot of money is right before your eyes." I proudly stated.

I could tell that everyone including Lance was impressed as they stood there motionless perusing the contents with their eyes. I hopped up on the base of the box and reached to the top of the neatly stacked load and retrieved a black suit-case like box.

"What the hell is that? The container has a 'black box'?" Ron asked.

"Yeah sure, so if it gets lost we can track it down." I said as I placed the black box on the edge of the stage. The group crowded around as I released the clasps that held the box shut. I opened up the box to reveal its foam lined inside which housed a letter and a fully charged satellite phone.

"It looks like something the Navy Seals or the FBI would use." Andy commented.

"It uses the same technology and the same communication and GPS satellites that they use." I answered.

"How did you get your hands on that?" Lee asked.

"Well, let's just say that I am 'the man'". I answered with a grin on my face.

"Stan the man!" Ron added.

Lance was getting a little jealous and was overwhelmed by the contents of the box and the attention it was getting. He changed the subject and asked "So what does the letter say?"

Before he could grab the letter from the box I answered. "The letter states that this is Lance Duncan's personal phone and line of communication to his beloved wife Jasmin. No need to try to use this phone for any other purpose as it only dials her number. Furthermore, all calls placed to her on this phone have been deemed a national security priority and will be transmitted in 32-bit encrypted 1800 mega-hertz wavelength signal strength." The group got a chuckle as Lance snatched up the letter from the box and unfolded it.

"I'm glad you see the importance (and humor) in a guy staying in touch with his wife. How many more black boxes are in there Stan? If you had a dedicated phone for each of your girlfriends, they would fill up the cargo container!" We all chuckled over Lance's comment.

Ron interjected "Which phone dials up the blond over there?" Ron gave a little head nod in Sarah's direction as she was on the far side of the stage with Robbie contemplating the placement of some more palm trees. "She is freakin' hot!" He added.

I reached in my pocket and pulled my personal cell phone out. "That's Sarah and this is the only phone that dials that number up!" Just to make a point I popped in my earpiece and dialed her number. The guys watched as she fetched her phone from the holder on her slender hip. "Hey girl, walk around the stage - I want to introduce you to some people." She looked over in our direction as she hung up, smiled and placed the phone back on her hip and began walking our way.

"You've got to be kidding me! Just like that - at your beck and call?" Ron exclaimed.

I smiled and didn't say a word. I knew my brother's single friends would love to meet her and I knew Robbie would enjoy the view from behind once again as she walked over to us. She was hot and she knew it and didn't mind showing off to anyone. She quickly sized up the group crowded around the cargo container doors as she stopped to pull two long-stemmed Stargazer lilies from an arrangement on the stage. She approached us with a huge smile on her face and extended a lily to Elizabeth and Jasmin. It was an act well received by the only two ladies in the group and a smart move by Sarah to dispel any possible jealousy from the other women. Sarah was good with the guys and the ladies too. She introduced herself to the group and then turned her attention to the open doors of the cargo container.

"Wow, Stan you have packed quite a load for this trip. I had no idea what to expect."

She climbed onto the base of the cargo container with her high heels. She extended onto her tip-toes to see as high as she could into the container. Her calves flexed as all of the guys stared a hole in her backside as she looked into Connie. She knew what she was doing. I called it 'pre-party entertainment'. Lance focused his attention to the letter from the black box to avert his stare and avoid any disrespect to Jasmin. He began to read the letter to further divert attention from Sarah.

The letter read: "Chet, G'day Mate! Hope all is well in your world 'down under'. Thanks for receiving my precious cargo. You will find the key along with the bill of lading and packing list in this envelope. Open the cargo box and you will find a black box in arm's reach. In the black box located top center overhead you will find a satellite phone. The phone will link up as soon as you turn it on. My number is programmed in speed dial - just hold down the #1 key until it says "dialing Stan". I am eager to hear from you as soon as Connie arrives. Please go to Rahiti and alert Hoanui and Arenui upon arrival as well. Thanks for your assistance and lending us a boat to unload and transport the contents. My brother and I will be en route as soon as we hear from you. Take care and I look forward to hearing from you soon. Stan"

Lance seemed puzzled. "So bro, I thought you had this thing planned out better than this." He said with doubt in his voice.

Before he could question me further I explained the situation he perceived as a dilemma. "Lance, the letter goes into the envelope containing the bill of lading. I just put it into the black box so that I wouldn't forget it or lose it. Tomorrow morning I will give the letter and the key to Clyde so that he can pack it properly. Chet will get the envelope when Connie gets there and he will know what to do. Don't worry about a thing. I've got it all covered."

Although Lance was my brother and knew me better than anyone, he had always remained my biggest skeptic. His skepticism was unwarranted as I had never once disappointed or let him down. I think that if he didn't plan it himself, it was in his natural instinct to doubt. I quietly pushed and held the #2 key on the satellite phone as I hid it in my pocket. Moments later Jasmin's cell phone chimed in her purse. She pulled her phone out and looked at the screen.

"Who the heck is calling me? All of my friends are here." She said as she fumbled to open her phone. She looked at the screen of her phone with a confused expression on her face. "It's a sixteen digit number I don't recognize."

"Well, why don't you answer it?" I asked.

She did just that. "Hello?" She said.

I turned my back to the group and pulled the satellite phone from my pocket and put it to my ear. "Can I speak to the object of my brother's affection please?"

The group got a chuckle from my antics. I handed the satellite phone over to Lance and he said a few words. He and Jasmin commented that the clarity of the reception was unbelievable. "Isn't it amazing that in a nano-second my voice is transmitted from this phone hundreds of miles into space and then beamed back down to earth to her phone when she is standing only a few feet away from me? No delay at all and clear enough to hear a pin drop in the background."

"It is really amazing" Jasmin agreed.

"So how much did that moment of fun cost to make the call?" Of course Lance had to express some concern over the cost.

"Who cares bro? The phone and account is in my name and I'm not worried about it right now. I will remind you of the cost when we get to Rahiti and you start burning up the minutes talking back home. I will transfer the bill over to you at that point. For now, let's just be thankful that it works and works well." I said.

"Agreed." He said and nodded his head as he handed the phone back to me. Ron reached out to intercept the handoff.

"Can I see that phone? I've never seen anything like it. It looks like something out of a sci-fi movie." He said.

"Sure, pass it around." I said as I let him take the phone from Lance. "It is a sweet piece of technology. It can connect to anywhere in the world from anywhere in the world. There is a built in GPS and global clock as well as tide charts, currency translator and tip calculator. There are other applications too - games etc... But I doubt I will be using much of that. The phone is strictly for us to keep in contact with you guys back home verbally. However, I can also connect the laptop to the internet via the phone in case the internet satellite link on the Toughbook laptop fails. I have another sat phone in Connie too just in case something happens to this one."

"Dude, were you a Boy Scout? Because you are always prepared!" Adam chimed in.

"Hey Stan, can I get the number to that Satellite phone too?" Sarah asked.

"Yeah, it's 757-236-1111" Ron interjected with a smile as he handed the phone back to me.

"Slick." Sarah said as she winked at Ron. I dialed Sarah's number on the sat phone and she began to ring instantly.

"Save the sixteen digit number into your cell phone. It will dial directly to this phone and shouldn't cost you anything extra to call from your local network. I don't plan to give the number to very many people as I am leaving to get away and out of contact for a bit, but you are special - so there you go." I said as I completed the call and put the phone back into the box.

"What about me? Am I special too?" I heard the familiar voice behind my back and then felt arms wrap around my waist and gently squeeze me. From the look on the guys' faces and from the voice and smell of her perfume, I knew that Claire had arrived. I turned and came eye to eye with my beautiful red-headed friend.

"Great to see you, Claire." I said as I returned her hug and she kissed me on the cheek. "Perfect timing - It's a party now! I was just about to lock up Connie. You can peek inside before I do so. First, let me introduce you to everyone."

I went around the group and introduced Claire to everyone and ended with Sarah. Claire glanced into the container a moment, raised her eyebrows and then returned her attention to us.

"So, what can I do to help?" She asked with eager excitement in her voice.

Sarah spoke up "Stan, I would like to get Claire's opinion on some of the flower and plant placements if you don't mind."

"Nope, not at all. You girls decorate until your heart is content." I dismissed them as the two of them headed over to the other side of the stage.

"Can we help out too?" Elizabeth asked. "Let's give the guys some time alone Jasmin."

Jasmin looked at Lance for approval before she accepted the invitation and followed Sarah and Claire over to the floral truck.

"You're in trouble now man!" Andy said to me.

"What do you mean?" I said as I closed up the black box.

"Don't play like you aren't dating both of those women. Now they are all over there comparing notes and whatnot. You're gonna be toast." Andy's cocky comment went unanswered by me as I non-chalantly placed the black box back inside Connie and locked her up.

"Dude, seriously - are you dating both of those women? They may be the two hottest girls I've ever seen - a blond and a red head too! I didn't know there were girls like that in Richmond. Wow!" Ron bubbled over with both jealousy and excitement. I just smiled and didn't say a word.

"So bro, how many girls are going to be here tonight that you have dated?" Lance asked with a tone of sarcastic jealousy in his voice as the other guys were all ears for my response.

"Out of eleven hundred guests?" I replied with innocence.

"Don't be coy man, no wonder you don't go out when you are at the beach - you've got your plate full in Richmond!" Adam added.

"My guess is about half." Lance chided.

"Dude, there is only one woman you should be concerned with and that's your wife - keep her close tonight." I sarcastically fired back at my brother.

"You don't have to worry about that - I always do. If anyone even looks at…" Lance was cut off abruptly by Ron.

"Chill, Lance - let us all live vicariously through your brother and learn from his ways. He is obviously the man. I had no idea." Ron said with resolve.

"Ok, seriously guys - it's not like that. Those two women as well as the rest of the party you will meet tonight are some of my best friends. It is irrelevant whether we dated or not - we are friends regardless. Just look." I pointed over to Sarah, Claire, Jasmin and Elizabeth as they were inspecting the tropical arrangements and chatting as if they had been lifelong friends. "That's how I roll. When you respect the ladies as I do, they will respect you back the same. Sex and 'dating' is secondary in my world. Friendship is what matters most."

"Yeah, and the looks are the icing on the cake." Lee added.

"Whatever, gigolo." Lance mumbled in a jealous tone. "So what time is the party over tonight?"

"Bro, you just got here. The party hasn't even started yet and already you are asking when it is over? Just chill and enjoy your time here." I said with frustration.

"The surf is going to be good in the morning and I want to get home before too late so I can get a dawn patrol session in tomorrow."

Lance couldn't stop talking about surfing no matter where he was or what he was doing. Surfing was everything to Lance. I enjoyed it as well, but it was a small fraction of my being whereas it totally consumed Lance's life. His whole life revolved around surfing and all of his plans and decisions were based on the surf report. It was an addiction, but a healthy addiction to him. He was passionate about the sport and passion to me was a necessary ingredient in a happy life. Seeing him happy on the surfboard made me happy as well, but tonight I wanted to see him happy at the party.

"So are you telling me that you are going to drive two hours back to the beach tonight?" I questioned his plans for the night.

"Uh, yeah - I never said I was staying the night. You should come back too and hit the surf in the am." His friends rolled their eyes at his comment.

"Surfing in the morning is the last thing on my mind tonight. There is no way I am driving two hours tonight or in the morning. I have eleven hundred people to entertain and a major cleanup to oversee in the morning. I really can't believe that you are not staying tonight."

"Dude, I never said…" Lance continued.

I cut him off before he could continue. "I know you never said you were staying tonight - I just assumed you were. I have plenty of room at my place for you and Jasmin and your friends. Plus, my friend manages a hotel downtown and he said he can hook up the rooms at a good rate for us. I even have limos to take you there." I said as I looked at my watch as to mimic Lance's constant worry about leaving in a hurry. "Why do you have to be such a homebody all of the time? You haven't been to Richmond in months. Stay and visit a bit. Go see some family in the morning and then we can catch up for brunch later tomorrow."

Lance shook his head and shrugged his shoulders. "I'll talk to Jasmin."

"I'm staying the night, Stan." Ron said as he stared over at Sarah.

"Me too." Andy and Lee added.

"So, who wants another beer?" I asked. The acceptance was unanimous and we all migrated over to the beer truck. I let Keith pour the beer as I made my way over to my truck and retrieved my I-pod. I went to the sound system and hooked the I-pod up, turned down the volume and played some reggae music. The pizza arrived right on time. I whistled for everyone at the terminal to come on over and feast.

The Departing Party

The party had unofficially begun. The VA Beach posse entertained themselves while my crew finished eating and then continued to set up. Sarah and her crew finished the meticulous placement of the plants and decorations and headed out. The port-o-potties came, the limos arrived and everything came together nicely. Clyde and Jim knocked off and headed home to change clothes and get their wives. I left Robbie in charge of the terminal briefly as Claire and I inconspicuously slid away to go to my place to change into our party attire.

On the short drive back to my place Claire made some observations. "I really liked talking to the girls. Sarah is a cool and beautiful girl. Elizabeth is a sweetheart. I think Jasmin wants to stay the night and is not happy that Lance is planning to drive back tonight. She said he rarely leaves the beach. How in the world did you convince your brother to leave her and go on this trip with you for six months?"

"Surfing. I tempted him with lots of surfing." I said with a smile. "This trip is going to be a huge challenge for both of us, but the rewards will be high. Lance will get limitless surfing, I will get the opportunity to experience a different life and we will both get some quality time together to bond and grow our brotherly love. This will be a life changing event for both of us. It's something that I've wanted to do all of my life, but now it is becoming a reality. The timing is perfect too."

"So the only way you could get him away from the beach is to take him to a place with better surfing?" Claire inquired.

"Pretty much." I answered.

"What about Jasmin? I only met her and Lance briefly, but it seems like they are pretty attached to each other. How did you pry him away from her for several months?"

"Well, although I really wanted it to just be a brotherly trip for a few months, I also extended an invitation to her out of courtesy to come as well. She declined and said she thought Lance and I needed some time alone together. I was glad she recognized that fact."

"So do you and your brother get along?"

"For the most part - yes. Most of our relationship is based on surfing and hanging out at the beach, but his entire lifestyle is only one dimensional compared to mine. I think he has always been slightly jealous of my ability to be diverse and fit in with any crowd at any time in any place. When I throw a party, hundreds, if not thousands, show up. When he throws a party, a dozen close friends show up. That's fine for him, but I like to be well networked and I love to host. This party and trip are prime examples. He wants equal recognition even though he contributed less than 10% of the cost financially and virtually no time planning and prepping. I really don't care though. I'm ok with putting my ego aside and giving him some credit too. My brother and I have been highly competitive all of our lives. In some cases our competitiveness turned into jealousy or heated battles over the most trivial things, but we love each other nonetheless. This trip gives us reason to have cohesion and really find out how we can complement each other by letting our strengths compensate for each other's weaknesses. I think it is going to be great for our relationship." I wrapped up the conversation as we pulled up to my place.

Claire grabbed her handbag and followed me inside as I held the door open for her. Within seconds of stepping inside, we were embraced in a passionate kiss.

"I better get my time in with you now. I'm sure you will be busy hosting all night." She said as she pulled my shirt off.

Within seconds we were completely naked and engrossed in a sensual lovemaking session. Claire was a passionate lover and wasn't afraid to demonstrate it. Ten minutes turned into an hour as we pleasured each other in every way possible. I adored everything about Claire from her sweet smell, to her silky smooth skin, her bright blue 'bedroom eyes' and her seductive tone as she moaned with pleasure. Our 'quickie' culminated with a simultaneous climax that the neighbors three doors down will be talking about for days.

After a few moments of post coital bliss, we cleaned ourselves up and then donned our party digs. Claire put on a beautiful knee-high dress that accentuated her curvaceous body. The autumn colors of the dress highlighted her red hair. It was tempting to stay and play longer, but I didn't want to leave the terminal too long.

Claire didn't take long to get ready - it was a trait I loved about her. She was naturally beautiful and required little or no makeup and styling. Her hair seemed to fall into perfect place as soon as she rolled out of (or into) bed.

In no time we were out the door and back on our way to the terminal - basking in our orgasmic glow the whole way. We were only gone briefly, but long enough for the guys to realize what was up. I caught a few jealous stares from the other guys when we got back.

Within an hour of our return, the party guests started arriving in droves. The reggae music still played quietly in random order from my Ipod. The limo drivers acted as valets at the front gate when guests arrived. My excitement grew as each car entered the terminal in eager anticipation of seeing someone I hadn't seen in a while. I did a double-take as I almost didn't recognize the handsome African-American gentleman clad in a three piece suit who was standing at the main gate. I quickly made my way over to the gate.

"Clyde, what the hell are you doing man? You're not at work tonight! Where is your wife?" I asked as I gave Clyde a little nudge.

"Hey Stan, great turnout so far. The wife is over there with Jim and his wife. I thought I would just come over here and... I feel comfortable at my post." Clyde said shyly.

"Nonsense, come on over here with me. I want to introduce you to some people." I said as I put my arm around his shoulder. I walked him over to the beer truck, grabbed two beers and then introduced him to a group of my friends. "This is the man responsible for the whole terminal. In fact, he also made the party possible." I started the conversation off and then left him with the group as they began to ask him logistics and details about the terminal. Clyde smiled at me in appreciation as I walked away.

I surveyed the party with my eyes. Lance and his VB posse seemed happy and content. Claire was being a great hostess and acting as a liaison between groups, but still finding a second or two to give me a wink with her bedroom eyes in passing. Robbie and my employees were dressed in crisp company uniforms and hats as they mingled in the crowd with beer in hand. A couple hundred people had arrived so far. The food was out and in full service. Everything was set.

I heard a chorus of female voices call out my name from behind. I already knew the deal before I turned around. Two limousines full of ladies pulled up behind me. It was the ballerinas. About two dozen young ladies rolled out of two different limousines as the drivers held the doors open for them.

I had been a sponsor to the Richmond Ballet for years and had become best friends with a few of the ballerinas who worked part time at the smoothie shop. I was like a big brother to the girls. On several occasions I had even hired them to help hostess some of my previous parties. Tonight it was their turn to be pampered.

The girls filed out of the limos in exquisite evening attire and lined up single file to hug me and kiss my cheek. Talk about a rock-star moment. Everyone at the party was aware of their arrival - and their affection toward me. I played it cool and escorted the ladies over to the food and wine. Some of the girls went straight to the dance floor and began showing off their dance moves to the reggae. I glanced over to Lance's friends. I thought I may have to call in the paramedics in case the guys had a heart attack! Ron gave me a 'thumbs up' from across the party.

I couldn't stand to watch over a dozen beautiful ballerinas dance alone on the dance floor, so I did the proper thing - and joined them. I busted out some dance moves of my own to the dancehall reggae as I alternated between the ladies - spinning them, dipping them and impressing them with my moves.

Everyone stood around and watched in amazement, but no one joined in until I managed to coax some of the guys onto the dance floor to introduce them to ladies in need of dance partners. I danced my heart out and my legs off as cars steadily streamed into the terminal. There was a short backup forming on the ramp onto the interstate. I was glad my friend Gunner was working security and traffic detail as an off-duty police officer tonight.

Suddenly, my attention was immediately diverted to a tall, black gentleman dressed in a blue suit, yellow shirt and green tie with matching green top-hat. He was standing off to the side with two gorgeous young black ladies dressed in full evening gowns and excessive jewelry. They stuck out like sore thumbs at the party. I slid off the dance floor and made my way over to them.

"Sorry I wasn't here sooner, Stan. Traffic on the Jersey turnpike was brutal."

"Not a problem - your timing is perfect. You ready to take the stage?"

"I'm always ready."

"Do you want an introduction?"

"Nah, this reggae jam is the perfect intro. I'll handle the rest."

"Do you need anything?" I asked.

"I just need a microphone, but can you set up my ladies with a table somewhere? We got some CD's and stuff to sell if that's alright."

"Of course." I motioned for Claire to come over and I introduced her to Mista Beat and his lady friends. She escorted the ladies over to a table by the food while I walked Mista around behind the stage and Connie - out of sight from the crowd. I grabbed a microphone off the stage as we passed and handed it to him.

"Crank the bass and tell the sound guy to kill the reggae after the next song is over." Mista instructed.

"No problem, man. Good luck." I tapped him on the shoulder and I reemerged from behind the stage. I walked over to Todd and passed the instructions along to him.

As I walked back into the party crowd, someone stopped me and asked "Who is the pimp?"

"You'll see." I responded with a smile on my face.

No sooner than I got the words out of my mouth there was a loud "Boom!"

People looked to the sky in unison as they expected to see a thunderstorm moving in. It was no thunderstorm though. It was the booming bass of Mista Beat.

He remained off stage and out of sight, but broke into a beat that mimicked the rhythm of the reggae. "Boom, boom, boom - boooom. Tacka, ticka tack-tah,tah,tah. Shaloka-loka- Baummm. Boom, boom, boom - boooom. Wah, wah, wah, - wooom."

The crowd looked around to see where the sound was coming from. It was amazing as it echoed off of everything in the terminal making the source of the sound indiscernible. This was gonna be good I thought to myself.

His beats grew in volume and pace with the song. People who weren't previously dancing began to nod their heads and sway their hips to the rhythm.

"Tah, tah, tah - booom."

Mista built his own crescendos with the reggae and then faded off harmoniously through the song. At the ending of the next song he began a drum roll like I've never heard with his mouth.

"BBBBRRRRRAPPPP-tap-tap-ticky-tap-tap-tap- baummm-wocka wap."

The music stopped and he jumped onto the stage and busted into a musical medley with only microphone in hand. The sounds he made were amazing and immediately captivated the audience. The dance floor became packed as people flooded closer to the stage.

"Oh yeah, I thought. This is definitely gonna be good." I was a huge fan of bass and there was no shortage of that in our sound system tonight.

Todd ran over and found me. "Dude, this guy is incredible! I just hope he doesn't blow out our sub-woofers before we get to play."

"Yeah, he's pretty talented isn't he?"

"How does he make those sounds with his mouth?" Todd asked.

"I dunno, but my ears like them."

"I think he should have been the headliner and we should have opened for him. He is going to be a tough act to follow." Todd commented.

"You'll be fine. I know you like to jam all night so I didn't want to limit your time by putting you on first."

Todd nodded in agreement and walked back over to the sound board. Other party goers gathered around me to find out more info about this guy.

"Stan, who the heck is this guy? How does he do that with his mouth?" Everyone asked.

I remained cool as I bobbed my head to the beat and answered "Yeah, he's pretty good isn't he. He's got some CD's for sale over there." I pointed to the table where the two ladies were setting up with Claire.

43

"What's his name - where is he from?" The questions continued.

"His name is Mista Beat - and he rarely misses a beat!" I assured.
I jumped back onto the dance floor and cut a little rug with the ladies. Claire joined me and we both took turns dancing with some of the ballerinas too.

What a great time. The sun was beginning to set. Cars were still rolling into the terminal. The place had come alive. By my estimation there were almost a thousand people here already. The food and booze were holding out nicely and all of my help were manning their posts graciously. The party was going smoothly due to the hard work of others and my meticulous coordination of the event. Ironically both had also led to the overwhelming success of my contracting company over the last 9 years as well. It was great to see a plan come together whether it was building a house or throwing a party.

Mista Beat worked the microphone for two hours non-stop until he tossed his top-hat into the crowd and signed off with a final "BOOOOOMMMM." I jumped up on stage and took the microphone from him and gave him a thank you and post-performance introduction.

"Ladies and gentlemen... Mistaaaaaaaaa..... Beat!" I said in my radio announcer voice.

I loved to hear the bass in my own voice carry across the crowd and echo back to me from the banks of the river and the cargo containers in the lot.

The crowd began to chant "Mista Beat, Mista Beat... Mista Beat!"

He took a bow and leaped off the stage and into the crowd. I watched as people flocked to him with CD's and pens in hand - ready to get his autograph. Mista looked back up on stage at me as he smiled and winked.

"If you haven't already done so, make sure to pick up Mista Beat's CD which is available for sale to the left of the food." I informed the crowd as I pointed in the direction of his lady friends. "Now please allow me to bring up another very special guest." I scanned the crowd. "Lance, where are you?" I didn't see him. "Lance Duncan - please come to the stage."

All of a sudden Lance came into sight as Ron and Andy ushered him through the crowd toward the stage - apparently against his will. He wants recognition, I'm going to give him a heavy dose of it! Lance got to the stage and reluctantly climbed up to join me.

"Family, friends, business associates and all - please give a warm welcome to my brother Lance. He came all the way up from Virginia Beach to join us this weekend and he will be going all the way to the South Pacific to join me on 'the trip' for the next several months. Give him a warm round of applause because, without him, this trip and party would not have been as special." I decided to put him on the spot. "Lance, have you got anything to say to the crowd?" I asked as I handed him the microphone.

He stammered for a moment and then composed himself enough to say "It was great to meet some new people tonight. Thanks for coming out to see us off. Jasmin, I'm gonna miss you baby. And... Surf's up Dude!"

I knew he would throw a surf reference in there. He handed the mike back to me and hopped down off of the stage and slid back into the crowd.

I continued speaking to my party people. "So many of you have been asking me what this 'trip' is all about. Some of you have even questioned my sanity for leaving my business and home for so long. Some of you have expressed desire to join me. And almost all of you have some curiosity as to what the heck we are doing and why."

The crowd cheered and jeered at me. Some people even began to chant "Stan-the-man, Stan-the-man." Even though I loved the affection, I quieted the crowd and began my story with a simple question.

"Have you ever just wanted to get away?" Everyone burst into jubilation over my question.

"Have you ever wanted to do something different?" The cheers continued.

I waited for the noise to subside.

"Well that's where my life is right now. I've built a business, a reputation and a great network of friends here in Virginia, but now I want to share my success with some friends far removed. As many of you know, I am a traveler. And thanks to my travel agent mom - where are you at mom?"

I scanned the crowd and immediately noticed her standing near Lance - my stepfather was holding his hand up pointing down to her.

"Hi mom - everyone say hi to my mom." The crowd obliged.

"Well, thanks to my mom, I have had the pleasure of seeing some exotic places. I have met some amazing people and experienced totally different cultures and ways of life. One such place was a chain of islands in the South Pacific known as the Society Islands. You may be familiar with such places as Tahiti, Bora Bora, and Moorea (where the book Mutiny on the Bounty took place). But you've probably never heard of the island of Rahiti. That's our destination. I spent two weeks island hopping on an outrigger canoe in the Societies and landed on the small, sparsely inhabited island of Rahiti. I absolutely fell in love with the island natives that live on Rahiti. Their way of life is so different than anything you can imagine. There are no cars, no traffic, no cell phones, no computers, no nine-to-five jobs and most importantly - NO BILLS!"

The crowd erupted into cheers.

"Money doesn't matter in Rahiti. What matters is family and friends. What matters is what you can contribute to society. What matters is appreciation for nature, the environment and healthy organic home-grown food and clean refreshing water. With that being said, I want to take this opportunity to thank some of my great friends and acknowledge their efforts that helped make this party such an amazing success tonight. Their contributions were priceless and abundant. I want to thank Ellwood Thompson and all of their wonderful employees for volunteering their services and providing the amazing and healthy food tonight. I want to thank Keith for all of the refreshing beverages tonight."

The crowd erupted into applause.

"Thank you, Sarah from the Flower Shop for all of the lovely decorations and plants. Thanks to John for the sanitation and bathroom usage. Thanks to River City Limos for providing transportation to anyone who needs a ride home tonight - PLEASE don't even think about drinking and driving. Your car will be safe here overnight - take a limo home. Thanks to Mista Beat for regaling us with his oral attributes and thanks, in advance, to Todd and the Earthtones who will play the remainder of the night. Thanks to my "FBI guys" for all of their help. Thanks to Gunner - you out there? - for providing security and a lawful presence."

Gunner heard me from all the way across the terminal and he sounded his siren to acknowledge my accolades.

"A big thank you goes out to Clyde and Jim and the Richmond Terminal folks who made it possible for us to utilize this amazing location for the party. Most importantly, thank you - everyone who came out to party tonight. I hope you will enjoy it."

Everyone cheered loudly and began chanting "Stan-the-man, Stan-the-man" again. I tried to act humbled, but soaked up all of the attention like a Christmas ham soaks up honey glazing.

"So the reason for the party - as if we really need a 'reason' to have a party - sits behind me. Ladies and gentleman, the star of the party - Connie."

I turned and gave a bow in front of the big green Conex container behind the stage.

"Connie here has been my life, my wife, my project, even some may say my obsession for the last nine months. I have packed her full of supplies every day for the last nine months. She contains everything from concrete to lumber, solar panels, laptops, surfboards - and even a collection of seeds from 47 different species of fruits and vegetables. Everything we need to survive and thrive in the islands is in there. The purpose? As I stated earlier, I want to make a difference. The supplies in Connie are more than sufficient to build a typhoon-proof community shelter on Rahiti to house the villagers during incoming storms. The seeds I collected from my vegetarian diet over the last year will bring a bounty of new non-native fruits and vegetables to the island. I have the materials and supplies necessary to build a gutter and canteen system to collect, capture and store rain water to bridge gaps during dry seasons on the island. The computers, solar panels, tools and satellite technology we are taking there and leaving behind will not only help my Rahitian friends become more educated and better prepared for approaching storms and life in general, but will also enable them to still maintain their self-sufficient lifestyle without compromising their culture."

I paused to take a breath, a sip of water and reflect for a moment.

"When you go home tonight, imagine your electricity, water, cable and phone have all been turned off - that's life on Rahiti. But they don't miss those things because they've never had those things. The next time you open a door or look out a window - whether it's on your car, your home or your office - realize that there are places in the world and people in the world that have never seen a door or a window. The next time you plan a vacation and book your hotel room or cruise cabin - ask yourself this - 'Am I really seeing a different world and experiencing a different way of life?'"

I paused a moment to let the crowd absorb and internalize the rhetorical question I'd just posed to them.

"For some of you it wouldn't be a pleasant option to give up the things you are accustomed to in life - and that's ok. Just know that there are many other cultures and customs that are different, but good in their own rights. Imagine how much more peaceful the world would be with that kind of acceptance and appreciation. Just know that there are still areas of the world that have managed to evade the modern world's influences. I plan to make a difference in Rahiti, but I plan to do it on their terms and with the utmost respect to the environment and their culture. My Rahitian friends have extended an open invitation to any of my friends that would like to come and visit. Hit me up on Facebook for details. Once Lance and I go, we will be posting pictures and updates on Facebook often to document our lives and progress on the island. I will miss everyone and hope to see you again soon - either in the South Pacific or at the next party!"

The crowd showed their appreciation by responding with a wave of head nods and smiles.

"Without further ado - I turn the party over to the Earthtones for the remainder of the night." The crowd erupted into cheers as I jumped off the stage and tossed the microphone to Todd. The Earthtones took over the stage and struck the first notes on the guitars.

Claire was the first to greet me in the crowd. "Wow, some speech. I think you missed your calling. You should have been a DJ or a sports announcer." She said.

"How about a dancer?" I replied as I grabbed her hands and started spinning and swinging her on the dance floor.

We danced for over an hour. Besides dancing with one of my best friends, I was in heaven because I was with 1100 other people who all seemed to be having a blast too. I even noticed Ron and Andy on the dance floor in the midst of a group of ballerinas. Ron saw me look over at him and he gave me the thumbs up sign. I scanned the crowd but didn't see Lance and Jasmin. I figured they were having fun too somewhere. I hoped that Lance would change his mind and stay the night. No sooner did I get the thought out of my head when I felt a tap on my shoulder. It was Lance and Lee.

"Great party, bro. We're taking off though." Lance informed me.

"The party was a 'Stan-dunk', dude!" Lee said with certain authority as he held us his hand to hi-five me.

"A what?" Lance asked of Lee.

"You know, like a slam-dunk, but instead a Stan-dunk - as in like, 'Stan Duncan'. The party went off like a slam-dunk man. What an epic event, bro." Lee added as his hi-five turned into a brief brotherly hug.

Lance rolled his eyes in somewhat jealous disgust.

I looked at my watch. "It's not even midnight yet. Stay the night, man. We are all going to go to brunch tomorrow once my cleanup crew gets started."

"Nah, I want to get home before too late so I can get up early for..."

I cut him off and finished his sentence ..."Dawn patrol surf session. I know, but can't surfing wait this time?" I asked with a bit of frustration.

"No way man. You should come too. You need to get all of the practice you can before we hit the South Pacific swell." He argued as Lee mimicked him in jest.

I cut my eyes over to Claire who was clinging to my left arm. "Trust me when I say that surfing is the last thing on my mind right now. We can surf until our hearts are content in a matter of a couple of weeks. This is a once in a lifetime party. I'll even let you use my bed tonight if you stay." I fired back.

Claire chimed in agreement "Yeah Lance, it would mean a lot if you stayed. It will be fun."

"No chance. Everyone is already in the cars waiting. Except Ron and Andy - I think they are going to stay." Lance answered.

"Yeah, Ron and Andy aren't going anywhere." I said as I looked over at them on the dance floor as they were engaged in some intense dancing with the ballerinas.

"I'm out of here, bro. Thanks again." Lance gave me a pat on the back and then he and Lee headed into the parking lot.

"Oh well, now I've got you to myself" Claire consoled as she kissed me on the cheek. "Let's mix and mingle a little."

We made our way through the crowd and made sure everyone was well fed, drunk and having fun. We ran into one of my good friends Jeff who I had somehow managed not to see yet tonight.

"Hell of a party - Stan, you are the man!" Jeff said as he greeted me in a slightly drunken state.

"I know, Bro." I answered.

"Hey do you rhyme all the time?" He asked.

"You're a poet and didn't know it!" I fired back.

"Oh I knew it, you just blew it!" He laughed and fell into me. "Who is the lovely lady?"

"Jeff, this is Claire." I said as Claire extended her hand for a handshake.

Jeff grabbed her hand and kissed it. "Not only have you been hiding from me all night, but how long have you been hiding this beauty from me? Why haven't I met you yet, honey?" Jeff said as he staggered and leaned into Claire.

"Pleasure to meet you, Jeff." Claire said as she side-stepped Jeff's advance. Jeff stumbled and fell to the ground.

"Glad you are enjoying the drink, Jeff. Make sure you take a limo home, okay?" I said as I helped him up.

Claire and I slipped away and sought out some less intoxicated people to chat with.

Mista Beat came over and gave me a knuckle-bump. "I sold over 300 CD's so far. I feel like I should pay you for the privilege to play tonight Stan. Anytime you have a party - you can call on me to beat-box it."

"No problem, Mista. You deserve it - you rocked the terminal. Everyone loved you." I said with satisfaction.

Claire complimented his performance as well.

"Everyone loved the party too. Great job Stan. This may be the best gig I've ever played." Mista's compliment meant a lot to me.

"You've got a lot more great gigs coming your way. Your talent is going to make you big time. Hey, have you got a place to stay tonight?"

"Yeah, me and my girls got a suite reserved over at the Plaza." He said.

"Great, let me get a limo to take you there." I offered.

"Not necessary. We cool to drive. Thanks anyway." Mista shook my hand and took off for the night - top hat and all.

It seemed like once Mista left the party started to wind down in spite of the fact the Earthtones were still jamming out. Claire and I made our rounds through the remaining crowd and made sure that everyone was sober enough to drive or that they were taking advantage of the free limo ride.

Ron found me and pulled me to the side. "Hey man, where is that hotel you said we could get some good deals on rooms for the night? Andy and I have got these two ladies and we need a place to go to continue the party." He said as he nodded his head over in Andy's direction.

I looked in the direction of his head gesture and spotted Andy with Vicky and Valerie - two of my ballerina friends.

"Good choice man - good girls for you guys." I said as I reached into my pocket. I dug out my keys and pulled my house key off of the key ring. I tossed the key to Ron and said "No hotel is necessary tonight. Take the girls back to my place."

"Thanks so much. You are the bomb. Where are you going to stay tonight?" Ron asked.

"I will probably stay at Claire's house. But one more thing - promise me that you will take a limo. You definitely should not drive. You car will be fine here tonight."

"Done deal man. Thanks again." Ron said.

"The girls know where my place is and can give the driver directions." I said.

"Yeah, I'm sure the girls also know where your bed is too." Ron said laughing as he walked away with my key in his hand.

I didn't mind hooking a friend up with my place. I loved to host and share my possessions with friends in need. I trusted Ron and the girls and had no worries that they would treat my house with respect and appreciation.

I walked back over to Claire and informed her of the situation. "I just gave my house up to some of my out of town friends for the night. So I guess I'll be going home with you."

Claire smiled seductively and said "That was my plan for the night all along."

She leaned over and kissed me on the cheek.

The party had thinned out significantly and there were only a couple dozen people remaining as we approached the 3 o'clock hour. The band was wrapping up their final set and the caterers were packing up the leftover food. Most of the beer taps had been floated but there was still a little drink left for those who remained.

I decided that my job as host was done for the night. I wanted to let Claire in on a little secret. I grabbed her by the hand and discreetly pulled her away from the party. I led her across the cargo yard toward the river. We slipped into the shadows of the terminal lights and into the trees by the river bank. I hoisted her onto my back piggy-back style so that her high-heeled shoes would not sink into the soft ground.

I walked in the dark through the narrow hidden trail leading down to the river. I knew the trail like the back of my hand and had every footstep memorized. Claire was apprehensive at first, but was delighted to see the end result at the end of the trail.

I lowered her down from my back onto the soft, clean section of grass on the river bank.

"This is my secret spot. I've been eager to show you this all night." I told her.

"Wow, it's quite impressive. How did you find this place?" She asked.

"Months of visiting the terminal every day to unload cargo into Connie peeked my interest in exploring the wilderness adjacent to the terminal. I'm not even sure if the guys who work at the terminal know about this spot. I sneak off of the cargo lot and come here occasionally to rest, relax, think and meditate." I said as I took her hand and coaxed her to the ground.

We sat on the river bank and stared out over the moonlit water. The band's timing was impeccable as they just finished playing.

"Ahh, peace and quiet - finally." I sighed.

"So why are we here tonight?" She asked as she turned and looked into my eyes.

"I thought you may like to see this spot. It is one of the best views of the river in the whole city."

"The spot is great, but it is you who I really want to see. I'm going to miss you more than you can imagine." She said as she drew near to my face. I put my arm around her shoulders and pulled her close to me.

"I will miss you too, but I will be back - I promise." I assured her.

"I think I have fallen in love with you, Stan." She said as she kissed my neck.

I felt the same way too, but my response wasn't indicative of my true emotions.

"Absence makes the heart grow fonder." I whispered to her as I began to kiss her.

I held my verbal expression of emotion for another time and indulged in the physical aspect of my feelings for the moment. Our passion was accentuated by the sounds of nature and the millions of stars as they shone down on us out of the cloak of darkness in space. As we lay there on the river bank in each other's arms I looked to the stars and thought "what a perfect ending to a perfect party."

The Arrival

The next couple of weeks after the party were a blur to me. I was definitely in vacation mode. My mind was in the South Pacific, but my body was still in Richmond, VA. I call it short-timers syndrome. It was a phrase I used when employees gave me their two week notice before quitting. I learned that once someone gave notice their efforts were usually minimal and worthless. So I made it a practice that when an employee gave me their notice, I would simply hand them a check for two weeks pay as severance, thank them and send them on their way. It was an efficient way to part company and usually made whatever situation that led to their quitting amicable so that they left on good terms.

Now, I had essentially cashed my own two weeks check and was awaiting the start of my new "job" and temporary new life in a new location. My business was already off and running on autopilot. Robbie had taken over the reins and already started the next project. I wanted to insulate myself from work and resist the temptation to get involved. I wanted to see how things would run without my involvement before I left. It should give me a good indication of how things would go once I was gone. So far things were going well.

I didn't have much to do except think about the trip. All the planning was done. I had no packing to do because everything I needed was on Connie. I tried to imagine where she was - in the Atlantic? - The Pacific? - Maybe in the Panama Canal? Wherever Connie was, she was in route halfway around the world to the place of my dreams. The anticipation of joining her was driving me crazy. I think it was the most excited I have ever been about anything in my entire life.

I passed the time and made a few trips to VA Beach and got a few surf sessions in with Lance. I continued my daily yoga sessions, runs, exercise and other routines. I waited and counted the minutes of every day until I would depart. The days leading up to the party had been hectic and time had flown by beforehand. Now, time seemed to tick slower. I also had a void in my schedule now that Connie was gone. It was an hour or two each day that I didn't have to go to the terminal and unload cargo. I missed that daily chore, but was happy that it was done.

I ended up substituting my Connie time with Claire time. Since the party we had gotten much closer, but I intentionally kept her at arm's length and stifled any serious relationship from developing as I didn't want to burden myself with any obligations before my trip.

I got a couple of calls a day from friends and family who were checking in with me to see if I had left yet. I read the dozens and dozens of thank you emails that I received in appreciation for the party. I perused hundreds, if not thousands, of pictures on Facebook that people had posted from the party. Soon I will be posting pictures of my own from a different world I thought.

Nineteen days had seemed like an eternity, but finally the call came. I remember the moment very clearly. It was late afternoon. I was driving in my truck coming home from the gym and listening to a favorite reggae band. My cell phone rang and I looked at the 16 digit number on the caller ID and I knew right away who it was. I almost dropped the phone with excitement as I hurriedly answered it. I heard Chet's Australian accent as he said "G'Day Matey" on the other end. His voice on the satellite phone was crystal clear considering it was beamed into space and half way around the world. The call meant only one thing – Connie had reached her destination!

Chet and I chatted for a while in exuberance. He couldn't believe the cargo had finally arrived. He couldn't believe it was actually all true. He couldn't believe that we would be reunited again in a matter of days. We bantered back and forth with personal details for a few minutes and then got down to the logistics of unpacking and transporting Connie's load.

Chet gave Connie her own private and easily accessible space and gave Hoanui 24 hour access to her at the terminal port in Tahiti. Chet also gassed up the pontoon boat for Hoanui and was ready to head over to Rahiti to meet him and the other Rahitians right now.

When I hung up with Chet, I immediately called my international flight consolidator and booked two flights to Tahiti that would depart in two days. My next call was to Lance to tell him the news. Lance was shocked to hear that we would depart so soon, but readied himself to head out. He arranged for Jasmin to chauffeur us to the airport so that he could spend every last second possible with her.

Their goodbyes at the airport rivaled even the most nauseatingly romantic movie. I thought Lance was never going to stop kissing her and telling her how much he loved her and was going to miss her.

"Get over it, you'll be back" I thought to myself.

I figured we would miss the flight because Lance didn't want to enter the security screening and leave her behind in the terminal. I pried them apart and Lance and I breezed through the security since we had no luggage and our flip-flops were easy to remove. We caught a little flack about not having any luggage, but I explained the situation multiple times to security who seemed puzzled by the fact that someone could travel internationally and not take anything with them.

The Jet Blue flight from Richmond to LAX was great, but paled in comparison to the international flight on Air Tahiti Nui from LAX to Papeete, Tahiti. Flying coach on Air Tahiti is the closest thing to flying first class at a reasonable price. The beautiful female Tahitian flight attendants are all dressed in Pareas and have flowers behind their ears and leis around their necks. Their service is impeccable and the comfort of the airplane made the 14 hour flight a lot more tolerable. We took advantage of the free cocktails as well since I knew it may be our last opportunity to drink alcohol for quite some time.

As we flew over the open water of the Pacific Ocean, I looked out the window and thought how great it was to be able to jump a flight that takes you halfway around the world. Only decades ago there were no flights this long. For hundreds and even thousands of years, man's mode of transportation was much slower and limited to his feet, horse or by boat. Today we take for granted that we can travel so far so fast. I remembered people in line in front of us in the terminal in LAX complaining about having to take their shoes off to go through the metal detector at the security checkpoint. I imagined these same people having to pack for a month long trans-ocean voyage by sea. Whatever their objection was to the security screening would be minimal compared to the effort it would take to get to their destination without air travel.

As we came into our final descent and approached Tahiti, I gazed out the window of the plane and snapped some photos of the awesome aerial view of the islands below. The deep blue color of the open ocean had given way to teal green waters inside the shelter of barrier reefs. Lance commented that he could see waves breaking even from our altitude. Even at thirty thousand feet, surfing was still on that guy's mind.

We landed on the Tarmac at the airport in Papeete and instead of pulling up to a jet-way at the terminal, the plane stopped short of the terminal building. Stairs were deployed and we all exited the plane directly onto the ground outside the terminal. I knew the drill because I had been here before, but Lance and other first-time passengers were surprised by the curb-side drop off. The terminal building looked like a series of interconnected Tiki huts and it was obvious that it was not your typical international terminal - aside from not having a jet-way into the terminal.

It's customary that all of the passengers are greeted by a welcoming committee consisting of good-looking Tahitian guys and girls who are ready to "Lei" all visitors to their island. Aside from being adorned around the neck with a beautiful hand-made Lei of fresh flowers, a Tiare flower is also placed behind your ear. The Tahitian Tiare flower is the equivalent of our Gardenia flower back in the States. The Tiare flower is also the equivalent of a wedding ring according to Tahitian custom.

Lance was a little "taken aback" when a beautiful Tahitian girl asked him if his "love was taken" or if his "heart was vacant for love". Lance took the question as a proposition. Whereas having been there before, I knew the customs and the reason why they asked. He was quick to nervously reply that he was "happily married". She placed the Tiare flower behind his left ear to signify that he was unavailable. I smiled and winked at the Tahitian Wahine and she instinctively knew to put the flower behind my right ear to signify that I was single and "on the hunt".

Lance shook his head at me and commented. "Player!"

"What?" I responded with innocence.

"We haven't even gotten off the runway and already you are hitting on the locals! How many girls are you going to screw while we are here?" Lance chided.

"Dude, I just... never mind." His comment didn't even warrant a response.

A tall, dark and handsome male terminal worker whistled and waved a Tiare flower behind his head as he motioned for the passengers to follow him toward the terminal. The waving of the Tiare flower behind one's head was another Tahitian custom that simply meant "follow me." This gesture was also commonly used in a seductive nature by women, but coupled with a familiar hand gesture; it worked in this instance too for those who didn't know the custom.

We followed the Tahitian and the other passengers toward the terminal and mingled under a Tiki canopy to escape the heat of the South Pacific sun as the airline workers unloaded luggage directly onto the runway and wheeled it over to us on carts. A group of locals played congo drums and a banjo under the canopy to entertain the visitors. Lance and I were free to go because we didn't check any luggage. We proceeded through customs with our passports in hand. Customs entry was a piece of cake compared to the B.S. that a foreign visitor must go through in the US. The customs official was smiling as if he really enjoyed his job. We handed him our passports.

"Iorana. Welcome to Tahiti. What is the nature of your visit?" The friendly officer asked Lance.

"Surfing" was Lance's one word response.

"Very well, enjoy your stay and your surfing." The officer said as he stamped his passport and handed it back to him.

The customs officer flipped through the pages of my passport and noticed that I had traveled extensively. He coincidentally stopped on the page of my passport that had been previously stamped on my prior visit to Tahiti.

"Welcome back, sir." The officer said as he smiled at me.

"I couldn't stay away from this place." I answered as I smiled back.

"And what is the nature of your visit?"

"I'm visiting friends in Rahiti and building a community shelter on their island for the next 6 months."

"No luggage?" He asked as he glanced at my small carry-on bag.

"We shipped everything here in advance in a cargo container." I responded without hesitation.

"Very good. I'm sure your Rahitian friends will be happy to see you - in fact, I think there is a group waiting for your arrival in front of the terminal building." He stamped my passport and directed me through the gate.

"We're finally here." I said to Lance as we walked through the front main doors of the terminal.

Before Lance could say a word we were greeted by a chorus of Rahitians "Iorana, Stan." The words rang out to us from a group of five waiting eagerly on the sidewalk. Lance turned his head in amazement. I don't think Lance expected there to be a greeting party of that proportion at the airport waiting to see me.

Seeing my Rahitian friends was surreal to me. It had been several years since I last saw them, but they hadn't changed a bit in appearance.

Chet was the obvious one as he stood 6 feet tall with bleach-blond shoulder length hair. He wore board shorts and a billabong tank top. His Aussie body was nicely tanned, but relatively white in comparison to the 4 natives that stood next to him. Hoanui was taller than Chet and almost my height at 6'2".

Hoanui was very muscular and well built for his tall frame. He had a well-groomed short haircut and wore khaki cargo shorts and a T-shirt. Arenui was short and stocky in comparison to the other two and his long, black hair extended well past his shoulders and covered the portion of them that his tank-top did not. He wore blue board shorts with bright pink hibiscus flower print on them. The two "Nuis" almost mirrored Lance and me in height and build - they were like a dark haired, well tanned version of my brother and I.

Last, but certainly not least were the two lovely Tahitian girls Tania and Maruia. Both ladies were clad in wrap-around pareas - a traditional South Pacific garment for the ladies. Their flawless, blemish free dark brown skin and ultra healthy black hair were testament to the effects of healthy, natural, stress free living in the islands. Tania and Maruia, although not related, could have been twins. Their late-twenty-something bodies were lean and lithe, but curvaceous where it mattered. Their beautiful ear to ear smiles bore the island greeting that I so desired to see; however, Hoanui was the first to approach me. He gave me a big hi-five and then embraced me in a hug.

"Good to see you again my American brother." He said affectionately with a Rahitian accent.

"Likewise my Rahitian friend." I answered. "Speaking of brothers, meet my brother Lance." I introduced Lance to Hoanui, Arenui, Chet, Tania and Maruia.

"You're finally back, brah!" Arenui said as he also embraced me with a hug.

"I told you I was coming back, man."

"Yep, ya did it dude." Arenui agreed.

"It is impossible to stay away from this place too long - hey?" Chet added.

Tania placed another lei around Lance's neck as she kissed his cheek and said "Welcome to Tahiti." Lance nervously accepted the lei and the kiss and then turned to me and looked as if he had the guilt of just cheating on his wife.

"It's cool - South Pacific custom." I said to him.

Maruia approached me with a lei as well. She placed the beautiful floral necklace around my neck as I bent down to accept the gift.

"So glad to see you again, Stan. It has been too long. I'm not going to let you leave me this time."

Her words were followed by a long kiss on my lips, not cheek and then she put me in a bear hug and squeezed me tightly as if she wanted to crush me. I enjoyed the hug and the smell of her fragrant skin and hair. She was the most beautiful sight that the islands had to offer. Her long black hair shone in the bright Tahitian sun and her teeth were the whitest teeth I had ever laid eyes on. Her bright blue and yellow parea wrapped around her body and accentuated all of her womanly figure. I had missed her tremendously, but maintained my cool for the time being.

"You blokes ready to roll?" Chet asked.

"Yep, let's do it. Where are we heading?" I asked.

"We are walking over to the port and we will take the boat to Rahiti." Chet answered in his Aussie accent.

We began walking down the street in the direction of the port which was visible in the distance from the airport. Maruia grasped my hand and held it tightly - pulling me close to her side. Chet, Arenui and Lance took the lead and engaged in some surf-related conversation. Hoanui and Tania walked behind Maruia and me.

"You guys picked an excellent time to come. The weather has been very favorable lately." Hoanui said.

"Isn't the weather here always beautiful?" I asked.

"Well yes, but it has been exceptionally beautiful lately." Tania replied.

"Not as beautiful as you guys though." I commented as I glanced at Maruia and traced her figure with my eyes. She smiled and winked at me. She was even more beautiful than I remembered. I had looked at her pictures on a weekly basis for the last couple of years even though her image was engrained in my mind. Seeing her again in person was incredible. No picture could do her justice. Her perfection was limitless.

We had arrived in the middle of the day. The sun shone down brightly overhead and the heat of the day was reaching its peak. I estimated that the temperature was in the upper 80's and an occasional breeze made it very comfortable. The smell of the flowers on the lei around my neck as well as the smell of the fresh, clean salt air pleased my nose.

We walked down the narrow two-lane street leading from the airport to the city as an occasional car passed by and honked briefly as if to say "Hey welcome to Tahiti - I'm passing you" rather than "get out of my way."

It was such a great feeling to finally be here again. We all chatted about our flight and arrival until we reached the port. The port in Tahiti was very different from the terminal back in Richmond. The street outside the terminal was lined with street vendors selling everything from food to shirts to trinkets - and Hinano beer. We stopped at a stand and grabbed seven Hinanos from a vendor.

The beer was cool and refreshing on the hot day. I missed the taste of Hinano as it was not sold anywhere near home - only in Tahiti. The beer was native to Tahiti, but non-existent in Rahiti. I enjoyed every refreshing drop as I knew it would be my last beer for a while. I was totally cool with that.

Chet lead us into the port. There was no security outpost like Clyde's here. People came and went through the port freely. The cargo yard was shared with everyone who was departing by Cruise ship, motorboat or sailboat - or just parking their cars in the lot to visit a nearby store or vendor. The terminal was much smaller in overall size than Richmond's but it was much busier to both pedestrian and vehicular traffic. Fishermen lined the dockside on one of the piers. There were no large ships in port at the moment, but a whole group of sailing yachts were moored just offshore. The multi-million dollar vessels were beautiful. I asked Chet "So which one of those yachts are we sailing to Rahiti today?"

Chet laughed and answered "I've got a special ship for us."

He led us through the cargo lot all the way to the back. I immediately saw the big green box labeled 'Conex'. "Connie!" I exclaimed as I pointed over to her.

"Yep, she's here mate." Chet said as he directed us over to her. He fetched a key from his pocket and opened up her doors.

As the doors swung open, I was shocked to see an area about 12 feet deep was already empty.

"Wow, you guys have been busy huh?" I said with surprise as I was impressed with the amount of work they had already done.

"Yeah, we already made 4 trips in the last two days." Hoanui answered.

"Where are the surfboards?" Lance asked as he peered into the container. Of course he had to ask that question.

"Already unloaded and waiting in Rahiti with your water, brah." Arenui quickly interjected. "I like your choice of sticks man." Arenui said referring to the surfboards that we brought.

His comment sparked more surfing conversation between him and Lance. I knew those two guys would get along great. They could talk surf lingo until their hearts were content.

"You really brought a lot of stuff - and a ton of water too." Hoanui said. "Why did you ship so much Fiji water? It took a whole boat load to carry it all. How many bottles are there?"

"Yeah, I told you I was bringing a load. I had 100 cases of Fiji water shipped directly from Fiji to Tahiti to meet up with Connie here."

"What? Why did you ship water here from one island to another? That seems a little crazy." Lance commented.

"Dude, I love my Fiji water. I like the square plastic bottles better than coconut canteens too." I added.

"Yeah, but 100 cases - 1200 bottles? A little excessive, bro." Lance stated.

"You can never have enough water. I plan to recycle all of the bottles too. Everyone on the island can have their own bottle to keep and reuse. We will fill them with rain water and reuse all of them over and over. I think they will be handy. Plus, my instincts told me to bring a lot of water - you never know." I stated with confident resolve.

"Whatever, dude." Lance said.

"No worries, brah. Your water is safe and sound and waiting for you at home." Arenui said.

"How difficult is it going to be to transport the rest of the load to Rahiti?" I inquired as I stared into Connie.

"Well, we made 4 trips already - maybe another 40 trips should do it." I nodded in agreement as it appeared that less than 10% of the cargo had been unloaded.

"I'm glad the load is packed in the order in which we will need it. It looks like you got the basics for the foundation off already as well as the valuable electronics and tools. The rest of the stuff can stay and we can bring it over as needed." I said.

Chet nodded in agreement. "The dock space is yours as long as you need it. And the pontoon boat is available 24/7 for you to use."

"Awesome." I said. "How long is the ride to Rahiti by pontoon boat?"

"Just over an hour at full speed. Fully loaded takes much longer." Hoanui answered.

The travel time involved made me appreciate the fact that they had made two trips in one day for the last two days. It was going to be a lot of work to haul the rest of the stuff over. Chet led us down to the dock where the pontoon boat was tied up.

"Here she is guys. This is your ride to Rahiti. She's not the most beautiful vessel in the yard, but she is very useful and durable." Chet said as he jumped onto the 25' flat bottomed double-pontoon boat. "She is stable and capable of carrying about 1500 pounds of total cargo." Two men and a thousand pound load I thought. I did some quick math in my head and confirmed that we were probably looking at about another 40 trips to finish the move.

I was eager to get on the boat and head to Rahiti, but Hoanui suggested that we take a little walk around Papeete since Lance had never been here before. I agreed as my legs were eager to stretch and move some more after the long flight. We walked back out of the terminal and across the street into the busy city.

Papeete was certainly no major metropolitan city in comparison to our standards in the US, but it was the epicenter of activity in the South Pacific. There was mild traffic congestion, but mostly foot traffic everywhere. The striking thing that I was reminded of was that no one seemed to be in a hurry to get anywhere. I liked the island time concept of "I'll get there when I get there."

We made our way through the narrow streets past jewelry stores selling black pearls and diamonds and shops selling wood carvings and souvenirs. Handmade tapestries hung from racks outside of some stores and cheap tourist T-shirts were on display in others. Lance slid up beside me and leaned toward me to say "I thought we left the US to escape the 'concrete jungle'."

"Dude, we are in the South Pacific, but we are still a world away from Rahiti. Papeete is possibly the only city in a thousand mile radius. Enjoy 'civilization' for a moment because where we are going will be nothing like this at all. You have to understand that the one hour boat ride from Rahiti to Papeete removes the Rahitians from their way of life in about as profound a manner as our 14 hour flight removes us from our world as we know it. Civilization as we know it is much different than anything our friends here have experienced." I explained to Lance as Hoanui concurred.

"Good." He responded.

"Are you guys hungry?" Chet asked.

"You betcha." I answered quickly.

"There is a great eatin' place that I frequent almost daily right around the corner." Chet said as he took the lead of the group.

"It will be the last meal you will have to buy during your stay here." Maruia assured. "The rest of the meals and cooking will be on us."

Chet quickly interrupted "Actually, lunch is on me today. I know the owner of the restaurant and I did some work on his boat so he is working off the debt with food and drink."

I loved the bartering system here. That is what enables my Rahitian friends to get educated and acquire an occasional material item from the island with no money.

We scarfed down a delicious lunch of fresh fruits and veggies, met the restaurant owner and a few of Chet's acquaintances before making our way back to the port. Both Lance and I were very eager to get to our destination and our friends could sense that. We said goodbye to Chet for the moment and the six of us jumped into the pontoon boat and Arenui shoved us off of the dock as Hoanui took control of the wheel.

The boat ride from Papeete to Rahiti was beautiful. It vividly reminded me of why I had fallen in love with this place and why I longed to come back. The teal green waters were placid today and the boat cut through the water with ease. Hoanui navigated the boat as he narrated the ride like a professional tour guide. He pointed out dozens of small "motu" islands and called them by name.

"There are hundreds of islands and small motus in the Society Islands. Some of which are only visible at low tide as the sandy remains of the atoll seem to emerge from the water. It is important to remain alert in these waters and know the tide charts. It would be unfortunate to run aground on an atoll or a reef at full speed in this boat." Hoanui explained as he drove from a standing position.

I remembered visiting many of the small motus on my kayak adventures on my previous visit. I was happy to be back again. I snapped some photos of us on the pontoon boat as we motored through the sea. Tania and Maruia loved posing for the camera. They were very photogenic and would certainly make beautiful models. Lance and Arenui posed together and made hand gestures of "hang loose" and peace signs. Hoanui took his eyes off of the water long enough to smile for the camera as well. Lance took over camera duty and took a couple of remarkable shots of Maruia, Tania and me. I couldn't wait to post these pictures online on Facebook so that everyone back home could meet our new friends and see that we had arrived safely in the islands.

"There she is." Hoanui exclaimed as he pointed to an island on the horizon. "We're almost home."

I recognized Rahiti from a distance. The island wasn't as majestic as some of the other larger islands, but like the other islands, Rahiti was formed millions of years ago from volcanic activity deep under the sea. Rahiti was a relatively flat island compared to others and had only moderate elevation in the middle, but she was beautiful nonetheless.

A school of dolphins surfaced in front of the pontoon boat and momentarily took our attention off of the island. There were about a dozen or so of the graceful creatures jumping, diving and undulating in the water next to our boat. I snapped a few shots of them as well and enjoyed watching them frolic next to us.

"Rahitian welcoming committee" Arenui said as he pointed to the dolphins.

"They are the best surfers in the world!" Lance added referring to their ability to ride the wake of our boat.

The dolphins followed us all the way to Rahiti and dazzled us with their aquatic abilities.

As we drew near to Rahiti, the lush green tropical island came into focus. A gorgeous white sand beach encircled the entire island and tall palm trees rose out of the sand and danced in the gentle breeze as if to wave us into the beach. The palms and the dense flora in the jungle growth gave Rahiti a rich, green color and a fragrant smell that wafted into our noses as we neared the beach.

Hoanui instructed everyone to go to the rear of the boat as he throttled the boat a little and beached it smoothly on the white sand next to several wooden outrigger kayaks. I could also see a stack of materials from Connie that had been delivered and neatly placed and covered up with plastic on the beach. Hoanui hit the air horn on the boat to announce our arrival and within seconds a throng of Rahitians came running from every direction to the beach to greet us.

Tania's little sister Fetia was the first to greet us on the beach. "Mr. Stan, welcome back to Rahiti." She said in her sweet little ten year old voice.

She had grown up a lot since I last saw her, but her bright green eyes hadn't changed a bit. She ran and hugged my waist and squeezed me tight. I wished I had some kind of souvenir to give her, but I figured my presence here would be enough to suffice for now.

Maruia's friend Puatea and about a dozen or so other locals all gathered on the beach to meet us. We were greeted by the locals with hugs, kisses and were adorned with more fresh flowers and leis around our necks. I felt like I may topple over from the weight of all of the flowers on my neck.

Everyone seemed thrilled to see us with the exception of Tane who reluctantly extended his hand for what seemed like an almost forced obligatory handshake. Apparently his affection and constant unwarranted pursuit of Maruia had embittered him even more and now my presence had once again stoked the jealousy fire in him. Maruia made it clear to him that her relationship with him went no further than the platonic level. She had told me that everything was cool with him since my departure, but she was concerned that my presence would provoke his jealous side again. Her fears were validated instantly. It didn't take a psychic to tell that he wasn't happy to see me. Maruia was relieved in a way that I was here so that he might finally get the message that there was no hope of future relationship between them. I didn't care what he thought anyway. There were dozens of other villagers who were thrilled for us to be here. I could deal with one jealous competitor.

I could sense that Lance was overwhelmed by the greeting that we received. The villagers made us feel like we were kings returning home to take the throne. I could also tell that Lance was surprised to see that many of the locals were topless or wore tops made of palm thatching or coconuts - both men and women. "I told you we were going 'native'. Enjoy the natural beauty that the island has to offer." I said to him.

Fetia remained latched to my leg and she tugged on my shorts to get my attention. "Mr. Stan, come to the village - I have something for you." She pleaded in her girlish voice and Rahitian accent.

Fetia took my hand and led me from the beach into the jungle and down the trail heading to the village. She was so excited to see me that she was about to pull my arm out of the socket as she coaxed me down the trail. Lance and the other villagers followed behind. I couldn't help but wonder if Lance was thinking that I had fathered a child on a previous visit here since Fetia was so attached to me as if she were my own child. I laughed the thought away and hoped that Lance would realize that I really had made a great impression on everyone the last time I was here.

We made our way down the trail through the dense jungle until we reached the clearing at the village. It was exactly as I had remembered it. The clearing was sheltered amidst the surrounding jungle and there were several dozen grass huts scattered randomly along the perimeter of the clearing. Tall palm trees with thatched hammocks tied between them separated many of the huts. A large bamboo and thatched open-sided tiki hut canopy was in the middle of the clearing. Inside the tiki hut were multiple banquet-sized wooden tables piled high with fresh fruits, herbs and fish. There were stone fire pits on one side of the central tiki hut that were emitting smoke from their smoldering coals and ashes. The smell of food filled the air and my mouth watered at the sight of the fruit.

"I'm sure you guys are hungry after your long voyage. We have prepared a feast for you today." Puatea said as she took the lead and invited us into the tiki hut.

"Yeah, and I helped too." Fetia added.

"It looks wonderful ladies. My mouth is watering for this delicious food." I said to compliment their efforts.

The meal we had eaten in Papeete had previously fulfilled my hunger, but the sight of this feast made my stomach churn in anticipation of the fresh fare. This was one more reason I had desired to return - fresh, delicious home cooked meals gathered and prepared by the community every day. Fetia grasp my hand and led me to the seat next to the head of the table. Puatea instructed Lance to sit across from me. Maruia claimed the seat next to me and the rest of the tribe took their usual seats as well.

Within a few moments, Matahi emerged from a hut closest to the tiki canopy. He was dressed in full tribal outfit - a grass skirt, a thatched tunic and a feathered headpiece. Nanihi wore a beautiful full-length red and green parea and followed him from their hut to the table. Matahi hadn't aged a bit since I left. He was in remarkably great health and was exceptionally mobile for a man of his age. No one really knew exactly how old Matahi was. He was rumored to be well over 100 years old, but he didn't look a day over 70. Nanihi boasted her same timeless age and health as well. They were both a testament of what good, clean, natural living can do for one's health and anti-aging. Matahi approached the head of the table. I stood up and motioned for Lance to do the same. I bowed and lowered my head slightly in respect to the elder of the village. He placed his hands on both of my shoulders and said a few words in Rahitian which Hoanui was kind enough to translate.

"Welcome back my son." Hoanui said as he translated. "I prayed for your safe return since the day that you departed. I am glad the day has arrived that you join our family again. You and your brother are now Rahitian brothers with the rest of the tribe. We are grateful for the gifts that you bring, but most importantly we are enlightened by your presence here once again. Please make yourselves comfortable on our island and consider Rahiti your new home away from home now."

"Maruru." I said to say thanks and acknowledge Matahi's kind words.

Matahi and I kissed each other's cheeks and then he turned to Lance and placed his hands on his shoulders in the same fashion.

"Welcome, my new son. What is ours is now yours on this island. We hope you will enjoy your stay." Hoanui translated from Matahi to Lance.

"Maruru." Lance said as he mimicked my one word response.

Matahi took his seat at the head of the table next to Lance and me.

"Let us eat!" Hoanui announced as everyone sat eagerly awaiting the command. It was customary for the elder to serve himself first, but in this case Matahi invited us to go first. The table, bench seat and all of the place settings were different from anything Lance had ever seen before. Everything was all natural and was made from materials on the island. The "plates" or platters as they looked were carved from wood and the "cups" were carved out of coconut canteens. The bottoms of the coconuts had been shaved down flat so that they would sit upright on the table. The coconuts were filled with coconut milk. There were no knives, forks or spoons as it was customary to eat with your hands here. There were also no napkins or paper products, so a quick cleaning in the ocean or at least a good finger-licking was also customary after the meal was finished.

Lance seemed puzzled as he looked for some type of serving spoon or utensil to gather his food from the serving platters in the middle of the table. "Dig in with your hands bro." I said to him. "There are no germs as we know them on the island. It is perfectly sanitary and normal to eat with your hands here. You will get used to it and will never want to use a fork again when you go home. There's nothing like "feeling" your food before you eat it." I added.

"Touching one's food with his hands before eating it is a South Pacific custom. The first touch is said to begin the digestion process as it prepares the body and soul to receive the food and digest it properly." Maruia said.

Her comment invoked thoughts of "food foreplay" in my mind, but I kept my comment to myself. I wasted no time indulging in the bounty of fresh food. I piled my plate high with mango, papaya, pineapple, Tahitian Noni fruit, Acai berries and an assortment of fresh greens and herbs. Maruia squeezed a large green pomello fruit over my plate and let the juice drizzle onto my food as a dressing. She even convinced me to break my vegetarianism and try a piece of freshly caught fish.

The food looked delicious, but I hardly had a chance to eat as all of the locals were eager to hear stories of my travels and life back in the US since I left. In between bites I regaled them with stories of my preparation for the trip and the 'departing party' that we hosted only weeks ago. I told them about Mista Beat and I even did a poor impression of him as I tried to unsuccessfully mimic his beat-boxing. Everyone at the table hung on my every word and they all competed to ask me the next question. Maruia sat quietly next to me and stroked my arm lovingly. Tane sat across from us and stared a jealous hole in both of us.

Meals were an important part of Rahitian culture. Not only did we eat to nourish our bodies, but we gathered to socialize and bond with each other as well. I think that it is this bonding and quality time that is now missing from our culture back home. Eating fast food and eating on the go has outweighed the importance of the social aspect of the meal. Convenience outweighs wholesomeness back home. As a single guy, I often ate solo back home and although I ate healthy food, I often ate in my truck while working. I was very glad that the Rahitians placed a high value on meal time in their culture. I looked forward to the day when I would have a family and implement this tradition in my lifestyle. But for now, the Rahitians would be my family and meal time would be sacred.

After dinner, Lance had immediate business he had to tend to. "Where is the sat phone?" He asked me.

"Dunno, bro." I replied. "Hey Hoanui - did you guys transport the sat phone from the terminal to here?"

"Of course, man. That along with the laptop and other electronics is stowed in the Rubbermaid container in your hut." He hollered back. "Let me show you your setup."

We rose from the table and thanked the girls for the wonderful meal and then followed Hoanui across the clearing to our new dwelling. Our hut was about 12'x12' square and the roof was about 7' tall. It was like a large tent made out of bamboo, thatching and twine. The floor was sand and there were two thatched beddings or makeshift mattresses on either side of the hut floor separated by Rubbermaid containers of our personal belongings. "Home sweet home." I exalted as we stepped inside the hut. It was close quarters inside compared to what we were accustomed to back home, but I didn't plan on spending much time in the hut other than to sleep. Lance and I chose sides of the hut and unpacked some of our stuff. Lance wasted no time fetching the phone from the container.

"How the hell do you work this thing?" He asked me as he fumbled around the complicated looking display and keypad.

"Who you callin?" I sarcastically asked.

"Your mother." He quipped back.

"Hey, my mom is your mom too sucka." I said implying that two could play this childish game.

"Who do you think I'm calling bro?" He finally conceded.

"Just hold the one key down. It is programmed to speed dial Jasmin. I hooked it up like that for you."

He held the button and the screen lit up and began connecting and dialing. He exited the hut and walked away with the phone to his ear without saying another word to me. I watched as he walked and talked down the trail to the beach. I understood he wanted to call his wife and let her know he got here safe and sound, but I hoped that this wasn't indicative of how things would be. I hoped he would spend some time bonding with me and the locals rather than constantly chatting with the woman he had spent every day of the last nine years of his life with. I considered telling him that the phone had a maximum minute usage on it so that he would be forced to ration out his time on the phone.

I looked at Hoanui and shook my head in disapproval of Lance's call. "Married life." I said.

"Why didn't you ever marry?" Hoanui inquired.

"I've had some good options, but I guess I haven't met the right one yet. Plus, I've been married to my business for the last 10 years."

"Aren't you afraid that you are going to miss out on a lot working too hard on your business and not enough on your life?"

"That is precisely why I'm here, my Rahitian brother. I just got fed up with the stress of work and modern society and all of the limits and pressures that come with the lifestyle. I was so eager to come here and experience a different life, get in touch with myself and nature, and help others - because I wanted to, not because I had to. Besides, it's never too late to marry." I said with resolve as I sincerely addressed Hoanui.

"Well, we are so glad to have you and your brother here. And there are no shortages of wives here to choose from." Hoanui said as he raised his eyebrows and gave a head nod in Maruia's direction as she and Puatea were across the clearing cleaning up after lunch. "That girl has counted the minutes until your return and hoped and prayed that you would come back to her with a vacant spot in your heart. She wishes to marry and leave the island just as bad as you desired to leave America and come here. Plus, having you around would certainly get Tane off of her back. You have been foremost in her thoughts since the day she met you."

"I know. She will make a fine wife regardless of who she marries." I said as I admired her from a distance. "I don't think I could remove her from the island though. The tropical paradise she is accustomed to attributes to her infinite beauty. To remove her from this environment would be like cutting a flower from the plant that gives it life."

"Maybe, but as an outsider it is easy for you to love the beauty and island lifestyle because it is still new to you. But when you have lived the same life on the same small island with the same small group of people all of your life, you eventually desire to break away and explore the rest of the world. She is ready - trust me." Hoanui said as he winked at me.

I pondered the thought for a while as I stood at the entrance of my hut and watched Maruia tend to the chores of post-meal cleanup. She would be a fantastic wife and a great mother. She would probably stay young looking and healthy until the day she died. Her exotic looks, culture and family values had been well preserved in the virgin society in which she lived. I reassured myself that it would be a crime to take her away from it. For a moment I teased my intellect with the thought of marrying her and giving up everything at home to stay here with her. It was a novel thought, but only a remote idea.

"We are having a big tribal ceremony tonight to celebrate your arrival." Hoanui added and broke my concentration on Maruia.

"Really? When and where?" I asked.

"Dusk - right here in the village clearing." Hoanui said as he pointed to the area between our hut and the tiki hut where we had lunch.

"Do we need to do anything to help prepare for it?" I inquired.

"Nah, we do this all of the time. The girls have made tribal gear for you and your brother to wear. Just wear that and your dancing legs." Hoanui said as he pointed to a grass skirt-looking thing and a thatched tunic and feathered headband which lay neatly on my thatched mattress bedding. "I'm going to go and do some quick chores. Why don't you relax and get some rest for a bit." He said as he left my hut.

I bent down and picked up the tribal outfit from my bed and held it up. "Wow, this is gonna be 'cute'" I thought. There is no way Lance was going to go along with wearing a grass skirt and feathers. I could bear wearing it for a bit to go along with custom, but there was no way in hell that any pictures were going to end up on Facebook of me in this garb! I leaned back down and placed my hand on the thatched mattress that lay directly on the sandy floor of my hut. The mattress was thin in comparison to a normal mattress back home, but it was surprisingly soft and cushiony. I gently laid down on it and the natural fibers tickled my back, arms and neck. The natural smell of the palm thatching was very pleasant to my nose as well. I knew that I would be comfortable here no matter what I had to sleep on. The mattress was an added bonus especially since I knew that it had been handcrafted with love by the Rahitian girls.

I lay in my new bed for a bit and looked up at the ceiling of the hut above me. The roof and ceiling were together one in the same and consisted of a series of intricately interwoven bundles of palm thatching that were tightly cinched together with twine and then lashed to bamboo framing. The roof seemed to be relatively waterproof based on the density and strength of the work, but I could see how any substantial amount of wind could render the hut useless in a storm. At least if it did leak, the floor was sand and would soak up any water that intruded.

The walls were thatched in the same fashion as the roof, but utilized longer, less dense strands of leaves that were bound straight vertically rather than concentrically like the roof. The 'door' consisted of two flaps of thatching that could be tied together in the middle or tied back to either side of the hut to allow light in or easy entry or exit. The hut was just enough to offer privacy and basic shelter from the elements, but it was in no way, shape or form secure or stable. But it was home for now. I vowed to appreciate it. Certainly no one was going to break in and steal anything. And, after all, millions of South Pacific Islanders had lived in this type of home for thousands of years. I became more motivated to build the community center and give safety and security to the Rahitians.

I relaxed a bit on my 'bed', but couldn't even begin to sleep. My mind raced a million miles per hour now that I was finally here. I contemplated setting up the laptop and the satellite internet connection, but quickly dismissed the notion as I knew it would be better left in the weatherproof Rubbermaid container. Everything native to the island handled water and weather well and always dried out; however, the same was not true with the electronics we brought (except for the waterproof camera).

The rest would remain safely stowed in the containers until we needed them or until the community center was done. Plus, I just simply didn't feel like messing with anything electronic. I felt like surfing. I exited the hut and found Arenui milling around the village.

"Hey dude, do you know where the boards are?" I asked of the salty Rahitian Arenui who had just poked his head into the hut.

"Yeah, brah - they be chillin on back of my hut. You ready for a ride man?" He responded in his Rahitian accented surfer dialect.

"Yep, let's go." I already had my board shorts on and I quickly shed my shirt as I followed him to his hut.

I had a chance to briefly glance inside the door flaps of his hut as he tossed his shirt inside. It was quite a mess in there as it looked like a typhoon had just blown through his hut.

"The maid was off this week, brah." He said as he laughed off the embarrassment of the dirty dwelling. We walked around to the rear of his hut and there were a bunch of surfboards, kayaks and other junk strewn about the backyard between his hut and the dense jungle behind it. Our familiar boards were obviously visible amongst the other wooden and extremely used fiberglass boards that Arenui had. Lance and I brought 4 boards total - 2 long boards both about 9'6" in length and 2 'fun' boards about 7'4" long. The interesting thing was that although all of Arenui's boards were strewn about the ground, ours were lashed upright to a palm tree with twine.

"Why are our boards tied up man?" I asked with bewilderment.

"Don't want them to catch a breeze and blow away, brah. Trust me, I've lost a many that way and it's no kinda fun to chase them down." He said as he began to untie our boards.

"So why don't you tie all of them up - not just ours?"

"Don't really care dude. If mine blow away I'll carve up a new one or wait for it to blow back. Lost a few, gained a few, but I've always got a stick around to ride." A quick flip of his hair out of his face and he handed me the two longboards. "It was aching me not to ride your boards the last two days, but I waited for ya brah."

"You could have ridden them and I wouldn't have cared. I trust you." I said as I laid the boards on the sand face up and began waxing up the face of the smooth, clean deck.

"Didn't trust myself, brah. A quick, clean stick like that - I wouldn't know what to do with myself. I'd be straight tearing up the face and busting the lips off some waves."

"Grab my 7-4." I said as I pointed to the blue and white striped board still lashed to the palm tree. "I'm riding this long board and taking the other to Lance." I said as I put the final waxing on Lance's bright green long board.

"Really brah?" Arenui seemed surprised by his tone.

"Really." I said as I gestured to the board on the tree.

"Cool." He said as he wasted no time grabbing the stick and waxing it up.

We headed past my hut and I tossed my shirt inside of it and then we walked down the trail to the beach and followed Lance's footsteps right to a tall palm tree. I found Lance sitting on the beach, his back against the palm with the phone pressed to his ear. I didn't say a word - I simply tossed his board gently on the ground next to him and then pointed to my watch as if to say he had been on the phone long enough. In fact, he had been on the phone long enough - it had been well over an hour.

Arenui and I strapped the leashes of the boards to our ankles while in stride to the water. The short Rahitian surfer hit the water with speed and didn't miss a stroke as he paddled through the chest high shore break. I turned to look at Lance before I hit the water and he put his index finger in the air as if to signify one more minute. Wow, there was something more pressing to him than surfing - unbelievable.

I hit the water and busted through the shore break with a quick duck-dive and a few hard, smooth strokes. The water was refreshing, salty, teal green in color and crystal clear. I righted myself and straddled the board in a sitting position when I reached the outside break and pulled up next to Arenui.

"Wow, I can see my feet in the water - and all the way to the bottom too. I forgot how clear the water was here. Much different than that murky, dirty water on the east coast of the US." I commented in amazement as I stared into the clean, clear water. Thousands of miles from pollution I thought.

"This is me, brah." Arenui said as he wasted no time paddling into the next wave that jacked up behind him. He made the drop on the chest high wave look easy. Then from my vantage point behind the passing wave I could see him carving up the face as he smacked the lip a few times and then ended the ride with a floater that sent him over the backside of the wave. He gracefully landed the floater on his chest flat on the board and stroked back outside toward me without missing a beat. "Your turn, brah." He shouted as he cocked his head to the side to signal the incoming wave behind me.

I acknowledged his signal with a big smile, angled my board, arched my back and stroked into the wave as it welled up behind me. It was my first Rahitian wave in years and I couldn't believe I was riding one before Lance. I let out a "whoop" as I made the drop down the smooth face of the wave. I hit my bottom turn just right and went vert back up the face of the wave, smacked the lip and then ripped back down the face again to pull off a wicked roundhouse cutback. I then launched airborne over the backside of the wave and let out a loud "wooo-hooo!"

I must have gotten Lance's attention because once I righted myself from my plunge, I turned to see him trotting down the beach toward the water with his board under his arm. In no time he was outside next to us in the lineup.

"Glad you could join us." I sarcastically said. "You checking the surf report on the phone or getting the wife's permission to surf?" I taunted.

"Funny." He said as he rolled his eyes. "Hope you enjoyed that one wave, cause the rest are mine." He fired back as he turned and stroked into the next wave.

"You dudes are straight Houlis!" Arenui said as he shook his head in jest - implying that Lance and I were 'tools'. He paddled into the next wave before I could hit him with a response.

The three of us caught wave after wave - passing each other as we alternated dropping, ripping, shredding, duck-diving and paddling back outside to the lineup. It was exhilarating, exciting and 'epic' as Lance put it. Arenui wouldn't stop raving about how much he enjoyed riding my surfboard. He was delighted to hear that I was leaving both boards behind for him when I left to return home.

"No way, brah." He said with delight. "I'm gonna treat it like it was my own, I promise dude."

I had visions of his messy hut and his boards strewn in the back yard versus our boards tied safely and neatly to the trees.

"Better treat them like mine for now." I said as I patted him on the back.

We concluded our early evening surf session as the sun began to fall below the palm trees and their shadows reached out into the water as if to beckon us ashore.

"I think it's time to head in boys. Hoanui said we are having a tribal ceremony tonight at dusk." I announced.

"Right on, brah. That's totally accurate. You guys gonna love the festivities." Arenui added as he waited for his next wave. "See ya on the beach, brahs." He hollered as he dropped down the face of the next wave.

"Yeah, and you are going to love the outfit we get to wear tonight." I said to Lance with a devilish grin on my face.

"What the..." He started to ask as I paddled into the next wave and left him in the wake.

72

I rode my wave toes-to-the-nose all the way to the beach and literally stepped off onto dry sand. "Curbside service." I said to Arenui as I pulled my board out of the water. Lance was right behind me on the next wave and pulled the same stunt, only not as gracefully as his fin caught sand and stopped the board abruptly sending him stumbling into the beach. "Smooth." I sarcastically said to him.

"You dudes really tore it up out there today. I'm stoked for ya and glad ya brought some talent with ya from the states." Arenui said as he flung his long, wet hair back behind his ears and shoulders.

"I brought talent and Stan brought 2 boards." Lance jokingly added as he stopped to pick up the sat phone which he rolled in his shirt and left on the beach.

"Dude, that wasn't even funny. If you are going to crack on me, make it good. I don't want the Rahitians to think Americans aren't funny." I said in quick defense to Lance's failed attempt at joking me. We all laughed and walked back up the trail to the village. We parted company with Arenui at our hut, propped our boards up against a tree and shook the rest of the water from our bodies before entering the hut.

The thing I liked about the Rahitian sand was that it was easy to shed. It was fine, soft and powdery, but shook loose from your skin and returned to its home on the floor of your hut. I liked not having to worry about tracking sand in the house - since the floor of my house was made of sand! No vacuuming would be required here.

I picked up my tribal gear off of the bed and held it up for Lance to see. "Yours is over there." I said as I pointed to the head of his mattress.

"No way I'm wearing that ridiculous shit, man." Lance said in disapproval of the garb.

"So are you going to deny custom and be the only one not wearing it?"

"Yep." He said as if that were his final answer - and the norm.

"Look bro - when in Rome, do as the Romans - right?" I reasoned with him.

"We are not in Rome Stan. And I wouldn't go to Rome anyway - there is no surf there!"

"Okay, let's say there is a huge surf party somewhere. All of the pros are there and they are all wearing togas because it's a toga party. Are you going to go against the grain and show up in shorts and a T-shirt." I argued.

"Depends on which pros." Lance answered.

"Ok, whatever man. I'm here to experience the culture. Someone spent a lot of time making these clothes for us and I think it would be disrespectful not to wear them - not to mention the fact that they are having this ceremony as a welcoming party especially for us. Don't be a tool." I urged of him.

Before he could argue any more there was a female voice outside the hut. "Stan, Lance - are you guys dressed yet?"

"We are dressed, but not in our tribal gear if that's what you mean." I said as I stuck my head out of the door flaps to see Tania and Maruia standing outside with some feathers and wooden containers on a tray.

"Oh, we are here to put the final touches on you for the ceremony. Hurry up and get dressed." Maruia urged in her sexy voice.

I wasted no time shedding my wet board shorts. I pulled the grass skirt up to my naked waist and found the fiber drawstring and pulled it tight and tied it. I then donned my thatched tunic which fit loosely around my neck and shoulders and was open under the sides under my armpits. I then popped my headband and feathers on my semi-dry, salty head as Lance stood and watched in disbelief.

"You look like a jackass." He said as he laughed at me.

"I feel like a Rahitian." I responded with pride. "You are gonna be the only jackass wearing shorts and a T."

I shook my head at Lance and then emerged from the hut to meet the girls outside. "I'm all yours, ladies."

I sat down on a wooden bench made of driftwood just outside of the tent as the two Rahitian ladies began to prep me for the tribal ceremony. The first order of business was for them to place some war paint on my face with their fingers and feather brushes. I felt like I was getting a makeover at Macy's; however, I had never had a makeover - let alone at Macy's. The smell of the war paint (makeup) was earthy, yet intoxicating. Even more intoxicating was watching the ladies apply it to my face and then the rest of my body. I was glad I was sitting down to hide my arousal from under my grass skirt as the two ladies who worked on me were wearing only their coconut-clad bras and grass skirts. They were the sexiest sight I had ever seen. I was so charmed by them that I would have worn anything they told me to wear. Not only were they beautiful and convincing, they were also great artists too. I surveyed my body and noticed the intricate designs they were painting on my arms, belly below the tunic, sides and legs too. I couldn't see my face due to lack of a mirror, but I imagined it looked pretty cool in a tribal kind of way.

I was dying to see what I looked like so I called for Lance to bring my camera from the hut. Lance emerged from the hut moments later with camera in hand, but he was still wearing board shorts. He had changed into a dry pair and a T-shirt, but he was definitely still wearing surf gear, not tribal gear.

"What the…" He said as he snickered at me and laughed at my appearance.

"Shut up and snap a picture." I said as he was already aiming the camera at me and laughing his ass off.

"What are you laughing at? You are next." Tania said to Lance.

"Not a chance." Lance responded as he snapped a few more pics of me as the girls continued to tattoo my body with their tribal paint.

"Let me see how I look, bro." I asked as I extended my hand for the camera.

"You look like a fool." Lance said as he tossed the camera to me.

I hit the display on the camera and clicked through the last few pictures while the girls continued to apply paint to my body. It was absolutely not what I expected. I was surprised how awesome I looked. The outfit fit me perfectly and the makeup accentuated my body, my muscles and natural definition. The girls really did a great job decorating me and I appreciated their efforts. The look was certainly different for me, but I was honored to share in their tribal custom and I was more than happy to have two beautiful girls tending to me and my body. Lance retreated back into the hut without saying another word, but still laughing at me.

"Is he really not going to wear his tribal costume?" Maruia asked me.

"We made it for him. Everyone will be dressed in theirs." Tania added.

"I know, but what you have to understand about my brother is that he is very stubborn and set in his ways. He even has a specific spectrum of colors that his clothes must fit into or else he won't wear them - blue, green, white, beige, gray - that's about it. Same styles, same colors, same usual Lance." I said in his defense, but also to diffuse any sense of disrespect for their culture.

"Ok, but I should talk to Matahi in advance so he is not surprised or offended to see Lance not dressed traditionally." Tania said with slight embarrassment.

"Not necessary. I will handle it." I stood up as the girls finished applying the final touches to my body. "Wait here one second." I walked into the hut to find Lance fumbling through one of our containers. "Look man, all joking aside - either wear the tribal outfit or stay in the damn hut tonight. You are going to make a big deal out of nothing and offend our hosts or you can sit your ass right here and miss out

altogether. There is no flexibility on this subject. Make your decision now - the girls are outside waiting."
I said with firm resolve.

"Okay, okay - I'll wear it." He said as he slapped the lid closed on the Rubbermaid container.

I walked back out of the hut to give him a moment of privacy to change as well as to inform the girls that they had another makeover to do. Moments later, Lance reluctantly emerged from the hut. He was wearing his headpiece, tunic and grass skirt, but he was also wearing his tighty-whities under the skirt. I know he is a little shy and very conservative compared to me, but I realized that maybe he wore the undies because his grass skirt was a little more sparse and revealing than mine since it was the same size, yet forced to cover more area. Lance's slight pot-belly and larger mid-section and hips caused the draw string to reach its max and the grass to have to spread thin. Oddly enough, it would have been much less noticeable if he was naked underneath the grass versus displaying the bright white underwear. I snickered to myself and choked on my laughter. I didn't want to do anything to provoke him to change his mind and retreat back into his 'surf wear'.

"You look... tropical." I said in a neutral tone with a well concealed hint of sarcasm.

"Are you ready for your tribal body art Lance?" Tania asked as both girls cut their eyes down to do a double-take on his underwear situation.

"Sure, paint me up - I already look ridiculous enough." He said as he took a seat on the driftwood. He crossed his legs as the girls began working on him. Meanwhile, I discreetly snapped some candid photos from behind. 'Priceless' I thought to myself. Although the girls had more 'surface area' to deal with on Lance, they finished his body art much quicker than mine as they did not put the same obvious care and detail into him that they had done for me. I think that his lackluster attitude and reluctance to wear his tribal outfit contributed to their lessened effort.

When they were done with the painting, Maruia took me by the hand and led me over to the clearing where the tribe was already gathering. Tania escorted Lance behind us. We took our seat on the sand around a campfire along with the other tribe members already present. Various tiki torches back-lit the area behind us and cast alternating shadows around the fire as the sun had almost totally set now. Maruia sat next to me on the left and held my hand while Lance and Tania sat to my right. Puatea came around the circle carrying a tray with small wooden cups on it. She bent down and offered one to me first. "Kavaty" She said as she handed me the cup.

"Kavaty?" I asked as she had already handed one to Maruia and moved on to Lance who reluctantly took the offering as well.

"Kava, Kava Tea" Maruia whispered in my ear. "Good for relaxing the mind and body."

"Ahhh." I sighed as I tipped the cup to my lips. I had heard of Kava Kava before since I was in to health and natural supplements, but it was not what I was expecting at all. It tasted nothing like tea and it was neither hot, nor cold - just 'air temp'. It was an earthy taste that teased my nose and taste buds. I took a swig and by the time I had swallowed, I noticed a tingling, numbing sensation on my lips and tongue. I grimaced slightly at the unexpectedness of the potion's effect.

Maruia saw my expression and whispered to me "You're going to love it once you get accustomed to it."

I got the feeling her comment implied more than just the tea.

I felt empowered in my tribal gear, but at the same time I felt humored looking at Lance in his. It was ironic that he had laughed at me when he first saw me dressed in mine, when in fact I looked like an authentic Rahitian and he looked like a tourist wearing an outfit he didn't belong in.

I fit the part in so many ways. My tall, trim, athletic body fit perfectly into the skirt and tunic and my tanned skin matched the natural fibers perfectly. The body art that the girls had carefully painted onto my skin was ideal for me. I am sure that all of the symbols and signs they had painted had significance, but there had been no explanation about that yet.

Lance, on the other hand, was pale in comparison to everyone else. Even though he surfed back home almost every day, he wore either a long sleeved shirt or wetsuit to cover his body and SPF 45 lotion on his head and face. I preferred to go natural in the sun and soak up the rays and let my body defend itself the way it was intended to. Rahitians were testament to the sun's healthy effects on the skin sans sunscreen.

I surveyed the scene around the campfire. Everyone was mellow and seated in a relaxed position. I glanced over at Lance - his face was illuminated by the fire and Tania was on his other side looking off at the sunset. Most of the village was present and seated, but some notable people were not present including Matahi, Hoanui, Arenui and Tane. I wondered what the rest of them were up to, but before I could ask Maruia, I was startled by a loud crash and booming of drums.

An entourage of Congo line proportion stormed into the tranquil environment and began chanting loudly and wildly while moving their bodies in total discord as if their spines and legs were made of rubber. Hoanui led the procession and tossed a handful of powder-like substance into the fire as he neared it. The powder caused the flames to dance higher and sent an eruption of sparks airborne into the dusk sky. Arenui and Tane were also in the dancing procession along with about 5 other males. They were all wearing the exact same tribal costume that Lance and I wore.

After about 5 laps around the fire, they circled and spread out and took a position at even intervals around the fire like numbers on the face of a clock. Arenui and Tane and one other guy all had Congo drums of different sizes hanging around their necks by a lanyard and they tapped them with methodical rhythm as they moved their legs side to side while their bodies stood perfectly still. Another tribesman played some sort of wooden flute -which in between the carefully timed drum beats emitted a shrill sound that pierced the night sky.

Hoanui threw his head back and bellowed out a tribal chant in Rahitian or some sort of indiscernible dialect. "Haaiiiiiiiiiieeeeeeee-kalawaiiiiiiiieeeeee-oooooonaho." He called out to the heavens at the top of his lungs. He paused for a second and then let out the same chant again.

I turned my head to look at Maruia. "He is asking the Gods to bless this meeting and welcome new friends." She whispered to me.

"Wow." I thought - all of that in just three long, exaggerated words; however, I realized that one word in Rahitian can mean a sentence in English. I appreciated the language and their culture and was honored that they were sharing it with me and my brother.

The drum beats quickened and the volume increased as if a crescendo was in the making. When their hands could not possibly slap the Congo drums any harder or faster, the drumming stopped abruptly in unison. Then the woodwind instrument kicked in with a solo.

The shrill pitch of the instrument echoed into the night as it whistled from note to note almost as if to charm a snake or something. The other tribal dancers stood perfectly still and silent as the solo flute player carried on his tune. 'This was awesome' I thought to myself as I pulled my digital camera from the waistband of my skirt. I didn't want to snap any flash photography to disturb the mood of the moment so I took advantage of the motionless group and clicked a bunch of flash-free still shots from the campfire light. They would definitely be the best pictures I have taken so far. The environment and aura of the tribal ceremony was like something out of a fairy tale. It was too different for words to describe.

The flute player played passionately for a couple of minutes before stopping abruptly. All was silent and everyone was still until a deep male voice broke the silence and hollered out from a distance "IORANA".

The entire gathering responded together in unison "IORANA".

Then the same male voice bellowed out the same chant that Hoanui had cried to the heavens only moments earlier. "Haaiiiiiiiiiieeeeeeee-kalawaiiiiiiiieeeeee-oooooonaho."

And all of the villagers responded by loudly and passionately chanting back the same as they all threw their heads back and looked to the heavens. Then the drum beats and the flute started instantaneously and the tribal dancers began dancing wildly as they circled the fire. Matahi emerged from the darkness on some sort of bamboo Rickshaw carried by four tribal males. They sat the Rickshaw down at what was evidently the head of the circle and as soon as it touched the sand, the dancers stopped dancing and dropped to their knees and bowed down in some sort of 'child's pose' yoga position facing in Matahi's direction. The rest of the tribe did the same from their seated position. Maruia and Tania cued Lance and me as to what to do and we followed only a second or so behind the perfectly timed synchronization of the rest of the tribe.

Matahi uttered some Rahitian phrases in his weathered and wise old voice. The crowd responded with "Iorana" and then rose from their worshiping bowed position to a seated position and the dancers returned to standing. The drum beats started again, but this time slower, lower and rhythmic.

"So what did all of that mean?" I whispered to Maruia.

She turned to me and her face was only inches from mine as she answered in a quiet, sultry voice "First Hoanui and the dancers summoned the attention of the Gods with their music and salutations to open the door for Matahi to speak directly to them. Then Matahi asked the Gods to bless our ceremony and to welcome our new guests into the family and offer them safety, health, prosperity and love during their stay here." She winked at me and I got the impression that maybe she threw in the 'love' part on her own. "Next, it will be your turn to participate. I hope you have your dancing legs on."

Before I could respond or ask anything else, all of the males in the tribe stood up and made their way toward the fire and joined Hoanui's group. Maruia motioned for me to go and Hoanui came over to meet Lance and me. Lance required some coaxing to get him off his ass and on his feet - me, I was ready for anything. At least I thought I was ready for anything!

The drum beats started and the flute chimed in. The guys all began 'dancing' with motionless bodies and crazy legs. Their feet remained planted, their legs alternated in and out - side to side as if the knees were knocking, their arms were raised out to the side at shoulder height and were bent at the elbow with the thumbs pointing in to the chest. I got the motion instantly, but Lance tried to retreat back to his seat as he was having difficulty.

Hoanui convinced him to stay and try "Good for surfing and balance" he told Lance. He knew how to persuade him.

Just when I had the whole pose and motion down-pat, they had to go and add another element to it. Instead of keeping the feet planted, they began to walk methodically while the knees and legs continued to rapidly knock. I tried unsuccessfully multiple times to maintain the motion and rhythm in my legs while stepping my feet forward, but it just wasn't possible. It was about as hard as patting your head while rubbing your belly, chewing gum, standing on one foot, reciting the alphabet backwards while solving a calculus equation all at once - no joke!

"Focus." Hoanui said as he put his hands on my shoulders and looked into my eyes.

Arenui took charge of Lance. The rest of the men formed a large ring around the fire while the women remained seated on the outskirts. Lance and I took our place in the circle as well under the direction of the two Nui's. Hoanui remained face to face with me as the rest of the men turned to face the women.

"Control." He said in a stern voice. "Watch my legs." He insisted as he stepped forward and backward - one step forward, one step back as the legs vibrated like a plucked guitar string.

It was amazing to watch. I looked over at Lance who was engaged in the same practice with Arenui. We caught each other's gaze and smiled and shook our heads at one another.

"FOCUS!" Hoanui said with stern determination in his voice. "Your body will do what the mind wants it to do." He said as he nodded in approval of my continuing efforts. "Control" he reminded me as he looked into my eyes.

And just like that I took my first rhythmic step forward and then back without breaking the motion of my vibrating legs. The vibration was easy - the steps in concert with the vibration had seemed almost impossible until I finally did it! Hoanui nodded in approval. I got the rhythm instantly and I'm not going to say it became easy, but it became 'manageable'.

I stepped forward and back, knocking at the knees. I looked over at Lance who was still trying in desperate frustration. The fact that I had gotten it aggravated him even more. Arenui didn't give up on him though. They remained engaged face to face and Arenui encouraged him the same way that Hoanui had done for me, but Lance gave up too easily.

I glanced around the fire at the sight. It was amazing - several dozen men all knee-knock dancing in unison. I looked back at Maruia to find that she had picked up my camera and was videotaping me! Holy wow! I mouthed the words "don't do that" to her as I was pretending to not want to see myself doing this later. I was actually stoked that she had taken the initiative to tape me. It seemed like a big deal that I had gotten the dance down so fast.

It was obvious that my tighty-whitie wearing brother wasn't going to get the knack of it anytime soon. I got very comfortable in my dance and started to have a little fun with it as I took two steps forward, three steps back and then three steps forward and two steps back. My comfort in the dance was momentarily distracted by my curiosity as I noticed one of the tribesmen had approached the fire with a tool with a long handle on it and was raking coals out of the bonfire and corralling them into a small circle just about the distance from the fire where the ring of men were standing. I got the feeling I knew what was about to happen.

"Relax and watch this." Hoanui said to me as he took his place in the circular line next to me. Arenui gave up on Lance for the moment and stood next to him as Lance just kind of half-heartedly moved his legs around.

The drum beats picked up. The circle of men rotated clockwise one degree or so and the man that had been standing next to the newly formed pile of flaming hot, glowing red coals stepped sideways into the circle of coals while not missing a beat with his legs and feet. The rotation of the circle of men stopped for at least ten seconds as the human-hot-potato and the rest of the guys including myself continued our leg motion in a static stance.

The tribe began to chant together "Hola-wola-wola-hi, hola-wola-wola-hi."

The guy in the coals danced with his legs and moved his arms from straight out at shoulder height like a T to bent into his chest. He stepped his feet up and down to mimic footsteps although he remained in the same spot. It looked like some version of the "Monster Mash" dance or something.

I counted in my head and figured he had been in the coals for a good ten to fifteen seconds. It was amazing, but not unbelievable to me.

The group kept chanting "Hola-wola-wola-hi, hola-wola-wola-hi..." until finally the fire dancer hollered back "Hiiiieeee!" Thus signaling the circle to rotate one more person to the right. He hopped from the coals onto the sand and never once broke his leg rhythm or concentration. Talk about focus. I was intrigued as I watched the next fire dancer do the same thing for a good ten seconds or more. I could see flames and sparks flying off of the coals under his feet as the tribe chanted "Hola-wola-wola-hi, hola-wola-wola-hi..." It was quite a "feet".

I heard Lance say "There is no damn way I'm doing that crazy shit!" I turned to him and smiled.

Hoanui stood between both of us and said "You don't have to do anything you don't feel comfortable with. The last thing in the world I want is for you guys to get hurt. Just step behind the coals when your time comes and say "Hiiiieeee!" so the circle will rotate again and relieve you of the position."

We were almost at the farthest point away from the coals so I had plenty of time to watch the other dancers hit the coals while I practiced my new leg motion and dance. I also figured that the coals would have time to cool down a little before I got to them. I was wrong - after about 5 or 6 guys had done their fire dance, the rake came back out and more fresh coals were added to the circle. "Keeping it hot" I said to myself.

The circle had rotated about 90 degrees and Maruia and Tania were now visible across the circle from me instead of behind me. The two beauties remained seated "Indian style" with their legs crossed in front of them. They had a perfect vantage point of the fire dance from their front-row seats. The girls chanted along with the tribe as they watched me from across the fire.

The circle kept rotating and the chant kept going "Hola-wola-wola-hi, hola-wola-wola-hi..." So far about 15 guys did the fire dance and only 2 bypassed the coals and stepped to the rear of the circle. There seemed to be no shame in not doing the dance. The guys who didn't do it were of average age - not young, not old. Some elders and pre-teenage boys did the dance without hesitation.

81

Maybe the guys who bypassed it were still recovering from burns from the last dance. There were still more than a dozen guys in front of me. My heart raced and my legs quivered every time the circle rotated. "Hola-wola-wola-hi, hola-wola-wola-hi..."

I knew I could do it, but I also knew it was a long way to the hospital. Hoanui placed his hand on my shoulder as I drew nearer to the coals. "It's okay to step back" he said. I ignored him and kept my concentration on the fire in front of me and the coals to my left. I cut my eyes over to Maruia momentarily to see if she was still watching me. She was not only still watching me, but she was also still videotaping the event. I let myself become mesmerized and hypnotized by the fire.

"Stan" Hoanui whispered to me. I ignored him.

"Hola-wola-wola-hi, hola-wola-wola-hi..." I chanted out loud.

The circle rotated again and I was now one guy away from the fire. "Don't do it if you don't feel comfortable." Hoanui urged. "It takes a lot of concentration." He added.

"Hola-wola-wola-hi, hola-wola-wola-hi..." I chanted even louder as I ignored Hoanui and concentrated on the fire in front of me.

He finally got the message that he was breaking my concentration when I ignored him again and kept my gaze on the fire. One more guy to go I thought. My heart raced at a million beats per minute. My head was spinning with excitement. My body was bursting with adrenaline. But before we rotated a fresh batch of coals got raked out into the circle. I could feel the heat radiating from the freshly laid coals from several 'feet' away.

The coal raker signaled the rotation to start again with a "Hiiiieeee!" and then instantly the guy to my left stepped behind the circle on the rotation. He did a brief dance outside of the coals and then hollered "Hiiiieeee!" to signal the rotation. Shit - I was all prepared to do it, but fresh coals and then the native next to me chickened out. Damn! What the hell, I thought as I took a deep breath and dance stepped into the fire without further hesitation.

'Cool sand, wet sand, cool sand, wet sand' I thought to myself as I danced in the fire and continued my chanting. My legs knocked in rhythm, my feet stepped up and down in concert with the motion. My voice carried the chant "Hola-wola-wola-hi, hola-wola-wola-hi..."

I was standing on flaming coals, but my mind told my feet it was cool, wet sand. I did not feel the heat although I knew it was there. The only burning I felt was from the muscles in my legs as I continued my dance. I incorporated my arm motion into the dance, bending and straightening them.

I estimated that I had been in the fire for well over ten seconds. Just when I thought I could go longer, a searing pain shot momentarily through one of my feet. I instinctively let out a "Hiiiieeee!" and jumped from the fire pit back onto the sand to the left of the fire. I realized I had gotten too cocky and had broken my concentration on the cool, wet sand when I started to focus my attention on moving my arms.

The pain in my foot subsided almost instantly though. I didn't dare to stop my dance to look at my feet. I figured if they were smoking, someone would toss water on them and put it out. I looked over at Maruia who was smiling ear to ear. She gave me the big thumbs-up sign and mouthed the words 'good job' to me. I turned to my right as Hoanui was doing his fire dance next to me. He animated his facial expressions and elevated his steps as if he was marching with rubber legs. He must have done this a thousand times or more in his life.

I wondered if my performance had been enough to motivate Lance to give it a try. I knew I would find out as Hoanui gave his "Hiiiieeee!" and signaled the rotation. Lance stepped to the rear of the fire and immediately signaled the rotation with a lackluster "Hie".

Arenui also stepped to the rear as if to reassure Lance that it was okay to not jump in the fire. I was glad I had done it and I knew not to tease Lance about choosing not to. It was a personal choice and a very scary one at that.

The last few guys in the circle did their dance and then the entire circle stepped back a couple of steps to enlarge the ring. I was back in front of Maruia and Tania. I cut my head back to see what she was doing. She locked eyes with me and blew me a kiss. Lance witnessed the gesture and rolled his eyes at me.

The circle continued their leg motions as the drum beats intensified and built up to crescendo. The chanting also sped up too. Then, in unison, the entire group of men yelled "Hiiiieeee!" to end the ritual and break the circle. My legs did not want to stop moving and they almost collapsed when I suddenly stopped. I felt like I was invincible, but I also felt like I had rubber legs that were still vibrating.

Maruia sprang to her feet and hugged me. Her embrace was welcomed and comforting and reinforced the importance of what I had done. Tania greeted Lance and gave him a customary kiss on each cheek which he reluctantly accepted.

"You are amazing!" Maruia said as she leaned her head back to look into my eyes. "How did you do that? It takes some Rahitian men years of practice and courage-building to be able to do the fire dance. You just jumped right in! I am so impressed."

I smiled at her and simply said "It's amazing what the body can do when the mind wants it to."

I kept the real truth under my hat though. I had actually done a fire walk through 40 feet of hot, flaming, burning coals years prior at an Anthony Robbins motivational seminar. I had learned the power of mind over body at that experience. I knew that if the mind was in the right state, it would not allow the body to be burned. It was an amazing principle, but was proven true by those who believed time after time. I was so focused and empowered at the seminar that nothing could stop me.

I had learned to summon this focus and mind power whenever I needed it in my life. It was one of the most powerful and fulfilling things I had ever done. When I returned to my seat in the seminar, I was amazed to discover that not even a hair on my toe had been singed by the heat of the fire.

One bold naysayer had challenged Tony Robbins in front of the seminar crowd of hundreds and offered an explanation to the fire walk. He said to Tony "Isn't it true that coals burn internally and the surface is actually cool, thus allowing your skin to contact it without burning - especially when pressure is applied to the coal?"

The naysayer was sarcastic in his questioning to Tony, but Tony remained 'as cool as coal' and answered his question with another question. "How does the heat from a coal fireplace heat a room if that is true? Or how does the radiating heat from the coals in a campfire cook a hot dog or roast a marshmallow?" Tony asked with calm resolve.

He then invited the naysayer to reach his hand into the fire and fetch a burning coal and apply pressure to it by squeezing it in his hand. The naysayer bent down near the fire, but backed away about five feet shy of even being able to reach into it. Instead of berating the naysayer in front of the crowd, Tony simply put his hand on the guy's shoulder and said "The only answer is that sometimes there are no answers. There are things in life we cannot and will not understand. The power of the mind can be one of them."

I took away a very important message from that life changing seminar. It had helped me in many facets of my life - both in personal and business, emotional and physical. Now I got to use this power for fun. I was glad I had never told Lance about my previous seminar experience as it would have given him reason to minimize my effort today.

Puatea came around right on time with a refill of Kava Kava tea. I enjoyed the beverage much more this time since I knew what to expect. Tania and Puatea both commented on my bravery and dancing ability. I didn't get to relish in my feat too long before Hoanui offered up another challenge to me.

"Your dance was great and your time in the fire was commendable. Do you want to ascend to the ranks of fire-handler now? It is an elite group of Rahitians that have a focus and concentration level that has enabled them to master fire...and their minds and bodies." Hoanui asked as he placed his hand on my shoulder.

I looked over at Maruia and she stood expressionless and motionless as if to leave the entire decision up to me. I knew that she wouldn't let me do anything that would cause me to hurt myself, so I accepted the invitation.

"I'm in. What do I have to do?" I asked Hoanui.

"You don't have to do anything you don't want to do, first of all. Just watch and follow the lead. It is really quite simple. Let's find out how brave and strong you really are." Hoanui said as he winked at me and led me back over to where the coals were placed for the dance.

Several other tribesmen were convening there as the rest of the crowd still mingled and shook their legs out from the dance. Puatea poured some more Kava into my cup and topped me off. I sipped it down as Hoanui directed me to sit down cross-legged in front of the fire pit. Five other guys including Hoanui and Tane joined me.

Within moments of us sitting down, the Congo drums began beating. The drums seemed to signal the rest of the crowd to take their seats as well. I sat across the circle from Hoanui this time instead of next to him. A tribesmen from outside of the circle raked six coals from the fire into the middle of the circle and then pushed one coal in front of each of us with his tool. All of the coals were equally sized at about the size of a plum and they were all glowing red hot. I knew where this was going.

The drum beats hastened and intensified. I knew what I had to do. And the first thing I had to do was take my eyes and my mind off of the glowing red coal in front of me. I stared across the circle to Hoanui. I locked eyes with the tall, lithe, dark skinned Rahitian. We cracked simultaneous smiles at each other. The drum beats sped up more - and so did my pulse.

Matahi stood up from his Rickshaw for the first time during the ceremony and stood presiding over our circle of six. He raised his hand and then said "Soma" as he dropped his hand.

I gathered this was the signal to start the challenge as I saw the guys in the circle reach to pick up the coal. I breathed deeply and let my mind slip into a trance-like state. I instinctively reached down and grabbed the coal. I kept my focus on Hoanui as he did the same to me. I instantly heard the guy to my left cry "Hiiiieeee!" as he dropped his coal immediately. I kept my focus and ignored him. 'Cold stone' I told myself 'cold stone'.

I squeezed my 'cold stone' firmly in my left hand. I kept eye contact with Hoanui. I didn't break my focus as both Tane to his right and the guy to his left both gave in with their "Hiiiieeee!" and tossed their coals.

From my peripheral vision I could see that Tane clutched his hand and Puatea immediately came to pour water on it. Three down, three to go. I estimated it had been close to five seconds so far. Five seconds sounds fast, but can be an eternity when you are holding a flaming coal in your bare hand!

'Cold stone' I reminded myself. I didn't see the guy to my left give in, but I heard his "Hiiiieeee!" and I knew that it was just Hoanui and I left standing.

I sat in a trance and transferred the heat from my hand to my eyes as my eyes burned a hole in Hoanui from across the circle. This had turned into a game of pride between two friends. This was a game of 'chicken' and 'hot potato' rolled into one.

The drums beat faster and faster. 'Cold stone, cold stone, cold stone.' I repeated in my head.

I knew it had been well over ten seconds and maybe approaching twenty. I didn't know and I didn't care - I had lost all sense of time. My goal was to win this contest. I had come this far. I had learned an impossible dance and then done it while standing in flaming coals so far tonight. Sitting with a 'cold stone' in my hand was easy in comparison I convinced myself.

I didn't blink, I just stared at Hoanui from about eight feet away. We leaned in closer to each other. Neither of us flinched. Our faces remained emotionless. Our eyes remained opened. Our hands remained clinched. I felt a searing pain piercing through my left hand, but I ignored it and squeezed tighter. I would not say that word first, I would not give in. 'Cold stone' I told myself.

I kept eye contact with my friendly adversary and noticed his face began to change. He pursed his mouth and squinted his eyes and started to scream a long "H-h-h-h-h-hiiiiiieeeeeeeeeeeeeee!" before finally dropping the coal and clutching his hand to his chest. Puatea was quick to pour water on his hand as he opened it.

I clenched my fist tighter around my coal, sprang to my feet and exclaimed "yeeeeeeah!" as I spiked my coal into the sand as if I had just caught the winning touchdown in a super bowl game. I then closed my fist tightly again and told myself 'ice cube, ice cube'. Puatea quickly offered to pour water on my hand, but I declined the offer.

The tribe erupted into tribal chanting. Hoanui sprang to his feet and hugged me. Tane reluctantly did the same and the other members of the circle also congratulated me. Maruia, Tania and Lance had crowded closer during the intense event. Maruia kissed my cheeks and hugged me and then handed me the camera. "I got it all on recording." She said with a smile.

Lance bent down to examine the coal that I had spiked. I thought for a minute he was going to pick it up as he extended his hand in such a fashion, but he jerked back at the last second only millimeters from the coal.

"Good job, bro." He said as he patted me on the back. "I thought maybe you got a dud or something, but not the case. How the hell did you do that?" He asked.

"Focus, courage, strength, concentration, mind over matter, will-power and... a LOT of BALLS!" I answered as I busted out laughing.

"Let me see your hand, bro." Lance asked as he tried to grab my arm. I extended my arm out to him and opened my hand and spread my fingers. "Oh my God!" he exclaimed as he examined my palm. "Not even red. Maybe pink." He said in disbelief.

I looked over on the other side of the fire as one of the girls was applying something to Tane's hand as well as one of the other guys who dropped out first.

Lance kept looking at my palm and fingers in utter amazement. "Jesus Christ. That is a 'Stan-dunk' if I've ever seen one!"

"Stan-dunk?" Maruia asked of Lance.

"Yeah, never mind - it's an inside joke between Stan and me." Lance shrugged off his own commentary with no further explanation, so Maruia turned her attention to me.

"In basketball when a player jumps up and forcefully slams the ball directly through the hoop - sometimes even hanging by their wrists on the rim for a second it's called a slam-dunk. It is the most profound way to score in the game. The term is also used in business when you strike a great deal or when you succeed in other major accomplishments in life. Lance and some of my friends just substituted my name 'Stan' for 'slam' since it kind of rhymes and because I am always accomplishing amazing things." I explained to her with a less than humble tone.

"Let's not get carried away now." Lance said to diffuse the attention away from me.

"I'd say the term applies nicely to you, Stan." Maruia said in a coy, sexy tone and she placed her hand in my unburned palm.

"Yeah, I will second that Stan-dunk comment." Hoanui added. "Stan, I've been doing the circle of fire since I was 15 years old - that's almost 20 years ago. It took 15 years of watching my father and others before I built up the courage to participate. My first dozen or so times lasted about one second before I dropped the coal. I've been burned dozens more times - once the blisters lasted over two weeks. I was truly scared for you to try this tonight. You danced well in the fire, so I knew you would have the courage to try this, but I honestly assumed that you would be the first one out and immediately drop the coal. I said a quick prayer to the Gods for you that your burns would not be too severe. I am certainly burning right now and expect to have limited use of my hand tomorrow. I cannot understand how..."

I cut Hoanui off before he could finish his sentence and I interjected a borrowed quote from my Tony Robbins experience. "The only answer is that sometimes there are no answers. There are things in life we cannot and will not understand. The power of the mind can be one of them." I cracked a smile and left it at that.

A flute sounded and the drums began beating again.

"It's our turn now. Sit down and make yourselves comfortable guys." Tania said as she took Maruia by the hand and headed over to the fire. The rest of the female contingency did the same as the guys all sat in the sand around the other perimeter of the fire.

"No way - are they going to do the fire walk also?" I asked Hoanui.

"Nope, not a chance. It's much better - they are going to do the fertility dance." He answered. "Sit back and enjoy the show. Our work is done for the night, brother."

"Good." I said as I wiped the sweat from my forehead with the back of my hand. I immediately realized that I had smeared the tribal face-paint with my hand. Lance and Hoanui laughed at my smudged face.

"According to our tribal custom, the guys must first impress the ladies with a display of fortitude, courage and will power. Next, the ladies will then seduce the men that have proven themselves worthy with their seductive dance. After that, it's lights out for the married folks and the courting ones also if you know what I mean." Hoanui said as he nudged me.

Arenui ran up behind us and then plopped down in the sand between Hoa and I. "Nice, brah!" he said as he extended his fist to knuckle bump me.

"Thanks, man." I said as I noticed that Arenui was holding a smoking pipe in his other hand.

Arenui took a quick toke on the pipe and then passed it to me. "Tane is crying like a baby about his burns over there and the two real men are sitting here laughing. You dudes rock." He said as he placed his arms on Hoanui's and my shoulders. "Now let's watch the ladies and enjoy. Smoke that thing, man." He said as he passed the smoking pipe to me.

I took a quick toke of the pipe and almost choked on the strong herbal essence of the smoke. I recognized the faint taste and smell of marijuana, but it was heavily masked by something else that it was mixed with. I hit it again and this time it went down much smoother. I passed it to Lance who wasted no time putting some smoke in the air.

"You and Hoanui handle the fire and Arenui and I will handle the smoke" Lance said as he exhaled.

I laughed and turned my attention to the ladies who had begun their sensuous dance. I sipped on my Kavaty and leaned back on my elbows and dug my toes into the sand. The girls circled the fire in the same fashion that the guys had done - the only exception being the absence of the fire pit in the line-up.

Their dance was very similar to the one I had learned except that their motion originated in the hips rather than the knees. They danced sort of belly-dancer style and moved their waists erratically as if their spines were made of rubber. Their mid-sections swayed back and forth with the rhythm of the drum beats. The circle of ladies rotated every few seconds so that a different girl was centered in front of us and the whole group got to show off their skills to everyone. The dance was intoxicating and compounded the effects of the Kava Kava and the herbal peace pipe.

"Brahs, the ladies dance like this for a while and then they break the circle and go to the guy they want to seduce." Arenui informed me as he leaned over.

It was interesting to me. It was like a tribal strip club, but you didn't have to pay, the girls were all stunning and healthy and kept their 'clothes' or tribal wear on. This must have been where the whole strip-club concept started. The concept certainly got lost in translation along with a lot of morals and values by the time it made it to the states!

Maruia was the first to break out of the circle and she made a bee-line straight for me. She knelt down in front of me as she continued to undulate her hips from her crouched position only inches from my face.

Wow - it was the best show I'd ever seen. Granted, I hadn't been to many strip clubs, but I knew it couldn't get any better than this. She coaxed me from my comfortable seated position and took my Kavaty from me. She held the cup to my lips and gently tipped the bottom of the cup to pour the remaining liquid into my mouth. As soon as I swallowed, she tossed the cup on the ground and then locked her lips around mine and planted a long, sensuous kiss on me. We danced in front of the guys for a bit. I did my male knee-knocking dance in sync with her female hip undulation. We made perfect tribal dance partners.

Hoanui grabbed the camera and snapped some pics of us dancing. We impressed all of the tribe with our dancing ability as well as our passion for each other. Finally, I couldn't take anymore and we decided to retire for the evening. Most of the tribe had already done the same. We said goodnight to everyone who remained and Maruia walked Lance and me back to our hut.

I had resisted the urge all night, but could no longer hold back. Lance was walking a couple of steps in front of Maruia and me. I put a quick haste in my step and sidled up behind Lance and grabbed hold of his tighty-whities and pulled them halfway up his back into a massive wedgie. I heard something tear with the amount of force I put into the motion. I hoped it wasn't his ass crack - cracking more!

"Real funny, jackass!" Lance shouted as he quickly turned to face me. He was pissed as I knew he would be and he gave me a push. "Didn't we quit giving wedgies in the 5th grade?" He sarcastically asked.

"No, but I quit wearing tighty-whitie underwear in the fifth grade!" I shot back quickly.

Maruia and I were both having a hard time controlling our laughter as he picked his underwear out of his ass crack from under the grass skirt. I saw the flash of the camera as Maruia instinctively snapped a shot of Lance in his embarr'ass'ing state.

"Real funny, guys. That pic better not end up on Facebook. I mean it." He said in disapproval.

"I'm thinking album cover or even profile pic - either way it's definitely getting tagged!" I said as I choked on my words with laughter.

Lance continued to grumble as he guarded his back while we followed him to the hut. He immediately went into the darkness of the hut and I stood outside with Maruia. I glanced up at the pitch black sky dotted with stars above and then down into Maruia's eyes. The silhouette of her face was barely visible in the darkness of the night.

"What an amazing day. I'm so happy to be back here with you again." I said as I leaned down and passionately kissed her on the lips, face and neck.

"You have no idea how happy I am too." She said in between breaths and kisses.

"Good night my Rahitian beauty. See you in the morning." I said as I kissed her one last time and entered my hut solo.

Ordinarily I would escort a lady home and not leave her standing on my doorstep to find her own way home, but in this case I felt Maruia was more than capable of finding her own way in the dark. She probably knew the island like the back of her hand. Plus, my legs could hardly take another moment of walking or standing after all of the dancing.

I pulled off my headpiece and tossed it to the side. I pulled the tunic over my head and dropped my grass shirt. I fumbled around the floor of the hut until my hands felt the familiar micro-fiber material in my board shorts. I slipped the shorts on and crashed onto my comfortable mattress. My head was spinning and my body was almost floating on air. I was high on life, high on energy, high on love, high on Rahiti and maybe a little high on Kava Kava and the herb smoke too. I passed out within seconds with a huge smile plastered on my face.

Rahiti

I awoke early the next morning at sunrise. My first night's sleep in Rahiti had been exceptional. The sounds of nature filled the hut. A gentle breeze blew through the thatching on the hut walls and roof - "Air Conditioning" I thought.

The mattress I slept on was exceptionally comfortable. Although it was woven and stuffed with palm thatching and grass, it rivaled the comfort of my $3000 hypo-allergenic pillow top mattress at home. This mattress was special to me because I knew it was handcrafted with love by the Rahitian girls.

I was unbelievably comfortable and I slept like a baby. Even though I had gone to bed elated and with a buzz from the tribal ceremony, I woke up well rested and energized with the exception of some muscle aches in my legs from the excessive knee-knock dancing. It was wonderful to wake up feeling great – free from hangovers and any jet lag.

I looked at the palm of my left hand and then compared it to my right hand – nothing out of the ordinary! My hand looked just as normal as if I had never clenched a hot coal for umpteen seconds last night. It was an amazing feat that reminded me of what I was capable of if I put my mind to it.

I let my mind wander about all of the things I intended to do while I was here for the next six months. I was so thrilled to be here with my friends again and to have some quality time with my brother too. I heard Lance stirring on the other side of the hut as he woke and rolled over to face me.

"What time is it dude?" He asked.

Time for another wedgie I thought to myself, but answered "Who cares dude?" I responded. "I took my watch off when we got on the airplane in LAX and I don't intend to wear it again while I'm here."

"Why did you do that?" He asked.

"Call it part of my stress reduction plan. You got somewhere you need to be at a particular time?"

"No, but it's nice to know what time it is."

"Actually it no longer matters to me. I'm going to make the most of every minute I'm here regardless of what time it is. Time no longer matters to me." I said with definite resolve.

We chatted briefly about the festivities last night and some of the sounds we heard in the night while sleeping and about how incredibly comfortable the bedding and the temperature of the hut was. We then exited the hut, grabbed our boards and headed down to the beach. Lance wasted no time paddling out into the surf. I stayed on the beach and started practicing my yoga. From my yoga pose positions I watched Lance carve up the shore break right in front of me.

Maruia, Puatea and Tania were busy doing their morning chores when we left the village but I noticed them as they walked down the trail to the beach and found me in a warrior pose. They questioned my position and I told them a bit about yoga. The girls shed their parea wraps as they were not conducive to yoga poses. The three of them stood nude next to me as I instructed them on some different yoga positions.

The girls struck the same pose as me in perfect form. We went through some Vinyassa flows and sun salutations. I had an extremely 'hard' time concentrating on yoga and teaching them the poses as I was totally distracted by their naked beauty. I played it as cool as possible though as I thought about 'Sesame Street, Mr. Rogers, Sesame Street, Mr. Rogers' to stifle my burgeoning erection. It was a stunt that had worked for me all of my life to both prevent embarrassing situations as well as to prolong love making sessions. This situation tested the validity of my mind/body control to its max. Dancing in a fire and holding a hot coal in my hand paled in comparison to the self control it took me to control my libido around these beautiful women!

I totally forgot that Lance was even in the water surfing as I engrossed myself in the moment with the ladies. I focused on my form, my breathing and setting a good example for my lady friends as they attempted to imitate all of my poses. We flowed from pose to pose - linking our body movements and shifting our poses in accordance with our breath. We spread our feet hip-width apart and pressed our toes into the sand and then spread our fingers and pressed our hands into the sand as we piked our bodies back into a perfect down-dog position. I raised my head for a moment to make sure the ladies were exhibiting good form. I lost my breath for a moment - wow, what a sight! 'Where is the damn camera now?' I thought.

Then I dismissed the thought as it would be highly disrespectful to photograph the ladies in their natural beauty in such a precarious and 'vulnerable' position. I decided to just take a mental snapshot and capture the image in my mind and file it among my 'favorite things I've ever seen' place in my memory bank.

We continued our yoga session on the white sandy beach as we stretched, breathed, relaxed and engaged core strength when necessary. I had practiced yoga for over a decade in many different environments and with many different people, but this was by far my best session ever - plus, I was in control and leading.

After about 30 to 40 minutes of yoga, my legs had almost fully rejuvenated after the tribal dance from last night. Our practice on the soft sand felt great, but our bodies had accumulated sand on about every inch of our skin.

"Bath time." Tania said with a smile as she rose from our final resting pose on our backs.

I momentarily gave thanks to the yoga Gods before following the girls down to the water to bathe. Even though I was wearing board shorts and was about to get them wet surfing anyway, I shed them on the beach at the edge of the water since the girls were naked. To a native Rahitian this was just as normal as us waking up and taking a shower in the privacy of our own bathrooms at home every morning. This was the routine that they have known all of their lives. There was no shame or embarrassment in their nudity or public bathing. It was almost like they never got word that Eve tempted Adam with the apple in the Garden of Eden. Being one with nature and exposing their bodies was natural and normal. This was going to take some getting used to for me as I struggled to keep my burgeoning erection at bay and fight off my natural urge of male arousal. It was a sensory overload for me - yoga, the sunrise, perfect weather, crispness in the air, the fragrant smell of flowers, three beautiful naked Rahitian girls frolicking in the water right in front of me. It was the kind of thing that guys dream about. 'Sesame Street, Mr. Rogers, Sesame Street, Mr. Rogers' I kept reminding myself.

I concluded my bathing with the ladies, exited the water with them only to put my board shorts on, grab my board and join Lance back in the water. He had been trying to surf while watching the girls out of the corner of his eye. He must have a hell of a love for surfing to choose it over yoga on the beach with three lovely ladies. The ladies stood nude on the beach to "air dry" for a bit as they watched me paddle out to meet my brother.

I ducked a few waves and stroked my way to Lance with a big smile on my face. "So, how gay is yoga now?" I asked him with every ounce of sarcasm I could muster.

"Ok, I'll chalk up one more Stan-dunk to you. That was pretty incredible to watch even from out here. I'm starting to realize that my brother is the man." He said with a hint of hidden anguish.

"Stan the man." I shouted egotistically as I turned and paddled into an oncoming wave leaving Lance in the lineup.

I screamed down the face of the wave and shredded it up a little to impress the ladies who were still standing on the beach watching us. They were impressed with our surfing and we were impressed by them. The thing that really struck me about the Rahitian natives was their overwhelming natural beauty.

The girls could wake up in the morning and look just as beautiful as they did in the middle of the day - without the benefit of makeup, hair products, curling irons, hair dryers etc... The fact that they bathed in salt water and didn't have conditioner for their hair other than the natural coconut and plant oils that they extracted and used as lotions made their beauty even more impressive. All of the 'potions' and lotions that they used were all derived from the natural flora on the island. Their hair seemed to air-dry naturally and fall into perfect placement every time. Their skin was blemish free and required no drugs or artificial products. Their beauty was definitely testament to clean, natural, stress-free healthy island living. The ladies stayed on the beach and watched us catch a few waves before waving goodbye and heading up the trail to the village.

A short time later, Arenui and Hoanui came down to the beach. Arenui was dragging his stick with him and paddled out to join the surf session with Lance. I paddled in past Arenui and headed up to the beach to meet Hoanui who was eager to chat with me.

"How is your hand my fellow fire-handler?" Hoanui asked right away.

"Fine." I said as I held up my wet hand to reveal an unscathed palm.

"Me too, but Tane - not so fine!" Hoanui said with a laugh as he held up his palm next to mine.

"He must have had Maruia on his mind and not been concentrating on his health." I said with a snicker.

"Actually, keep this between us, but it was the first time in a very long time that he did the fire-handling. I believe he made a last minute decision to do it when he learned that you were going to give it a try. Last time he did it, he burned the hell out of himself also. I think he desperately wanted to 'one-up' you. He just doesn't have any mind control." Hoanui explained in confidence.

"Hence the jealous attitude all of the time." I replied.

"Exactly." Hoanui nodded. "Let's take a walk."

"I've got a better idea - let's take a run." I said to my Rahitian friend.

"Ok, what did you have in mind?" He asked.

"Does the beach circle the entire island and is it unimpeded?" I asked.

"What does unimpeded mean?" He responded.

"Are there any obstacles that would keep us from running smoothly around the entire island by way of the beach?" I clarified.

"Nope. Are you sure your legs are up for a run that long after your dancing last night?" He questioned.

"I guess we will find out." I said as I broke into stride on the beach.

Hoanui followed next to me. I settled into a comfortable, yet aggressive pace that the Nui could keep up with. We talked and surveyed the island from the beach. I looked out over the beautiful landscape and thought how different it was from the urban setting I was accustomed to back home. I loved it, but thought 'if only there were a smoothie shop here'. Oh well, I would have to learn to substitute fresh fruits, coconut milk and kava for my wheatgrass shot.

94

Hoa started out talking about all of the areas of the island, but his conversation became shorter and then non-existent as he became winded from trying to keep pace with me. We ran side by side for about two or three miles until Hoanui started to lose pace. "Are we halfway around the island yet?" I asked.

"Not quite." He managed to squeeze out a quick response in between gasping for air.

"Ok, why don't you turn back in the direction we came from and meet me back at my hut? I'll continue on the long way around. Let's race." I challenged.

"Done deal!" He said as he gasped for air and turned to head back.

I picked up my pace a bit and began to stride more freely not having to worry about losing a partner or embarrassing anyone. I planned to embarrass him by getting back to the hut first. I had no idea how much farther I had to run nor how much of a head start I had given my friendly adversary. I didn't care - it was more of a competition with myself to just run my best.

I had run on soft sand back home in VA Beach hundreds of times, but it had been a while and my calves weren't quite ready for it - especially after the workout my legs got last night. I pushed anyway. I picked up my feet and lengthened my stride. I breathed the fresh, crisp, salty island air into my lungs. I smiled as I ran like a gazelle across the white sand beach parallel to the teal green water. I didn't have a watch on so I had no idea what my time was and couldn't gauge my distance accurately, but I estimated I had run over 6 miles by the time I started to see familiar territory again.

I had almost rounded the entire island and still felt great. I picked up my pace to a sprint until I reached the beach where Lance and Arenui were still surfing. I didn't see Hoanui yet, so I turned on my 'burners' and hit full speed up the trail to the hut. I sprinted faster than I had remembered running in recent memory. I reached the hut just as I had not another ounce of energy to exert. I had paced myself and timed the run perfectly to my ability. I stopped sprinting and slowed to a trot as I circled my hut and then meandered through the village. I didn't see Hoanui anywhere, but my sprinting had caught the attention of many of the villagers. I asked a few of them as I passed "Have you seen Hoanui in the last few minutes?"

Everyone responded "No" with concern as they assumed there was some sort of problem.

I returned to my hut and stopped to stretch. Puatea walked over to me and asked "Is everything okay?"

"Oh yeah, everything is good. I just had a race with Hoanui and I was looking for him." I replied.

"Well, I guess you beat him at one more thing." She said as she smiled and walked away.

I contemplated walking back down the trail to the beach in case he stopped to talk to Lance and Arenui. I figured if he wasn't there, I'd start to back-track the island in the opposite direction until I ran into him. I went into the hut to grab a bottle of water to take with me on my victory walk. I came out of the hut a moment later to see Hoanui walking toward my hut, but from a different direction than the trail to the beach.

"You've got to be kidding me!" He said as he shook his head.

"What, bro?" I asked as I tried to be a little humble to hide my glowing victory.

"I have a confession to make." He said with a grin. "I cheated and you still beat me!"

"What do you mean?" I asked with curiosity.

"I mean, I took another trail - a shortcut across the island back to the village. I figured I could take it easy and still beat you. We only ran about a third of the way around the island on the beach. I had a huge head start on you. I cut across the island and… damn you are hardcore!" He said as he extended his arm to hug me. "I can learn a lot from you. You will push me to do my best from now on."

"Ok, I will be your coach and motivator and you can be my host." I said with resolve.

"Look, take a swim and cool off and relax for a few and then I will meet up with you and we can start getting to work. I can't wait to see if your work ethic is the same as your fire-handling and running!" He said as he patted me on the back and walked away.

I walked down to the beach and took a quick dip and then watched Are and Lance tear up some surf as I 'air dried' on the beach. A little while later Hoa came walking down the trail and told me he was ready to get started.

Hoanui decided to start out by giving me a tour of the entire island to refresh my memory of the layout and to make sure there wasn't a better spot that he hadn't thought of to build the community center. First he showed me the spot that he had in mind for the construction and explained his rationale for choosing the spot. He noted all of the pros and cons of the spot and pointed out several attributes including its proximity to one of the only fresh water springs on the island. We staked it out and surveyed the plot and measured all of our angles and cross-reference points. Just to make sure that he had chosen the most optimum spot, he decided to cover almost the rest of the entire island with me as well.

He showed me the remainder of the island for the rest of the day - the watering hole, the palms, the rock outcroppings, the beaches, and the jungle. As he toured me across the island, I realized that there was a network of trails all over the island which all seemed to originate on the beach and culminate at the clearing in the center of the island at the village. Most of the Rahitians lived in the village in a series of inter-connecting huts, but some chose to live in outlying areas secluded in the jungle off of one of the trails. Hoanui referred to the jungle huts as the "suburbs".

My dancing and fire-handling ability made me somewhat of a celebrity on the island. Everyone already knew who I was, but today everyone we passed went out of their way to stop and congratulate me. Surprisingly, Hoanui didn't mind the attention I was getting - especially since it was he who I had defeated. If it had been Lance, he would have been eaten up with jealousy and his eyes would have rolled out of his head by now. A couple of islanders who couldn't speak English simply made a fist and mimicked my "Stan-dunk" spike I did with the coal after I won. It was a great feeling to be respected and liked in a new place so soon.

There were just over a hundred Rahitians who lived on the island full time and probably another couple dozen who lived on other islands but visited frequently. About 10 or so Rahitians spoke English fluently including Hoanui, Arenui, Tane, Maruia, Tania, Puatea and Fetia and about another dozen spoke enough broken English to hold a very basic conversation. I was glad to have a well-educated guide in Hoanui to translate and introduce me to all of the locals. I made it my goal to try to learn everyone's name and something about each one of them by the time I left. Hoanui was the perfect person to help me accomplish this goal. Our initial tour of the island coupled with my attention from the tribal ceremony last night was making it immediately possible to meet everyone.

During our tour, Hoanui also introduced me to much of the island's flora and fauna. I was very pleased to learn that there were no poisonous spiders or bugs, no snakes and no poison ivy - there was virtually nothing harmful to man living on the island. It was, however, a very fragile and self-contained eco system. Everything and every animal relied on other things for their existence. Much the same as the people in Rahiti relied on Mother Nature to bring rain, the seas to bring fish, the skies to bring sun and the soil to bear plants and fruits. It was Rahitian culture to not fish with nets and wipe out whole colonies of fish, but rather to catch one at a time and leave the others behind to mate and produce more future generations of the species. The Rahitians also tried to preserve nature and never cut down plants or trees unless absolutely necessary. They understood that picking fruits and leaves off of the trees did not kill the plant, but left it alive to produce more fruit and foliage for future consumption.

Hoanui stopped and knelt down by a small, knee-high bush with big green leaves about the size of my hand. "Kava Kava" he said.

"Ah, this is the tea we were drinking at the tribal ceremony last night?" I asked as I pinched off a leaf and smelt it.

"Yeah, but the tea does not come from the leaves, but rather the roots." He answered as he dug a small patch of soil from around the base of the plant with his hands to expose its roots. He put two fingers under a root about the size of a pencil and snapped it off about six inches from the main stalk of the plant. He then carefully pushed the remaining root back into the ground and covered it up with soil. "That will grow back again and be ready for harvest in several months." He said as he shook the dirt off of the root he had excavated. He rolled the root between his fingers and twisted it in half and then handed me one of the equal portions. He popped his in his mouth and we started walking down the trail again. I held my root in my hands and explored the earthy item with my fingers and my eyes. I put it to my nose and smelt the herbal, natural fragrance from the juice that flowed from its broken ends. I would normally wash all of my produce thoroughly at home before eating it. There was something natural, yet dirty that kept me from popping the root right into my mouth.

"Oh, go ahead and chew on it." Hoanui said as he noticed my hesitation in eating the root. "It's not going to kill you - in fact, it's very healthy. A little dirt never hurt." He added with a smile.

I gave it a final shake and popped it in my mouth. It tasted surprisingly good - dirt and all! The flavor was very pungent and earthy, but after all, I was a vegetarian and loved for all of my food to be 'natural'. I chewed on the root and sucked its juice Huckleberry Finn style. Within moments my lips, gums and tongue began to tingle and become slightly numb. "Interesting taste and sensation" I said to Hoanui. It was the same sensation I felt in my mouth last night while sipping on the tea.

"The effects are better than alcohol, plus it is healthy and there is no hangover or addiction." He said.

"Cool" I thought.

"The Kava Kava plant has been an integral part of our culture for thousands of years. It is a part of our normal diet, tribal ritual and medicine too. It soothes the mind and body and relieves you of stress and pain." Hoanui explained as he chewed away on his root.

"Really?"

"Yeah, you can make tea by simply boiling the roots in water and then drinking the water. You can grind the root into powder and add the powder to water or put the powder directly onto your skin or mouth to soothe pain. Or you can do like I do and just chew on the root. It never gets old - I've been chewing Kava Kava roots for years. It keeps your teeth and gums clean too. Better than flossing!" Hoanui added as he turned to me and nodded his head.

He looked pretty funny with the root hanging from his lip and his mouth pursed open on one side as if to exaggerate his enjoyment from the herb.

"And if the Kava Kava can't handle your ailment and satisfy your stress, the cannabis certainly will." He said as he pointed from the trail into the woods at a large marijuana plant full of buds ready for harvest.

"Wow." I exclaimed as I stared at the green and purple five-leafed plant. "Haven't ever seen one in the wild like that" I added.

"Grows natively everywhere here - peace pipe filling!" He said with a smile. "It certainly keeps the peace too. It's hard to want to fight when you are soothed and relaxed by the herbal remedies on the island. The people respect the power of the plants and use them in moderation and never abuse them - especially when there is work to be done. You will see" He said as he winked at me.

During our tour of the island we found a perfect spot for me to plant my garden. The soil was very fertile and moist and there was low-lying surrounding growth and ample sun all day long. I made a mental note of the spot and starting laying out the planting pattern in my head. The island of Rahiti was relatively flat, but it has some small elevations from the ancient weathered volcano which once formed the island. There were a few random rock outcroppings where the fertile soil had been eroded off of the underlying volcanic rocks. Overall, the island is a flat oasis full of lush, dense tropical vegetation - a perfect environment for any plant to grow.

After touring the entire island for the better part of the day, I concurred with Hoa's choice of locations for the community center as it was relatively free from tall palms which could be a hazard in high winds, plus the spot was well sheltered by dense low-lying vegetation. The spot was also easily accessible and central to the village and outlying huts. The few tall palms that were within falling distance of the structure we tagged and marked for removal to reduce the possibility of typhoon damage.

Hoanui introduced me to his crew of Rahitian laborers who were ready, willing and able to make another trek to Tahiti to load up pontoon boat with more cargo from Connie. We decided that Hoanui should make the supply runs to Tahiti with his crew and that I should stay on the island with the other half of the crew and oversee the starting of the ground work and foundation. This suited me fine because I had no desire to return to 'civilization' and leave the peace and tranquility of Rahiti. I was also the only one capable of reading the plans properly and instructing the labor how to begin the construction process.

So Hoanui split his crew in half based on their skills and physical abilities. He would take several guys with him to load and transport and leave me an ample crew to start the construction. We ate dinner and discussed our plans for the next day and then retired to bed early. It had been a very busy two days on the island so far.

The next morning I started off the usual way with my morning yoga session. The three girls joined me for yoga and then we bathed while Arenui and Lance surfed. I skipped the run this morning and rendezvoused with Hoanui in the village. Hoa hooked me up with my crew and made sure they could understand what to do and then he took off to Tahiti with his crew on the pontoon boat.

My crew wasted no time in getting busy clearing out vegetation in the construction zone. The guys uprooted trees, cleared undergrowth, dug holes and excavated and moved soil. The tools that I brought them to use were a very welcomed and pleasant surprise. I think that using the tools made the job fun and less like work for them. Compared to the primitive tools they had on the island, my tools were a dream come true. They were extra happy to learn that I would be leaving them behind for them to use in the future. I taught them to respect and care for the tools because if they broke, we had no replacements. They used my tools with the same care and respect that they placed on their own hands. It was awesome to see how much a Rahitian appreciated the use of a steel-tipped shovel with a fiberglass handle and rubber grip.

It was clear to me how technology has really allowed modern society to thrive over the last hundred years and enabled man to do things that were previously impossible. Back home - large, national chain stores are able to operate and ship and track merchandise and inventory all over the country, tracking each sale of each item. UPS, Fed Ex and the postal service are able to deliver millions and millions of pieces of mail every day all over the world. With the help of computers and software programs, engineers and architects are able to design and build amazing structures that can withstand even the most profound forces of nature.

My project here in Rahiti was small on the scale of greatness in the world, but huge on the Rahitian scale of technology and importance. The small amount of tools and technology I brought here to this isolated island would make a huge impact on their way of life and their understanding of the world. From the hand and power tools they used to the computer we would show them and the movies and pictures we would see - they were all amazed at the ability of man to invent it and me to possess it.

I reiterated to myself that it was not my purpose to change this beautiful Rahitian culture, but just to enhance it a little bit. I felt like I was successfully doing just that. I didn't want to reinvent their wheel, I just wanted to grease it and make it roll a little smoother and safer. I wanted to add a little sugar to the tea and sweeten their perfect lifestyle.

I gained a great respect for the Rahitians and their way of life on the island. And I gained a great sense of appreciation for tools, materials, plans and technology that I brought in comparison to what was available on the island. Connie's load would bring their construction ability from the stone ages to modern standards immediately. It was amazing to take part in the transformation.

The ease of the undertaking and the smooth success was great testament to my planning and packing abilities. Everything went like clockwork. Everything was unloaded and transported in the order in which we needed it.

By the time Hoanui had returned from a four hour round trip with another load of cargo, my guys had cleared a substantial portion of the lot. We had even begun digging several footings. I didn't anticipate a tremendous amount of manual labor help from Lance based on his past history. Plus I knew it was only his third day on the island and surfing was first and foremost on his mind. It didn't bother me that he and Arenui chose to surf well past noon. When they did finally join us at the site, it was in perfect concert with lunch time - how coincidental! The girls had prepared a delicious and gorgeous lunch for us which we ate at the tiki hut. Hoanui and his crew had worked up a tremendous appetite as well. I had to restrain Lance and remind him to let the people who had 'worked' up an appetite eat first.

We worked in shifts unloading and carrying cargo, clearing brush and digging holes. All total we had about 12 Rahitian laborers helping us in addition to myself, Lance, Arenui, Tane (with only one good hand) and Hoanui. It was a brilliant crew and I was happy that it was free labor. I didn't have to worry about payroll on Friday or filing taxes on withheld wages and workers compensation insurance etc... It felt great to be free from the responsibility of being an employer in the US. I didn't have to worry about micro-managing anyone since they were working for free and they were not costing me by the minute. The ironic thing is that, although working for free, they worked harder than any other workers I had ever supervised. It was quite an anomaly. No one came into work drunk. No one took cigarette or coffee breaks. Everyone was very happy to just be working and doing something.

It seemed as if the workers were almost competing with each other to see who could work the hardest and the longest. I would love to kidnap these guys and take them back home to work for my contracting company. As good as my staff was at home, I would take one Rahitian over five of my fellow American laborers. Their work ethic was phenomenal. Even the older Rahitians were just as able-bodied and strong as the guys my age and younger. Lifting and carrying the heavy concrete and lumber was absolutely no problem for them. They made it look easy and fun.

They appreciated the fact that I was there working to help them - also for free. It was a great relationship and we all developed a tremendous amount of respect for each other. I formed an instant bond with all of them. Even Tane put his jealousy aside and listened to every one of my commands and followed my orders to the "T". Tane also proved to be a great translator between me and the elder workers who did not speak English. I was glad he could "offer at least one helping hand" and translate for us - until his other hand healed from its severe burns.

Our daily ritual continued for the next week or so. I would wake up in the morning at daybreak without the use of an alarm clock or the obligation of a wrist watch. Lance and Arenui would surf a dawn patrol session each morning while I did nude yoga on the beach with the girls. Even some of the laborers decided to join in on the yoga sessions. When the yoga wrapped up, the girls would bathe while I caught a wave or two and then we would all start our work day. The girls had to work extra hard preparing extra food to feed the extra-hungry laborers every day.

Hoanui and I would make our plan for the day and discuss progress and then split up as he would return to Connie with his moving crew and I would get my guys going on a particular task at the work site. I hadn't gotten my hands dirty in years and I began to realize how much I really missed physical labor. The natural assumption was that I had paid my dues on the physical side and had graduated to a life of management - never to return to the depths of manual labor again. Not the case- working with my hands was very fulfilling and pleasant to me.

I really enjoyed every aspect of my role in the construction - especially taking daily progress pictures and posting them on Facebook. I marked a notch on a rock adjacent to the worksite so that I could place my camera in the same location at the same angle to take a picture at the start and finish of every work day. A great slideshow of our progress was developing.

It was such a high sense of satisfaction stopping at the end of each day and tracking our progress based on where we had started in the morning. I set up the laptop and the portable satellite and linked up to the internet. The villagers took turns crowding around to look at the 17" inch Toughbook screen after dinner each night. They were enthralled as I showed them how I could pop the memory chip from the camera into the laptop and transfer pictures to the big screen.

Matahi was especially curious as to how the pictures went from the camera to the card to the computer to the rest of the world. It took hours and hours of explanation and translation to make him even remotely understand and comprehend the technology. I created several albums on Facebook and uploaded all of the pictures from the flight to our arrival, surfing, the tribal dance and fire-handling videos and the construction progress on the community center. I took the time to caption each picture with a brief explanation. The response from my friends back home was immediate and overwhelming. Their commentary and chatting was so excessive that I couldn't even begin to respond to it. I just kept on posting pictures on a daily basis and I sent Claire and a select group of other friends and family some personal messages.

Within a week all of the footings were dug, pilings were in the ground, concrete was poured and the box framing was done. The rest of the framing was prepared and ready to be erected and installed. The Rahitians didn't quite understand everything I was telling them to do because they had never seen construction like this before, but they followed my directions remarkably well and when the project started to take shape they totally understood why we had done the things we did. It was great to see them gain a sense of understanding of modern construction.

Within two weeks, the entire structure was framed and the roof was on, the windows and doors were installed and functional, and the exterior siding was installed. The entire structure was now weatherproof. This was quite an impressive feat considering I was working with an inexperienced "virgin crew". And even more impressive considering we had to import all of our tools and materials from halfway around the world and then wait for them to be delivered by pontoon boat from Tahiti to Rahiti.

The look on the locals faces as they took turns opening, entering and closing the front door and then peering through the hurricane proof windows was priceless. Many of the Rahitians had never seen a door or a clear pane of glass before. It was hard to believe, but it was true. The Rahitians were as excited about opening the door to their new community center as I would have been opening the door to a new Bentley or Ferrari. I loved it. I loved teaching, planning, working and watching this project come together. This was, by far, my favorite construction undertaking of my life. Everything about this project was spectacular. I was thrilled to be able to improve the lives of the Rahitians and to add safety and security to the island.

Rahiti was the epitome of natural beauty and the people were the epitome of Rahiti. To say that the Rahitian lifestyle was different than what most people could comprehend would be an understatement of mass proportion. One notable difference was the lack of soap, shampoo and detergent. Most people would assume that the lack of these common essentials would mean that people would be dirty and smelly, but that was not the case here. Everything was quite the opposite - very clean and fragrant. I loved the smell of Rahiti and the Rahitians.

Hoanui explained that the salt water acted as a great natural astringent and disinfectant to the body, clothes, dishes and anything else that required washing and it eliminated the need for soaps and deodorants. The clean, natural healthy lifestyle on the island also kept their bodies clean and free of toxins that would normally emit odors during perspiration. Naturally, when your body is clean and healthy it doesn't produce foul odors. The only odors their bodies emitted were natural hormones and pheromones and the sweet smell of vitamin D as their skin produced it naturally with sun exposure.

Speaking of sun exposure, Lance forgot to put on his SPF 45 lotion and got sunburned to a crisp because he wasn't naturally adapted to the strong South Pacific sun. The locals introduced him the soothing effects of natural aloe vera and coconut oil. I was glad that I had visited the tanning bed regularly for two months before I left home. I had built up a nice base tan and my skin was very resistant to the effects of the intense sun of the South Pacific.

To fully understand the culture and lifestyle here, imagine a world with no money, no cars, no corporations, no jobs, no pollution, no grocery stores, and no concept of time. Time was valuable and appreciated, but it wasn't clocked the same way it was in my life back home. I still appreciated every minute of every day - in fact, I appreciated it more because I got to spend my time doing things that I felt really mattered more to me. The most important time was the time spent with friends and loved ones.

The Rahitians worked, played and lived all day everyday with loved ones and were productive together - giving themselves a tighter bond and sense of appreciation for each other. Back home, couples very rarely worked together. In fact, work was an 8 hour separation and distraction from most relationships. I imagined how many of my friends back home were spending their time sitting at a desk in a cubicle in front of a computer right now – "thinking inside the box". I wondered how many millions of people were stuck in their vehicles in traffic right now. I looked up at the sky through swaying palm trees and thought 'this is the life.'

When I wasn't surfing with the guys, practicing yoga with the girls, building the community center with my crew or eating and socializing with the tribe, I was spending every moment possible with Maruia. We loved to take long walks on the beach and talk. We loved to watch the sunset together. We practiced the Rahitian tribal dance together. We loved to kiss passionately and act romantically, but we never slept together. Maruia wasn't a true virgin, but she was to me. For some reason I wanted to keep it that way for now. It wasn't that I didn't want her - in fact, I had never been so attracted to someone so much in my life. I think that limiting our physical interaction built the anticipation and made me want her even more. I was so attracted to her in every way. Her smile, her pearl white teeth, her green eyes, her perfect hair and skin, her sweet smell and pheromones, her positive attitude and caring nature all made her the most ideal woman in the world. I wanted to preserve her innocent beauty forever.

We ended almost every night with a "walk and talk" on the beach as the sun set. We often ended up cuddling on the beach as we watched the stars rotate overhead, but we always ended up parting company and retiring to our own huts to sleep. Lance, on the other hand, spent his time when he wasn't surfing, eating or sleeping - on the phone with his wife. I didn't bother him about it even though I wished he would spend some time bonding with the Rahitians instead. In a matter of a month or so he would be back at home with his wife again and could talk to her 24/7 for free, but then he would have missed a brilliant opportunity to make new friends and learn about a whole new culture and way of life.

Despite a great dinner and our usual comfortable walk on the beach, last night turned out to be the most uncomfortable night on the island so far. It had rained many times in the last few weeks, but usually only briefly during the day and then the sun would come out and warm things up and dry things out. When it rained during the day, you would typically only stay wet for a brief period of time. Your clothes and possessions would get wet as well, but you could just hang them up in a tree or clothes line and they would dry rapidly in the sun and warm air.

Overall the weather had been very pleasant and hot. Last night was not the case - it was quite miserable. When I went to sleep, the weather was pleasant, calm and warm, but I was awakened in the middle of the night by a torrential downpour and strong winds. I'm not sure whether it was the wind and rain or Lance's bitching that woke me up first.

The wind cut through the hut as if it weren't even there and the rain poured in through the roof and the walls. Water pooled on the sandy floor of the hut faster than the sand could absorb it. Before I knew it I was lying in a pool of cold rainwater. I was very thankful that all of the electronics and water-sensitive items were stowed away safely in the Rubbermaid containers. I contemplated crawling into one myself. Lance got up and put his wetsuit on. It was a smart move, but I decided to tough it out in nature. The Rahitians had survived hundreds of rainstorms without the benefit of a wetsuit - and so could I.

I toughed it out shirtless in my board shorts, curled up on my thatched mattress in a pool of water that covered half of my arms. My body kicked in its natural warming mechanism and I began to shiver. I was freezing, but I decided to employ the same mind-over-matter attitude that had empowered me in my fire-dancing and fire-handling. 'Hot tub' I told myself as I pretended to be in my bubbly, warm Jacuzzi tub back home. 'Hot tub' I repeated again and again as I relaxed my muscles and stretched out. An interesting thing happened - my shivering stopped and my goose-bumps went away. It felt as if the temperature of the rain had increased although I knew it hadn't.

The rain continued to pelt me in my face and body as it penetrated the roof. Lance continued to bitch - even in his wetsuit with a poncho pulled over his head. I lay there in a pool of water and pretended it was exactly where I wanted to be. I once again proved the power of the mind over the body and the importance of attitude. Certainly bitching wasn't going to stop the rain. Somehow I managed to fall back asleep in the wet environment with a smile on my face. I allowed myself to slip back into slumber and not worry about the wind and rain. I was also able to totally tune out Lance's complaining. There was no point in worrying or complaining about something I had no control over - so I didn't.

I awoke the next morning still wet although the rain and wind had stopped. Lance was sitting upright wearing his wetsuit. He was hunched over with a poncho pulled over his head. I sat upright and shook the rainwater from my head and body. I stood up and my feet sank into the soft, wet sand on the floor of the hut. I reached into my container and retrieved my camera and snapped a couple pictures of Lance sleeping upright in his wetsuit and rain gear. I also snapped a few pictures of the pool of water which remained on my mattress. I grabbed my mattress from the floor and took it outside. I gave it a shake and then hung it on the limb of a nearby Banyan tree. I stuck my head back in the hut to wake Lance.

"Dude, get up. The rain stopped. It's a beautiful morning. Let's get wet and salty." I said implying that it was time for a surf session.

He lifted his head and grumbled. I snapped a picture of him as he looked at me from under his poncho. "Damn rain!" He mumbled.

"Get up, bro. I'll be over at the tiki hut eating. Meet me there and then we can surf." I said as I left the hut and walked over to the central tiki.

Maruia and some of the women were already there prepping fruits and other foods for breakfast.

"Yoga this morning?" Maruia asked.

"Of course." I replied as I sat down and grabbed a Pomello fruit and began to peel it.

Soon many of the other Rahitians had also congregated around the table for the morning meal. Everyone ate in peace and no one really spoke of the storm. No one complained about getting wet. Everyone just did the same thing as I did when they exited the hut - they shook out their mattresses and some of their belongings and hung them on a tree or clothesline to dry. Lance was the first to complain about the rain when he finally came to the table. He was still wearing his wetsuit and he was grumbling about being cold.

"Damn rain. I didn't sleep a wink - froze my ass off. All of my stuff is wet. Shitty situation." He complained to everyone within earshot.

"You slept a wink - you were sleeping sitting upright this morning when I woke up - I've got pictures to prove it." I interjected into his bitching.

"I don't have any idea how the hell you slept through that storm last night. That was crazy." He continued.

"That storm last night was nothing - a mere rain shower." Maruia said in a complacent tone. "Wait until a typhoon hits." She added.

105

"If that wasn't a typhoon, then I don't know what a typhoon is." Lance said.

"A typhoon is when you wake up in the night and your hut is completely gone!" Tania explained.

"How do you guys deal with that?" Lance asked.

"Well, first we thank the Gods that we survived it and are still here to build a new hut. Then we sleep in the woods or pack into the remaining huts for the next few days or weeks until we can rebuild what we lost." Tania answered.

"That's life in a hut." Maruia added. "You just get used to it."

"I don't know if I could ever get used to waking up in the middle of the night freezing my ass off in a puddle of water. It's just not right." Lance argued.

"We've done it all of our lives." Tania said as Maruia nodded her head in agreement.

"I believe that the body can adapt to a wide range of situations - sometimes even extremely uncomfortable ones. Last night I woke up cold and wet too, but instead of letting it bother me, I changed my mindset and attitude about it. I told myself that the rain that woke me up and made me cold last night was the same rain that would fill our canteens with drinking water and also hydrate the soil and the plants that we depend on for food. I also pretended that I was lying in my hot tub back home instead of a cold puddle of sandy rain water. It worked and I fell back asleep in no time."

"Yeah - if you live your whole life that way it becomes normal and it doesn't bother you." Tania said.

"The beauty of water is that it's natural and it dries naturally" I suggested.

"When you live your life in weatherproof, climate controlled environment you become very sensitive to even the slightest temperature change. When you live in nature, your body becomes tolerant to a wide range of conditions." Maruia added.

"Living in air conditioned houses and driving cars with A/C and even wearing wet-suits does detach us from nature and make us more sensitive to change in climate. The human body is capable of living in a variety of climates and temperature ranges from desert at the equator to the glaciers or the Arctic Circle." I agreed.

"Screw the rain - let's get wet and salty and surf!" Lance insisted as he stuffed a papaya in his mouth and stood up to leave the table.

"Sometimes you have to have rain to appreciate the sunshine - even in a tropical paradise." I said as I stood up, kissed Maruia's hand and followed Lance to the beach. "See ya for yoga in a bit." I said as I turned my head back to the girls.

Mata Utu

This morning Lance and I sat on the beach with the two Nui's after an awesome dawn patrol surf session. The four of us had enjoyed a great Rahitian beach break surf session for over three hours. Copious amounts of clean, barreling waves had given us our exercise as well as our fill of surfing for the day. We all had our asses handed to us on at least one wave each as the punishing waves barreled hard right onto the beach. The name of the game this morning was fast takeoffs, quick drops and quicker bottom turns.

Hoanui and Arenui were impressed with how well Lance and I had adapted to the Rahitian surf. After all, it was a far cry from what we were accustomed to back home on the east coast of the U.S. I hated to even think about the little bullshit ripples that we called waves back home. I think the waves in Rahiti on a bad day are better than the best day back in Virginia Beach – at least it seemed that way. I was feeling very confident in my abilities to ride the big surf that the South Pacific offered up and I got braver and braver every day - charging larger and carving harder with each session.

As we sat there watching the tide roll in and flatten out the waves, the Nui brothers got a big smile on their faces and began speaking between themselves in Rahitian. I was curious as to what they were talking about, but I figured I would find out soon enough. I could tell that Arenui was the protagonist in the conversation and it seemed like he was trying to convince Hoanui of something as if he were a used car salesman trying to get him to take a test drive. They carried on their conversation in Rahitian a while until Arenui suddenly stopped and addressed us directly with a devilish smile on his face.

"So are you brahs ready to see some real South Pacific surf?" He asked as he raised his eyebrows.

Lance was all ears. "So what have we been surfing here? I do believe we are in the South Pacific, man."

Arenui answered my brother sarcastically. "These little ripples, they are starter waves bro. I was just telling Hoanui that you guys are ready for the big ones."

Lance's intrigue grew. "Dude, these waves are ripples? You should come back to Virginia Beach with us if you want to see ripples! So where are these "big ones" you have been holding out on us?"

Arenui's one word response was intriguing. "Mata". He repeated it again only slower and more exaggerated. "Mah-tah."

Then Hoanui chimed in "Ooo-too" as if he were chanting some tribal verse or mocking Arenui.

Arenui responded "Mah-tah" and again Hoanui answered "Ooo-too".

"So what is this Mata Utu?" Lance asked.

"Not what, but where..." Arenui chuckled as he pointed to the horizon in an easterly direction. "Brahs, right out there... lies the most beautiful island in all of the South Pacific. Mata Utu is her name. She is so beautiful that she is said to have been kissed by the Gods. The same kiss that blessed the island with beauty also reserved her only for the Gods. Are you guys feeling Godly?" he asked with a devilish smile.

I had no idea what to think of Arenui's statement. I didn't want to offend him. Religion is a very touchy subject for many and I respect that fact. Even though I am not religious, I am very spiritual. So I responded "I strive to be Godly in all of my actions."

Arenui followed up my statement with his own dissertation. "Godly or not, once you see this island, you will think you have been to heaven, man. Not only is it the most picturesque place you will ever lay your eyes on, but there is a reef break so perfect that it may be the best wave in the world – and it is perfectly hidden from the rest of the world too - not so much in location as in mystery." Arenui pointed to the east again. "About 12 kilometers or a good hour of kayaking if the current is right in that direction will take you to Mata-Utu."

"Mah-tah ooo-too." Hoanui interjected and chanted as Arenui continued his story.

"Mata is the easternmost island in the Rahitian Sea and has the best right break in the entire South Pacific. Dudes, even when there is very little swell elsewhere, the wave on Mata jacks up out of nowhere. The break originates at the point on the hip of Mount Mata and breaks the entire length of the three mile long island. Mount Mata is the tallest volcano in all of the nearby islands and acts as a beacon to the oasis surrounding it. The volcano itself makes up over a third of Mata Utu's real estate. It is said that Mount Mata guards and protects the island by summoning waves from the sea to crash hard on her outer reef to keep ships and visitors off of the eastern shore. The wave is both elegant and brutal as it barrels perfectly along the curvature of the outer reef. The face of the wave is always so clean and glassy that you can part your hair in the reflection while you are getting shacked in a double overhead tube, dude. The wave thunders and booms as its thick veil of water pitches and rolls before crashing onto the shallow reef below. The sound of the break can be heard all over the island and is said to be the 'heartbeat of the Gods'."

Hoanui interrupted again "Or the drumbeat of the Matains".

Arenui shrugged off the comment. "Dude, don't scare the crap out of them yet. Let them enjoy the vision of the wave."

"Scare the crap out of us?" Lance asked.

Arenui non-chalantly disregarded the question and continued. "So this wave goes on and on for minutes. It's not a wave that you can carve up and pull tricks on though – if you try, the trick will be on you as you are thrown over the falls and dashed into the reef. One wrong move on this wave can cost you your life, brah. I'm not joking dude. It is an easy launch and drop at the point and then very little work as you make your bottom turn – the wave does the rest as it propels you down her face and into the depths of her barrel. Just ride the tube and enjoy as you surf parallel to the most beautiful beach in the world."

Hoanui nodded his head in agreement as Arenui kept the tale going. "The hard part of surfing Mata's perfect wave is getting to it. The venture is long, but the ride is so worth it. It takes about an hour or so to kayak there and then add another hour to stroke back home. As you approach the island from the west, you are greeted by the calm, teal waters of Mata's lagoon. The sand on the beach of the lagoon is so white and pure that it will almost blind you if you don't have your shades on. The only relief from the blinding sun on the sand is the occasional patch of shade cast by one of the tall palm trees that grow scattered on the sandy spit between the leeward lagoon and the beach on the windward side of the island. To the right of the lagoon the southern end of the island is encompassed by a dense tropical rainforest. The rainforest is very forbidding from the southern coast as it ends abruptly on the jagged obsidian rock that makes up the shoreline on that end of the island. The rainforest extends from the southern shore all the way to Mount Mata's hip on the eastern boundary and the sandy spit on the northern side of the island. From the spit side the rainforest is very welcoming. The dense vegetation seems to part in one spot where there is a thousand year old trail that leads into the jungle. This trail winds through the forest past fresh water springs that collect and form small ponds throughout the jungle. You can't imagine the sights you will see as the sun pierces through the tree canopy high above your head. Some of the largest trees known to exist in the South Pacific are on Mata and these trees and plants bear some of the largest leaves and fruits ever seen. You will see mangoes, coconuts, papaya, lemons, limes, hibiscus, rose hips, kava kava, pomello fruit, figs and dozens of other fruits and herbs. Mata is home to just about every type of plant, fruit and herb found in the entire South Pacific. The plants thrive in Mata Utu because they have no predators. You will not see a single mosquito, bird, mouse, snake, lizard, monkey, fish, or any living creatures. Not so much as one insect lives on the island. Mata Utu is the most beautiful place you will ever lay eyes on and she is also one of the most interesting stories you will ever hear. Rest up tonight, boys – tomorrow we will introduce you to Mata Utu."

Hoanui shook his head in disapproval of Arenui's statement. "I don't know if you guys are ready yet. I mean you hold your own on the beach breaks just fine, but Mata has a fierce reef break. One bad drop, a missed bottom turn or a careless move will send you flailing over the double-overhead falls and into the most treacherous reef you never want to meet. Worst of all, if you are lucky enough to survive being dashed into the reef, you will surely bleed to death before swimming over a half mile into shore through treacherous secondary swell. Mata is no joke in more ways than one. Arenui is a little gung-ho guys. Plus we must consult Matahi and get his blessings before taking you there. Mata is not an open invitation for everyone. In fact, when was the last time you were there Arenui?"

"It's been a while bro, but I am totally ready to go. And so are these guys. Lighten up. If you are scared, you can stay home." Arenui lashed back at Hoanui.

Hoanui seemed concerned over Arenui's proposal. This concern fueled interest in Lance. I was perfectly content surfing the safe and convenient beach break right here in Rahiti, but I knew that Lance was eager to discover more challenging surf – no matter what the consequence.

We got up from our sandy seat, dusted off and headed in to the village. Hoanui and Arenui became quiet in silent opposition. What was the big deal? A reef break – no problem! Lance and I had surfed numerous reef breaks in our lives including Teahpoo. How bad could this one really be? I was intrigued and eager to discover what the hype was about. I couldn't help but wonder why no animals lived on the island. I also wondered why we had to get Matahi's blessing before visiting the island. I sensed there was more to Mata than just the reef break.

That night at dinner everything seemed commonplace. We had a delicious fare of fresh salad, fish, and roasted vegetables. Everyone was almost finished eating when Hoanui made a comment in Tahitian that got everyone's attention. All eyes fell on Arenui.

"What?" he said as he shrugged off everyone's glare.

Matahi addressed Arenui in Tahitian as if to reprimand him. Arenui responded back in an apologetic tone that had a slight air of sarcasm.

Hoanui then spoke to us directly. "Arenui has made an offer to you that must be granted by the elder. As I said earlier, no one visits Mata without consent from Matahi."

I couldn't take the suspense and tension so I asked "So what is the big deal about Mata? We have canoed to other islands and Motus – what makes Mata Utu so special?"

Tania spoke up quickly "It's a bad place. Mata Utu is haunted by the spirits of our ancestors and many others too. Bad things happened there."

Fetia backed her up and chimed in with her cute and innocent voice "Yeah it is a bad place. It's haunted and evil."

I felt a sense of uneasiness set in over the tribe. I wondered who would elaborate on Tania and Fetia's comments. Everyone remained silent. I looked at Maruia who busied herself with the food on her plate. I looked at Matahi whose eyes were fixated on Arenui.

"Ok, go ahead and tell them. Scare the pants off of them if you wish." Arenui defiantly directed at Hoanui.

Hoanui got serious and turned to address us. "There is a lot about our culture and history that you do not know. The peaceful serenity you see in the islands today wasn't always that way. Arenui doesn't have the same respect for tribal tradition that others may have. This lack of respect has enabled him to

111

make an offer to you that violates tradition. Matahi is not happy about the idea and may not grant his blessing for us to go to Mata."

I cut my eyes to Matahi who sat at the head of the table and had a serious demeanor about him as he looked at Arenui.

Hoanui cut the tension by elaborating. "First, let me say that Mata Utu is the most beautiful place in all of the South Pacific. I have not traveled outside of the islands, but I cannot imagine a more beautiful place in the world. As Arenui stated earlier, the island is as beautiful as if it were kissed by the gods, but it was also cursed by them at the same time. Mata is home to the most dense and lush rainforest vegetation which bears the most amazing fruits and herbs because there is no one or nothing there to eat them. The island has many fresh water springs that are as cold as ice and mineral rich, but no one or nothing is there to drink from them. The perfect conditions for life are there, yet nobody lives there. Mata is an oasis of life for everything 'non-living' so to speak."

I looked over at Arenui who rolled his eyes in sarcasm, but a calm seriousness came over the rest of the entire group as Hoanui continued.

"To understand the gravity of the situation, you must understand the history and folklore about Mata Utu and its former inhabitants. For hundreds (maybe even thousands) of years a tribe of cannibalistic head-hunters known as the Matains (Ma-tay-ins) inhabited the island of Mata Utu. The Matains were fierce cannibalistic hunters who would quietly paddle out in their outriggers at night to surrounding islands and kidnap the inhabitants of the other islands and bring them back as dinner. No other tribe had the ability or the courage to challenge the fierce Matain warriors - for this tribe was ruthless and feared nothing. Death was a way of life to them – hunting was how they ate – and humans were their prey. The skin of the Matains was stained with the blood of their victims and their teeth were pointed and sharp for tearing flesh from the bone. It is rumored that they looked so fierce that they could scare their prey to death even if their poison darts missed their target. The tribe was so ruthless that, when killed in battle, it was an honor for the dead Matain to feed his own people for dinner that night. Needless to say, everyone feared the Matains. Tribal committees and lookouts were formed to stand sentry on the other islands to protect their inhabitants; however, lookouts were futile against the stealthy tactics of the Matains. Plus, with so many other islands to choose from, the Matains would vary up their diet and their attacks over so many different islands that no one ever knew where or when their village would be attacked."

I could see both interest and fear in the faces of all of us at the table. Even the Rahitians who had surely heard the story dozens of times were enthralled. Lance and I turned to each other at the same time and gave each other a slight head nod and wink as if to silently say "Screw those Matains. We are gonna conquer that surf and ride the mighty Mata. And, oh yeah, I'm gonna eat you if you die!" We quickly returned our attention to Hoanui's story.

"Many tribes tried to fight the Matains unsuccessfully over history. Launching an attack against the Matains on their home turf was almost impossible and catching them at sea or on the prowl was even more elusive and difficult. The island of Mata itself was the best defense for the Matains. The island offered up the perfect refuge for its cannibalistic inhabitants. Mata was approachable only from the western leeward side. The other three sides were heavily guarded by nature and Mata herself. The outermost reef in the Rahitian Sea started virtually at the easternmost point on Mount Mata and then wrapped around the island on the east and then curved to the north. This outer reef was a great shelter to the island from some of the heaviest surf in the entire south Pacific."

Arenui broke his silence and interjected. "Ironically, the same reef and surf break that kept visitors off of the island is the very thing that has lured many surfers there. The heavy surf wrecked many a ship, broke many a surfboard and dashed passengers and surfers into the shallow, jagged reef. A collision with this reef surely means an ugly mess and a long swim back to shore. So don't wipe out, brah."

Not to disregard the warning, but Lance and I had no intention of coming in contact with the reef. We planned to dominate that surf and ride it with grace and respect while keeping our bodies above water and off of the reef.

Our excitement and interest grew as Hoanui continued.

"Clockwise from the point on Mount Mata, the south side of Mata is a steep, rocky, volcanic ridge that juts abruptly from the sea and rises skyward to form the steep outer wall of Mount Mata. Mount Mata seems to stand sentry on the island and protects her from both nature and man. The base of Mount Mata ends just as abruptly as it starts on that side of the island. A lush, dense tropical rainforest grows right to the rocky ledge of the volcano and all the way to the edge of the sea. Entry to the island from the north, east and south is virtually impossible. Many people have tried – and died. As uninviting as the other three sides of the island are, the western leeward side is surprisingly welcoming. A gorgeous lagoon flanked by a soft, sandy white beach lies nestled from the heavy surf and trade winds by Mount Mata and the rainforest. The fact that the lagoon is the only approach to the island meant that the Matains only had to be concerned about guarding and protecting one side of the island while nature handled the rest of the defense. To past visitors, the lagoon must have seemed welcoming and inviting. Legend states that the lagoon seems to pull you right into her calm, warm, teal green waters – and straight into a trap. The Matains would hide in the rainforest or climb high into the palm trees and surprise their visitors with poisoned darts or spears as they were helplessly trapped in the lagoon. The lagoon was a Venus fly-trap of sorts. It would lure you in and then wham – you never knew what hit you. Legend has it that the Matains had laser accuracy with their darts and spears from hundreds of feet away. They could hit you in a moving kayak in spite of a breeze. The poison from their darts acted so rapidly that the target would fall into slumber and immediate death before they could even pull the dart out of their neck. Poison tipped darts were the Matains weapon of choice. Legend says that, amazingly, the Matains were immune to the poison in their own darts because they had built up a tolerance to it from eating the flesh of their prey which was tainted with the poison."

I was amazed at the fact that you could actually build up an immunity to poison if you ingested it in small quantities over time... as a vegetarian, I was also amazed that people could eat human flesh – revolting thoughts entered my mind.

Hoanui got more serious and leaned forward across the table as his story continued.

"The Matains utilized all of the victim's body. The heads were ritualistically severed from the body and shrunken before the flesh of the body could be consumed."

This tribal ritual was eerie and repulsive to me. How could you shrink a head anyway?

"The Matains believed that if the head was not handled and blessed properly then the flesh would bring illness to those who ate the raw meat."

I found it unbelievable that so much care was put into the ritualistic handling of the head which would be retained as a trophy, but that the cannibals would savagely tear the raw meat from the bones with their hands and teeth and devour every last piece of flesh off of every bone.

"The bones were then thrown into Mount Mata as a sacrifice to the Gods. The shrunken heads were placed on bamboo poles as trophies along the path to Mount Mata. The shrinking process preserved the heads remarkably well and formed doll-sized head replicas of the former owners".

I wondered if the Matains would walk by someone's shrunken head on a pole and relish the thought of eating that person... "wow, I remember eating Bob – he had great tenderloin and a slightly salty finish!"... even in my jest, I struggled to hold down my dinner at the nauseating thought of cannibalism.

"We Rahitians and other peaceful, mostly vegetarian and fish-eating South Pacific islanders constantly and helplessly grieved the loss of our loved ones. Rahitians and our neighbors would eat dinner and then participate in tribal dances and peaceful socialization before retiring to bed – never knowing whether we would be darted and abducted in the middle of the night. In some cases, wives or husbands would awake in the morning to find their loved ones gone from their arms. Sometimes the only trace of them would be a feather tipped poison dart lying on the ground. Often though, they disappeared without a trace. You see, the stealthy Matain cannibals had perfected the art of the sneak attack. They would invade an island, dart a few villagers while they slept and then carry them to their kayaks and strap their bodies to the outrigger as if they were a piece of cargo. No matter how prepared we thought we were, every abduction went unnoticed until the following morning when frantic family members awoke to find their loved ones missing. "

Chills crawled up my spine at the thought of being darted and captured in my sleep. It had to be a helpless feeling for those who were attacked by the cannibalistic hunters. I just hoped that the poison was strong enough to kill them so that they would not wake up later while being eaten alive.

Hoanui kept up his tale as he animated the story more vividly with body language and emotion.

"There was no point in a retaliatory attack or invasion of Mata Utu to retrieve the captured. They were dead shortly after the point of abduction thanks to the poisonous venom in the dart. The Matains wasted no time in killing, beheading and eating their prey – they liked to eat the flesh while it was still fresh. Tribal folklore claimed that the Matains were the fiercest and most efficient hunters and warriors to ever inhabit the South Pacific. They held this reputation for two reasons – first, they tactfully eliminated the strongest, healthiest and most able bodied competitors - and second, according to their religion, the souls of their prey became part of the strength and soul of the Matains since their bodies were ingested into theirs. The Matains were very good predators who chose to eliminate and eat mostly male victims who could potentially be their strongest possible challengers. The cannibals were also smart – they often left the women alive to breed more victims for them to eat later and the children were left alone so they could grow larger to provide more flesh when they were ultimately eaten as full grown adults. The Matains were savage cannibals, but had no interest in enslaving, raping or robbing their victims. Their prey simply provided food for their survival. Their weird head-shrinking habit was part of a long tribal ritual of their religion. The strength and success of the Matains was largely due to the fact that they stayed aloof and reclusive from the rest of the islands. Taking living prey or slaves back to their island increased the chance of invasion of their secretive and secure island world. The Rahitians repeatedly attempted to join forces with other island tribes to plan an attack on the Matains, but our efforts went unsupported. It was almost as if the other islanders had accepted the occasional cannibalistic abductions as a natural cause of death. Since there was virtually no disease or other predators to kill people, the Matains were one of the natural causes of death. Death by cannibalism was an accepted way to die."

This was an interesting concept to me – people preying on people to feed and strengthen their bodies and souls and control the population. It was not survival of the fittest though. Instead it was feast on the fittest, and the strongest, healthiest men were the meal of choice. Wow.

"The thought of attacking the Matains on their home turf at Mata Utu seemed daunting especially since we could not even defend ourselves in our own homes, let alone protect our own islands or even detect or anticipate the secretive Matain attacks. No one knew the layout of the terrain on Mata Utu because no one had ever seen the island. No one knew how many Matains existed because they only traveled in small packs of two or four while they were out on the hunt. No one had ever challenged the Matains; however, the Rahitians seemed like the most likely tribe to challenge them. For that reason the Rahitians were a more likely target for the Matain attacks. The Matain philosophy seemed to be the best way to increase your own strength and chance of survival is to eliminate your competitors – especially since their religion gave them the opportunity to gain the strength of the souls of those they ate. The Matains must have loved some Rahitian flesh and soul. Countless Matain abductions went unanswered, yet heavily grieved until one day when they chose to take the wrong victim. One kidnapping led to the ultimate defeat and downfall of the entire Matain culture. One brave Rahitian single-handedly challenged and fought the Matains and changed the course of history in our culture. I will give Matahi the honor of telling you the story tonight after we finish evening chores." Hoanui said as he concluded his tale for now.

Talk about a cliff-hanger. I was totally engrossed in the story and was not ready for the unexpected intermission. Lance and I hurriedly finished up our chores and even helped the girls with theirs in an attempt to expedite the evening tribal gathering. We built a fire on the beach and boiled up some Kava-Kava tea. We lit the torches and packed up the peace pipes with herbs as the sunset illuminated the sky with hues of red and pink. My haste with the chores had caused me to work up a sweat. I excused myself momentarily and walked down to the water where I took a cool, relaxing dip.

I was so eager to hear Matahi's story that I couldn't stand the suspense. As I came out of the water from my dip, I saw the tribe gathering around the campfire on the beach. I didn't even go back to the hut to dry off or change clothes, just straight to the fire where I took my seat in the sand next to Lance and Maruia. Matahi took his seat on the driftwood throne next to the fire as the glow from the flames illuminated his weathered old face. He was in full tribal garb and had his headpiece on. Matahi loved his rituals and loved to tell stories. I loved to absorb the culture and listen. Even though this ritual was hundreds of years old, I felt as if they were doing it only for Lance and me.

Matahi began his story in Rahitian as his elderly voice echoed and cracked with experience and wisdom. Matahi would slowly and deliberately talk while animating the tale with his hand and facial gestures, pausing long enough for Hoanui to translate between every few sentences. His tale unfolded as we all sat in quiet and respectful attentiveness as Hoanui relayed every word in English.

"I was only a young boy. My mother Kania and father Hoku and I lived a very happy family life in this very same village we live in today. In fact, three generations ago, me and my father fished from this very beach and climbed these very palm trees. My father was an excellent fisherman and was the best swimmer in Rahiti. He was well known and liked by all of the Rahitians and he was often the sole provider of fish to the whole island. He seemed to be able to catch fish when no one else could and this made him a champion fisherman and hero. More importantly he was a family man and loved my mother and I with all of his huge heart. In fact, he loved our family so much that he and my mother were expecting a second child soon as well. It was a big deal to me as I was preparing and expecting to be a big brother soon. I had become very attached and attentive to my mother and had taken over many of her chores as she neared childbirth. One day while my father was out fishing, my mother and I walked through the forest gathering fruits. All of a sudden, she collapsed and turned pale and blue. I frantically tried to revive her – thinking that she had become ill or that the heat had gotten the best of her. Her skin began to quickly turn pale and deeper blue. Then I noticed the dart in her neck. I immediately removed the dart and attempted to suck the poison from the gaping hole in her neck. I scanned the forest, but saw no one. I took the dart and ran lightning fast back to the village to seek help – all the while screaming for anyone who could hear me. Father was out to sea, but I was able to gather some Rahitians who followed me back to the spot where I had left my mother. Nevertheless, she was gone. We quickly followed several tracks of footprints in the soil down to the beach where we saw two outrigger canoes several hundred yards off shore and already heading out to sea in the direction of

116

Mata Utu. I screamed at the top of my lungs for my mother. I ran to the water and fell to my knees and wept. I wanted to swim, I wanted to fly, I wanted to walk on water to rescue my mother, but I knew my efforts would be fruitless. I screamed in agony and cursed the Matains and the Gods too. The tribe subdued me and comforted me. We returned to the village where I impatiently awaited the return of my father from his day at sea."

Emotion and sorrow filled Matahi's fire-lit face as he recounted the ordeal that day. Tears seemed to well up in his ancient eyes and his voice cracked with the painful words. He paused and took the peace pipe into his mouth and smoked.

"When my father Hoku returned from his day fishing at sea, he was happy and proud as he carried the many fish he had caught that day. But instead of being greeted by the usual happy and appreciative villagers who were pleased to see him come back with fish for them to cook and clean, he was greeted by the entire village as they sat somber and silent on the beach eagerly awaiting his return. Immediately he sensed something was wrong by the look on everyone's face and the attitude in the air. I was terrified to confront my father for fear he would blame me for not protecting my mother. I was afraid he would not think I was enough of a man to protect her. I was young, but I was proud and very scared at that moment. It was the most critical moment of my life. I approached Hoku from the crowd gathered on the beach. Before I could say a word, he dropped his fish and ran to embrace me. I whispered in his ear "Mommy is gone. I am so sorry, Dad." He fell to his knees and screamed to the heavens. He wailed so loud that I am sure the Gods and the Matains heard his roar. I will never forget that sound – his cries still ring in my ears after all of the years."

Matahi took a long pause as he toked on his peace pipe again and stared off into the distance in deep reflection. Hoanui finished translating the last sentence and then waited in silence for Matahi's next words. No one said a word. We all sat in silent suspense as we waited for Matahi to continue.

Seconds turned into minutes before Matahi spoke again. His voice sounded hoarse and wavering - as if he was choking on emotion when he started the story where he left off.

"My father was never the same again. In one instant his life changed. One Matain dart destroyed our family. One dart would change the course of history. Hoku sent me to live with relatives in the village. I didn't fully understand why, but I knew I couldn't blame him – he needed to be alone. I needed his support and love, but he needed something different at the time. I didn't understand why I had lost my mother to the Matains and then lost my father to solitude. I was too young to understand. I was too young to lose both parents."

Matahi paused again to smoke the pipe. The campfire crackled and spit some fiery ash into the sky and the fire grew brighter. Matahi began to speak again and Hoanui resumed his translation.

"In his anger, Hoku tried to rally support from other Rahitian men to lead an attack on the Matains. His attack plan went unsupported as the Rahitians offered up sympathy and condolences, but no support

117

for retaliation. Hoku became angry and unstable and the villagers began to talk amongst themselves about how to handle Hoku rather than how to handle the Matains. Hoku was smart and sensitive enough to sense the growing tension on the island. His hatred was directed at the Matains and not his fellow Rahitians even though they were not supporting him. He made a decision on his own to leave Rahiti. He left without even saying goodbye to me or anyone else. There was great speculation and rumors as to where he went and what he was doing. The assumption was that he had gone to Mata Utu to exact revenge on the cannibals, but no one could imagine the plan that he was concocting. Hoku was a great fisherman, sailor, swimmer and father – but a warrior he was not. He was strong, healthy and well built by Rahitian standards, but was no match for a Matain cannibal. Everyone knew that - except Hoku."

Matahi adjusted his headpiece and cleared his throat.

"For months after he left, my father kayaked from island to island trying to gain support from other tribes and convince them to attack Mata Utu with him. He told of the countless abductions that happened in Rahiti and how their loved ones were killed, beheaded and eaten. The other tribes would all sympathize and share similar stories with him. Every island had experienced at least one visit from the cannibals and had lost their own loved ones; however, no one was angry or motivated enough to retaliate. No one offered up any support for fighting them. No one knew anything about Mata or the Matain civilization. Everyone was scared and content simply praying to the Gods for their safety. No one did anything – until Hoku met a medicine man in Moorea."

Nanihi leaned toward the fire and tossed a handful of powder into it which made it blaze brightly for a moment.

"Praise to the medicine man." She said in Rahitian.

Matahi toked the pipe and exhausted the smoke from his lungs to the heavens and then continued his tale.

"This wise old medicine man took my father into his home. He listened to Hoku and felt his pain. The medicine man claimed to have dreams and visions of the Matains and their civilization and rituals on Mata Utu. Although he had never been there, he knew the layout of Mata well and recounted it to my father in great detail. The medicine man had also come into possession of a Matain dart that had taken the life of a Moorean tribe member. He had studied the dart and determined the origin and ingredients in the Matain poison. Not only did he claim to have an antidote for the poison, but he also concocted a poison of his own that was equally as potent as the poison in the Matain dart. He claimed that the Matains should not be immune to this poison because they had never been exposed to it. This medicine man intrigued Hoku and gave him some brilliant ideas. Hoku believed the medicine man's tales; although, the other Moorean villagers dismissed the medicine man as crazy and didn't take his stories or his medicines seriously. They would only come to him when they had injuries or illness and would ignore and disregard his stories about the Matains and Mata Utu. Hoku was the first person to listen to him."

118

Matahi paused to hit the pipe at the exact time a stiff breeze came out of nowhere and ignited the fire hotter sending smoke and ashes into the sky. The smoke from Matahi's pipe joined the smoke of the campfire on its journey skyward. The ambiance was perfectly captivating for his tale. Lance and I turned to look at each other in partial disbelief, but we both had a look of curiosity and interest painted on our faces. We couldn't decide whether this folklore was fact or fiction. The fact that the isolated breeze had come out of nowhere showed us that a natural mystic was playing in concert with the story and Matahi's pipe smoking. The smoke trail dissipated into the air and the fire calmed down as the breeze subsided and the story resumed.

"The medicine man gave Hoku the knowledge he needed to infiltrate Mata Utu and he also promised to provide Hoku with his special poison. The rest was going to have to be up to Hoku himself. According to the Mooreans, Hoku went into isolation and took up residence in the rain forest on their island. No one saw him in the village for months. Occasionally he was spotted scaling the side of the volcano on Moorea or swimming in Opanahu bay. He went into intense physical and mental training for the plan he was concocting. He began crafting darts from bamboo shoots and making other weapons and daggers from jagged volcanic rocks. After months of isolation he revisited the medicine man and picked up the poison potion as well as some additional advice. The medicine man had visions of Hoku while he was training. He saw the anguish in his eyes and felt the sorrow and hatred in his heart, but he knew that Hoku was not a warrior. He knew that underneath all of the rage Hoku was a peace-loving fisherman and family man. His advice to my father was that if he went to Mata Utu, he better be prepared to "kill or be killed". Hoku was prepared and was ready to sacrifice his life for his cause, but not before ending the Matain cannibal attacks on Rahiti. Hoku took the medicine man's potion and his advice and quietly left Moorea."

Tania interrupted the story by bringing a serving of Kava Kava tea to the campfire gathering. Suffice to say that the timing was impeccable as Matahi was just speaking of a poison potion. I took the tea anyway and wrote it off as coincidence.

Hoanui took a sip from the Kava Kava and the translation resumed.

"Hoku left Moorea in the same kayak he came in. He rowed back to Rahiti to pay me a brief visit. I remember the day distinctly. I had been living with my aunt for the last few months and she had taken me down to the beach to bathe that day. I was sitting at the edge of the water looking out to sea when I saw the familiar outrigger kayak appear on the horizon. I thought I was dreaming. It was just like old times when I would wait for my father to return from his daily fishing expedition. I stood up in disbelief, but became confident that it was him as he stroked closer. It was definitely him. No one else had the ability to row an outrigger kayak with such speed and ease. He beached the kayak and we ran to embrace each other. I was overjoyed that my father was finally home, but my joy quickly turned to sadness as he informed me he was not going to stay. He told me that he had missed me dearly and that he loved me with all of his heart. He told me that his love for me and his fellow Rahitians was sending him on a mission that he may not return from. He told me that he had come to say what would possibly be his final farewell. I begged and pleaded with him to stay, but he kissed me on the cheek and boarded his kayak and rowed away just as quickly as he had come. He did not visit or say a word to anyone else - just me. I was devastated all over again at the departure of my father. I wanted to keep him with me. I missed my mother so dearly and I didn't want to miss my father another day longer. I knew I had to be strong though. I knew by the seriousness and determination in Hoku's eyes that he had changed. He was a different man. He was a Rahitian on a mission. The best I could do for him was pray. I still pray for him every day."

Matahi stopped to smoke again and this time when he exhaled he let out a chant. "ooooohhhhhmmmmm."

The Rahitians answered with the same chant. And then Matahi broke into tribal verse in Rahitian. Hoanui leaned over to us and told us that he could not translate this chant and prayer into English because it wouldn't make sense to us. He told us to just "feel" what Matahi was saying.

Tane began to tap the Congo drums and Matahi burst into a loud but lyrical cry to the heavens. "Ouwwwwah-hauewwwwah-solawaaaaaaaah-Rahitiiiiiiah......" The tribe responded in unison.

The breeze returned and stoked the fire. Smoke and burning embers rose into the dark, starry sky. A chill came over me and goosebumps formed on my skin. I would like to think that it was the breeze that invoked the chill, but I knew the warm breeze had little to do with my chilling sensation. I was captivated by the story and the ritual. I loved it and my emotions overflowed. I couldn't wait to hear what happened to Hoku next.

Lance and I sipped our Kava Kava tea as the chant and congo drums continued. The sound of the drums and Rahitian verse echoed in the distance. This story and ritual was different than the rest of the tribal ceremonies we had experienced here and it may be the most interesting story I had experienced in my life to date.

As the chant reached its crescendo, I noticed a full harvest moon rising over the water. I pointed it out to Lance who was equally as awestruck. It was as if the Rahitians had summoned the moon to rise with their chant. I sat there taking in the sights and sounds and felt as if I were totally connected to Rahiti. I felt as if I was learning a great tribal secret. I was honored to be here.

The chant ended abruptly with a final tap of the drum and another long "ooooohhhhhhmmmmmmm." The Rahitians all remained still and focused on Matahi.

Hoanui turned to address Lance and me. "So, you guys want to know what happens next?"

Lance and I both answered simultaneously "Yeah!"

Hoanui picked a prime time to be sarcastic as he answered "So do I, but nobody knows."

The tribe erupted in laughter – even Matahi cracked a smile. It was the perfect ice breaker after the long prayer and chant. I sincerely hoped he was joking because I was enthralled in the story. I was already skeptical as to the validity of the folklore and ending it now would only cause serious doubt in my mind. I was relieved when Matahi spoke again and continued the story. I still couldn't get over the spectacle of the moon rising over the water. The timing was impeccable.

Matahi's wise and weathered voice spouted Rahitian again - fresh after his lung and throat-clearing chant.

"So Hoku rowed out of Rahiti and I shed many tears. I knew where he was going and what he was going to attempt. I knew the only thing I could do was pray – so I did – every day. And it is a practice that I still do. We are all fortunate that we are alive today to pray. We owe a lot of thanks and prayers to my father." With that statement, many of the tribe shouted Maruru Hoku – meaning "thanks Hoku" in Rahitian.

"Hoku left Rahiti with a purpose. He rowed toward Mata Utu and stopped halfway there. He knew that if he was to gain access to the forbidden island he was going to have to employ the same stealthy tactics that the Matains used to infiltrate our island on their attacks. He strapped his potion and some belongings to his waist and jumped from his outrigger kayak leaving it to drift at sea. He used his excellent swimming skills to swim the rest of the way to Mata to remain as inconspicuous as possible. He waited until sunset before finally approaching the lagoon. The island appeared to be just as the medicine man had magically described. The current seemed to push him effortlessly right into the lagoon. He swam quietly and partially submerged to stay out of sight and out of the way of incoming darts. He surveyed the scene and saw no one. He listened quietly but heard nothing. He stayed close to the beach on the lagoon, but made his way to the south and into the cover of the rainforest. He exited the water and entered the dense forest in the dark of the night. He was partially relieved as he knew he had successfully done something that no other Rahitian or any other islander had ever done – he had stepped foot on Mata Utu. To our society it was as great a feat as man stepping onto the moon. His accomplishment fueled his ambition and courage to complete the task he had set out to do. He wasted no time familiarizing himself with the island. He quietly made his way through the forest stopping only to drink some spring water to hydrate after the long swim. He came to a well-beaten path in the forest, but shunned it and stayed in the thicket to avoid being seen. He knew he had to make the best of his time and find shelter before the cover of darkness gave way to dawn. As he wandered through the jungle, he began to hear sounds of the Matains. He heard drum beats and tribal chanting. He smelt smoke and herbs burning. He knew he was close to their village. He kept going – walking barefooted through the densest plant growth he had ever seen, until he ultimately came to a clearing by the beach on the other side of the island. He saw dozens of grass huts and hundreds of Matains. They were in the middle of a cannibalistic ritual. It was dinner time. Hoku was hungry. He had not eaten in days, but the sight he saw enabled him to go many more days without eating. He watched in disgust as he witnessed the beheading of four men. The Matains danced wildly and whooped and hollered as they took turns running around with the bloody heads. He saw the four headless bodies lying on stone tables around the fire. The heads were placed into some sort of large stone cauldron and the Matains continued their tribal dance around the cauldron as they threw some sort of sand-like substance into the fire below the pot. Each handful of sand they tossed caused the fire to ignite wildly and sent flames and sparks into the air. The putrid scent of burning flesh and hair wafted in the breeze until it reached Hoku's nose. The smell was nauseating and, had he eaten, Hoku would have vomited instantly. The dance continued for what seemed like hours until it was halted by the tribal leader. He was presented four bamboo stalks by another Matain warrior. He jabbed the bamboo into the cauldron and skewered each skull raising each one out of the cauldron and handing it to a warrior. Each time a head came out on a stick, the Matains would erupt into tribal chant and a warrior would take off running down a trail toward the volcano with the bamboo stick which held the head like a flag. When the last head had departed, the Matains began their feast. The men surrounded the bodies and began to feast like lions tearing the flesh from the bones. The men would eat first and then throw scraps and entrails to the women and children. It was the most horrific sight ever witnessed by anyone. The feast enraged Hoku as he knew his wife and unborn child had met the same fate. He wanted to run into the village and immediately kill as many Matains as he could, but he was smart. He knew that he had to be very patient and remain hidden unless he wanted to become the next Matain meal. He surveyed his surroundings and knew that he was well hidden at the moment as the cannibals were focused on their feast, but he feared that sunrise would expose him. He watched the village closely as the four warriors who ran off with the heads earlier emerged from the trail and joined the feast. The village was in the exact location that the medicine man had described – in a clearing by the sea between the forest and Mount Mata. If the medicine man was right about everything, then he knew the trail he crossed earlier would lead him to the volcano. The volcano could offer up a good vantage point as well as shelter so that he could further study the Matains in the daylight. He knew now was the time to make a move while the Matains were feasting. He crept back into the depths of the jungle and made his way back to the trail. When he reached the trail, he followed it, but remained in the cover of the thicket next to the trail. He knew he could not risk being seen and give up the element of surprise. Surprise would be his best weapon. He skirted the trail until he was well past the clearing and the sound of the tribe had waned in the distance. He felt it was safe to exit the forest and make a dash down the trail toward Mount Mata. He ran as swiftly and as quietly as the wind through the darkness. He ran with ease and breathed deeply and efficiently as if he were swimming. He ran until his breath was stifled by the smell of rotting flesh. He stopped mid-stride on the trail as he realized that he was amidst a row of bamboo poles flanking the trail. He stopped to observe the heads which were proudly skewered on top of each one. He could vaguely see the silhouette of each face as he held his breath and walked with disgust. He feared the inevitable encounter with his wife's head, but he did not see any women. He gagged and wretched at the sight and smell of the grotesque display. He wanted to remove the heads and give them a proper burial, but knew that he could not afford to do anything that may alert the Matains as to his presence there. So he held his breath and kept on running until he reached Mount Mata. He must have passed a thousand heads along the way. Each head he passed fueled his anger more and more. He touched his neck in appreciation for it and vowed that his head would stay attached to his body. The trail led him out of the forest and into the open air. He looked up at the peak of Mount Mata which seemed to reach up to the heavens and stars above. The soft, moist soil in the forest had turned into hard, jagged volcanic rock. The painful stepping stones didn't faze Hoku as he began to climb the volcano. The climb was long and treacherous especially at night, but his training in Moorea had paid off and he ascended the steep mountain to its peak. He reached the peak just as the sun had begun to rise in the east. He scanned the island below in the light of the fresh dawn. Mount Mata cast its shadow over the rainforest and the clearing where the village was. All was quiet below. The nocturnal cannibals had retired for the time being."

I looked skyward as the moon had climbed higher on the horizon. A chill came over my body again in spite of the warmth of the night. I imagined the story vividly. Hearing the same story back in the comfort of my home in Virginia definitely would not have had the same effect. I was here. I was only miles from this "Mata" place. I was hearing the story translated from the native tongue of the legend's own son. Wow. I looked over at Lance who was staring intently at Matahi. He was captivated by the story. I couldn't resist the temptation to scare the crap out of him at this point in the story so I was very sneaky as I slid my hand over and grabbed his side and whispered "Boo." His reaction was more than I had anticipated. He sprung up a few feet off of the ground and let out a whoop in surprised shock. I got him good and I also gave the tribe a laugh. Matahi paused the story long enough to give Lance and me a look. Then he too cracked a smile before hitting the pipe and continuing. The chuckles continued from the rest of the tribe for a few minutes. Lance socked me on the arm and then held up one finger to signify that he "owed me one" now. I snickered at him and then returned my attention to Matahi and Hoanui.

"Hoku made his way around the top of the volcano and back down the windward side - out of sight of the rest of the island. As the sun rose in the east, he descended the steep volcano's back-side slope. The waves smacked the base of the mountain far below where it met the sea. Hoku did not fear the height. He knew he would find shelter and be safe. The Moorean medicine man had spoken of a cave on the sea-side of the volcano. Sure enough, Hoku discovered a cave on a rocky ledge halfway down the mountain facing the sea just as the Moorean had described. He took refuge there and got some rest. He awoke hours later and climbed around the side of the mountain until he could peer around its side down to the village and forest below. He knew he had found the perfect hidden lookout spot to keep a close watch on the Matains. For days he stayed in the cave watching and learning the ways of the cannibals. He would watch in the early evening as several kayaks would leave in different directions carrying two Matain warriors each. Later after dark, the warriors would return with dinner strapped to their outriggers. The women would enter the rainforest and return to the village with pails of water and fruits and herbs. The clouds also had their daily ritual as they would surround the top of the volcano like a halo in the morning and then migrate out to sea as the heat of the sun rose only to return to the top of the volcano at sunset and resume their halo position on Mount Mata. Hoku fought through exhaustion, hunger and thirst for days during his vigilant observation. When he reached the brink of dehydration, he contemplated leaving the safety of his position to retrieve a drink from one of the streams in the rainforest. He feared leaving the cave and being discovered. He prayed to the Gods to relieve his thirst. He waited patiently as long as he could until his mouth was so dry he could not swallow. The thought of the cool, fresh streams in the rainforest below were too tempting. He decided to emerge from the cave and descend to the jungle, but before he could leave – it rained. The rain poured down from an easterly direction, and ponded on the rocky floor of his cave. He fell to his knees and prayed thanks to the Gods.

123

He drank on his knees as he lapped up the cool, fresh rainwater like a dog. He worshiped the Gods in appreciation for the water."

I leaned over to Lance and whispered "down dog" in jest. I couldn't resist interjecting the yoga reference as an innuendo to lighten the mood.

Matahi kept going as if he didn't hear me.

"Hoku accepted and appreciated the gift of the water and it relieved his thirst, but hunger still gripped him. His empty stomach churned in agony. He once again prayed to the Gods to relieve his hunger. He held out, watched and waited. When Hoku reached his maximum hunger and contemplated going into the rainforest to retrieve food, something amazing happened. A bird flew into the cave carrying a large fish that he had just plucked from the water below. The bird had probably perched and eaten his fish there many times prior, but the sight of Hoku startled him and he flew away – leaving the fish behind. Hoku grabbed the fish, knelt and prayed to the Gods. He then ate the fish and thought it ironic how many times he had fished, but never caught one in this fashion. He appreciated the catch and the nourishment and prayed to the Gods once more in thanks. His good fortune gave him strength and confidence that he was in the right place doing the right thing. He got brave and comfortable with the terrain after observing and learning the Matains' schedule and rituals. Hydrated and nourished, he began to venture down the volcano at opportune times and enter into the rainforest. He got a chance to study the Matains closely. He kept his fears at bay and his senses keen as he prowled through the jungle dangerously close to the unsuspecting cannibals. He watched them as they drank and collected water from the springs and ponds. He watched them as they picked fruits and berries and herbs. He watched them with hatred and disgust as they had their nightly cannibal feasts. He watched them as they danced and skewered the heads of their victims. And he watched them when they slept. He counted over 200 cannibals. He knew his task was daunting, but he knew the first thing he had to do. While in the forest, he collected fruits and water to sustain him at his hideout on Mount Mata. He couldn't rely only on the kindness of the Gods to bring him rain and deliver fish every day. The Gods had now blessed him with something more important - they had given him the strength, courage and stamina to fend for himself. He stockpiled his own supplies and relied only on himself at this point. He collected bamboo and tree branches from the rainforest and picked up feathers that birds had shed while in the trees. He spent hours in his cave - crafting perfectly formed darts and spears from the bamboo and wood to add to the collection that he brought from Moorea. He carefully placed a ration of his poison potion on each one and stowed it away in the back of the cave for later use. When he felt he had enough weapons in his arsenal, he took the remaining poison to the rainforest and dumped it into the spring and let it feed into the pond where the Matains collected water. He repeated the words of the Moorean medicine man as he poisoned the water – "kill or be killed" he said to himself. Proud of his action, he returned to his perch on Mount Mata. He watched the next day as the women filled their pails with the water. That night the tribal feast was quieter and only half of the cannibals attended. The next day, Hoku was awakened at sunrise – not by the light of the sun, but by the screams of the cannibals as they awoke to find their loved ones dead. Apparently, the poison had worked and effectively wiped out over half of the tribe. That evening no warriors left the island in kayaks to go hunt. The feast was already at home. The remaining cannibals devoured their own dead. They handled the heads of their fallen tribe members in the same ritualistic fashion. They seemed to have no remorse or guilt as they ate their own dead families and tribal members. Dozens and dozens of heads were placed into the cauldron, cooked and then skewered. Warrior after warrior ran down the trail and planted the bamboo pole and head trophy into the lineup. Each head that emerged from the pot made Hoku smile wider with satisfaction of his success. 'One more dead Matain' he thought. The ritual continued almost all night until all of the dead had been beheaded and devoured. The tribe concluded their feast late into the night and retired for sleep. But the remainder of the night and early morning was not as quiet and peaceful as usual. Hoku was kept awake by the groans, moans and vomiting of the Matains who were experiencing the mild effects of the poison from the flesh they had devoured. The next day started with the same loud cries of the Matains as they awoke to find many more dead cannibals. No kayaks left that day either. That night the same ritual took place in the same manner. Dozens more of the dead cannibals were devoured by the remaining cannibals. Hoku couldn't figure whether it was pure stupidity or the insatiable desire to devour flesh at any cost that drove the Matains to once again eat their own dead. They obviously had no clue he was there and responsible for the massacre. The effects were not as profound this time around as the poison had been diluted past its potency. Hoku went in for close observation from the forest and counted only 20 or so remaining Matains. The smell of the rotting heads tainted the air with their pungent odor, but it was the sweet smell of victory to Hoku. However, the remaining Matains had finally figured it out that something was very wrong. They drank from a different stream and ventured into areas of the rainforest that they didn't normally frequent. Hoku knew they were on the prowl. He knew that he had to act on the offensive again before he was discovered. The windward side of the volcano offered up perfect refuge, but it would only take one curious Matain to spoil his hideout. Hoku carried his poison tipped weapons into the forest and began to systematically dart the Matains one by one as they were alone in the forest. "Kill or be killed" he would say before he darted each cannibal. When they fell unconscious and into immediate death from his darts, he would then hoist their bodies on his shoulder and carry them back to the hip of Mount Mata where he would throw them into the sea so their bodies would not be discovered. He knew the Matains couldn't figure out how the majority of their tribe had been poisoned, but they would surely recognize a dart wound to the neck and know that they were being hunted by an intruder. For days Hoku darted and tossed over a dozen Matains into the water undetected. He returned to the hidden safety of his cave each night. He knew the island and the forest like the back of his hand now. He calculated there were less than 10 remaining Matains. The strongest men had seemed to be the only survivors. They would be the most challenging to defeat especially since he was out of poison and darts. Hoku emerged from the forest carrying his last kill back to Mount Mata for disposal as he saw four of the remaining cannibals climbing around the hip of the volcano toward his lair. He knew it would be discovered. He was happy he was not there for their visit, but he knew he could no longer return to his safe haven. His mind raced as he formulated his next plan. He lightened his load and ditched the dead Matain into some thick undergrowth and then sprinted down the trail to the lagoon. Dozens of Matain kayaks were beached there. He knew what he had to do. He pushed each kayak into the water with enough force to set it adrift into the sea. No one was leaving the island by boat. It was him and the remaining warriors. Hoku vowed to finish the job. He reentered the forest on the trail with no regard to being seen. He ran like the wind down the trail in the open daylight. He hurried through the forest with speed toward the volcano again. He stopped in awe as he entered the section of the trail where the bamboo head trophies were. He hadn't been through this spot since his first night on the island. He hadn't seen the spectacle in the daylight. He walked past hundreds of heads of both cannibalized Matains and other islanders. He froze in his tracks as he saw the distorted face he once kissed. My mother's head was familiar and relatively well preserved. He wept a moment, but his eyes quickly ran dry."

Matahi stopped a moment and hung his head in sorrow. He too wept a moment, but righted his face and wiped his eyes to continue the tale.

"He removed her head from the pointed bamboo pole, kissed it and then gently placed it under a shrub and covered it with soil and leaves to temporarily bury it. He then grabbed the bamboo spear that his wife's head had rested on. He pulled it from the ground and wielded it like a sword. He took off down the trail in a rage – determined to finish the Matains. He didn't miss a step as he exited the forest at the volcano. He had taken that section of the path dozens and dozens of times in the last few weeks and he knew every rock on the trail like the back of his hand. He knew every nook and cranny on the face of Mount Mata. He quickly ascended the volcano along the same path that the warriors had taken in route to his hiding place. As he rounded the hip of the volcano, the warriors came in to sight. They were emerging from his cave. He charged up the steep, narrow slope toward them. They spotted him and began to rapidly descend in his direction as well. Enraged by the sight of his wife's head, he was determined to kill the cannibals. He met them in a fierce clash on the edge of the volcano. The width of the ledge on which they stood caused the Matains to line up single file. The advantage was to Hoku as he stabbed and pushed the cannibals off of the ledge one at a time until they had all fallen into the sea below. He didn't have time to celebrate his momentary victory as he saw four more Matains scaling the volcano behind him. He was trapped and he knew it. There was nowhere to go. He hurriedly climbed the rest of the distance to his cave. He entered it cautiously - not knowing whether a Matain had stayed there to ambush him. When he found it empty, he entered and retrieved from a hiding place in the cave the antidote to the Matain poison that the Moorean medicine man had given him. He quickly drank it down and exited the cave to the ledge. The cannibals were approaching quickly with their spears drawn. Without hesitation, Hoku jumped from the ledge and into the air where he plummeted into the water far below. The Matains watched in amazement as he fell hundreds of feet and into the water – narrowly missing jagged rocks and reef. The fall would have killed any ordinary man – even a mighty Matain – but Hoku was no ordinary man – and certainly no Matain. Hoku was unaffected by the fall and quickly began to swim like the fish that he was. He rounded the hip of the volcano well out of the range of the Matain darts and spears. He swam around the southern side of the island with the rainforest as cover and separation between him and the four Matains. The lagoon was his destination. He knew the Matains would head there to board their kayaks and come after him. He got there first and waited in the middle of the lagoon. Before he could catch his breath, a dart whizzed by his head – followed by another and another until one lodged into his shoulder. He quickly pulled it out and squeezed the blood from the wound. He waited and hoped the poison wouldn't affect him – and it didn't. As more darts flew, he submerged deep under the crystal clear water. Darts and spears plunged into the water, but harmless at his depth. He reemerged to the surface for air and to taunt the Matains. He beckoned them to come into the water and fight like men. Two of them obliged. The two biggest men he had ever seen reluctantly dove into the water and swam toward him. He could tell by their hesitance and their motion in the water that they were not proficient swimmers. They may be the fiercest hunters and warriors on land, but their swimming skills paled in comparison to Hoku's. He let them get very close before he dove and submerged beneath them. He grabbed both of them by the feet and pulled them under. He used his strong swimming kick to pull them deep into the water. They thrashed and kicked wildly, but Hoku did not let go. He kept pulling them deeper and deeper. Even out of breath from his day of fighting, his leap from the volcano and the long swim to the lagoon, he was still able to hold his breath longer than the Matains. He pulled them down and held their feet tight as they struggled. He didn't release them and vowed not to resurface until their lifeless bodies stopped moving. When their bodies became still and lifeless, Hoku resurfaced and saw two more Matains running down the beach to enter the water. He invited them to join the fight by taunting them with the dead bodies of the two cannibals he just killed. "Here is your lunch – come and get it guys" he shouted. The Matains shot their remaining darts at him from a distance, but Hoku avoided another strike. The anger and fear in the Matains had evidently affected their concentration and accuracy. Either that or all of the good darters had perished already. The two Matains cautiously entered the water with spears in their hands and waded waist deep toward Hoku as he stayed just out of their range. The Matains took aim and hurled their last two spears toward Hoku with all of their strength. One spear missed and the other grazed his arm as it flew by. He quickly grabbed the spear as it plunged into the water. Hoku emerged from the water with spear in hand and thrust himself like a dolphin toward the Matains. He plunged the spear deep into the chest of one of the cannibals as the other turned to run back onto the beach. Hoku gave chase and ran the Matain down and wrestled him to the ground. Hoku's rage was strong and enabled him to subdue the bigger Matain. He choked the cannibal with all of his might until his face turned redder than his blood stained hands and mouth. The mighty Matain warrior was helpless as he pleaded with his eyes for his life to be spared. Hoku looked deep into his eyes and cannibal soul and said "kill or be killed." Then he snapped the neck of the last Matain. The ordeal had exhausted him. The struggle and swim had dehydrated him. The poison of the dart and spear was finally affecting him. His blood coursed though his veins and his breath got deep and heavy as he fell into slumber. He hoped and prayed to the Gods with his last bit of energy and awareness that he had killed the last Matain. He knew he would be easy prey now as he passed out in the sand on the beach. Time melted away. No one knows how long he slept there. No one knows how much poison was in his body. He had come close to death, but cheated it thus far. The sun rose and set multiple times as he lay there unconscious on the beach. Ultimately, Hoku awoke to find that he was alive and well rested. He was amazed to discover that the current and tide had reversed at some point and brought one of the Matain kayaks back into the lagoon and onto the beach next to him. He gained his senses and checked his surroundings – not knowing whether he was safe or not. He rose to his feet and pulled the spear from the dead Matain who was lying face down on the beach by the water. Hoku proudly, but cautiously entered the forest. He went straight to a spring by the trail that he had not poisoned and he drank until he had his fill. He plucked some fruit from some trees and ate until he had his fill. He walked with confidence as he made his way back onto the trail toward the Matain village. By his count, he had killed them all. The very fact that he had survived lying on the beach for so long was testament to that. He searched the village and found no one. He searched the forest and saw no Matains. He climbed Mount Mata and observed the island from the high peak – and saw no one. He raised his head to the sky and let out a loud "oooohhhhhhmmm" and then began the same tribal verse that we Rahitians still practice to this day. He prayed to the gods and thanked them for his victory. His mission was complete and he was now ready to leave Mata. But he had one final task to complete. He descended the volcano and walked back down the path through the head trophies. He began removing all of the Rahitian heads that he recognized and carried them back to the lagoon and placed them in the outrigger on the kayak. He wanted to return them to Rahiti for proper burial. His wife's head was the last one to go into the kayak. When the cargo was loaded and secured with palm thatching, he shoved off and said goodbye to Mata Utu for good. He stroked out of the lagoon and into the open sea on his way back to Rahiti. He hadn't gotten far before a terrible storm developed in the sky around him. The wind howled and woke up the seas. Dark clouds formed above him and Mata Utu. Thunder boomed and lightning struck all around him. He turned back to look at Mata as she was struck multiple times by lightning. Fires erupted on the island as the lightning had ignited parts of the rain forest and the Matain village. Hoku kept rowing, but his progress away from the island halted. The current was pulling him back toward Mata. He fought hard to maintain his position, but couldn't distance himself from the island. He struggled until his kayak was ultimately overrun by waves and capsized. The shrunken skulls of the victims spilled into the water as the kayak sank. Hoku tried to grab my mother's head as it sank just out of his reach. Lightning struck in the water all around him, but Hoku remained fearless as he turned his head to the heavens and prayed. He begged for survival so that he may be able to relay his story to the Rahitians and see me once again. He prayed that he could tell me and the rest of Rahiti that we were free from the cannibals. His prayers were granted as the storm quickly subsided just as rapidly as it had formed. Smoke filled the air and the glow of the fires on Mata Utu filled the sky behind him. Hoku floated on his back and rested until he had enough strength to swim in the direction of Rahiti. No ordinary man could have made the swim especially after the days of fighting tirelessly. But once again Hoku reminded us that he was no ordinary man."

Matahi smiled with satisfaction and pride in his father.

"Hoku returned to Rahiti a hero, but a very different man and father. He shared his story with the island and they celebrated their liberation from the fear of the Matains. Hoku, however, could not celebrate with them as returning to Rahiti only reminded him of the loss of his wife. Hoku single handedly wiped out the Matains, but could not conquer the pain and suffering of losing his wife. Within days of his return, Hoku fell ill and died. Some say it was the Matain poison in his system that finally got the best of him. I say that he died of a broken heart. Some say that it was the curse of Mata Utu that killed him. I say it was the pain in his heart. At least I got to see my father the hero again and hear his story of victory first hand."

Matahi paused in reflection and deep thought as he toked on his pipe. Tane began to tap the drums again as the tribe began to chant "Hoku, Hoku, Hoku…" in rhythm with the drum beats. The chant of appreciation and remembrance lasted a few minutes before Matahi concluded his story.

"Hoku profoundly changed our way of life here in Rahiti. No longer do we have to fear the cannibals. No longer do we have to sleep with one eye open. Hoku's bravery was honored by all of the islands and he is now heralded as a legend. He eliminated the only natural predator and leading cause of death in the islands – and he did it singlehandedly except for the help of the medicine man. Had it not been for the poison and knowledge that the Moorean shared with him, he would not have been able to successfully conquer the Matains. Had it not been for his strong faith and belief in himself and the Gods, he surely would have perished and met a cannibalistic fate as well. Hoku proved that wisdom and faith combined with a burning desire can conquer even the strongest, most fierce civilizations. Not only did Hoku singlehandedly conquer the mighty Matains, but he conquered mysterious Mata Utu as well."

Hoanui took advantage of a brief pause in Matahi's dialect to interject some of his own.

"By the way, Hoku was a master fire-handler as well. It was said that he once extinguished a burning coal in his hand." Hoanui said as he looked directly at me.

"Wow" I thought as I took the comment and Hoanui's eye contact as a huge compliment to me for having handled the coal as well.

Hoanui continued to translate as Matahi resumed his legendary story.

"Weeks after Hoku's passing, some Rahitians formed a posse and set out for Mata Utu to explore the uncharted territory. They set out on an expedition to see the mighty Mata for the first time. They were all a little timid and feared that some Matains may have remained hidden or returned from sea after Hoku left. They armed themselves just in case. Upon approaching Mata, they knew Hoku's tale was true. Everything about the island was just as Hoku had described. They entered the lagoon and were on the lookout for poison darts, but none came. They discovered the dead Matains that Hoku had slain on the beach. They cautiously entered the rainforest at the trail and made their way past the crystal clear springs, but they didn't dare drink from them for fear that the water was still poisoned. They noticed the abundant fruits and herbs, but didn't dare partake of them for fear of angering the Gods. They reached the Matain village at the clearing and discovered that it had burned to the ground when it was ignited by lighting during the storm when Hoku left. They made their way down the path to Mount Mata and were repulsed by the sight of the remaining head trophies lining the trail. They were spared the trauma of seeing their fellow Rahitians' heads due to the fact that Hoku had removed them and the storm then put them to rest at sea. They ascended the volcano and rounded the hip to the cave where Hoku had sought refuge in hiding. The wooden viles that once held the Moorean poison and antidote still lie on the floor of the cave. The Rahitians took in the full beauty of the island from the top of the volcano. All was quiet on Mata – in fact, too quiet. The Rahitians noticed that they didn't hear the familiar sounds of life that they were accustomed to back home in Rahiti. No birds flew or sang, no insects buzzed about, no monkeys called out from the tree tops – there was no sound of life. The eerie and quiet calm on the island sent chills up their spines, but also gave them the courage to explore the island more. They found every type of plant and fruit known to exist in the South Pacific, but they did not find one living animal. They did not know why there was no life other than plants on the island. It is very lush and inviting and a perfect home, but no birds flew overhead, no fish swam inside the reef and no animals inhabited the soil. Nothing ever lived on that island again after Hoku left. The Rahitians assumed that the island must be possessed by the curse of the dead Matains. In an attempt to rid the island of the curse, they began removing the heads and dead Matain bodies and dumped them into the volcano as they prayed to the Gods to restore friendly life to the island. The Rahitians fell in love with Mata that day and decided to stay the night. The next day half of the Rahitian posse remained on the island to continue the cleanup of the dead. The other half rowed back to Rahiti to gather more of the tribe to return and help. Their entire time on Mata had been peaceful – until they left. Half way back to Rahiti another fierce storm erupted and nearly sank their kayaks. They watched Mata in the distance as the storm seemed to encompass the island. They prayed for their safe return home and for the safety of those who remained behind on Mata. The kayakers survived the storm and returned to Rahiti in spite of a strong current that tried to draw them back to Mata Utu. Exhausted from the ordeal, the Rahitian expedition told their story to the village upon their return. They then retired to get rest and planned to go back to Mata Utu with reinforcements the next day. The next day never came for them as every one of the Rahitians that returned from the island fell ill and died. This terrified the Rahitians and everyone feared that the Matain curse had been brought to Rahiti. Reluctantly, a group of four Rahitians returned to Mata the next day to retrieve the Rahitians that remained. When they got to Mata all was quiet and peaceful. There was no storm on the island as was there was no life either. They searched the island from side to side and from the peak on Mount Mata to the tip of the spit at the lagoon. They found nothing – no Rahitians, no heads or no dead bodies. There was absolutely no sign of life whatsoever. Scared and bewildered by the situation, they immediately returned to Rahiti before sunset. The four that returned prayed that they would not fall ill and perish. They prayed that the curse be contained to Mata Utu. Their prayers were answered and they safely returned and survived to tell of their puzzling discovery."

Lance and I looked at each other with a look of intrigue on our faces. Lance raised his eyebrows in disbelief.

Hoanui continued the translation. "Hoku's story was told to all of the islands and word of the curse spread through all of the South Pacific. Everyone avoided the temptation to visit Mata Utu like the plague and left the island alone as they had always done. For a hundred years nothing lived on Mata, but ultimately the curse was forgotten and islanders ventured back to Mata to experience her beauty. The visitors found no life on the island on any of their visits. It took bravery to go to Mata, but no one had enough courage to spend the night there. No one had stayed on the island past sunset that we were aware of – until two years ago. A sailor found himself shipwrecked on the outer reef of Mata. He managed to survive the wreck and struggled through the heavy surf to the beach. He was not aware of the history and the curse of the island and he thought he had stumbled into an oasis of paradise. He took up refuge for the night and made himself comfortable in the rain forest. He was so enthralled by the beauty of the island that he did not notice the lack of life there at first. The next day his attitude changed and the quiet solitude turned from pleasure to fear and began to drive him mad. He knew he had to leave the island immediately and feared for his safety. He had no boat, but his desire to leave was so strong that he decided to swim for freedom. As he began to swim away from Mata, a fierce storm blew up and the current began to pull him back to the island. He fought and struggled all day until he finally distanced himself from the island. Later that night, he washed ashore in Rahiti – exhausted and dehydrated from his ordeal. He barely had enough life left in him to tell his tale. That night he fell ill and died. His story renewed the fact that the curse of Mata Utu was still alive and well."

"Mah-tah - ooooo-toooo." Arenui chanted as he tapped the Congo drums lightly.

Hoanui relayed more of Matahi's Rahitian words. "So now that you know the story of Mata Utu, I have one question for you guys."

Matahi's attention and focus turned to Lance and me. All eyes of the rest of the tribe fell on us as well. I knew what he was going to ask before the words came out of his mouth.

"Do you still desire to visit the mysterious island of Mata Utu?"

Lance and I turned to each other as if to see what the other was thinking. I knew Lance was imagining the story of that perfect wave that Arenui had initially shared with us. I knew that the surf would outweigh the curse in Lance's mind. The adventure and mystery was my chief motivation to visit the island and I had slight concern, but little fear for the curse. I had not been raised religiously and both Lance and I rarely subscribed to folklore. In my mind, I could easily dismiss this story as a great legend but a fictitious legend nonetheless.

Lance nodded his head at me in approval and we both answered Matahi with a resounding "Yes!" at the exact same time.

Matahi raised his hand to the sky and blessed our trip with his words. "I hereby grant you access and permission to travel to Mata with one condition. You must leave the island before sunset. I will pray for your safe return."

Arenui was the first to rise from his seated position around the fire. "Well there you have it dudes - the tale of Mata Utu. Get some rest tonight. Tomorrow we will surf the mighty Mata Utu."

We agreed with his statement and thanked Matahi for the story and his permission. We thanked Hoanui for translating before we retired to our huts. I asked Lance what he thought about the story and he winked at me and said "I'm ready."

I was enthralled by the story and how it animated and enhanced the history of the culture we were visiting.

Lance and I didn't know what to make of the folklore. Neither of us were religious and we could hardly comprehend the religious references and significance of prayer in the story. Hoku had prayed and received rain. Hoku prayed and received a fish delivered by a bird. Hoku prayed to defeat the Matains - and he did! I contemplated the Moorean medicine man's prophecy and connection to Mata Utu even though he had never been there. We wondered how much of the story was true and how much had been embellished into a fable. Certainly the passionate storytelling and the environment in which it was told made us believe. I believed in Hoku. I believed in the human spirit - regardless of religion. Belief and knowledge were powerful themes to me. The moral of the story to me was to have faith and believe in something. I also believe that determination, planning and follow through can bring profound results.

I was thankful I had taken an extra couple of shots of Kava Kava last night during the story, but even so – I still had some crazy nightmares of head-hunting cannibals. In spite of my dreams, the next morning Lance and I woke with excitement. The stories of Mata had not deterred our will and desire to see this mysterious place. In fact, we were both so intrigued that we hardly slept. I couldn't wait to discover a new place. Lance couldn't wait to see this perfect wave. I was a little concerned about Matahi's reluctance to grant passage to Mata Utu, but was glad that he had conceded. We may be doing something against tradition, but at least we had permission. The forbidden nature of the island added to the excitement. We ate our breakfast and finished our chores quickly. Lance was the first to head down to the beach. I was almost done with my water replenishment, when Maruia approached me.

"Be careful today. Mata can change you. I don't want you to get hurt." She warned as she grabbed my arm.

"It's okay, I'm a big boy. And I'm sure if I do get hurt, you can nurse me back to health." I answered.

"Yes, but Mata Utu can hurt you in ways that I cannot nurse. Be careful." She held my arm tightly in an urgent plea.

I was unsure how to take her concern. I didn't want to seem less than brave and bold in the face of a new adventure, yet I didn't want to seem so callous in regards to her feelings.

"Look, Maruia, would it make you feel better if you accompanied us as well? That way you can look out for us and bless us with your kind heart?"

"Absolutely not, I will stay here and bless you from afar. I have not been to Mata Utu in years and don't plan to return any time soon."

"So be it. I will see you this afternoon and you will see that everything will be okay." I kissed her hand and turned to walk away. I passed Tane on my way to the beach. I was pretty positive that he had been watching my conversation with Maruia from afar.

"Break a leg" he said as I passed him. His comment went without response. I would like to break his leg sometimes. Jealously is a wicked emotion.

I made my way on down to the beach where I found Lance and Arenui already waiting. They had dragged two outrigger canoes down to the water and had three boards already strapped to the outriggers. I jumped right in and handed them the fourth board which happened to be my own. We went over the short check list of shit we needed to take for the day trip. Wax – check! Water – check! Lighter – check! Suntan lotion – check! Balls – double check! Hoanui – missing!

"Dude, did Hoanui chicken out?" I sarcastically asked.

"Nah, bro – he was here – I think he went to drop a 'morning deuce'. It's a long paddle in the kayak. I suggest you do the same. Plus, I don't want you guys to shit yourself when you see Mata's wicked right." Arenui loved to talk shit – especially about shitting!

"I'm all good to go on that bro. I'm ready to roll." I answered.

"Me too - Let's do it." Lance was always ready to surf – regardless of anything else.

I decided to start a little yoga session while we patiently waited for Hoanui. Maruia and Tania saw the three of us guys in the down-dog position and decided to run down to the beach and join us. We did a few Vinyassa flows and some deep breathing followed by some sun-salutations and some core stretching to get us relaxed and limbered up for what seemed like it was going to be a long paddle and a long voyage. I loved yoga in the morning. In my opinion there is no better way to start the day than with a sunrise yoga practice on the beach followed by a dawn patrol surf session. Whenever my day started with yoga, it seemed that I was a little more positive, productive and prepared. I had the notion for some reason that today Lance and I would need all of the preparation and strength we could get.

We were on our second sun-salutation series posing in a reverse triangle when I heard Hoanui approaching in a hurry. "Ok, guys – finish up your synchronized gayness and lets' paddle."

I looked over at Maruia and Tania as they both cracked a big smile at Hoanui's comment. I admit the scene would have appeared a lot 'gayer' had the two girls not been there with us. Gay or not, I loved the way yoga made me feel. Getting teased by the guys for doing it was nothing new either. I didn't care – it was my thing and I was happy to share it with all who cared to learn. The five of us wrapped up our series as Hoanui pulled the kayaks into the water. I said goodbye to the girls as I waded into the water and jumped into the two man kayak behind Lance.

"Race ya to Mata guys." Arenui and Hoanui challenged from their kayak.

"Easy for you to say – we don't even know where we are going!" Lance splashed back the challenge with his words and a stroke of the oar.

"Follow the rising sun in the east. It's like a beacon to Mata Utu. That's why we always go to Mata first thing in the morning – the rising sun seems to rise from Mount Mata. And also it gives us plenty of time to exit the island before nightfall. Keep the sun in your sights and Mata will magically appear. Or just follow us as we leave you in the dust." Arenui laughed.

As much as Lance and I loved a challenge – especially in the sport and fitness arena, we felt it might be wise to conserve our energy for the return trip home – and for the surfing too. Plus, it is hard to pace yourself and know how much energy to exert when you really have no concept of how far you are going to have to go. Lance and I were no strangers to the two man outrigger kayak, but we felt as if we were going into uncharted territory. Certainly paddling in the open water outside the protection of barrier reefs was much more daunting than the short-range island hopping we were accustomed to. Nonetheless, we set out on the trek and established a good alternating stroke and found ourselves at a good pace that kept us side by side with the Nuis.

A school of porpoise joined us on the venture and entertained us with their frolicking and undulating movements as they occasionally surfaced next to us as if to check us out and taunt us with their graceful swimming ability. I told the guys that we should figure out a way to lasso them and have them tow us all the way to Mata. At best guess, I figured there were about 8 porpoise around us and under us. Having porpoise close by is a comforting feeling since apparently they ward off sharks. It is hard to believe that such a peaceful and seemingly harmless animal could defeat such ferocious hunters as sharks. It made me think of how Hoku, a peaceful fisherman, had wiped out the fierce Matains.

Hoanui explained that it was the porpoises' speed, agility and intelligence that enabled it to defeat the sharks – much like the same characteristics that Hoku possessed in defeating the Matains. I hoped that Lance and I possessed enough of those same traits to conquer Mata's surf – and any sharks we happened to encounter along the way.

I took a couple of short breaks from the paddling to snap several digital pictures of our new fish friends as they were kind enough to model for me by breaking the water's surface and splash down next to us. No zooming was required with the camera since they were almost close enough to us to reach out and touch. They swam close, but just far enough to remain clear of our oars as we methodically stroked through the water. The water was so crystal clear that I was able to reach over the side of the kayak and place the camera under water and snap some amazing pictures of them swimming under us. Lance got on my case for not pulling my weight in the paddling as I looked at the pictures on the camera's display screen. I told him to chill because he was not going to believe how cool the pics looked. I knew my Facebook friends would love to see them later too.

We remained relatively quiet during the paddle - partly to conserve our breath during the physical exertion but mostly to just take in the beauty of nature around us. I glanced at my watch in between strokes and realized that we had been paddling for over 30 minutes, but Mata was still not in sight. I had to ask in a sarcastic kid-in-the-backseat tone "Are we there yet?"

Arenui replied back almost as sarcastically "Do you see a freakin' island yet man? Quit your whining and keep stroking!" Everyone laughed and dug in deeper with our oars. Not more than a couple of minutes after the sarcasm, I saw something appear on the horizon out of nowhere. It looked like the clouds were connecting with the water. Minutes later, I could see more clearly as a defined mountain rose from the water to meet the clouds. It almost appeared to be an optical illusion or maybe an oasis at sea.

"There she is guys. Meet Mata Utu!" Hoanui was the first to make the introduction. The directions were right on point as the sun seemed to rise directly from the top of Mount Mata. The direct sunlight glaring off of the water had kept the island backlit, but hidden from our eyes. The island now came into focus and seemed deceivingly close in proximity. My pulse raced and I felt an adrenaline rush surge through my body. We picked up our stroking pace. Every stroke seemed to get easier. Every stroke seemed to bring us there faster and faster. Every stroke brought the island into focus more vividly right before our eyes. The island seemed to draw us in like magic. I stopped stroking for a second and Lance followed suit. I pulled out my camera again and began snapping picture after picture. This time I didn't take the time to view the pictures on the camera. The image in front of me was pure and absolute perfection in every way – just as had been described.

When I first laid eyes on Mata Utu, a sense of euphoria came over me. Imagine the most beautiful place in the world – and then multiply it by ten. That's how I felt when I saw Mata magically come into focus on the horizon. The island appeared enchanted by rays of sunlight that seemed to rain down through the clouds from heaven above. A giant volcano crowned with a halo of puffy white clouds rose from the sea skyward on the east end of the island and was a beacon to us as we continued to stroke across the sea. Mata appeared to be larger than the size of Rahiti and the volcano looked huge in comparison to the older, weathered volcano on Rahiti. As we drew nearer to the island we became sheltered from the wind. The sea turned into glass as we paddled across crystal clear teal green and blue waters which revealed an incredible view of the world's largest and most beautiful aquarium.

Our paddling became less laborious as the island seemed to pull us in to its sheltered waters on the leeward side. The water became so calm and glassy that the only disturbance on the surface was the ripples from our kayaks and paddles. My excitement grew with every stroke. A beautiful lagoon flanked by a c-shaped beach came into our sights. The scene was so picturesque that it took my breath away. I Immediately pulled out my camera again and began snapping dozens of photos from every angle possible. I couldn't wait to post these pictures on Facebook later. I knew pictures wouldn't do it justice, but no one could imagine the beauty of this place without seeing it in person. Not only was the sight unbelievable, but the smell of tropical flora filled the air. There was a sweet, organic scent wafting from the island in the gentle leeward breeze. I became so enthralled by the island that I didn't even notice that our porpoise friends had departed.

"What happened to our flippered friends?" I asked.

Arenui answered quickly "They split a while ago, bro. They won't come near Mata. Neither will sharks or anything else either."

His comment invoked thoughts of the tales from last night. It put more believability and truth to the outrageous Mata tales that I had partially dismissed as folklore. At this point I didn't care. We were here and I was ready to meet Mata.

We glided into the lagoon with very little effort. I have to admit that I was still a little paranoid and was on the lookout for poisoned darts and spears. Hoanui and Matahi had portrayed the island perfectly in their stories last night. It was only natural that I would have some residual fears based on the tales we heard last night.

When we reached the beach, we disembarked the kayaks and dragged them up onto the bright white sand. Hoanui and Arenui began un-strapping the longboards from the outriggers while Lance and I stood in amazement as we took in the full beauty of the island. The beach at the lagoon had the whitest sand I had ever seen in my life. The granules of sand were so fine and soft that it felt like we were walking on cashmere. I reached down and grabbed a handful of sand and let it run through my fingers. It was so fine that it seemed to evaporate into the air before it hit the ground. I had walked on dozens, if not hundreds of beaches in my life and had never seen or felt anything like this. The beach started as a narrow spit to our left on the far western side of the island and then gently curved around the lagoon for close to a mile until it met a mangrove and tropical rain forest that extended all the way to the water. The beach was narrow at the spit and then narrowed at the forest end, but was very wide and flat in the middle with tall palms scattered randomly across the sandy paradise. I turned away from the island and admired the lagoon - it looked too perfect to be real. Blue and green are my favorite colors and the waters in the lagoon displayed the most natural, colorful, clean and clear shades of blue/green that I had ever seen.

Mount Mata cast a shadow from the rising sun that extended all the way across the island and into the lagoon. An occasional light breeze from the east managed to find its way around the volcano across the island and to the beach where we stood. This light breeze began what I perceived to be a "floral dance". The thousands of flowers and leaves began to sway and flutter in the breeze and then went back to perfect rest as the breeze stopped. The breeze came and went with almost predictable regularity. It was as if Mount Mata was breathing a gentle breath and then exhaling it down across the island to us.

The beach was peacefully quiet with one exception. Our pulses increased with the sound of loud booming sounds in the distance. The source of the sound came from the other side of the island. To a non-surfer it may have been interpreted as an approaching thunderstorm or the drums of a cannibal tribe, but we all knew the source of the sound. Our pulses raced and the adrenaline flowed. Lance made a dash across the beach and I followed him to the other side of the flat, sandy spit. The island was very narrow on this end and was mostly sand and tall palm trees. The spit probably looked like a tail on the island from above.

Lance and I had left the Nui brothers behind with the kayaks as we sprinted through the powdery sand. We couldn't wait one more second to see the surf. Lance was the first to reach the beach on the other side and he stopped dead in his tracks. I stopped next to him and we both stood in silence. Our eyes fixated on the panoramic landscape in front of us. Our ear drums reverberated with the booming sounds of the waves crashing in the distance and the echoes they sent off of Mount Mata. The sound reminded me of Mista Beat and how his beat-boxing had echoed in the terminal yard at the party. "Boom, boom, boooom. Boom chalak, boom, tat tat ta, booooom." Lance and I broke out into a momentary beat-box session in jubilation.

"Hey - you 'mista beat'." I said to Lance.

"I never miss a beat, man." He responded as we continued our beat-boxing. "Boom, bam, boom-boom-boooooooooom."

The emerald green and teal blue water of the vast sea gave rise to walls of water which grew until they peaked and then, as if pushed down from heaven above, the top of the wall collapsed and thrust forward forming the most perfectly hollow barreling wave. The barrels formed from the initial break at the point on Mount Mata which was barely visible to the far right from our vantage point on the beach. The barrels peeled down the reef parallel to the beach thundering their mighty bass tone as tens of thousands of tons of water horizontally spiraled for what was definitely the longest right point break we had ever seen. Each thundering collapse and close-out yielded a white frothy foam and spray that formed rainbows in the clear blue sky. We were awestruck. We stood speechless for minutes as we watched the perfect sheet glass faces of the waves break and become cloaked by barrel after barrel. As we watched in amazement, we began to count the seconds from the first visible break at the point on Mount Mata to the final closeout directly in front of us at the spit. I turned to Lance with a big smile and said only "ninety-two". He smiled back and said "I counted one-o-four". Either count meant a perfect ride for over a minute and a half!

My brother and I immediately exempted ourselves from the curse of Mata Utu. We dismissed the past and focused on one small aspect of its present. However, one rumor was true – Mata certainly had the longest right surf break in the entire South Pacific and possibly the world. Off in the distance, we could see the rocky reef outcropping that Mount Mata formed as her giant base plunged deep into the sea forming a point which was rightly named Point Mata. This point was strategically placed in perfect concert with the forces of nature to form the perfect conditions for the perfect wave. The prevailing winds in conjunction with the water currents traveled for over a thousand miles unimpeded - building up momentum and creating a long, powerful and forceful wave. This right break unleashed its wrath of the windward side of Mata Utu repeatedly – wave after wave. The first contact point the wave encounters after its thousand mile journey is Point Mata. The point initiates the break and the underwater barrier reef perpetuates the break forming of one of the most hollow, pitching barrels I've ever seen. The wave just peels along the length of the windward side of the island from Point Mata all the way to the sand spit adjacent to the lagoon. Wow. We stood there for minutes staring in disbelief. My fear of the Matains and the curse quickly turned into the fear of breaking my neck or drowning on the reef. My mind grappled with the notion of wiping out on the reef break, but my sense of adventure kicked in. It was a bold move for me, but I came here to surf Mata and I was going to do just that.

We returned to the lagoon where Arenui and Hoanui were waxing down their boards and waiting for us. Arenui was eager to hear what we thought of the break. "Dude, did I tell you or what? Isn't it incredible?" Arenui excitedly asked.

Lance wasted no time in concurring with him. We all grabbed our boards and followed the Nuis onto the island.

We walked down the sandy spit toward the jungle that separated us from Mount Mata. It was hard to believe we were about to follow the same trail that Hoku had once walked. I began to get flashbacks from the story last night. I couldn't help but scan the treetops and look over my shoulder for Matains hiding and waiting to attack. Hoanui noticed my paranoia and teased me a little bit. "Stan, the Matains have been dead for almost a century. Relax. As long as we are off the island by dark we will have no worries." He said as I laughed and shrugged off my fear.

The sandy spit ended abruptly and the sporadic palm trees turned into dense jungle with the exception of one opening where the trail started. When we entered the rainforest, I imagined it was like entering the Garden of Eden but with no serpents. Fruit was abundant on almost every tree. The temperature seemed to drop about ten to twenty degrees as soon as the tropical canopy's shade engulfed us. Dew drops the size of quarters were puddled in the leaves. I would venture to say that this was the most fertile place on earth – at least that I had ever seen. It should be a haven for life of all types, but I felt quite fortunate that we were the only living things on the island. With no mosquitoes or spiders to bite us or sharks or other wildlife to attack us, this paradise felt secure. It was heaven on earth. I wanted to capture this moment in my brain forever. I was in the most perfect place with the three greatest guys in my life. Nothing else mattered as we walked through the forest. I was totally enthralled in the moment, the environment and the company. I snapped some more pictures.

I commented on my feelings about the place. "Dude, this place is awesome. It is exactly as you described it. It is total paradise. No offense intended - because I love Rahiti, but I want to live here."

Arenui reminded us "No animals can live here on the island at all. No snakes, no birds, no lizards, no nothing – not even a mosquito – especially not a Rahitian. In fact, I don't think I've ever even caught a fish near this island. Don't get too comfortable - we are leaving when the surfing is done."

Lance chimed in "Good, because I don't want any sharks or bugs eating on me while I surf."

Hoanui added "The only thing that seems to "live" here is plants. These plants bear some of the best fruits you have ever seen or tasted in your life. Seems like the plants and fruit were the only things the Matains managed not to eat and totally destroy."

Good thing for me I am a vegetarian. My mouth watered at the thought of a paradise of nothing but fruits with no bugs or critters to spoil them.

Why was there no animal life of Mata? It was eerie and strange, but more confusing than anything else. It was such a lush, tropical paradise – a vegetarian's dream come true. I dismissed any negative thoughts about the situation and looked at it as a sign – it was a place I was supposed to be. Hoanui veered off of the trail and shimmied up a tree and began tossing down fruit. You name it – it grew here. There were mangoes, bananas, limes and lemons, pomello fruit, avocado, figs, and of course, coconuts all ripe for the picking. One thing that amazed me was that you could pull a fruit off of a tree on a 100 degree day and when you peeled it and bit into it, it was cool. Somehow the rainforest acted as nature's refrigerator. We sat on the cool, soft, mossy ground in the jungle and feasted on the most delicious fruit I had ever eaten. I couldn't wait for my garden project in Rahiti to come to fruition.

I was in absolute heaven as I sat in the jungle among my friends. Mata Utu was such a cool place and added a whole new adventure and dimension to our trip. It was a pristine island with a perfectly hidden and safe lagoon. There was lush rainforest vegetation rich with fruits and edible plants on the majority of the island except for the rocky volcanic reef outcropping and Mount Mata on the windward side. The island was about a mile and a half long and the width varied from a couple hundred feet to almost a mile on the volcanic end. The island was a perfect oasis, seemingly untouched by man. It had a lure and an enchantment. I would have never known that such a brutal tribe once practiced such atrocities here. However, the absence of life and all of the landmarks and sights we have seen so far totally validated Matahi's story. That fact and the subsequent myths and stories spread throughout the other islands was more than ominous enough to keep anyone from inhabiting this island. Even the most die-hard surfers and island hoppers were kept away from this paradise by their fears of its past. I was determined to not let the myth ruin my day here and I was equally as determined to not let the curse follow me home. Mata was awesome, but not worth dying for.

We wrapped up our snacking and hit the trail again with our boards under our arms. We were facing about an hour long hike to the point. The booming of the waves echoed through the forest and resonated in my chest – causing my heart to beat more rapidly with excitement. I put fear out of my mind and imagined how awesome the ride on Mata's right break would be. After today I would be able to say that I surfed the longest, most barreling wave in the whole world. Probably less than a few thousand people world-wide had ever heard of this place and probably less than 10 had surfed it. Incredible!

As we made our way through the forest, I pulled out the digital camera and began snapping photos of the wilderness around me. Rays of sunlight pierced the canopy of the forest high above and shone down on the leaves glistening their dew drops as if they were diamonds. The place seemed magical. I was absorbed into the nature around me. I could stay here forever – the only catch is that I have to leave by sunset.

Soon the dense jungle parted and we came to a clearing by the beach. Hoanui pointed it out first. "Guys, that is where the Matain village was for over a thousand years. Not a trace of it is left. It is crazy to think how many people – how many of our ancestors were eaten there in that spot. If it had not been for Hoku we may have made a fine Matain meal as well."

"If it had not been for Hoku, we certainly wouldn't be standing here right now on this island" Arenui added.

"What happened to the remains of the village?" I asked.

"Well, the lightning from the storm that blew up as Hoku kayaked away from the island with an outrigger full of Rahitian heads struck the village and then burned it to the ground. The ashen remains deteriorated with weather and washed away in storms. In fact, there is no apparent trace that anyone ever lived here." Hoanui answered.

"Well, I bet if you looked hard enough you could find something." Lance commented.

"Yeah, if you crawled down into the mouth of the volcano you would probably find 100 year old skeletons from human remains." Arenui answered.

"No thanks." I said.

We passed the clearing and entered the trail that lead to Mount Mata. I got the eerie sensation that this is the trail that was flanked by the skull trophies. I also got the sensation that something, if nothing more than the trees was watching us. I got the same chill down my spine that I had experienced last night as I listened to the story. It wasn't a good feeling in spite of how happy I was to be there. I kept on walking and focused my attention on the gigantic volcano ahead. It was definitely the tallest volcano that I had ever seen firsthand. I wondered when it had last erupted. I wondered if the island would get mad at us for being here and spew hot lava down onto us. It would be one more chapter to add to the mystery of Mata.

The trail ended abruptly and the jungle opened up to the sky when we reached the base of Mount Mata. No longer did we have soft mossy soil to walk on. The ground turned into hard jagged rock. It was a little painful on my feet, but I thought of Hoku and how he had scaled the mountain barefooted with Matains chasing him. I sucked up the pain and carried on. Climbing with a long board under ours arms was a bit challenging, but we did it. We climbed about a quarter of the way up the side of Mount Mata to the "hip" and then headed left to the point. The view from the volcano was spectacular. The island looked even more beautiful from above. We could see all the way back to the kayaks in the lagoon by the spit. We had a great vantage point of the waves as they rolled in from the east. The crashing of the waves echoed off of the volcano and carried across the island. I put down my board and took another amazing series of photos.

Our trek finally culminated at the point. The point was a narrow, rocky ledge that jutted out into the water on the easternmost point of Mount Mata's hip. We had to descend down the backside of the volcano to get to it. Gravity seemed to be obsolete as climbing downhill proved to be harder than going up. It had been well over an hour of hiking since we finished lunch by the spit. What a journey to ride only one wave. I knew it was going to be good because walking back for a second would be a time consuming and calorie burning event. As I stood on the point watching the waves roll in and crash on the point, I felt like I was on top of the world. I also felt a few butterflies welling up in my stomach as the waves were more than slightly intimidating.

I listened intently as Arenui spouted out some final instructions and words of wisdom. "First of all, time your jump just right or you could risk being dashed into the rocks on the point. Secondly, you have to jump and launch on your board off of the ledge which is about 10 feet above the water – depending on the tide. Third, you have to paddle hard and quick as the wave jacks up behind you. And fourth you have to make the drop and pull off a perfect bottom turn tight into the barrel. If you get out ahead of the wave you are sure to get tossed into the reef by the lip as it pitches into you. Stay high in the tube in case you need to drop more and pick up some momentum. Feel free to lag deep in the barrel, but no more than about 6 board lengths or so. If you feel the tube closing too quickly behind you, pump the board and drop a little to gain some momentum. You do not want to get caught in a closeout and get thrown over the falls and into the reef. Stay cool and in control. Don't get too crazy and pull any tricks yet. I want you guys to be around to do this again. When the wave starts to bend around the spit and subside, be ready to get spit out of the tube and prepare to launch off of the backside. The water is deep there and there is no reef so feel free to get some air. Just don't let your board hit you on the way down. We will all meet back on the beach at the spit. Any questions?"

"Nope" Lance quickly responded.

it sounded easy enough, but looked much more difficult in reality. Arenui insisted that Lance or I go first, but we both refused. I wanted one of them to launch off the point first so I could see exactly how they pulled the stunt off first.

Arenui was hesitant to go first and he expressed his concerns. "Dude, if I go first and Hoanui goes next there is no one left to make sure you guys launch. If you chicken out it's a long walk back to the spit. Basically there are three ways to get back to the spit. You can walk, surf or swim. You don't want to swim. And if you walk back, we will make it a walk of shame as we harass you for being a wimp. As for me, I'm gonna surf." Without further ado Arenui grabbed his board by the rails and pulled it tight to his chest as he bent over and jumped off of the point. "Watch and learn, boys." He said as he went airborne.

He hit the water perfectly and immediately turned and began stroking. A huge wave jacked up behind him and the white water started to form on the peak of the wave at the point. The wave looked to be well over twice as tall as Arenui. He let out a whoop as he popped up and made the drop. I saw him scream down the face until he was shacked by the breaking tube. We watched the wave break and roll along the reef from behind. I could barely make out Arenui's body through the crystal clear wall of water on the back of the wave. We watched until distance distorted our view. Hoanui told us to pay close attention to the end of the wave at the spit as we would see him get spit out of the tube in a moment. The distance was over a mile or so and from our perspective he would look like a speck. But sure enough we saw him come flying out of the end of the tube and launch airborne as a mist of water and foam sprayed into the air behind him. What an awesome sight.

Lance was ready and was already making his way to the edge of the point. It was obvious he was eager, but I sensed that even he was a little nervous too. This would be one of the most daring things I had ever done in my life. It was certainly the most awesome, yet most dangerous wave I had ever surfed. Hoanui counted the sets as the waves rolled by.

"Get ready Lance. This one is yours." Hoanui said. "Okay... now!" He instructed as he pointed to the spot where Lance should land.

Lance turned his head briefly and gave me a head nod as he launched into the air off of the point. I stepped forward to the edge in time to see him splash into the water below. He had landed perfectly and maintained his grip on his board. He turned to face the beach quickly as the wave jacked up behind him. He pulled a couple of quick strokes to gain pace with the wave as it lifted him skyward. He angled the board, popped to his feet and let out a "whoooooaaa yeah!"

I watched him make the drop and the perfect double-overhead wave. He hit his bottom turn perfectly and pulled into the barrel. I could see him inside the tube through the back of the wave. I watched for over a minute until he was spit airborne at the end of the tube in the same fashion Arenui had exited his wave. I could see Arenui jumping in celebration on the edge of the beach at the spit.

"Ok, Stan - your turn. You ready?" Hoanui asked.

I wasn't so sure I was ready, but I summoned my courage and answered with certainty. "Right on dude!"

Hoanui counted and timed the sets for me. "I'm gonna find you the perfect 'first wave'." He said as he placed his hand on my shoulder.

My toes curled over the edge of the rocky point. My feet and legs crouched in preparation to launch my body and board from the edge. My hands gripped the rails of my board tightly and my arms bent to pull the board close to my chest. My heart pounded and my mind raced with excitement. Butterflies churned in my stomach. "I can do this." I thought to myself.

Hoanui began to count. "Okay, go on seven." He said.

Each count fueled my excitement and fear simultaneously. When he said "seven" my legs flexed and my toes straightened and propelled me from the rocky ledge. The free-fall into the water was brilliant. Although it was a short fall of only about eight to ten feet, it felt monumental. I splashed down into the water and gripped my board tightly. I submerged only briefly and popped to the surface. I instinctively paddled with one arm to turn myself toward the beach and achieve proper angle on the wave. Once my angle was right, I paddled several quick, powerful strokes. My arms pulled the board forward against the force of the rising wave behind. I felt the wave lifting me and I glanced back briefly to see the wall of water rising around me. In an instant I heard the sound of breaking water hitting the point and then felt the immediate thrust of the wave behind me. I sprung to my feet as gravity and the force of the mighty wave took over and propelled me. I dropped down the face of the wave quickly and smoothly. I hit the bottom of the trough and then shifted my weight and my feet slightly to the right to pull me back up the face of the wave and parallel to the wave. The wall of water to my right was easily twice my height. It looked like teal green glass. A rumble behind me intensified as the breaking wave sounded like a freight train chasing me. I crept my feet forward on the board toward the nose and leaned back slightly to slow my momentum. I felt the wind generated by the barreling tube behind me. I felt the spray from the veil of water that began to break over my head. The sunlight was drowned out by the shadow of the tube of water as it engulfed me. I was in the barrel - I was getting 'shacked' at Mata.

I maintained my balance well and leaned my head back slightly to see the awesome sight above me. My speed was intense as I raced with the breaking water. I purposefully leaned back a little more to slow my speed and let the tube engulf me a little deeper. The spiraling, pitching barrel pulled ahead of me and swallowed me into its cavernous recesses. I wanted to take a picture, but was afraid to fetch my waterproof digital camera from my pocket. I didn't want to lose it and I didn't want to lose my balance either. I decided to engrain the image into my head instead. There would be many more opportunities for pictures later.

I could feel the spray and the thunderous booms intensifying behind me. I knew I was nearing the end of the ride. I pumped the board and crouched to lean forward a bit. My speed rapidly increased and I emerged from the hollow tube and into the sunlight just as a tremendous blast of water and air hit me from behind. I turned my feet and shifted my weight hard right. The motion sent me up and over the remaining wall of water in front of me. In an instant I went from surfing to flying. The board dropped as my feet lost contact with the fiberglass deck. I snapped my head around to the right in time to see Lance and Arenui raise their arms in jubilant celebration. I estimated I was a good 15 to 20 feet in the air. I tucked and rolled my body into a ball as I plummeted and splashed into the water. I hoped I wouldn't hit my board on the way down. I splashed down cannon-ball style and immediately emerged and reeled my board in to me. I began to paddle the short distance to the spit where Lance and Arenui eagerly awaited. I saw Lance and Arenui pointing behind me and I turned my head just in time to see Hoanui launce airborne on the very next wave. His launch must have been much more graceful than mine as he extended his arms and legs into a full swan dive. His dive landed him in the water not too far from me and he quickly recovered his board and caught up to me as I reached the beach.

The four of us high-fived each other and celebrated our victorious ride.

"Congratulations, brah." Arenui said as he slapped my hand. "You did it - you rode the mighty Mata!"

"Right on! I conquered that wave!" I exclaimed.

"That was undoubtedly the best tube I've had in my life." Lance added as he smiled ear to ear. "I've surfed a lot of waves too - that was the best ever!" Lance continued.

"No matter how many times I have surfed here, every time always gives the same sensational rush." Hoanui said.

We stood on the beach talking surf lingo and celebrating for a while. We contemplated making the hour-long hike again and riding a second time. Lance was the only one who was gung-ho to do it again. I was content with my one successful ride for the day. Although it was exhilarating, I was happy with only one ride.

"Don't get too greedy, brah." Arenui said to Lance as he convinced him to leave it at one. "There is always a wave here and plenty of days left to enjoy it." He consoled as we headed to the outriggers in the lagoon on the other side of the spit.

"I can't wait for tomorrow!" Lance said as we strapped our boards onto the kayaks and shoved off for the journey back to Rahiti.

The paddle back to Rahiti was easy. We stayed stroke for stroke alongside the Nuis as we joked and recounted stories of the emotional first ride at Mata. The dolphins appeared and escorted us all the way back to Rahiti. We thanked the Nuis for introducing us to what would become our new daily morning ritual. And I thanked God that I had experienced and survived such an awesome day.

The Production

It was tough to keep up our usual daily routine now that we had been introduced to Mata Utu. Mata had gotten into our souls. Lance and I talked non-stop about the island and its perfect wave. Mata consumed about 99% of all of our conversations. I wanted to go back there every day, but I didn't want to lose focus on my goals for Rahiti. The Nui brothers promised to take us back there very soon once we got a few things done at home, so I used that as my motivation to expedite the construction efforts.

Hoanui and his crew had efficiently unloaded all of Connie's contents and transported the last load to Rahiti today. It took exactly 47 total trips in 22 days - not bad considering the bulk of the load and the fact that there were days with slightly turbulent seas. Now that the transporting was done, Hoanui's moving crew was able to join forces with my construction crew on-site. The increase in labor should easily double our progress and effort - especially since the most difficult aspects of the job were done. The entire exterior of the structure was completely built which gave us a weatherproof environment in which we could now store all of the materials.

The community center was built strong and looked beautiful. There was just over six thousand square feet of total interior space divided into five different sections. The entrance foyer and central meeting room comprised almost half of the total area and then there were three different sleeping quarters - each of which had enough space to sleep about 30 people. The fourth area was to be utilized for storage of tools, equipment, food, water and emergency supplies. The center had a total of 4 bathrooms. The bathrooms were not your typical bathroom as they had no running water and only a urinal which piped liquid-only waste out of the building and away from the community center into the sand about 50 feet away. There was a kitchen in the main meeting room, but there was no refrigerator or stove. The kitchen did have running water in a large stainless steel sink. The running water was sourced and mechanically pressurized from the aqueduct system that collected and stored rain water from the gutters on the building and there was also a water outlet piped to the deck side of the building outside. A total of 5 multi-angle intersecting hip roofs gave plenty of surface area for rain water runoff and ample linear footage for the 6" PVC gutters to collect it. The roof was made of 6x9" faux-slate rubber shingles that were rated to withstand 150mph winds. The shingles were light and easily transported and installed flawlessly. I had the shingles pre-painted with a special white-oxide elastomeric finish to reflect sunlight to keep the eaves of the building cool in the intense South Pacific sun. The white roof was also easy to keep clean. The PVC gutters ran the entire outside circumference of the roof and fed into downspouts which housed re-usable filters that filtered out debris such as leaves and sand that may blow onto the roof and wash into the system. Five different fifty-five gallon plastic drums were buried underground at different depths and were interconnected with PVC plumbing. The downspouts were piped into the drums and the system was sealed with the exception of the ABS valves which allowed the system to breathe and flow. Out of all the aspects of the community center, I was most proud of the water system - because a plumber I was not! I was skeptical of how it was going to work even though the prototype we tested back home months prior had worked like a charm. I got help and advice from one of the best plumbers in Richmond. I gave him tens of thousands of dollars worth of work for several years and he gave me invaluable advice and help with this system which would hopefully work effortlessly with nature for decades to collect and provide over 250 gallons of fresh rain water at once for an entire island community. Water was a priceless commodity and necessity and I felt like this was my greatest contribution to the island. The entire tribe gathered in the meeting room of the center and rejoiced after the first rain when I turned on the faucet and fresh water flowed from the tap. I filled several of my plastic Fiji water bottles and passed them around the room for the Rahitians to sample their first glass of running water. The response was as tremendous as if I had invented the light bulb.

Speaking of light bulbs, I installed low-voltage LED lights in the ceilings of all of the rooms. They were the first permanent artificial lights ever installed on the island. The LED lights were powered by solar panels which we had integrated into the roof system on the north side of all of the roof angles to maximize sun exposure. The solar panels were flat and paralleled the roof angles to minimize wind resistance and damage during storms. The solar panels fed the energy into a series of ni-cad battery packs that were capable of storing over 35,000 watts of power indefinitely. One 12 hour sunny day could offer enough solar power to provide enough energy to power all of the lights, the computer and recharge the tool batteries for almost a week. I couldn't help but think that since it was so easy to power a village on an island with natural energy - why couldn't we do it back home in the States too?

I finally wired up the laptop and connected it to the permanent satellite that I mounted on the roof of the center. Although securely affixed, I made sure that the dish could be quickly removed from the roof in the event of a big storm. In one of the final crates that was transported from Connie there was also a 32" flat-screen LCD TV/Computer monitor. I had honestly almost forgotten about the TV. It had been almost three months since I saw a TV and hadn't missed it one bit. My brief semi-daily visits to the internet kept me informed and in contact with my family and friends - that was enough for me - screw "reality TV". This island and life on it was my reality. I had no intention of starting to watch TV again now, but the large monitor would definitely make it easier to show pictures and the internet to the entire tribe. I also brought surround speakers and an amplifier that would add a whole new dimension to our entertainment. With over 3000 MP3 music files on my computer, I was ready to introduce the natives to new sounds and genres of music they had never heard of before. I couldn't wait to bust out the knee-knock tribal dance to some MC Hammer or Lady Gaga. Hearing the music played on the surround system for the first time was astonishing to the locals. It was the first time in the history of Rahiti that pre-recorded music had been played to the public. Certainly the educated Rahitians had experienced radio, TV, Cd's and computers while attending school in Papeete, but those things were left in Tahiti and not brought back home to Rahiti. I was curious how the tribe would respond when I introduced the technology to their culture. I didn't know if I was breaking tradition or violating religion, but the music and the computer were surprisingly very well received. In fact, many of the locals instantly chose favorite songs and began to sing the lyrics even though they had no idea what they meant. I figured it would be a great way for them to start learning English. The addition of music to the building also reinvigorated the work force as well. The guys danced and nodded their heads in time with the music as they worked.

The projects that remained for completion on the center were adding the 1200 square foot exterior decking which would be covered by a thatched canopy. The Rahitian girls had already begun work weaving the canopy from palm leaves. The footings and deck pilings were already completed when the foundation of the main structure was done. We waited until the structure was finished before building the deck in case we ran short on materials - we could shrink the size of the deck and use additional lumber from it on the structure if we had needed to. Remarkably, we had no shortages and were able to build the full deck according to plans. I was pleased not to have to compromise the deck because, along with the Rahitians, I enjoyed outdoor space. The deck would make the perfect eating, meeting and dancing area.

We made use of some local materials and made a stone fire pit adjacent to the deck, but far enough away so that there was minimal risk of fire hazard on the new building. The fire pit would serve for cooking as well as offer up heat and ambiance for our tribal ceremonies. I converted some of the crew from carpenters to furniture makers as the need for labor on the structure was decreasing as construction was nearing completion. Of course some of the locals were already very adept at making things from wood and other natural materials so I naturally chose them to take on the task of furnishing the community center. Connie was so packed full of building materials that I was unable to bring any furnishings other than a few basics. That didn't matter to me at the time because the priority had been to build a safe, weatherproof structure with a water collection system. Once the construction neared completion, I realized we now had an enormous building with nothing really in it. The kitchen had a huge bar with a sink and a few cabinets, the bathrooms had urinals and the storage room had shelves, but other than that it was pretty much open, empty floor space - a lot of it.

I was able to divert the use of some of the tools from construction to fabrication of furniture. The furniture makers were very pleased to be able to carve, sand, nail and assemble things with the use of the new technology. With the help and oversight of Nanihi and Matahi, I turned them loose to build whatever they wanted to put in the building. They began carving benches, seats, tables and other furniture out of Banyan trees, palm trees, bamboo and even stone. I was amazed at the daily production of furniture.

Since the construction was running on auto-pilot, I decided to start a new project. I had my eye on an area of the island away from the village that would be perfect for a garden. A fire caused by a lightning strike had burned an area of the rainforest a couple of years prior. The jungle had begun to grow back immediately in the fertile soil, but the larger trees were gone and only small undergrowth was there. It was a perfect situation for the garden because the absence of large trees meant there would be ample sunlight for our new plants. Plus, in the spirit of 'going green' we wouldn't have to cut down any existing trees. We only had to clear out the undergrowth and till the soft, rich soil. I enlisted the help of the tribe members who were not working on the center to help me do just that. Within a matter of days we had planted all of my seeds. Avocados, pomegranates, strawberries, tomatoes, cucumbers, basil, mint, squash, lettuce, corn were just a few of the dozens of plants we seeded. I showed the tribe pictures of the fruits and veggies we were planting on the internet and explained each of the non-native plants to them. I couldn't wait to share strawberries with the island for the first time. The island was rich with its own bounty of native fruits and plants, but there were many things that didn't grow here naturally - until now. We worked hard and planted with love. The rest would be up to Mother nature.

Meanwhile, my construction crew framed up the entire deck in a matter of two days and even had enough scrap lumber left over to build some bench seating in lieu of railings in certain sections. The girls wove the canopy and my 'roofers' installed it underneath the gutters on the deck side of the building. The canopy would be the only "expendable" part of the structure. If a typhoon hit, the canopy could be removed if there was enough time in advance or if it blew away it could easily be rebuilt and installed again. It was really only there to offer shade and enhance the natural look of the exterior of the building.

On the interior, I had several crews working in different areas of the building each doing specific tasks. There were three guys installing wooden paneling on the walls and vaulted ceilings. Then I had an assembly line of Rahitians nailing down sections of pre-finished bamboo plank flooring. The flooring was natural, beautiful, durable, light weight, came in compact packaging and was easily installed. Another crew followed on the heels of the flooring guys and applied base board trim and window and door trim as well. Then I had two guys with caulk guns sealing up all the cracks with silicone. The guys worked at lightning speed and within a matter of a few days, the building was almost done. Matahi and Nanihi began to become more involved as my role of construction manager was almost over. I was more than happy to hand the reins over to them. After all, I built the community center for the Rahitians and I wanted the Rahitians to finish it off and furnish it in a way that would make them feel comfortable and proud to call it their own. Every Rahitian had contributed to the center in some way. It was truly the pride of the entire island.

Every evening we gathered around the center to admire the day's work and to look at slide show pictures on the computer monitor as I posted them to Facebook. I snapped pictures and videos of all of my Rahitian friends and proudly posted them on the internet as well. I had posted over 500 pictures already and my friends back home had shared plenty of commentary on them. The Rahitians were amazed that people halfway around the world could connect and see us in an instant. It was cool to share the technology with the locals while keeping in touch with friends and family back home as well.

Meals were now prepared and served at the new center instead of the old tiki hut across the clearing. Tonight's dinner was special as it marked the final completion of all of the construction. Every last bit of material from Connie had been used - right down to the last nail. I breathed a sigh of relief and sat down at the table next to Maruia. Matahi said a prayer to bless the building and to thank everyone for their efforts. Before we could begin to eat, Hoanui addressed the group and said "Now that the community center is done, we must give it a name. Does anyone have any suggestions?" His question invoked conversation among the villagers. I heard a myriad of different names being discussed between each table, but it was Maruia who stood up and addressed the village first.

"I have it!" She said. "I know what the name HAS to be!" She said in English and then repeated her statement in Rahitian.

"What is your idea?" I asked as she stood there smiling in silence.

"Let's hear it, Maruia." Puatea urged as Maruia just smiled and then looked down at me as I sat there in anticipation of her idea. She purposefully remained silent for another few moments as if to build anticipation and to get everyone's full attention.

She finally broke her silence with two words. "Stan-Dunk!" She said with absolute resolve. The entire village repeated the words over and over as they became the focal point of a debate. Lance rolled his eyes and shook his head side to side in subtle disapproval. With the exception of Hoanui, Arenui and a few others, the Rahitians didn't initially understand the significance of the name until Maruia explained the double-connotation to them. Once they understood the meaning of the term and its significance as it applied to me, they all stood up at the table in the midst of dinner and began to chant "Stan-dunk, Stan-dunk, Stan-dunk...." So that was it - it was decided that the community center would now be known as 'The Stan-Dunk'. I was cool with it and so were all of the Rahitians - except for maybe Tane, but he remained silent and kept his jealous opposition to himself. Lance wasn't thrilled either, but even in their opposition both of the guys realized how much of my heart and soul I had put into the building. Lance's financial contribution to the trip was minimal and his efforts on the construction were even less. Plus, I didn't really care what he thought. The building now belonged to the Rahitians and they were free to furnish it how they saw fit and name it whatever they wanted. In my (totally unbiased) opinion the name was brilliant. The building truly was a "Stan-Dunk" as far as I was concerned. It was my greatest construction achievement yet and also my greatest contribution ever. I felt the name was very apropos and the tribe unanimously agreed.

At the conclusion of dinner, Maruia and I excused ourselves and took our usual walk on the beach. "Thank you for the wonderful gesture of naming the building after me." I said once we were in private.

"You are more than welcome - it is the least we can do to show our appreciation. That building is YOU - and you are a part of our family. Now whether you are here or elsewhere there will always be a part of you here on Rahiti." She said as she held my hand and gently massaged the top of it with her thumb. "I hope that someday I will truly get to show my appreciation to you and return the favor somehow."

I didn't know exactly what she had in mind, but I thought maybe she was implying marriage. I decided to redirect the conversation down a more comfortable path. "Just being here with you and your tribe is repayment enough for me. I appreciate the fact that you have welcomed my brother and me onto your island and into your tribe. You share your food, your water, your surf..."

Maruia interrupted me in mid-sentence as she stepped in front of me. "That's not what I meant..." She said with a seductive tone. Before I could respond, she hooked her right leg behind mine and swept my legs as she gave my chest a firm push. She tripped me and then landed on top of me, straddling my body with hers as we hit the soft sand. She leaned down and put her lips on mine and began to kiss me passionately while stroking my head and neck with her hands. Her affection was appreciated and well received as I quickly returned the emotion. We rolled around in the sand and played as we tickled, kissed and massaged each other's bodies. She began to shed her Parea in the heat of the passion, but something other than her beautiful exposed body caught my attention. Tane was standing in the tree line where the forest met the beach. He must have been hiding behind a palm tree watching us, but stepped into the clear to reveal himself in an attempt to thwart our romance. I didn't care - I made it clear that I had seen him by my head movement and eye contact as I kept the passion alive with Maruia. I kissed every square inch of her naked body from head to toe and then she returned the favor to me. After a while of observing our passion, Tane disappeared into the woods. I guess he could no longer tolerate our display of affection - I didn't care - he had no business spying on us in the first place. Our kissing and caressing continued until we had both reached climax. We lay there on the sand in total bliss as the island became cloaked in darkness and the stars began to become visible and illuminated the sky.

We got dressed and walked back up the trail to the village and I escorted Maruia to her hut and kissed her one last time for the night. I then walked to my hut with a stride and bounce in my step congruent with the passion that I had just experienced. I was also still elated over the fact that the new community center was finished - and named after me! My positive state was interrupted as I was surprised to see that my hut was illuminated by lantern light. My good spirits were shattered as I entered into the hut to find Lance sitting on top of my Rubbermaid container holding a gun.

"What the hell is this, Stan?" He asked in a pissed off tone.

'Shit' I thought to myself. How the hell did he come across that? "Well, it kinda looks like a gun bro." I innocently answered.

"Damn it. I thought we had an agreement. Why did you disregard our conversation and my request for you to leave the gun at home?" He said as he tapped the barrel of the gun on his leg in nervous fashion.

"To be honest, I really didn't think it was a big deal. Safety was a primary concern for me and the gun offered up some protection." I answered with little remorse.

"Protection? From what - the seagulls? We came here to the islands to escape the violence and all of the bullshit of our society back home. Why bring a weapon to such a peaceful place?" He argued as his temper flared.

"I didn't know what we may encounter on this trip or what to expect..." I answered, but he promptly cut me off.

"Bullshit - you've been here before. You know what is here." He said as he shook his head in anger. "It's not so much the fact that you brought the gun as much as the fact that you hid it from me."

"Honestly, I forgot that I brought it." I told a lie that I quickly regretted.

"Screw you, Stan. Do you think I'm stupid?" He retorted.

"Maybe a little moody and irrational." I fired back.

"Did you forget about these too and the whole other container you hid from me?" He said as he pulled out my infrared binoculars and dangled them by their lanyard.

"Be careful with them. They are infrared binoculars and they are very sensitive." I said as I reached out to grab the binoculars.

"And probably expensive too - why the hell do you need these?" He said as he tossed them to me in an arrogant tone.

"Actually, I didn't pay a penny for them. A friend of mine lent them to me. They are military spec binoculars - the same ones the Navy Seals use. You can see body heat and thermal signatures with them and…" I said as I was interrupted.

"What, so you can shoot stuff in the dark with your little gun here?" He said as he waved my gun and continued to plunder through my Rubbermaid container. He tossed out my dry suit, rope, repelling gear, compass, transistor radio and some other personal items that I had acquired on loan from my friend in the military. He threw all of my stuff onto the sandy floor without regard to damaging it.

"All free, but all fragile and sensitive to sand." I said as he handled my items. "Can you please stop…"

"So what - it was free!? It still took up valuable space in the container and…" Lance argued for no reason.

"Don't worry about space - I had room for everything. In fact, I have room for everything except for your attitude." I said as I began to pick my items up and place them back into the Rubbermaid container that I pulled away from his grip. "What the hell is your problem Lance?"

"My problem is you - hiding this from me - bringing all of this unnecessary shit. We left the US to get away from these kind of things, yet you bring them and hide them from me. I don't trust you now."

"Well, I agree that these things may be unnecessary, but I wanted to be prepared. I packed Connie at my own discretion and I don't need your input now. You sure don't mind using the phone I brought - that seems like unnecessary technology too. How many hours have you wasted talking to Jasmin? Why don't you just give me the gun, the phone and everything else unnecessary and I will take care of it from now on."

"The phone is not going to kill anyone." He snapped at me.

151

"Yeah, well guns don't kill people either - people kill people. It takes a finger to pull the trigger." I said defensively as I continued to pack up my stuff. I opened the lens covers on the binocs and peered through them to make sure they still worked. I glanced through them at Lance and they picked up a very red thermal signature as he was "heated" with emotion. I could also see the glow from the embers of the fire pit outside and the torches that lined the village.

Lance threw my gun onto my bed along with the clip full of bullets and then he plopped down on his mattress. "I'll keep the phone." He said with authority.

"I'm sure you will." I said sarcastically in tune with his hypocritical nature. I continued to pack up my belongings into the Rubbermaid. I then snapped the lid closed and folded up my mattress and neatly placed it on top of the container. I stood up, grabbed the container and left the hut before Lance could say another word. I made my way over to the "Stan-Dunk" and decided to be the first to take up refuge and sleep inside of it. I must say that other than the discomfort of arguing with my brother, the thatched mattress was much more comfortable when placed on a sandy ground rather than a hardwood floor. I could hardly sleep, so I took a long walk on the beach and contemplated the situation. I couldn't imagine why Lance had made such a big deal about the gun and the other items. I rationalized the situation with the fact that he had been harboring some jealousy since the beginning of the trip. I think my relationship with Maruia and the tribe, as well as my successes on the island with surfing, fire-handling, dancing and completing the center had finally boiled over and come to a head when they named the community center after me. It was the only logical explanation. I later returned from my walk to the "Stan-Dunk" to get a few hours of sleep before sunrise.

The next morning, Maruia was surprised to find me sleeping in the new building instead of my hut. I ate breakfast with her and some of the tribe on the deck before heading to the beach for yoga. I explained the fight with Lance to her during the yoga session. Everyone noticed that Lance was not surfing this morning and was nowhere to be seen. Questions ensued and I was forced to share the story with everyone.

"Why did you bring the gun? And why did you hide it from him?" Maruia asked as we began our yoga session.

I didn't expect her to understand my decision to bring the gun and I didn't mind her questioning me about it. I knew that she had probably never even seen a real gun in her life and I was prepared to explain my actions to her. "Look" I said as I addressed the girls from my down-dog position. "I hope you understand that I had no intention of bringing violence to the island. The gun is a defensive tool to me and I would never use it offensively." I explained. "In my line of work back home I was constantly exposed to threatening situations. I carried a lot of tools and sometimes cash into areas of the city that weren't necessarily safe. Having the gun with me brought a sense of security. I became accustomed to it and decided to bring it along on this trip - just in case. My intuition and instincts told me to bring it along. Maybe a wild boar or rabid animal may ransack the village - I don't know what I was thinking, but I don't want it to be a big deal. I stashed the gun last night in a safe hiding place on the island. It is out of sight and out of mind for now. I will decide how to handle the situation with Lance later. I just ask that you trust me and my decision." I pleaded.

"I trust you 100% percent and I don't think that you have the heart to ever hurt anyone. There is not a cruel intention in your body, Stan." Maruia said as the other girls agreed.

I had the same conversation with Hoanui later who also agreed to trust me. The situation really didn't affect his attitude at all and he had no problem with the gun. Lance, however had gotten to Arenui first and pleaded his case to him from his side of the story. Arenui sided with Lance which caused a rift between the two of them and the rest of the tribe.

Several days of estrangement ensued before Hoanui and Arenui offered an amicable resolve. The Nui's suggested that we take another trip to Mata Utu to quell the awkwardness and give us some time to talk it out. Arenui dragged two outrigger kayaks from the beach down to the water and strapped on the four surfboards as I finished up my morning yoga session with the girls. Hoanui beckoned for me to join them as the three guys waited at the kayaks. I wrapped up the yoga and skipped bathing with the girls. The two Nui's jumped into one kayak and left the other for Lance and me to share. Lance entered the kayak from the rear and stayed in the rear instead of sliding forward to make it easier for me to enter. I hesitated a second as I waited for him to slide forward. 'This is going to be as awkward as a hemorrhoid operation' I thought to myself.

"What, you can't jump in from the side, Rambo?" My brother said sarcastically.

"Whatever, man." I said as I waded into the water and climbed up and over the side of the wooden vessel.

"I don't want you sitting behind me in case you decide to shoot me in the back." He continued his sarcasm.

"Let it go man." I said calmly as I picked up my oar and began to row.

This trip to Mata was not going to be nearly as enjoyable as the first one had been. Lance and I didn't say a word to each other once we began paddling. We couldn't even find rhythm in our paddling strokes which caused us to splash each other erratically, thus fueling the stress. It also caused us to lag behind the Nuis who rowed much more efficiently as a team.

"Let's just let this argument die and let's have fun surfing, okay?" I pleaded to Lance.

"That's the plan for now." He said in an emotionless tone with a stoic look on his face.

When we reached Mata, Lance and Arenui grabbed their boards and took the lead down the trail while Hoanui and I lagged behind. I had hoped that today would bring us together in a positive state again, but apparently it was a pipe dream. I just couldn't fathom why Lance had such a bug up his ass about the gun and the other items I brought. It really didn't make sense. I pondered the situation in my head and wished we could all just enjoy this beautiful day, the lush island and the brilliant wave we were all about to surf again.

Lance and Arenui picked up their pace as they walked just out of earshot in front of us. My board seemed heavy under my arm today - maybe it was because of a heavy heart from feuding with Lance.

"I've had enough of this situation." Hoanui said to me as he stopped abruptly and whistled to get Arenui and Lance's attention. They both turned their heads to look back over their shoulders as Hoanui beckoned for them to turn around and come back to us. Reluctantly they dropped their boards on the trail and followed Hoa's command. "I've got the perfect fix for this situation. Wait right here." Hoa announced as he stepped off of the trail and into the thick jungle. Moments later he emerged with a handful of cannabis buds.

"Right on, brah." Arenui said with a smile. Even Lance cracked a smile at the sight of the herbal treat.

"We don't have any fire or a pipe, so we are gonna have to eat it boys. Call it an early lunch." Hoanui said as he broke up the buds and divvied them up into equal portions. "Eat up, there is much more where this came from." He said as we filled our hands with his offering.

I had never eaten pot before (with the exception of a few brownies). I must say that it tasted very "tasty". The moist, sticky buds were easy to chew, but difficult to swallow without water so we made our way into the jungle to a stream where we all drank on our hands and knees as if we were animals in the wild. It was an awesome, natural feeling. Arenui couldn't resist the urge to push Hoanui into the water face first while he was in his drinking position. We all laughed our asses off as Hoa emerged from the water and shook off like a dog.

"You know this is supposedly the very stream that Hoku poisoned when he wiped out the Matains." Hoa said with a raised eyebrow and water dripping from his face.

"Really? And we are drinking from it?" I asked.

"That poison washed away a hundred years ago, brah. Drink up. We've been watering at this hole for a long time. It's cool now." Arenui assured us.

"Ok, but if the poison kills me, I'm gonna come back to curse you." I said as I put my face into the crystal clear, cool stream.

"Or he will come back to shoot you." Lance sarcastically added.

My face was buried in the water, but my ears were not as I heard Lance's comment.

"Ok, bro - you seriously need to let it go. Enough is enough. I'm sorry for bringing the gun, but it really shouldn't be a problem between us anymore." I said with a serious tone as I made eye contact with my brother.

"You are a liar, Stan and I don't trust you now." Lance answered.

"Look, I never lied to you - I may have disregarded our conversation about the gun before we left, but I never lied. If you had asked me if I brought it, I would have admitted it. Keeping it from you was innocent in my mind. It was none of your business and it shouldn't affect your trust in me."

"Bullshit." Lance said as he turned and lowered his body to drink from the stream.

"You two Haloes are definitely brothers. You need to knock it off or fight it out or something." Arenui said as he stuffed some more buds into his mouth and then washed them down.

"I have no desire to fight my brother - especially over something so damn ridiculous." I stated as I chewed on a pot stem.

"Look, you guys should appreciate each other and be fortunate that you are together. Your time together here in the islands is limited and your time on earth is also limited, so make the best of every moment." Hoanui said as he addressed both of us.

"Agreed." I quickly responded. I stared at Lance and waited for him to say the same. Instead he just pursed his lips and nodded his head with little emotion on his face. I guess that was his humble way of agreeing.

"Dudes, let's get the blood flowing so the buds will kick in faster. I'll race ya to the point." Arenui challenged as he sprang to his feet.

I hadn't seen Are move that fast the entire trip. I guess the guy was eager to surf or at least break up the tension from our conversation. We all rose from our crouched positions at the stream, but I decided to bend back down and get one final sip of the refreshing spring. Hoanui took full advantage of my position and bumped me into the water as Arenui had done to him. I was a good sport about it and came up laughing. I charged after the guys toward the trail as they all had gotten a head start on me. By the time I reached my surfboard back at the trail, Lance and Arenui were no longer in sight. Hoa lingered at a slower pace to give me an opportunity to catch up since he put me at an unfair advantage. We both picked up our boards at the same time and started the race equally. We ran side by side down the trail at a brisk, but comfortable pace.

"You feeling it yet?" He said as he turned to me with a grin on his face.

"I feel the breeze in my hair, the salt air in my lungs, the sun on my skin and the soft soil under my feet." I answered.

"That's not what I'm talking about, bro." Hoa said with a huge smile as he tried to hide his labored breathing from the run.

Before I could respond again, I lost half of my body weight and half of my speed as well. Everything began to move in super-slo-mo. The green of the jungle became more vivid than ever. I could actually see individual rays of sunlight piercing through the leaves as they danced in the wind. I couldn't feel my feet, but I knew they were still there and functioning because I was still moving - but where was I going? And why was I running? Was I in a hurry? Oh, yeah - we were racing. But why race? 'He who gets there the slowest enjoys the journey more' I told myself.

"Hey, Hoa." I called out, but turned to realize he was right next to me. "You ever realize that the volcano looks like a big stone pimple sticking out of the face of the island?"

"Nope, but I did just notice that you are stoned." He said as he began to laugh uncontrollably.

"Nah, not possible bro." I said as I changed my run into more of a school-kid skip. Hoa slowed his pace a bit to stay side by side with me. The nose of my surfboard slammed into the ground and jarred me under my armpit sending me back into brief sobriety.

"Smooth, dude." Hoa said as he continued to laugh. "Eatin the buds has a different effect than smoking them. It creeps up on ya and hangs around to make your entire day irie."

"Huh, I'm still not feeling it yet." I said unconvincingly as I stared off at the tops of the trees. I bumped into Hoa as he steered me back onto the path. "Why are we running man?"

"We are racing. Your brother and Arenui are beating us."

"Let them win. Lance needs a victory over something. Jealous bitch." I said as I stopped skipping and began to walk at a leisurely pace. Hoa continued his trot for a second before stopping to let me catch up and join him.

"I have a stupid question dude." Hoa confessed.

"What is a 'bitch' exactly anyway. I know it is a popular word in your language, but what is it really mean? And why is it use so much?" Hoa stammered to get his words out.

I began laughing uncontrollably and had to stop a moment to compose myself. I laughed so hard that a bit of drool came out of my mouth which caused Hoa to start laughing again which made me laugh more and then my face began to hurt from all of the laughter.

156

"A bitch is Lance right now." I said through my laughter.

"I know you already called him that. That is why I asked you for the bitch explanation."

"Okay, literally a bitch is a female dog. But in this case it refers to someone who complains all of the time. Bitch can also just be used to make a statement if something unexpected or bad happens." I explained.

"Lance is literally a female dog who complains a lot? What is literally mean?"

"Literally is a direct translation of something. We are literally walking right now. My head is literally spinning around right now. My face is literally hurting from laughing. My...my...my eye... I forgot what I was going to say." Hoa's comment was followed by more laughter as we tried to focus on walking again. My board jackknifed into the ground and brought me to an abrupt halt. "Bitch!" I said laughing.

"Statement Bitch?" Hoa said as he choked on his laughter and staggered into me.

"Good English lesson. Damn that was some good herb." I commented as I brushed the dirt off of the nose of my board and inspected the fiberglass for damage.

"Herbal medicine." Hoa said with a wink.

"Ok, let's get serious, catch those guys and surf." I no sooner got the word out of my mouth as we came around a bend in the trail and discovered Lance lying face down in the trail with his board still under his arm. Arenui was standing over him bent double with laughter.

"AHHHHH." Lance groaned as he struggled to right himself from the mud hole that he had tripped and fallen into. "What the hell. Damn stupid shit. Bitch." He cursed as he sat upright in the middle of the mud.

"Statement Bitch - there are no dogs on the island." Hoa said as he smiled and nodded his head at me.

I couldn't contain myself as I immediately busted into full-blown laughter. Hoa dropped his board and fell to his knees laughing. It was the funniest sight I had seen in forever - the entire front of Lance's body was completely covered in black mud. The only thing visible were his teeth and eyes and even his teeth had some mud on them. Why the hell didn't I have my camera right now - it was a priceless photo opportunity. After a few moments of all out laughter, Arenui extended his hand to help Lance up out of the mud bog. Lance decided to give us more to laugh about as he pulled Arenui into the mud on top of him. I saw it coming. I knew Lance wouldn't miss the opportunity to share his pitfall with someone else. The two surfers began to roll around and wrestle in the mud. Hoa grabbed their boards and pulled them out of the way so they wouldn't be damaged in the frolicking. Hoa and I stood there watching the mud fight go down as Arenui and Lance turned their attention to us. Both of them decided to include us in their dirtiness as they picked up handfuls of mud and attempted to lob them in our direction. They were so high and muddy that they couldn't hit the side of a barn and the mud balls fell well short of us. Hoa and I had been the victims of previous "prankery" and had both been pushed into a crystal clear stream - Lance and Arenui got to wallow in a mud bog - how apropos given Lance's 'shitty' attitude and Arenui siding with him. Hoa and I kept our distance from them as they emerged from the pit. My stomach and face both hurt from laughing so hard. I just couldn't control myself - they looked like a couple of tar-babies. It was hilarious and it was the perfect comic relief for the mood today. It couldn't have happened at a better time and to more deserving people. 'Perfect' I thought as I looked over at Hoa and winked.

We all got back on track and decided to walk the rest of the way as an earlier rain had apparently made the trail muddy and wet in certain places. I had no desire to run any longer and certainly had no desire to slip into a mud pit. Clumps of mud dried and fell from Lance and Arenui's head and bodies making us laugh every time it happened. The two of them were eager to get to the point and hit the surf just so they could wash off. Once again I was wishing I had my camera. I took a permanent snapshot of the situation and stored the memory in my brain to recall later when I needed a good laugh.

"Do they really look that funny or is it just the herb making me laugh?" I asked out loud.

"No, they look pretty damn funny dude." Hoa quickly answered.

Even Lance finally cracked a smile at the situation.

When we reached the point, although eager to launch and surf, Arenui reminded us of the importance of watching the wave sets roll in and timing the take off right. "One wrong launch and you may be taking your life into your own hands, brah. You gotta time it right or you are gonna eat reef and rock." He said as he blinked his mud covered eyelids and stretched his mud covered lips to reveal his teeth.

"Does reef and rock taste better than mud?" I asked in jest - evoking more laughter from everyone.

"This really sucks by the way." He said as he laughed at himself. Of course his laughter then invoked another round of laughing from all of us again. This was the best effect I had ever had from cannabis or alcohol - or both combined. I think we all proved today that pot could be a great anti-depressant and positive mood enhancer.

Under Arenui's direction, Lance was the first to make the launch. He paddled into a head-and-a-half high wall of water as it welled up behind him. He made the drop, snapped a quick bottom turn and then pulled into the tube - still partially covered in mud. Arenui followed suit on the very next wave. Hoa and I were left standing on the point alone for a moment.

"Your brother loves you, Stan. Let his bullshit bounce off of you. He really loves you. Maybe a bit of jealousy in the love, but love nonetheless. You are the big brother and a bigger man - be proud of that." He said as he patted me on the back and gave me the green light to launch off of the point as the next set rolled in.

I made the plunge and I thought about what he said as I paddled ferociously. I felt the lift coming behind me so I turned at a 45 and popped up to my feet. In an instant I was screaming down the face of the wave. I hit the bottom swiftly, busted my turn and then climbed back up the face before settling into the tube. There is something about getting shacked by a wave that just puts everything into a different perspective. The wave boomed and rumbled behind me as the tube closed out. I pumped down the line and sped up dramatically, pulling myself out in front of the veil of water overhead. I put my toes on the nose and leaned back on the board. The beautiful beach to my left paralleled my ride and enhanced my smile. I could see Lance and Arenui had already reached the sandy spit at the end of the island. I would join them momentarily, but for now I enjoyed the rush of the wind in my face as I sped down the line with my toes hanging over the nose of my board. I was high on life, high on nature and high in the air as the barrel closed out and spit me over the backside of the wave. I tucked in mid air and plummeted into the water. I felt so free and happy that I momentarily forgot all about the tension with my brother. As I paddled toward the spit, I turned my head just in time to see Hoa launch airborne off of the backside of the next wave. I waited up for him to paddle over to me.

"What a ride dude. This will never get old." I said as he nodded his head in agreement.

We took our time paddling back to the spit. When we met Lance and Arenui back at the lagoon we all talked about our ride for a bit before strapping the boards on the outriggers. Although not totally back to normal, everything seemed to be cool with Lance for the moment. The herb and the surf had mellowed everyone's mood for the time being. For the paddle home Lance and Arenui took the same kayak while Hoa and I took the other. The rest of the day was lazy and peaceful as the effects of the herbs still lingered. We all had the munchies for the rest of the day so dinner was a feast and I gorged myself and then passed out on the floor of the Stan-Dunk. Today I had figured out how to get along with my brother in spite of a bad attitude - eat pot - a lot of it. I also figured out what I had to do to put an end to this argument.

The next morning I woke, fetched the gun, skipped breakfast and yoga and paddled out to meet my brother and Arenui who were surfing the usual beach break. I tucked the Glock into the waist of my board shorts and paddled my surfboard out to the spot where Lance and Arenui were surfing. I pulled up next to Lance in the lineup and he immediately noticed the grip of the gun that was visible above the waistline of my shorts.

"What, did you come out here to hunt for some dolphins?" He said sarcastically. I guess the effects of the herbs had worn off and he was back to his old self.

"No, actually I brought the gun out here so I could end this ridiculous situation and argument with you once and for all. You are making a big production out of nothing." I said as I drew the gun from my shorts. "I have owned this gun for years and never once used it or brandished it maliciously, but it has brought me great security and comfort many times in my line of work in the city back home. I obviously don't need it here - and the discomfort it is causing you is not worth keeping it any more. So here we go." I said as I hurled the gun into the sea. "It's gone now. No need to worry or be pissed off anymore."

He nodded his head in agreement, but didn't say a word.

"As for the binocs and the other equipment - I plan to take them back home with me since they are not mine. Is that a problem for you?" I asked.

Lance shook his head no, but smiled briefly in agreement before turning to paddle into the next wave. That was his way of saying he was done being a bitch.

Island Life

It was amazing how fast our first couple of months in Rahiti flew by. Lance counted the days until his departure back to the states while I enjoyed every moment of island life. Three months away from Jasmin was too long for him as he was ready to go now. His nightly hour-long conversations with Jasmin on the sat phone kept him occupied, but perpetuated his home sickness. I left him alone and did not taunt him at all. We were finally getting along great and I wanted to keep it that way. While Lance could not wait to go back home, I was glad that I was staying for six months instead of three. Several of my friends back home were making plans to come and visit after Lance left. Claire was the one who was most eager to come, but I was hesitant to invite her because of Maruia. Even though I was not obligated to anyone, I knew it just wouldn't be the right thing to do. Everything on the island was peaceful and tranquil and I did not want to stir up any drama. Life was perfect here just as it was.

I had adapted quickly and well to the island life and didn't miss much about life back home (Claire being the exception). Once the construction was done and the 'Stan-Dunk' center was built, I was able to relax and really take in all of the beauty of island life. My mind, body and soul blended perfectly with life in Rahiti. It was everything I had imagined it would be. From the minute we got off of the plane in Tahiti, I felt like I belonged here. The people are so warm, friendly and welcoming, plus Lance and I were getting along great once again. The weather and environment meshed perfectly with my attitude. The smell of freshness and cleanliness abounded and filled my senses with the purity of the place. I was in heaven and found a new energy and spirit within my own body. The place was all natural - and 100% me.

It was very easy to settle into a daily routine of morning yoga, running, surfing, gardening, fishing, eating, dancing and socializing with the tribe during the tribal rituals. Life here was different, but easy and laid back and virtually stress free. The burden of the daily grind back home was totally forgotten. All stress of business, money and daily chores melted away rapidly. I felt free to do whatever I wanted with my day. For years, I lived by a rigorous and demanding schedule which necessitated performance and responsibility. For once, I felt in total control of my time and energy. I felt that everything I did in the Rahiti mattered so much more than anything I had done previously. It is ironic how difficult it was for me to wake up early each morning back home at 6am when I had to do it for work, but how easy it was to wake up for sunrise at 5:30am here when I didn't have to. This was my chance to really live. This was my chance to make a difference in a village community. It was also a prime opportunity to get in touch with nature and my brother. I planned to make the best of every moment of this trip so I woke up at daybreak each day so that I wouldn't miss a minute of any day.

I loved everything about Rahiti, but my most favorite things included: the people, nude yoga on the beach with the girls, the fresh vegetarian food, the family environment of the tribe, our dances and tribal rituals, the weather and my ultimate favorite was Mata-Utu. Lance and I made it our daily ritual to go to Mata - with or without Arenui and Hoanui. We woke up every morning with Mata on our minds. We would chant Maaaataaaah - ooooootooooo all day long in passing. We had our ritual. We would paddle from Rahiti to Mata every morning on the two person outrigger canoe. We would strap our boards on the outrigger and drag it down to the water. The outrigger canoes and anything else wood could not be left in the water due to a waterborne wood eating parasite in the water. The parasite was like a termite and would eat any wood that remained in the water, but it couldn't survive in the open air - so therefore the kayaks were never left in the water unless they were in use.

Some days the trip to Mata was as easy as pulling the canoe into the water and letting the current carry us over with no effort in a matter of 20 to 30 minutes. Other days, we found ourselves paddling against the current for well over an hour or two. Some days the current would reverse and carry us home too or make us fight both ways – we never knew. There was no rhyme or reason to the ever changing current and tides. But there were two things that were certain – the sun would rise in the east and Mata Utu would have a long, right, barreling point break. It was this certainty that made the uncertain paddle worthwhile every time.

The kayak trip and the hike to the point on Mount Mata became a spiritual routine as well as a great workout for both of us. Lance began to lose weight and get into the best shape of his life. The three hour journey burned hundreds of calories and, along with the healthy diet on the island, energized both of us and made us feel years younger. Not only did we feel years younger physically, but we relived our long lost childhood memories on the trips as well. We were finally getting the bonding time that I envisioned for the trip.

As for the surfing, my skills had improved dramatically and I no longer had the least bit of fear for the huge break on Mata. Although absent of fear, I still maintained respect for the wave. My brother had superior experience and technique when it came to paddling and surfing, but I made up for my lack thereof with strength and stamina. I quickly learned that even the strongest paddling in the world could not help you if you got caught in the impact zone and got pounded and pitched a few times by some double overhead barrels. So I learned real fast to perfect my duck-diving instead of increasing my power. A well executed duck dive could save you time and lots of energy as well as possibly your life too.

Surfing the perfect wave is so righteous that it is essentially "baptism by barrel". We surfed Mata every day - it was mostly just Lance and me, but occasionally Arenui or Hoanui would join us. We alternated who launched first. Today, it was my turn to go first. I clocked the wave sets and sized up my perfect ride rolling in. I timed the launch perfectly as the wave jacked up in front of me. I stroked a few quick strokes and then I was off. I made the drop and bottom turn and went to pull up the face when I hit a sudden bump in the water. I lost my footing for the first time in Mata and wiped out. I found myself flailing as I was in the water in a pitching barrel. It only took a moment before I was sucked over the falls and tossed against the reef like a rag doll. The impact was brutal - equivalent to jumping off the roof of a four story building - plus the added insult of tens of thousands of pounds of water crashing down and driving me harder into the reef. Every ounce of air was knocked out of my lungs upon impact. The left side of my body took the brunt of the damage and seared with pain. My board tombstoned on top of the water. I instinctively grabbed the leash to pull myself to the surface, but the leash was only attached to the remaining portion of my tattered board which I easily submerged with my pull. I was disoriented and had no idea which way was up. I took my chance and guessed right. I used every last ounce of energy in my body and thrust myself to the surface. I gasped for air when my head cleared the water, but I took in a mouthful of foam from the whitewater. I choked and spit and tried to clear my lungs and throat. My left arm and hip hurt badly and I noticed the foam in the water around me quickly turning red and orange with blood. Imagine jumping off a four story building and then getting hit by a bus and then the bus landing on top of you - that was how I felt. The salt water, frothy foam and air added insult to injury - talk about pouring salt into a wound. My board shorts were torn and bloody. I panicked and pulled myself onto the remaining chunk of surfboard just as another wave crashed and spit on top of me. I was trapped in the impact zone, disoriented, out of breath and bleeding profusely. I barely recovered and rose to the surface after being dashed into the reef once again from the second impact. I grabbed the leash and pulled the jagged tail of my broken surfboard to me. I grasp it tight to my chest as if it were a kickboard and began to float and kick backwards as I watched the next barrel forming in front of me ready to deal the final blow to my tattered body.

I was in trouble and I knew it. I couldn't sustain another blow like that again. I was extremely lucky to have survived two impacts thus far. It was going to be a very long and painful swim to the beach from the reef as I was over half a mile out. I could take my time once I got clear of the impact zone. I had to put every bit of effort into getting out of my current position before I got hit again. My board was a joke and would barely keep me afloat. I was thankful there were no sharks in the water due to the Matain curse because they would have surely swarmed to my blood. I tried to kick with my legs, but only my right leg responded. My left leg was cramped and shocked and rendered useless by the reef impacts. Just as I was certain I would get pounded a third time, I heard a whoop and a holler and saw lance dropping in on the same wave that was bearing down on me. He didn't make his bottom turn, but instead shot straight down the face and pulled ahead of the whitewater and headed straight for me. He got out ahead of the wave and pulled a roundhouse cutback and dropped to his belly on the board. Somehow he managed to pull out of the wash and paddle toward me. His momentum brought him within a few feet of me as he rolled off the board and pushed it in my direction. I released my hold on my tattered board and lunged for his - grabbing it with all of my might and I held on for dear life. I managed to hang on to the rails of the board and I kept the nose of the board up and pointing perpendicular to the beach. The crashing white water behind us sent us shooting through the water in the direction of the beach. We were able to ride the whitewater in past the impact zone. We both clung to the longboard as Lance kicked and paddled. We doubled on the board and both paddled as hard as we could. Once we were past the impact zone, we weren't totally in the clear as the secondary waves formed from the initial break of the outside sets were just as capable of drowning us. These secondary waves ultimately pounded the shore forming a nice shorebreak that any surfer would be stoked to surf. I thanked Lance repeatedly for risking his ass for me. He told me to thank him once we were safe on the beach. In the meantime, Lance instructed me to slide as far forward on his board as I could. He mounted the rear of the board and we both stroked hard. I could tell Lance was concerned by the tone of his voice when he said "Stan, we've got to get you to shore quickly."

"Is it bad, bro?" I asked.

"It ain't good man. You are losing a lot of blood." He answered.

I knew I was losing a lot of blood, but the fact that Lance made a point to alert me of it made me even more concerned. We hunkered down and paddled together in unison. We were overcome by another secondary wave and both of us got tossed off the board. Thank god we were clear of the reef this time. I surfaced and choked on the foamy water again. Lance quickly reeled the board back with his leash and helped me on board.

"This isn't working well. We've gotta try to catch one in." Lance said.

I was game for anything. "Ok." I answered. I had no idea what he intended to do, but I resigned myself to try anything to get back onto shore.

"The next one - we are riding in. Paddle on my count and pull your feet up. I'm gonna pop up and steer us in. You stay on your belly as far forward as you can."

The plan sounded good, but we had definitely never rode a wave together in this fashion before. This was a hell of a time to practice such a stunt. Lance made the call that the next wave was building. I slid forward as far to the nose as I could go without submarining us. I arched my chest back as I felt the wave pulling us back. I bent my knees and painfully drew my feet back to my butt. Just as I felt the thrust of the wave, I grabbed the nose of the board and held on tight. I turned my head back to see Lance popping up to his feet. It was a go. We made the drop and Lance steered us into a hard-right bottom turn. We were riding - thank God. We paralleled the beach as we drew nearer and nearer to the sand. I wasn't quite sure how Lance planned to dismount the wave, but I figured he had something planned. I figured right as Lance cut back hard left and got out ahead of the wash. We coasted ahead of the whitewater until we were within 20 feet of the beach. Lance told me to hold on as he jumped off of the board. The weight shift as Lance exited caused the board to flip, but I held on tight. The whitewater pushed me and the board until the slack in Lance's leash ran out and brought us to an abrupt stop. I let go of the board and rolled up onto the beach. Lance hurried up behind me.

"Lets have a look at you." He said. I was covered in bloody sand so he helped me wade into the water to clean up a bit. The combination of salt water and air caused excruciating pain. When the sand and blood washed away it revealed a mess of torn flesh. The worst spot was just above my left knee. There was a chunk missing out of my thigh a couple of inches deep and several inches wide. The exposed white muscle and flesh were gushing blood. Lance thought quick as he unstrapped the leash from his board. He wrapped the leash around my leg like a tourniquet to slow the bleeding.

"Lay down and elevate your leg. We need to slow this bleeding down. I can only get the leash so tight." He said.

I tried to stay calm, but had visions of my leg having to be amputated. There was no hospital anywhere close. I had lost a lot of blood. Plus we were still a mile or two away from the outrigger.

"I can do this bro." I said with conviction in my voice.

"I know you can Stan. Just take it easy for a little while until I figure out how to get you home." He said with encouragement.

"I can't lay here and bleed to death. I can walk. I can make it." I said.

"No way - standing up and walking is going to make it bleed much worse. You need to lay down and keep it elevated." He built a pile of sand under my left leg and put my leg on it to keep it higher than my heart. "Look, if you can wait here and remain calm. I will paddle back to Rahiti and get help."

"I'd rather go with you. Don't leave me here alone. It's going to take you at least two hours to return. I will still have to stand up when you return. I can make it." I insisted.

"I was going to get Hoanui and Arenui and others too. They can help me carry you to the outrigger. Maybe I can even call to Chet and have him bring the boat."

"Dude, listen to me - I can and will make it." I rolled over and rose up. I was lightheaded, but determined. Lance stood by my side and I put my right arm around his shoulder and leaned on him. "Let's go." I said.

He began to walk - I hobbled on my one good leg. I felt blood streaming down my lower left leg. I didn't care. I was getting off the island on my own power. I picked up my pace, but Lance urged me to slow down.

"The faster you go, the more elevated your heart rate gets and the higher your blood pressure - causing you to bleed more." Lance said as he urged me to stay calm and slow.

He was right and I knew it. I felt nausea overcome me and I got a metallic taste in my mouth. The leash was tied tight and digging into my thigh, but the bleeding still continued. I tried not to look at my leg or think about it. I pretended I was doing a three-legged race like we used to do in grade school. Mind over matter I told myself. I had to stop several times - once to throw up. Lance reassured me that everything was going to be okay, but maintained a strong sense of urgency. It was undoubtedly the longest walk of my life, but somehow I made it back to the lagoon. I was so happy to see the kayak. Lance grabbed a bottle of water from the outrigger and gave it to me. I drank like I had never tasted water before. Lance helped me into the kayak.

"What about your board?" I asked as we prepared to leave.

"Forget about it for now. It will be fine on the beach overnight." He answered.

I took the front of the kayak and laid on my back with my legs elevated on the bow of the kayak's hull. Lance began to stroke away from Mata Utu.

"I hope the current is favorable." He said.

"If you need me to help row just let me know." I offered.

"No way, just lay there and take it easy." I was happy he declined my help. He put my sunglasses on my face. I laid there on my back looking up at the clouds. It was a crazy ordeal, but an inevitable one nonetheless. I was surprised that I had surfed Mata so many times without wiping out yet. I was due. I was just happy to be alive. I had never come so close to drowning in my life. It was a frightening experience, but now I was at ease - with the exception of the constant throbbing in my left leg and left arm.

I watched as the clouds passed overhead. The occasional splash from Lance's alternating paddling strokes kept me in and out of consciousness for a while. I finally passed out at some point. When I awoke, I heard Lance calling out for help. I sat up in the kayak as we approached the beach in Rahiti. Hoanui and several others heard his cries for help and ran down to the beach to help us in. They lifted me from the kayak and carried me up to the village. They gently laid me down in the shade on a clean patch of soil. I passed out again. My slumber was brought to an abrupt halt as I felt a searing pain in my leg. Matahi was standing over me. The villagers were all gathered around as Nanihi was putting some kind of powder on my wounds. I felt hands running through my hair as I tilted my head back to see Maruia running her hands over my head.

"You are going to be okay, just relax." Maruia said as she smiled at me. It was a comforting feeling. I heard Lance discussing the situation with some of the guys. They were contemplating taking me to Papeete for medical treatment. I really didn't want to leave Maruia and the comfort of Rahiti, but I figured it best to leave it up to their judgment.

I owed my life to Lance right now. There was no question that I would have drowned in Mata if I had been alone. I couldn't have mustered the energy in my disoriented state to swim over a half a mile back to shore alone. I couldn't have made the walk alone and I certainly couldn't have paddled all the way back to Rahiti. I would have been a victim of the Matain curse. Thank God for Lance's bravery and quick actions.

"Lance" I called out in a broken, wavering voice.

"He's over there. Be calm." Maruia said as she placed her hand on my forehead. Maruia motioned for Lance to come over with her other hand.

"Yeah, bro - you ok?" He asked as he stood over me.

"I just wanted to thank you."

"Not necessary. I know you would have done the same for me. Just take it easy. You've got a lot of healing to do."

Tania came to Maruia and crouched down beside her. She had a canteen that she handed over to Maruia. "Here, drink this." Maruia said. "It's Kava Kava."

I sipped the entire canteen full of the tea down. My mouth tingled from the effect of the herb. I got the chills even though it was hot outside.

"Thanks." I said. "Maruia..."

"Yes?" She responded.

"Don't let them take me from here. If this is how I'm gonna go, I want to be right here with you on this island." I said in delirious desperation.

"Stan, you are not going anywhere. Just rest." With her words still ringing in my ears, I was overcome with sleep again.

I awoke several times during the night and was pleased to discover that I was in the Stan-Dunk in Rahiti. I wasn't sure if I was dreaming or not, but I saw Maruia sitting next to me awake. It was the most comforting feeling in the world knowing that she was there with me. My dreams were confirmed in the morning when I awoke to see her lying next to me. Her eyes were open and gazing into mine. Every breath I took was painful and I could feel my pulse in my extremities, but my heart was beating for her at that moment. I tried to sit up, but she pushed me back down onto my back. I leaned my head to the left and looked down at my half-naked body. I almost gagged when I saw my leg. There was a nasty, puss-like mess coming out of the open wound. I reached down to touch it, but Maruia grabbed my hand.

"I know it hurts." She said. "It's an herbal remedy. It kills infection and heals reef wounds. Nanihi will clean it up and close the wound in a bit. It is better to let it breathe for now. At least the bleeding stopped for now. Just don't move a lot." I shook my head in agreement and passed out again.

I awoke again sometime later as Maruia offered me some Kava tea. There were several other people in the hut also, but I couldn't see who they were. They picked me up and carried me outside into the light. Nanihi inspected the wound and shook her head in approval.

"Ok, Stan we are going to give you some herbal painkiller. Nanihi will close up the wound once you are sedated." Maruia said in her comforting voice.

Lance, Arenui and Hoanui gathered around me and lit up the peace pipe. I smelt the herbal essence wafting through the air as they toked on the pipe. Each of them took turns shot-gunning the smoke into my nose and mouth as Maruia cupped her hands over my face to trap the smoke.

'This is so much better than a hospital or anesthesia' I thought to myself. It didn't take long before I was floating from the Kava and the herb smoke. They probably could have cut my leg off at this point. The throbbing was all but gone. I wanted to stay medicated as long as possible. My tranquil state was interrupted by a sharp pain in my leg. I tried to sit up to see what was going on, but Lance and Maruia restrained me.

"Nanihi is closing up the wound. Try to relax and stay still." Maruia said. 'Easier said than done' I thought to myself. My body tensed up as I felt the sharp, shooting pain hit my leg again. My stomach churned and I felt nausea overcome me. I passed out again from the pain. I awoke later that day feeling much better. Maruia was still by my side. I sat up partially and looked at my leg. It was stitched up nicely with some sort of organic thread.

"What's that?" I asked.

"Hemp thread. Nanihi stitched you up. Don't worry - it's all natural and very sanitary. You will heal fine. You just have to take it easy so you don't reinjure yourself."

I felt a pinching tightness in my left elbow. I rolled my head to the side and rotated my arm to see the back side of it.

"She stitched your arm also. It was bad too." Maruia said as she put a canteen to my lips and motioned for me to drink.

"Interesting." I said as I looked at about 10 stitches in my arm. "I didn't know I got my arm too. I guess my leg hurt so bad that I didn't even notice my arm."

"Yeah, it was pretty bad too. Reef cuts are the worst. They are vulnerable to infection."

I finished drinking and Maruia took the canteen from my face.

"I'm going to put some aloe on your wounds, okay?" She said as she looked at me with compassion.

"No problem." I answered. I watched as she stood up and pinched a section of aloe leaf off a plant that they had put in the room next to me. She sat down on my let side and began to squeeze the green gel from the leaf directly onto my skin. Another wonderful herbal remedy I told myself. Who needs a pharmacy anyway?

I looked at the stitched up wounds on my leg and arm. I touched my face with my right hand. I was so thankful that I had managed not to face plant on the reef and do the same damage to my head and face - or worse, knocked a few teeth out. The fact that my board had snapped into multiple pieces told me how lucky I was that I didn't break anything. Flesh will heal faster than bone I told myself. Lance entered the room and crouched down next to me.

"Bones of steel." I laughingly said.

"Skin of sandpaper." He joked back. He was right - my skin was torn to pieces on the left side of my body.

I was relegated to spending the next few days on my back resting and then the next couple of weeks on bamboo crutches. The injury slowed me down and allowed me to take in more of the island and appreciate things that surrounded me.

The Rahitians appreciated our presence and everything we did on the island. Mutually, we appreciated their hospitality and acceptance of us and our gifts to the community. The new Stan-Dunk brought an element to the island's life that had been missing. Certainly the locals had lived all of their lives without any of the technology we brought and that was remarkable to me. I had been engrossed in technology for years. I had become enslaved by technology and relied heavily on my cell phone, computer, truck, credit cards, and the internet. Finally, none of those things mattered to me anymore. I wanted to escape all of the things that I had come to rely on. I wanted to rely on nature and my mind and body. I didn't want any reminders of the stresses back home. Out of instinct we had brought technology on the trip with us. Our satellite phones, laptops, solar panels and tools made our mission here easier and allowed us to keep in touch with home, but these things were mundane to me. I realized what was mundane to me was a whole new world to the people here. Certainly the younger locals were privy to this technology and encountered it on their regular trips to Papeete, but actually having it within their grasp on their own island was powerful to them. There was no resistance on their part – only excitement. I limited my use of technology and let the others have a go at it. Lance enjoyed showing the locals the usefulness of our technology. Even the elders Nanihi and Matahi were intrigued by the TV, internet, digital photography and the music on the soundsystem. They would gather around the big screen as Lance showed them pictures from the day's activities as well as pictures and emails from friends back home. They would dance and mimic the lyrics to the songs I played. It was a great bonding experience and emulsification of culture.

The whole concept of digital photography was astounding to the villagers. I realized that not only did they not have cameras, but they also did not have mirrors. The whole concept of capturing ones' image was interesting to them. We take for granted how many times we look in a mirror each day. I admit to being slightly narcissistic and checking myself out when I walk by a mirror, but I had been over a month without seeing myself other than in the distorted reflection of the placid water. In the south pacific you know you look good because you feel so good. It didn't matter how you looked here – nobody cared. It was the smile on your face and the energy of your soul that showed your beauty. The girls didn't need a

169

mirror to put on makeup because they didn't wear any – they were naturally beautiful without it. There was no need for salons, makeup, fancy clothes or jewelry – just a smile on your face and fresh food in your belly. The absence of mirrors channeled one's focus from himself to nature and those around him. Your reflection is shown in those around you and how they interact with you. It was a novel concept to look and listen to others for a change. I liked it and didn't miss seeing my own mug for a second.

Lance made a daily ritual of posting our status and progress reports along with pictures on Facebook for all of our friends back home and in the rest of the world to see. The locals were amazed by this concept of networking and sharing with the rest of the world. Their culture survived for thousands of years by passing stories from generation to generation beside the campfire. Tribal rituals and ceremonies brought their culture together in close interaction. Very little changed in their society over thousands of years. In contrast, our society had evolved rapidly and was subject to constant change. One picture could tell a thousand words. I could write a novel alone about a Rahitian tribal dance. I could describe the attire of the women and men, the music of the congo drums, flutes and banjo. I could regale you for hours about the tribal dance and how the men could move their legs and feet in discord while still maintaining a fluid motion and perfectly still upper body. Lance practiced the dance for weeks, but cannot command his body to perform the motion. I have concluded that the way they move is a genetic trait that his body does not possess. The men's dance is difficult and unique and quite contrary to the women's. Watching Maruia and the girls move their bodies in unison with the music was surreal. Their dance hypnotized me. For thousands of years, women of the South Pacific mesmerized men into a passionate trance with their undulating hip movements. Their spines seemed to turn into rubber and their hips shook and bounced like basket balls. Their hand and arm motions were warm and welcoming and their eyes invited you into their soul. Their dance was quite possibly the most natural and beautiful thing I had ever seen.

My daily tasks were simple. I knew what I had to do to contribute and survive and had no problem doing it – even with only one good leg. The most important things in island life were clean water, fresh food and human interaction. The most valuable "thing" to the islanders was, no doubt, fresh, clean drinking water. So refilling my plastic water bottles from the faucet at the Stan-Dunk and making sure the collection containers and gutters were clean became paramount. I realized I was spoiled back in the states when it came to things we take for granted such as turning on a faucet and washing your hands or filling a cup. Previously, there were no sinks or plumbing, but clean, crisp water was abundant on the island most of the time. Hundreds of fresh water springs flowed from the volcanic rock and coursed their way through mineral rich soil and rock on their journey to return to the ocean. The tribe had to capture as much of that water as possible before it emulsified into the salty, undrinkable ocean water. They had performed this task through a number of age-old technologies. Coconut canteens were the easiest and most portable way to obtain the water. The coconuts first provided milk and coconut meat and then were "recycled" into water bottles. The empty coconut shells were waterproof and easily corked and transported, but the only problem is that they carried a very limited amount of water. Hundreds of coconuts could be loaded into an outrigger on a canoe and taken on sea voyages as island hoppers had done for centuries. Water for use locally in the village was channeled into cisterns made of impermeable rock. Gravity and hydraulic pressure allowed the water to be forced into large wooden buckets. These wooden buckets were not ideal for storing water, but rather transporting it to cisterns or storage containers. Now, the tribe had a sink and a couple hundred plastic Fiji water bottles to refill and reuse.

When the water chores were handled, I commenced to picking and gathering fruits, veggies and herbs. Even with a bad leg, my height really came in handy for this task as it allowed me to reach well past the reach of the average islander who would often miss out on the best fruit and end up leaving it for the birds. Although some of the tribe were very adept at climbing up trees like monkeys. I watched as some of the guys would race up perfectly straight palm trees with no branches. They climbed up the tree so quickly that it looked like they were running vertically on their hands and feet. This gravity-defying stunt was remarkable to me. Once my wounds healed, I began to practice tree climbing until I got the hang of it. The technique was really all about hand and foot strength and alternating pressure between them and the tree. Some of the males and me would race up the palm trees and then toss down the coconuts. I learned that falling coconuts were one of the greatest dangers on the island. Unlike Newton and the discovery of gravity, a coconut does a lot more damage to your head than an apple.

When I think of the island lifestyle I think calm, peaceful and laid back. It is no secret that marijuana has its place in the island culture as medicine and as part of religious ritual; however, I had discovered another secret island treasure with great medicinal purposes also. I grew to love Kava Kava tea or "Kavaty". The mellow, soothing beverage has a very earthy taste as it is made from the root of the Kava Kava plant. The Kava Kava plant is a small shrub with bright green heart-shaped leaves about the size of your hand. The leaves and tree itself are nice to look at, but pretty much useless except for the fact that they grow a plentiful root system. It is in the root of the Kava Kava that the good stuff resides. The Kava Kava plant has an inviting appearance and the fact that it has a shallow root system that thrives in loose, moist and well aerated soil seems to further invite you to harvest its roots. I mastered an island technique of harvesting the root without killing the shrub. Depending on the size of the shrub, I would excavate some soil by hand a couple of feet away from the trunk to expose the roots. I would then select a healthy root, grasp it gently, but firmly enough to exert just enough force to pull it from the soil. I would then break out my buck knife and cut the root off at a 45 degree angle a few inches below the surface of the tree. If I did this right and covered up the rest of the root cluster with the soil I removed, there was a very strong chance that not only would the plant survive, but the very root which I harvested would grow back to be harvested again in the future. In the islands it was important to be frugal and environmentally friendly. It was imperative to be in harmony with nature – your survival depended on it.

Once you've got the succulent root in your possession, you have multiple options. My favorite and most natural thing to do with the root is to chew on it. I love to stick the finger sized root right in my mouth and chew on it like a popsicle stick until all of its juices have been chewed and sucked out. The juice of the root has a very interesting numbing effect on your lips and the inside of your mouth. This wonderful nectar continues its effect into the stomach as well - where it has the amazing ability to soothe nausea and upset stomach. Highly bioavailable and easily absorbed into the blood stream, the kavalactones which are the active ingredients in the root course through your veins and ultimately unleash their tranquilizing effects on the brain. Kava Kava has the ability to relax and calm the mind without disrupting mental clarity. What a great relaxer it turned out to be. Although, there are no physically addictive properties in the root, I became mentally fond of it and always had a root nearby ready for chewing. If you don't like chewing the root, it can be soaked in water and gently boiled to unlock the juices into tea. The only problem with boiling the root is that temperatures above 140 degrees F can destroy some of the natural properties of the plant. This tea brewing was very traditional and was commonplace with meals and tribal ceremony. The last and most laborious option is to grind the root into a juicy powder on a coral stone and then dry the powder out in the sun. The powder can then be later reconstituted into beverage form with a little spring water. I tried it every way, but preferred to chew the root directly. As if the island lifestyle wasn't relaxing enough, the rooty goodness of the Kava Kava made the experience even more relaxing. I believe it is partly the reason why the islands have such a calm and mellow demeanor.

The sounds of hundreds of birds chirping harmoniously filled the air every day. I think there was every breed of some of the most colorful and interesting birds I'd ever seen in the world right here on this little island. I thought what a wonderful place for a bird to live. Surrounded by endless trees and vegetation in a society that appreciated nature, it must be an easy life for a bird. There is abundant fruit available year round and there is no need for seasonal migration. In this bird sanctuary no deforestation or pollution threatened their way of life. The birds must also be thrilled that there were no cats or snakes living on the island either. The life expectancy of an island bird must be exponentially longer than a bird back home. If I was a bird, this is where I would definitely choose to stay.

I finally strung up our two hammocks between two different pairs of palm trees. Nothing is as relaxing as swinging in a hammock while looking up at palm leaves swaying in the breeze. I was sure to shimmy up the tree and remove all coconuts so that we wouldn't get any Newtonian surprises. Apparently more islanders die from falling coconuts than shark attacks. I was glad I had finally mastered the art of monkey walking up the palm trees. Hoanui had been very patient with me and his training had finally paid off. Once you got the technique down, it was really quite easy. The danger of falling coconuts and the proper way to retrieve them were excellent tidbits of island knowledge I was glad to have acquired.

I didn't really miss my life back home, just my friends and family. I found myself lying in the hammock and thinking of Claire quite often in spite of my affection for Maruia. I felt like the two of them were twins in some aspects although a culture and a world apart. Claire kept in touch almost daily and was always the first one to comment on photos that I posted on Facebook. It was as if she was standing by waiting for any news from me and she didn't hesitate to let me know it. I really missed her in many ways, but looked forward to seeing her again upon my return.

There were so many things about life back in the States that I didn't miss. I was happy to be in a world without TV, phones, media, pollution, artificial foods, cars, bills, alcohol, cigarettes, money – and stress. I didn't even miss my comfortable bed –I really didn't miss much of it at all. Adapting to island life was easy in spite of the fact that these things were missing. Even though there was no soap, shampoo or deodorant, the natives did not smell bad and did not appear dirty – the salt water was a great natural cleanser. The islanders don't miss these comforts that we take for granted because they never had them. They don't miss them or even think about them. People lived tens of thousands of years this way, but back home we bitch if we go a day without a shower or an hour without power. Not being able to control the weather in your house is another thing that requires great adaption. We take for granted the dial on the thermostat on the A/C and heat in our homes. Going along with nature and adapting to natural temperature variations is great.

I wanted to leave behind the 'electronic leashes' that bound me to certain aspects of my life back home, but at the same time I didn't want to totally disconnect from the world I knew because I planned to return there and wanted to be in touch with everything when I got back. So I relegated myself to 1 hour of television four days a week - Monday thru Thursday. I continued my tradition back home of watching the Daily Show with Jon Stewart followed by the Colbert Report with Stephen Colbert. These two shows rolled all of the news and comedy I needed to stay in touch with life in the US and the rest of the world. I loved the honesty and unbiased reporting that both of these great pundits exuded. I loved how these two guys put truth to the news and had no problem calling people out when they were wrong. I watched these two shows online at my leisure as my reward for completing my tasks and goals for the day. If my day was too hectic or there was a tribal ritual instead, I would forego the shows until a later time. Lance continued his daily calls to Jasmin and he also took over posting pictures on Facebook with some of the tribe who took interest in the technology. I focused my attention on the island and what nature had to offer. The absence of exterior artificial light made for some brilliant star-lit nights which I usually chose to spend on the beach with Maruia. Millions of stars speckled the sky as we would lie in each other's arms on the beach at night and breathe in the fresh, clean salt air.

I spent a lot of daytime in the garden with the girls. The ideal growing conditions on the island had begun to yield some fruits and veggies. We began to harvest some berries and cherry tomatoes after only a few weeks. The cucumbers and squash began to bloom. Herbs seemed to really love the environment here as well. Basil, dill, cilantro, rosemary, thyme, oregano and mint went crazy in the garden very quickly. The pomegranates and avocados would take about 9 months or so to harvest, but they were taking off nicely. The natives absolutely loved smelling and tasting the new herbs and fruits. It was so exciting to see someone try something for the first time. Aside from the garden, the native rainforest is like a produce section in a grocery store. It seemed like there was a different edible fruit, leaf, stem, stalk or root on almost everything that grew here natively. Everything is all fresh, all raw, and all organic. The one thing I could never figure out though was how can fruits stay cool on the tree in spite of being in the heat of the sun. It was quite an anomaly.

I also learned to fish and weave palm thatching and how to make rope from hemp fibers. Arenui taught me how to carve wood and we made an Alia – a very thin hand carved wooden surfboard with no fins. Arenui and I also did some repairs to some of his old fiberglass surfboards with a resin kit that I brought. There was no fixing the board I broke in Mata on my last ride, but I still had a smaller fun board in reserve and Arenui had quite a collection of other boards to ride.

It had been several weeks, but I finally got up the courage to go ride Mata again. Lance and I woke up one morning and began the chant. "Maaaaataaaaah-ooootoooo, Maaaaataaaaah-ooootoooo, Maaaaataaaaah-ooootoooo." The chant inspired me and he and I set off in the outrigger on our way to Mata again.

The kayak ride to Mata was pleasant. Lance and I reminisced about everything except for our last trip to Mata. We both knew our time together on the islands was limited. Lance was due to leave in 4 days, so we wanted to make the best of the rest of our time together. My leg and arm had healed wonderfully with the exception of some nasty scars and I was back in action for the remainder of his stay.

We entered the serene lagoon on Mata and walked across the sandy spit to the windward side of the beach. It reminded me of the first day we ever stepped foot on the island. The perfect view of the perfect wave as it fired, spit, sprayed and barreled along the palm strewn beach builds excitement every time. I put all fear out of my mind. I had my one wipeout and survived. I was good to go again now.

The walk from the spit to the point was a spiritual journey today for Lance and me. We had some deep conversations on the walk as we watched the waves break on the reef through the jungle foliage. The walk was worth it to ride those waves back to the lagoon. The walk was worth it to spend time with Lance. Mata was a place of peace and tranquility for two brothers to get in touch with nature and harness its power in the surf, beauty and bounty of fruits and veggies. I plucked a couple of Pomellos to peel and eat. As we ate the delicious, juicy fruit I couldn't help but wonder why a tribe of people living on such a lush and dense rain forest full of delicious fruits, nuts and plant life ever needed to eat meat – let alone human flesh? Why did plant life thrive here now where animal life was void? These questions would remain a mystery for now.

When we got to the base of mount Mata, we usually veered left, but today we decided to put our boards down and take a little detour – an adventure. We hiked up the side of the volcano to the cave where Hoku had taken refuge. We chilled out in the cave and looked out over the sea for what seemed like a thousand miles. The view from up here was much different from anywhere else – almost Godly. We sat there in silence for a bit – except for the rumbling and echoing of the breaking waves off of the volcano and cave walls. The waves Sounded like a freight train with an earthquake behind it. I pictured us riding the waves with Hoanui and Arenui. I vividly imagined us screaming down the line and shredding up the face of the wave. I envisioned Lance and I riding the same wave as we high-fived each other in the barrel. These epic waves were "righteous rights" as Lance referred to them. Some days it felt right to dive off of the point and ride. Other days were filled with heavy contemplation and thought on the point; however, you passed the point of no return once you rounded the hip on Mount Mata. It was a long journey to turn back and walk back to the canoe without the thrill of the "Mata Express" to carry you back to the spit. "Surf, swim or walk dude – see you back at the boat" became our mantra.

"I'm gonna miss you when you leave, bro." I finally said as I broke the silence in the cave.

"Ditto, dude." Lance responded as we rose to our feet to go surf.

The Day

Today I started my day with my routine sunrise yoga session with the girls on the beach. Everything appeared normal and today looked to be a great day. Lance finished up his morning chores and we strapped the boards on the kayak and paddled to Mata as usual. It had been over three weeks since my wipeout - physically, I had finally recovered completely. Nanihi's herbal treatment along with Maruia's attentiveness had healed my flesh wounds nicely. My steadfast yoga exercise had all but eliminated my limp. Nothing but some nasty scars and some horrific memories remained from the incident. I had finally put my fear of the reef incident behind me and I wanted to put the negative images out of my head and replace them with some more great ones before Lance left. This would be one of the last trips to Mata with Lance as he was due to head back to the States in a matter of days. Mentally, I was once again comfortable surfing Mata and I wanted to make the experience enjoyable again.

I realized I was operating on island time for so long that I could no longer tell you what day of the week it was or what time it was - and I didn't care. The days had run together and every day was a Saturday as far as I was concerned. Hell, I couldn't even tell you what month it was. The only way I even knew the day and month was because Lance was constantly keeping track of his departure. It is easy to lose track of time when you live in a paradise where every day is beautiful and every day feels like a weekend. There is no 9 to 5 daily grind here. You work daily, but you do it for different reasons. You do it to contribute to life - because you want to, not because you have to pay bills. Chores were fun and meaningful. Surfing was fun and exhilarating. Yoga was fun and relaxing. Tribal rituals were fun and enlightening. Constructing the community center was fun and productive. Basically, everything was fun. It was my goal to make every minute of every day productive in some sort of way - and also have fun. But this one day would change things forever. From this day forward, fun no longer surrounded my life. This one day would be memorable and would start a new time and era for me and the rest of the world too. Today would never be forgotten. This one day would change the course of the rest of my life as well as mankind's too. This one day would stick in my mind forever. I should have enjoyed the ignorance and bliss of this morning a little bit more.

Lance and I jumped into the outrigger and paddled off toward Mata. Our kayak trip was accompanied by the dolphins this morning as usual, but they seemed to be a little more playful and energetic than usual. As always, they left us as we approached the lagoon on Mata. Lance and me beached the kayak, unstrapped the boards and began the hike down the trail toward Mount Mata. The sound of the booming waves was extra loud today and we could see that the swell was extraordinary even for Mata. We stopped on the trail to gather some fruit and drink some water. Everything other than the dolphins and the surf seemed to be ordinary until we got to the point on Mount Mata. Lance and I sat there on the point eating some Mango. We were counting and timing the sets of huge waves. It was a beautiful day, but a weird feeling came over me. I felt as if something were wrong. I wiped all memories of my wipeout out of my mind, but I got an odd feeling that I can best describe as a very intense appreciation of the moment. I was so happy to be standing there on the point with Lance at that time. There was no place I'd rather be and no person I would rather be there with. Little did I know that everything in the world that I once knew was changing as we sat there on that point. It was time to take one last innocent and brilliant ride. We just sat there in blissful ignorance and watched for the perfect wave to roll by, but I became paranoid about surfing because I felt something was going to happen to one of us - and not necessarily a wipeout. I had surfed Mata multiple times since the reef incident and had not had any problems nor any fears. Today something was different though.

Lance dismissed my fear and launched off the point without hesitation as he said "Walk, surf or swim, Dude. I'm surfing. If I'm gonna go out – this is how I'm gonna go." He dove off of the point and caught a good one. I shrugged off my own fears and followed his lead. Nothing unusual happened. We both had awesome rides and we met back at the spit, strapped on the boards and headed back to Rahiti. On the paddle back to Rahiti I felt a sense of uneasiness as my premonition and fears returned in spite of the fact that the Mata trip was safe and successful. My stomach became slightly upset which is very unusual for me. I developed a slight headache and tension in my body. I stopped between strokes several times to stretch my arms and rotate my head to ease my neck tension and headache. Lance busted my balls for slacking on the paddling.

When we returned from Mata by kayak, our approach to the beach in Rahiti confirmed that there was something terribly wrong. I realized how Hoku must have felt when he returned from his fateful fishing trip to find all of the villagers gathered on the beach waiting to greet him and tell him the news of his wife's abduction. I knew something was wrong by the very fact that the entire village was on the beach waiting for us. The looks on their faces were indicative of a huge problem. I had no idea what was in store for us as we paddled into the shore and beached our kayak. I had no idea the gravity of the life changing information we were about to discover.

Maruia was crying and was the first to run to approach me. She embraced me and hugged me tightly, but did not say a word. I scanned the group on the beach to see if anyone was missing. I thought surely a Rahitian had died and my first inclination was to think that Matahi or one of the elders had passed, but I was both pleased and puzzled to discover that everyone was present and accounted for. Maruia sobbed on my shoulder as Hoanui approached me and Arenui approached Lance.

"What's wrong guys?" Lance and I asked in unison.

"Please come. There is something you must see." Hoanui said with gravity in his voice as he led Lance and me down the trail to the community center. Maruia clutched my hand and wiped her tears with her free hand. Arenui put his arm around Lance and consoled him with a "Sorry, brah." The entire village followed us.

I repeatedly asked "What? What is going on? Please tell me." But no one said a word. I knew it must be bad.

My natural assumption was that since no one appeared to be dead that maybe something had happened to the community center. Was there a fire? Did it burn down? My assumptions were quickly erased as we discovered that the Stan-Dunk was still standing in perfect condition. When we reached the door to the building, Hoanui stood in front of the entrance and addressed Lance and me.

"My brothers, I am not sure how to tell you this, but I want to warn you before you enter and see for yourself." He said. "This morning after you left, Tania and I wanted to check and send some emails. We logged onto the laptop and the MSN.com homepage opened up as usual. We were both awestruck by the headlines that covered the entire screen. Apparently some very major developments occurred in the rest of the world last night and this morning. You are not going to believe what you are about to see." He said as he opened the door to the community center and we followed him in.

The laptop sat open on the bar in its usual place. The screen saver slideshow was rolling on both the laptop screen as well as the big-screen TV as the computer had entered hibernation mode from inactivity. Hoanui directed Lance and me to sit down in front of the computer. Maruia continued to clutch my hand.

"Are you ready, guys?" Hoanui asked with a grave tone in his voice and a serious look on his face.

I could not possibly imagine what we were about to see. Lance and I sat in silent curiosity as we both nodded our heads yes. Hoanui touched the mouse pad on the computer and the screen saver disappeared as the computer came to life. The image that appeared on the screen was an open web page browser. Lance sprung to his feet and screamed "Noooooo!" and immediately burst into tears. I sat in utter shock and amazement as I stared at the screen. My eyes attempted to focus as I held back tears that began to well up in them. My eyes fixated on the pictures displayed on the site. There were multiple aerial photos depicting huge explosions and mushroom clouds developing over what appeared to be New York City, San Francisco, Washington DC and other locations that I did not recognize due to the chaos. My eyes darted from picture to picture in disbelief. Maruia squeezed my hand tightly. Arenui and Tania embraced Lance and tried to subdue him from the angry rage that was building within him. I began to read the article.

"...amid mass confusion and terror, the world tries to make sense of what is the worst terrorist attack and catastrophe that mankind has ever known... Today at 9:11 am eastern time, nuclear explosions simultaneously rocked New York, Los Angeles, San Francisco, Washington DC, Chicago, New Orleans, London, and Israel. Subsequent explosions occurred in Baltimore, Boston, Norfolk, Miami, Galveston, San Diego and Seattle. The source of the explosions appears to originate from cargo yards as all of the attacks occurred in port cities. The size and intensity of the blasts indicate substantial nuclear weaponry of mass destruction... the military and national guard have been deployed and scramble to evacuate the living... millions of others are engaging in a mass exodus to leave all coastal metropolitan areas in fear of impending attacks. Communication, infrastructure, travel and resources are in shambles as the turmoil grows and confusion and chaos have taken over the US and Europe... Al Qaida has taken immediate responsibility for the initial attacks in retaliation for the capture and subsequent death of Osama bin

Laden. They have threatened future destruction if the US does not comply. With Washington DC under nuclear fallout and the whereabouts of the President unknown, it is uncertain what the government's course of action will be..."

My eyes had a hard time following the text as my vision was blurred out of focus by both tears and anger. I scrolled down the web page to see dozens of photos depicting mass destruction and chaos. The USA had turned into a war zone. Tanks and armored vehicles were seen entering rubble-strewn areas. Military soldiers wearing nuclear haz-mat suits and masks were pictured walking through streets as they were flanked by tanks as they looked through the debris. Buildings were leveled, cars were overturned, trees were incinerated and dead bodies were everywhere. I continued reading as Lance ran out of the center. Tania and Arenui left to follow him.

I scanned the captions of the photos and read the headlines. According to sources, the US military had captured Bin Laden in Pakistan days before. Terrorists living in the US had dirty bombs hidden already in multiple cities. In retaliation for his capture, the terrorists triggered their sleeper cells to detonate the bombs and then demanded immediate release of Bin Laden. The US went into full retaliatory mode - they didn't know where to launch their nukes, but they launched them at Afghanistan and Pakistan anyway. This blind retaliation triggered the second wave of terrorist explosions. The death toll was unimaginable - New York City alone was completely leveled and wiped off of the map. Millions and millions were expected dead. Transit and communication was in chaos. Plumes of debris and mushroom clouds could be seen from space by satellite imagery. The dust cloud had already started to encircle the globe. Nuclear winter was imminent.

After I had read the entire page on MSN.com, I tried to click and navigate through other news sources on the internet, but reception was spotty and many servers and hubs were down causing usual pages to not be available for display. The article, the pictures - everything depicted the end of the world as we know it. I waited impatiently for the internet to respond, but to my dismay the connection was lost.

The resounding theme of all of the news reports was that sources indicate that the source of the dirty bombs had one common denominator - port cities. I remembered that not too long ago the Saudis had attempted to purchase control of a large number of our major ports just a few years prior. The FBI had actually seized a cargo container - a blue "Hamburg" container had popped up radioactive, but the situation was kept hush-hush. To me, it always seemed likely that ports would be our greatest threat for attack. My time with Connie at the Richmond Deepwater terminal was resounding in my mind. There were so many containers just stacked up on the yard. Hundreds of other containers came and went daily and weekly. There was no way possible that all of the containers could be scanned and searched. Clyde and Jim were the front line of defense on that port. Wow. I remembered seeing several blue "Hamburg" containers there stacked in the yard. I remembered the name because I am a vegetarian and I pictured cows stuffed inside the boxes awaiting slaughter. Cows come in - hamburger goes out - I had thought. I wondered if Richmond had been hit as well. It was such a peaceful port, but such an easy target. It was adjacent to the most major interstate on the east coast and only one hundred miles away from both DC and Norfolk - both of which were confirmed nuclear attacks. My mind raced - I wondered if Richmond had been hit and if not, if it was far enough from DC and Norfolk to avoid total destruction.

I remembered how many times in my life I had been listening to the radio only to have my favorite song interrupted by the familiar tone of the emergency broadcast system. Three long horn blasts followed by a pre-recorded message that said that "this has been a test of the emergency broadcast system. In the event of a real emergency..." I imagined people back home driving in their cars as the emergency tone sounded. They reached for the radio to change the channel, but found that the tone and emergency broadcast was airing simultaneously on all of the channels. As news of the emergency was aired, people looked to the sky to see a mushroom cloud in the distant sky. People turned their cars around abruptly to head for safety or pulled over to take in the sight from a distance. Traffic jams began to form everywhere as people fled the vicinity of the disasters. Pandemonium set in as people realized the scope of what was happening.

I envisioned those people close to the blast who had no time to even realize what hit them. I imagined the initial blasts vaporizing everything in proximity. Chills shot up my spine as I thought about it. Those not fortunate enough to be instantly vaporized were hit from debris traveling at tremendous speed from the ensuing shock wave from the explosion. Buildings, cars - everything was sent hurling through the air as the shock wave spread concentrically away from the blast. My skin crawled and my stomach churned with nausea as the thought of the mushroom cloud flashed in my mind. The plume of fire, smoke and debris was formed by the destruction of hundreds of years of history - art, literature, artifacts, architecture, real estate, parks, wildlife - and lots and lots of innocent people. I couldn't swallow. I couldn't breathe. I could feel my heart beating outside of my body. I felt as if I had just been hit by the shock wave of the explosion and was awaiting incineration myself.

I got up and left the building. Maruia followed but I urged her to leave me alone for a bit. I walked to my hut, but found it empty. I passed Arenui and Tania in the clearing.

"Lance is at the beach and wants to be alone." Tania said with compassionate sorrow as they approached me.

"Thanks." I said as I nodded my head and passed them on my way to the beach.

I found Lance sitting under a palm tree on the beach with the sat phone in his hand. His face was stoic and emotionless. His eyes were filled with tears as they gazed out to the horizon. His thumb was pressed on the send button of the phone, but the display was not lit up.

"I was supposed to leave in three days. I was supposed to go. I should have been there." Lance said as he wept.

"Be thankful you were not. Be happy that you were here to avoid the destruction and certain death." I said as I consoled him.

179

"Jasmin - she needed me. And I wasn't there. Damn it. Three days. One last time to see her, to be there for her." He sobbed uncontrollably.

"Lance, I know this may be hard to fathom, but I am sure that Jasmin would have wanted you to be here and safe. There was no point in both of you perishing."

"I wouldn't expect you to understand. You don't know true love. You have women all over the place. If one dies, you can just replace her with someone else - somewhere else. You have no idea. Don't even try to pretend that you do." He said as his voice elevated in tone.

There was no point in trying to console him right now. He was too confrontational and determined to be mad. I was deeply hurt, confused and helpless too, but I didn't want to take my anger out on anyone undeserving. I wanted to find the terrorist bastards who had done this and rip their heads off. I just sat there next to Lance in silence for a bit. I tried to collect my thoughts, but couldn't. It was if my mind had just suffered and internal explosion.

"The sat phone..." I started to ask.

"Doesn't work." Lance said as he gripped it in his hand tightly.

"No signal or..."

"I tried a hundred times until the battery died. Nothing. Nothing at all." He said as he hurled the phone onto the beach.

I sprang to my feet to retrieve it. I put it in my pocket and returned to sit next to Lance. "I'll charge it up and we can try later. Maybe the signal will be restored. The initial chaos probably knocked out all communications." He did not respond nor did I continue.

I patted my brother on the back and got up and took a walk down the beach. I had so much nervous energy that I could not sit still. I wanted to dive in the water and swim all the way back home. I needed to know if everyone was okay. I wanted to help somehow. I paced back and forth in the sand as I tried to calm my nerves. Pacing was not going to do it so I took off on a run. My run started off slow, but quickly escalated into a full sprint. I ran like my life depended on it. I circled the island by way of the beach in record time. I passed Lance who was still sitting where I left him. I didn't stop to talk - I just kept running. One full lap of the island barefooted in the soft sand was normally enough to fulfill me, but I hardly broke a sweat or labored to breathe today. I kept running and running. Nausea overcame me and I stopped several times to vomit, but then immediately continued to run. Some of the tribe had gathered on the beach to gaze out over the ocean in the direction of my home. I didn't stop to speak, nor did I even acknowledge them. I just kept running. I wanted to calm the beast that had been awakened within me and running seemed to be my best outlet. I felt as if I had the energy of the millions of souls that had just perished in my body. My mouth was dry, my head hurt, and my stomach churned, but I didn't stop. I circled the island over and over again – passing Lance and the tribe who all seemed to be engrossed in their own form of mourning. I had to get the energy out. I had to release my anger and ease my stress. I had to rid myself of the wicked news that had been downloaded into my head and the demons that now controlled my thoughts. The vengeance and anger that was brewing inside me was out of control.

Finally, the sun began to set and it became difficult to see the ground under my feet. Additionally, it became difficult to feel the ground as my bare feet had become completely numb and raw. I found a secluded spot on the beach and concluded my running to have a seat and watch the sun set. The sun looked like a huge fireball in the sky. It invoked memories of nuclear explosions and the ensuing fireballs that must have obliterated civilization in the USA. I wanted to vomit again, but had nothing left in me. My mouth was even too dry to swallow. I just sat there choking on my thoughts as I tried to find peace within myself.

It was the longest sunset I had ever witnessed. Had the situation been different I may have deemed it as one of the most beautiful sunsets I had ever seen; however the red, orange, yellow and violet hues that illuminated the sky were eerie reminders of fire and destruction. I wanted darkness to come. I wanted this day to be over. I wanted to awake tomorrow and discover that this was all just a horrible nightmare that morning would terminate.

The negative thoughts continued as I sat there in a trance. The images were so vivid as if I had experienced the disaster first hand. I saw the vaporization of entire cities. I felt the shock wave of the explosions. Debris and bodies were hurled by me as I stood unfazed amidst the destruction. Fire engulfed my body, but did not burn me – I was impervious. I had conquered fire here on the island. The island had also given me refuge from the fire and destruction back home. Thousands of miles and a vast ocean insulated Lance and me from the disaster, but my emotions and the energy in the air connected me to the situation with absolute gravity.

The last rays of sunlight disappeared and night fell. The island became cloaked in darkness as millions of stars began to appear in the sea of black above me. I wondered what the earth must look like from space right now. I wanted to drift from my body into the sky and look down at the world. I wanted to close my eyes and see into my former world. I wanted to know that my family and friends were okay. I wanted to be home, if not more than a second to see what was going on. I wanted to help, I wanted to do something. But all I could do was slip into a deep, meditative trance. My mind and body were exhausted, but my soul was still running on adrenaline and anger.

The longest, most horrific day of my life was over, but the longest most miserable night of my life had just begun. I sat there motionless in a trance all night. Time seemed to stand still with the exception of the rotation of the stars in the sky above me. The moon was nowhere to be seen tonight. I let go of reality as I sat on that beach.

The Aftermath

I'm not sure if I actually slept or if I was just in a trance all night, but I finally came back to reality when the sun began to rise the next morning. I had hoped and prayed all night that the events of "The Day" had been a bad dream, but unfortunately the mere fact that I was still sitting in seclusion on the remote end of the island told me that the situation was real. I tried to stand, but putting weight on my legs proved to be a challenge as they were cramped and stiff from the ridiculous amount of running I did yesterday. I decided to commence my yoga practice instead. I remained seated and grounded my sit bones into the soft sand. My body connected with the energy of the earth and I felt extremely grounded. A chill shot up my spine – maybe partly from the moist sand, but probably more from the sensation of being connected to turmoil in the world. I shook off the chill and let my body relax. I sat with my legs crossed and placed my hands palms up on top of my knees with my middle fingers touching my thumbs. I took in a few deep, calming breaths. I let my mind go. I pretended that yesterday never happened. I imagined that I had dreamed it all – I pretended that I would return to the Stan-dunk to find the whole thing was a sick, twisted internet hoax. I let these thoughts carry me through my extended yoga practice. I needed it. I needed to stretch and relax my mind and body. Stress had put me in a million knots and this is how I would untie them. I flowed through my yoga practice and linked my body motion to my breaths. I breathed in the fresh, clean island air and exhaled out stress and anger. My body began to calm and relax. Even the butterflies in my stomach subsided. But the one thing I could not ignore was the dryness in my mouth. I hadn't had water in quite some time and I could hardly swallow. It was this dilemma that ultimately motivated me to end the yoga and head back to the village.

I took some long, calculated steps back to the village. I passed a few Rahitians on the way back to the Stan-dunk, but none said a word to me. They all looked at me with sympathetic eyes and pity. Their expression was that of confusion as they had no idea what to say to me. I kept walking and simply nodded my head to them as my eyes must have told them I wanted no conversation. When I entered the Stan-dunk, Maruia, Hoanui, Arenui, Tania and some others were gathered inside. Maruia sprang to her feet and came to greet me.

"Thank God you are okay, Stan. I was so worried about you. I walked the island, but could not find you anywhere." She said as I pressed my finger to her lips to silence her. Then I kissed her cheek.

I made my way into the kitchen and grabbed a bottle of water from the cabinet. I twisted the cap and broke the seal on my precious bottle of Fiji water. I took a swig and swished it in my mouth in an attempt to hydrate it and abolish the cotton-mouth that held my tongue hostage. I couldn't have spoken to Maruia if I had wanted to. I could hardly even swallow the water as I consumed it. My mouth was dry and my throat was swollen. I was disappointed that I had let myself get into this condition. It was horrible enough that the terrorists had wreaked havoc on the rest of the world. I had to remain steadfast and not let the situation affect my body too. Maruia remained by my side as I chugged an entire liter of water in record time. The rest of the group focused their attention on me as if they were waiting for me to say something. When I had taken the last swallow of water, I grabbed a mango off of the counter and took a big bite out of it. Its sweet, succulent juice flowed down my lips onto my chin. I savored the bite. Until this moment, I had not had an appetite since we returned from Mata yesterday. I still wasn't hungry, but I forced myself to eat. I knew my body needed nourishment and nutrition to counteract the effects of the stress. I took another bite and then offered the fruit up to Maruia's mouth. She hesitantly accepted the gesture as she took a bite, chewed and then swallowed with some difficulty as if she was choking on words she wanted to say as she ate. I finished off the mango and then broke my silence.

"Has anyone seen Lance?" I asked.

Everyone shook their head no.

"The last time I saw him was at sunset on the beach." Arenui said.

"Hmmm." I responded as I walked over to the laptop computer. The screen was blank as the screen-saver was on during the computer's slumber. I sat down in front of it for a minute. I stared at the blank screen, but images from yesterday's news were engrained in my mind. I wanted to touch the mouse pad and wake up the computer. I hoped that the internet was working and that the whole incident yesterday had been a very tasteless prank. I made a move to touch the computer, but resisted. I leaned back in the chair and breathed deeply. Maruia stood behind me and began to rub my neck and shoulders. I let her fingers do their work and I let my mind and body relax. Other than hearing from my friends and family, Maruia may have been the only thing that could put me at ease right now. The rest of the Rahitians watched me like a hawk out of the corner of their eyes. No one knew what to say or do. Maruia was doing the only thing that she knew to do. I let her continue, but I leaned forward in the chair and put my index finger on the mouse pad and then wiggled it. The screen came to life, but the internet browser had the familiar white screen with blue text "page cannot be displayed at this time – you are not currently connected to the internet". I tried to reconnect the satellite link, but to no avail. I sat there for a moment staring at the computer. I then grabbed the sat phone which had been charging all night. I powered it up, but got no signal at all. My efforts were pointless for now. I got up, grabbed Maruia's hand and led her out of the building.

Neither one of us said a word as I led her through the village and down to the beach. My spirit was lifted when I saw Lance on his surfboard on the outside break. Maruia and I sat down on the beach and watched Lance surf. He caught wave after wave and shredded each one before quickly paddling back out to the break to catch another.

"That's his best release." I said to Maruia.

"Yeah, surfing is a great outlet. Why don't you paddle out there and join him?" She asked.

"That's a good idea, but for now I just want to sit here with you."

I began to think the situation through logically to make sense of what our best course of action should be. The uncertainty of the situation was my biggest stress. I desperately wanted to know that our family and friends were okay. I wanted to get more news about what was currently transpiring. There was little chance that the internet or the satellite phone would come back into service, plus I couldn't sit by idly and wait for that miracle to happen.

"I think we should make a trip to Tahiti today to see if we can get some more information." I said as I turned to Maruia.

"I think that is a good idea. I will go with you guys and I'm sure that Hoanui and others will join us. Why don't you go out there with Lance and surf for a while and I will round up the others and pack the kayaks for the trip."

We both rose from our seats on the soft sand and headed up to the village. I grabbed my surfboard and headed back to the beach while Maruia headed into the Stan-dunk. I wasted no time paddling through the shore break to join Lance in the outside lineup.

"Good morning, bro. I'm glad to see you surfing this morning." I said as I shook the water from my head and ears.

"What else can I do?" He said as he quickly turned to paddle into the next wave.

He took off on the wave and thrashed the face of it with his board before snapping the lip and busting a floater over the backside. In a matter of seconds he was back in the lineup next to me. Before I could even comment on his ride he was paddling into another wave. Wave after wave, he unleashed his aggression with his fiberglass stick. He surfed with the same fervor that I had yesterday as I ran laps around the island. It was a great release for him. I caught a wave or two as I alternated through Lance's continuous rides. I managed to catch Lance during a lull in the surf as we waited to catch our next wave.

"Maruia and Hoanui are going to accompany me to Tahiti today to see if we can get more information on the situation. Would you like to come?" I asked him.

He sat upright on the board and dragged his fingers through the water. "Yeah, I guess." That was his only response.

"Okay, I'm gonna catch the next one in and go get ready for the journey. How much longer are you gonna stay out?" I asked.

I could tell he was exhausted as he dropped to his belly and began to paddle into another wave. "I'm gonna catch a few more. I'll meet you in the village in a bit." He said.

"Okay, save some arm strength for the kayak trip." I said as I prepared to catch my last wave in to the beach.

When I got back to the Stan-dunk I found Maruia, Tania, Puatea, Hoanui, Tane and Arenui preparing to depart.

"We loaded up 4 kayaks with water, food and supplies. Maruia and you will take one kayak, Lance and Arenui another, Tane and Puatea will pair up and Tania and I will take the last kayak. We can leave whenever you are ready." Hoanui informed me.

"Okay guys, thanks. Lance will be up here shortly. I'm going to take a walk and dry off." I said as I wiped my face with a towel.

"May I join you?" Maruia asked.

"Certainly." I replied.

She grabbed my hand and we walked through the village and into the jungle. Holding Maruia's hand as we walked through nature in silence was calming, but still not enough to calm the uneasiness inside me. My stomach churned, my mind raced and a hollow feeling gripped my heart. My mouth was still parched and I could barely swallow. I felt as if the lump in my throat would choke me. I was eager to get to Tahiti to find out any news I could, but I was also apprehensive about the trip as I knew the news may not be good.

I tried to relax as we walked and enjoyed the sounds of nature. The birds chirped, the breeze rustled the palm leaves and critters stirred in the brush. I couldn't help but imagine everything around me suddenly engulfed in flames and obliterated by the shock wave of an explosion. The images were so vivid in my mind that they caused nausea to well up from my stomach and into my throat. I buked (burped and puked) into my mouth and turned away from Maruia to spit the regurgitated mango into the woods. The acidy taste of the fruit was not pleasant the second time past my taste buds. I composed myself and wiped my mouth before turning back to face my Rahitian beauty.

"Are you okay?" She asked with sympathy as she patted me on the back.

I lied and shook my head yes, but kept my mouth closed for fear of a repeat of my gastric event. I kept walking with her and tried to focus on the beauty around me. I tried to appreciate the fact that it was still here and so was I. 'Everything for a reason' I thought as I tried to console myself. The taste in my mouth coupled with its dryness further nauseated me. I grabbed Maruia by the arm and turned back toward the village without saying a word.

We approached the Stan-dunk and I spotted Lance's surfboard propped up against the side of the building. I was pleased to see that he had returned from surfing and that we could now depart. The anxiety in my body increased as I opened the door for Maruia and followed her in. Lance was seated in front of the computer and the others were milling around inside the building. Lance turned his head around as we walked in.

"Any news or connection?" I asked.

"Nothing." He said as he shook his head and turned back around.

"Guys, lets go. We've got a long journey ahead of us today. There is no sense sitting around here depressed, let's go see what we can find out." Tane said as he grabbed his thatched satchel and rose to his feet from the driftwood bench he was sitting on.

For once, Tane had a good idea. I walked over to Lance and put my hand on his shoulder. My gesture was not readily received or reciprocated in any way. "Let's go, bro." I said to him as I turned to follow the others out of the building. I stopped to grab my water and some fruit, but Maruia grabbed my hand and pulled me away.

"I've already packed everything you need. Just bring your sunglasses." She said in a comforting way. It was nice to not have to worry about packing anything.

We all filed out of the community center as Lance brought up the rear. We made our way down to the beach where the 4 outriggers were packed and waiting. Matahi and Nanihi were present for the departure as well as many of the tribe. They blessed us and prayed for our safe return. Maruia and I waded into the water and climbed into our kayak while the three other pairs did the same. Not that it mattered, but I asked anyway "So how long is the trip?"

"About 4 to 5 hours depending on the current." Hoanui quickly answered.

I quickly calculated it to be about the same as two round-trips to Mata Utu. No problem I thought. I had enough adrenaline pumping through my veins to carry me all the way back to the USA. Without further ado we were off. Maruia sat in the front of our kayak and she stroked efficiently and effectively as her long, black hair blew in the breeze. We alternated strokes from side to side and the kayak responded nicely as it remained straight and true as it cut through the crystal clear blue water. Lance and Arenui had a slight lead on us as we lined up even with the other 3 kayaks. As I turned to stroke I noticed that Tane's gaze was fixated on Maruia. His head did not turn once nor did he blink as he watched her row my kayak. For the first time I felt sorry for him. I felt his pain – to want something that he couldn't have. I felt the same pain for the last day. I wanted news and contact with home, but could not attain it. I was far removed from the situation, yet emotionally connected so strongly. He, on the other hand, had to suffer every day as he was so close to Maruia physically, but yet disconnected emotionally by her barriers and lack of interest. I hated to think that I may never see my family and friends again, but I also imagined how hard it must be to see someone every day and not have the relationship with them that you desired so strongly. It was a tough predicament for both of us.

186

We all rowed with determination in silence. The splashing of the oars in the water and the wake slapping the hollow wooden hulls of the outriggers was the only sound to be heard. Hoanui was the first to break the silence when he commented "The current seems to be favorable today" meaning that it was heading in the same direction that we were paddling. That was about the only good news I had heard all day. I looked off at the horizon in the direction of North America. Everything looked so calm and peaceful. The sky was a deep blue and there were no clouds in sight. It was hard to believe that the world could be so peaceful here, yet in so much turmoil thousands of miles away. I wondered what the sky in the northern hemisphere looked like. I wondered if the sky was blue and the sun was visible or if it was hidden by a nuclear cloud of debris and destruction. I shook off the thoughts as I resolved myself to enjoy the peace around me.

We paddled the kayaks relentlessly, taking only short breaks to drink water and stretch. I could tell by the position of the sun in the sky that we had been on our journey for at least 3 or more hours. I expected to see Tahiti in the distance soon – and just as the thought entered my mind, the island entered my vision on the horizon. Elated by the sight, I began to paddle a little bit harder. Maruia and I pulled ahead of the other three kayaks. I dug deep and pulled hard on my oar as the kayak cut through the water.

"You in a hurry, brah?" Arenui shouted out as we pulled away from the pack.

"Yes." I replied between strokes.

"Okay then." He said as he and the others picked up their pace also.

Every stroke pulled us nearer and nearer to the island. I could begin to see the city of Papeete more clearly. There was an eerie calm surrounding the island. There were no ships moving in the water and no planes in the air. Everything seemed to be very quiet. This was my first approach to Tahiti by kayak and my first return since we flew in to Tahiti and departed to Rahiti on Chet's pontoon boat. As we got closer, I could see some cargo ships with full payloads sitting offshore awaiting entry into the port. The sight of the ships both scared me and excited me. I wanted to jump onboard one of them and cruise back to the States, but I wondered if any of the ships were carrying nuclear cargo. Maybe that was why they were not in port. Our approach to the island seemed to last forever until we were finally in the calm waters of the port. The busy, bustling port was quiet as no vessels were coming in or out – with the exception of our 4 kayaks. We tied up to the dock and jumped onto the wooden pier and made our way into the terminal. I heard Chet's familiar Australian accent as he was shouting out directions to someone. He was directing the Tahitian port authority police through the cargo yard.

"Iorana, Chet" I shouted.

"Holy shit – I didn't expect to see you mates today." Chet said as he embraced me and greeted the others. "I'm so sorry to hear about everything. I've got a bug up me ass today dealing with port

187

authorities. They are searching and scanning containers. They already turned away incoming ships for now until we can secure the port and be certain there is no threat here."

"Do you think Tahiti is in danger too?" Tania asked.

"Doubt it, but they're not taking any chances." He quickly responded.

"Have you heard any news about the States? Our satellite and internet is down – we can't get through to anyone." Lance stated in desperation.

"Yes, mates, unfortunately I have heard a lot. I cannot talk right now as I must deal with these blokes. I will free up in the next couple of hours. Go to the Marriott hotel over on Kahna Street and ask for Captain Riddell. He was the pilot on the last plane to land here yesterday. He was inbound from LAX when everything went down. Chat with him and I will meet you in the lobby of the hotel around dinner time." Chet said as he hugged me and went back about his business.

Hoanui took the lead as he knew exactly where the hotel was. We exited the terminal's closed gates which were usually wide open to the public. We walked down the street that was usually filled with pedestrians and street vendors, but was quiet and desolate today. It was weird being back in "civilization" anyway, but especially under the circumstances. We made our way through the quiet streets, passing only a few occasional people. When we entered the hotel, the desk clerk was quick to tell us that they had no rooms available.

"Good, because we don't need one. We need to talk to Captain Riddell. We were told he was staying here." I said to the clerk.

"Yes, let me page him for you."

"Okay, thank you. We will be waiting over there." I said as I pointed to the plush couches and fountain in the lobby.

We were all exhausted from the kayak trip and were happy to sit down on some comfortable couches. I did a little stretching and pacing to move my legs around before plopping down next to Maruia. We all sat in anticipation of meeting the captain. I couldn't help but notice the lack of people coming and going from the supposedly sold out hotel. I was hoping to have some interaction with someone who may know something, but the place was rather desolate. I sat back and sighed as I sank into the couch. Maruia stroked my leg and leaned over to kiss my cheek. I looked over at Lance who was nervously tapping his foot on the floor. His face was as white as a ghost and his expression was emotionless and stoic. I tried to relax and calm my nerves and doze off for a bit, but I was quickly awakened by a perfect American accent. I turned to see a tall American gentleman talking to the front desk clerk as she pointed over in our direction. The man had a serious demeanor about him as he strode across the lobby in our direction. I rose to my feet as my friends followed suit. I extended my hand to greet the captain and introduced myself.

"Hi sir, I'm Stan Duncan. This is my brother Lance and my Rahitian friends Maruia, Hoanui, Tania, Arenui and Tane and Puatea. You must be captain Riddell?" I said as I shook his hand and made the introductions.

"Yes, I am captain Riddell. How did you know to find me here?" He said in a perplexed tone.

"Our friend Chet at the port terminal told us we could find you here. We are desperately seeking any information we can get about the situation back home in the States. My brother and I are from Virginia and we are here visiting our friends in the islands and we just heard the horrible news yesterday, but all of our satellite communications are down. Please tell us what you know about the situation." I implored.

"The situation..." He started. "We better sit down." He said with a sigh as we all took our seats back on the comfortable couches. The captain sat on the edge of the couch and kept an erect posture either from the gravity of the situation or his normal stature – I couldn't tell. We all sat intently fixating on his every word.

"Well, I'm a pilot with Air Tahiti Nui. My flight number 1127 was the last one to leave LAX airport yesterday morning at 9:10 am. Everything was normal upon takeoff. I had contact with air-traffic control, I had my coordinates set and locked. It was my usual flight pattern and route that I had flown hundreds of times. It was an easy 14 hour flight – at least 12 hours of which would be on auto-pilot. As we climbed to thirty-six thousand feet, I felt a tremendous shutter in the plane as if we had hit unexpected turbulence. It was definitely unexpected because the wind and weather charts showed smooth sailing with no pressure gradients. My instruments went berserk and I lost contact with LAX air-traffic control. When we reached altitude, we turned to the south-west to steer on course to Tahiti. My co-pilot and I could not believe our eyes when we saw the giant plume of fire in the sky emanating from the coast below. It was the most horrific sight I've ever seen as it extended vertically probably close to 20,000 feet. I knew something major had happened. Although I had no contact with the ground, I was in communication with other pilots in the air who were reporting the same sights all over the country. Planes were stranded in the air with nowhere to land and no direction from air-traffic control. GPS and tracking systems were intermittent and signals were interrupted. From our altitude, we could also see a mushroom-cloud in the distance over the San Diego area." He stopped to compose himself and take a sip from a bottle of water as we all sat hanging on his every word.

Captain Riddell tried to remain composed as he continued, but tears began to well up in his eyes. "Guys, my family lives in Los Angeles. I just kissed my wife and kids goodbye just two hours prior. My oldest son had a big Algebra test today and my youngest son was taking a class field trip to Hancock Park at the La Brea tar pits. My wife was going to go shopping with some of her girlfriends on Rodeo Drive. I have not been able to make contact with them. All telecommunications are down. I wanted to land the plane back in LA and do something to help them and others, but there was no way possible to bring the plane into the area without risking damage. Protocol called for us to continue on to our destination unless the destination was in peril. It was the hardest thing for me to do – to leave my family and my country." He said as his voice cracked and tears began to flow down his cheeks. Tania rose to fetch some tissues for the distraught pilot.

We all experienced a few moments of silence as no one knew what to say until Lance broke the silence. "What do you know about the east coast?" Lance asked.

"Well, from hearing the chatter from other planes in the air, I know that New York, Boston, Baltimore, DC, Norfolk and Miami were all confirmed detonations. Pilots had no where to go and no direction from land. Many planes crashed as they ran out of fuel. Several pilots tried to touch down on interstate highways, but the roads were choked with traffic. It was pandemonium."

"What about Richmond, VA?" I asked.

"I don't know about Richmond, but I know that the Chesapeake Bay area was hit hard from the three explosions of the surrounding cities. How far away is Richmond?" The pilot asked.

"Richmond is 100 miles from both DC and Norfolk. How widespread is the damage?" I asked.

The pilot choked on his words as he tried to answer. "Dunno... I would say..." He paused as he put his hands to his forehead and bowed at the waist to support his elbows on his knees. He then let out a deep sigh as he continued. "I would guess that everything within a 25 mile radius of each explosion was completely destroyed. I have no idea how far-reaching the fall-out is guys. But they were massive explosions. If my plane had taken off ten seconds later, I would not be sitting here with you right now. Almost all of my passengers are US citizens and are in the same dilemma as we are. There was an uproar on the plane as many of the passengers wanted to return and land in the US somewhere so that they may try to reach and rescue their loved ones. It was a hard decision for me to make, but I followed protocol and continued on to Papeete. It was a very long 14 hours in the air with little or no further contact with anyone. I relied on radar to bring me in to the South Pacific until I could get into short wave radio reach with Tahiti air control. I just don't know what to do. The plane does not have enough fuel to make it anywhere else and the Tahitian government has put a freeze on all flights and a moratorium on jet fuel usage as they are rationing all fuel for emergency situations only. God help America and the world now." He said as he finally slouched into the couch from his upright commanding posture.

"Do you think the Tahitian government is going to allow anyone to leave?" Lance asked.

"Where are you going to go, son?" The pilot asked.

"Home – back to the States." Lance said with resolve.

"I doubt that is going to happen. The Tahitian government's primary concern right now is ensuring the safety of it's people and land. You better make yourself at home here for now." Riddell said as he wiped his brow and grimaced.

"What about my..." Lance started as he was cut off by the pilot.

"Look, son – we are all in the same predicament now. I don't know what to tell you than to be glad you are here and not there." The pilot stated sternly.

He was right. Although Lance and I both wanted to be home to help out our friends and family, we were very fortunate to have escaped the disaster. We were fortunate to be here. As painful as it was to be trapped here thousands of miles away from home amid the uncertainty of the situation, it was still a much better scenario than being there in the catastrophe. The pilot excused himself as he got up and walked back across the lobby. Although he didn't really give us any information that we didn't already know, he did reaffirm one thing – we should be thankful that we were here and not there.

"What to do now, guys?" Tania asked.

"Well, I guess we should wait here for Chet. Let's just try to relax and wait." I said as I knew my comment was easier said than done.

We sat there in the lobby as a few people came and went from the hotel. We heard people coming in who were complaining that the grocery store and local markets were almost wiped out of food as people rushed to stock up on food and supplies fearing that they may be limited. They were right – with no ships leaving or entering port, sooner or later imports would run out and the people would have to eat and survive off of local products. This had little impact on us as we had already been doing so since the day we got here. Rahiti was easily a self-sustained island and had more than enough food and water for its inhabitants – especially since the introduction of my garden and water collection system. Tahiti and the Papeete metropolitan area was much more densely populated and would have much more difficulty sustaining itself without imports and trade commerce. I realized the gravity of the situation.

I looked through the glass doors separating the hotel lobby and the adjacent sports bar. The bartender was flipping through channels on the big-screen TV as customers sat in eager anticipation of news; however, all channels came up blank with either a blue screen or static.

"I don't get it." Lance said. "Satellites are in space – far enough away from the explosions to be impacted. How is it possible all signals are out?" He asked in frustration.

"Well, the signals don't originate in space – they are sent from the ground and controlled from the ground. I guess the majority of communication satellites belong to the USA and Europe. Plus, I'm sure that any working satellite links have been taken over by the military for emergency use only." I explained in vain.

"It's bullshit!" Lance extorted as he got up and paced across the lobby and back before returning to his seat. Tania tried to comfort him, but he would have no part of it.

"Look bro, I know it sucks. I feel it too. We just have to try to remain calm." I said to him sternly, yet sympathetically as the Rahitians sat in silence trying to find the right words or mood to convey.

We all sat there in complete silence just staring at each other and the marble tiled floor. Maruia held my hand tight gently squeezing it from time to time. My mind began to wander as I imagined that I had been on the plane and witnessed the destruction from high above. I saw mushroom clouds all over the horizon as the fire extended from the ground up to the clouds. I felt the shock wave of the blast shutter through my body as if I were sitting on the plane right now. I felt queasiness in my gut as if my stomach had just jumped into my throat. I was afraid I was going to be sick, so I focused on my breathing and the fact that I was grounded and safe. The feelings I was experiencing now were the most helpless and confused state that I could ever imagine. We sat there for what seemed like an eternity until Chet finally entered the hotel lobby.

"Mates, I've had all I can take for the day." He said as he walked over to us. "They all but put a white glove up my ass. Port police – treating me like a suspect or something. They can search it all – I don't care. I gave them every key and bit of help I could. They gotta stop sweating me. I doubt seriously Tahiti is a damn target. If we were gonna blow, it would have happened by now. Terrorists aren't thinking about here. Their beef is not with Tahiti or Australia or anywhere down under." He carried on.

"Yeah, but better safe than sorry." I added. "Isn't it ironic that there is the Navy, Coast Guard, Homeland security, Customs and Port Authorities in the USA to protect the ports and virtually no security here – and it is the most heavily guarded ports in the world that got attacked while Tahiti remained unscathed."

"That's why they are heavily guarded – they are big damn targets for just such and attack. I guess the security proved to be inept." Chet said as he ran his fingers through his bleach-blond hair. "Look guys, lets get out of here and head over to my place. I've got some provisions and a little beer there. You guys can stay with me tonight as I'm sure you are too exhausted to make the return trip today – especially since sunset will be upon us soon."

He was right – paddling the kayak another stroke was the last thing on my mind right now. We headed out of the hotel and followed Chet down the street to his apartment building. Maruia clutched my hand tightly the entire way. Chet's apartment was located in the heart of Papeete, just blocks from the port terminal where he worked. His décor and furnishings were modest and minimalistic, yet comfortable. We invaded his small place and made ourselves comfortable as Chet fetched some beer from the fridge. I hadn't had a beer since our arrival in Tahiti and was excited by the proposition of drinking one. The cold Hinano beer was a welcomed treat to us all.

"I don't have much to share with you guys, but you are welcome to anything I have." Chet said as he verbally inventoried the rest of his fridge. "I needed to go grocery shopping before all of this crap happened – now, I'm not sure what the stores will have in stock. I heard they are wiped out right now due to the hysteria."

"Thank you for your generosity Chet. Why don't you come back to Rahiti with us tomorrow and stock up on some fresh food. We have plenty of fruits and veggies to share as well as water and some fish." I offered as the others concurred.

"I'm gonna take you up on your offer. I need to get away from here for a day or so anyway. Let's get some rest tonight and we can leave in the morning. I think we can tow the kayaks back and ride the pontoon boat to Rahiti. It'll save you guys from rowing half a day again." Chet decided.

It was a brilliant idea – except for the resting part. Sleep was the last thing on my mind right now especially since I was in Tahiti. I wanted to glean every bit of information I could find out before returning back to Rahiti. I knew the others were tired, but I was determined to get out and move around a bit.

"Guys, I'm not really tired, plus I want to see if I can get more info while we are here." I announced to the group. "I think I will head down to the hotel bar and put my feelers out."

"I will go with you." Maruia quickly added.

"And I'm going to go down to the port and sit by the water and see if maybe some sailors may know something. Or maybe the port police will talk to me." Lance said.

The rest of the group had settled in at Chet's place and gotten comfortable on the couches and the floor.

"Stan, if you're heading out, you're gonna need some duckets." He said as he dug into his wallet and handed me forty-some dollars.

"Thanks my brother." I said as I graciously accepted the money.

Maruia and I left the apartment taking care to notate where we were at so that we could find our way back to Chet's in the unfamiliar city. We walked around the streets hand in hand hoping to run into anyone who could tell us something we didn't already know. Our mission seemed futile as the streets were practically deserted. 'Where was everyone?' I thought to myself. Had people gone into total hibernation even when this far removed from the terror that gripped the rest of the world? Apparently so. We headed back to the hotel and into the bar in the lobby.

The bartender's name was Alia and she was very kind and outgoing to us. She gave us our first beer on the house as we began to tell her our story on how we came to visit the islands. She was very intrigued by the story and our generosity to the Rahitians. Of course, Maruia sang our praises as well.

"Maybe it was your generosity and contribution here that spared your life and kept you from being there during the catastrophe." Alia offered as a sympathetic comment as she busied herself cleaning the bar.

"That's what I'm telling myself, but it doesn't make me feel much better. Although, if I can't be at home with my family and friends, there is really nowhere else I'd rather be or no one I'd rather be with." I said as I put my arm around Maruia and kissed her.

"I'm glad you are here Stan. I don't want you to ever leave me. I don't want to lose you from my life." She answered before kissing me again.

Alia was impressed with our affection for each other and commented "You two are such a cute couple with such a nice love story. I wish to find the same in my life. Working at a bar allows me to meet people, but doesn't always get me the attention I want. I met such a cute couple today. They were on their honeymoon here and were supposed to fly back home to Chicago today. Needless to say, their plans changed. They are staying here in the hotel and don't know what to do. They are extremely distraught. They were ready to go back home and get started on married life. Now, they are stuck and don't know what to do."

"I know the feeling." I said.

"No one knows what to do. Everyone is in limbo. The world turned upside down it seems. Forget about business and money and life plans. It's all about surviving through this crisis." Alia commented as she ran her fingers through her long black hair as it fell back onto her olive skin and exposed shoulders. "I hope everything will be cool here."

"I'm sure it will be. Terrorists have no beef with Tahiti." I assured her.

"I know, but we rely heavily on tourism and trade to sustain our lives here in the city. No one will be traveling any more. And it is only a matter of time before our supplies here run out." She sighed.

"Yes, but the islands sustained themselves without tourism for thousands of years. It will require many lifestyle changes, but it is still possible to do it again. We have been living off of nature in Rahiti for the last three months. The island is completely self-sustaining." I answered.

"Feel free to come stay with us in Rahiti if you like, Alia." Maruia invited.

"I just may take you up on it some time." Alia said in thanks of Maruia's offer.

We finished up our drinks and attempted to pay for them, but Alia took care of the tab. We left the bar and exited the hotel back into the streets of Papeete. A beautiful sunset was in the process of occurring so we walked down to the port to get a better view and vantage point. I expected to see Lance somewhere around there, but he was nowhere in sight. Maruia and me sat down on the dock by our outrigger kayaks and watched the sunset illuminate the sky with beautiful hues of violet, red, orange and yellow.

"I used to enjoy the sunsets much more. Now it looks like a fire in the sky which invokes thoughts of the actual fire in the sky back home in the States." I commented.

Maruia put her arm around my shoulders and squeezed me tightly. "I know, Stan. I can only imagine how it must feel. I am deeply hurt because I know you are hurting. Me and the rest of the tribe have deep sympathy for you and Lance and the rest of the world too. You must be thankful that you are here though. You must appreciate what we have here."

"I agree. We were here at this time for a reason." I answered.

I scanned the port terminal. All was eerily quiet. There was no transit at all. Several port police still remained at the gate and on the opposite dock, but they were standing guard and not actively searching anything. The cargo yard was relatively empty as many of the containers had been exiled and relegated to stay and wait on incoming and outgoing vessels until they could be searched. I thought about the Richmond Deepwater Terminal and imagined it still there and unscathed by the attacks. I wondered what Clyde and Jim were doing. I hoped they were alright.

I put the thoughts out of my mind and focused on the beauty around me – starting with Maruia. She looked stunning in the sunset as the amber light illuminated her olive skin and shone on her long black hair. I looked into her eyes as they reflected the light from the sunset. I leaned over and kissed her lips. She returned the gesture and a long, romantic kissing session ensued.

"Please don't ever leave me, Stan. I love you more than I have ever loved anyone or anything."

I didn't comment, but I closed my eyes and kissed her again. For some strange reason, thoughts of Claire entered my mind. I tried to dismiss them, but they were strong. There were many similarities between the two girls – right down to the way they kissed. I diverted my attention from romance to another sight. There were dozens and dozens of sail boats moored in the harbor, but three very large sailing yachts were anchored in the harbor away from everything else. My assumption was that they were too large to fit into any of the available slips. I had noticed the same yachts months prior when we first arrived at the port. The ships appeared to be in the exact same position they were in before. I wondered who they belonged to. I wondered when the last time they had been sailed. I wondered how much they cost.

195

"Are you ready to go back to Chet's and catch some rest with the others?" Maruia asked.

I didn't immediately respond, but ultimately answered with an out-of-the-box thought. "I think Chet's place is going to be extremely crowded. We will have to sleep on the floor there with everyone else. I have a better idea, Maruia. You see those ships over there?" I said as I pointed in the direction of the yachts.

She followed my pointer finger with her eyes. "Yes, they are beautiful – and huge."

"I know. They are just sitting there unused. Do you think anyone is on board?" I asked.

"I don't know. If I owned it, I would be onboard it right now."

"Yeah, that's my thought exactly. Are you in favor of doing a little exploration?" I said as I cracked a mischievous smile.

"Sure, what do you have in mind?"

I didn't answer her verbally, but I stood up and then extended my hand to help her to her feet. I lead her down the dock to the kayaks and helped her into ours. We began to quietly row out of the dock and into the harbor in the direction of the yachts.

"You are not thinking about boarding one of them are you?" She asked.

I smiled and answered "Absolutely."

We approached the yachts quietly and with some degree of caution. With all of the craziness in the world, I didn't want to spook anyone who may be on board one of the ships. We circled the yachts, keeping a reasonable distance. The sails were down and tightly wrapped and covered on all of the ships. Only the national flags flew on each ship. Two of the vessels flew an American flag and the other an Australian flag. The American vessels bore the names "Wavelength" and "The Mareva." The Aussie vessel was called "Going Down Under." The two names were easily understood, but the Mareva stumped me. It was also the most beautiful of the three ships. It was sleek, very modern, clean as a whistle and gorgeous. I estimated it to be around 120' in length. My eyes were dazzled by the Mareva as we rowed the kayak closer and closer to the ship.

"Mareva – what does that mean?" I asked of Maruia.

"Mareva is Tahitian for a canoe that brings presents from one island to another. It is a trading vessel. We rarely use the term anymore, but trading is still alive and well between the islands. Marevans were traders who would journey from island to island bringing different fruits, stones and items that were not necessarily native to the islands they visited. These nomads were also responsible for spreading news and stories to remote tribes. All of the islanders liked to be visited by the Marevans and tribal ceremonies would usually take place upon their arrival." Maruia explained.

"So how does the name apply to this ship? It certainly does not resemble a canoe by any means. And I'm pretty sure that whoever owns it is not a trader or a nomad. In fact, I bet the ship hasn't been used since we have been here."

"I know." Maruia said. "But the word 'Mareva' also has another less common translation meaning departure or exit. This meaning was due to the fact that the Marevans would sometimes leave just as quickly and quietly as they arrived. Sometimes fishermen still use the term when saying goodbye to a departing ship."

"Hmmm... Interesting." I said as I approached the vessel from the aft. The yacht towered above the tiny kayak. I reached up and pulled down a retractable ladder on the rear deck. "Ahoy, Mareva – is there anyone on board?" I hollered out. I waited a few seconds before repeating my question – this time a little bit louder. There was no response.

"Hold on to the ladder for a second to steady the kayak." I instructed Maruia.

"Are you really going to board the ship? Do you think that is safe?" Maruia asked.

"No, WE are going to board the ship. And I think the ship may be one of the safest places in the world right now." I answered as I crawled up the ladder and onto the rear deck.

I surveyed the cockpit in the stern until I found a rope sufficient to use to moor the kayak to the side of the yacht. I returned to the rear platform and looped one end of the rope onto the rear cleat on the deck. Then I handed the other end of the rope to Maruia and instructed her to tie it to the wood between the outrigger and the kayak's hull. I then extended my hand and helped Maruia climb on board the massive sailing yacht.

"Wow, this is amazing." Maruia said as she scanned the ship in the last remaining light of the sunset. "What are you doing?" She asked me as I was fumbling around under the stern and stowage boxes.

"I'm looking for a key. The cabin is locked."

"Oh, what makes you think there is a key hidden?"

"I just have a hunch. I have sailed on many boats before and almost all of the owners had a key stashed somewhere on board." I explained as I continued my search.

It didn't take long before I discovered what I was looking for. There was a key with a small flotation device on it stashed up under the lip of one of the stowage bins. "Ah-ha!" I exclaimed.

"Awesome." Maruia said with excitement.

"Don't get your hopes up yet, though. Let's see if it works the cabin door." I said as I walked across the cockpit toward the sliding glass door that lead into the galley. I put the key into the lock and it slid in easily. I held my breath in anticipation as I turned the key. It worked – and the door slid open. "Awesome!" I said as I invited Maruia inside.

"Hello, is anyone here?" We both called into the interior of the vessel. All was quiet. I looked for the light switch and hoped that we had power as the sun's rays had disappeared over the horizon and left us in darkness. No one answered our call and the ship appeared to be uninhabited. I found a touch-pad on the wall which worked the lights. The lights came on and illuminated the inside of the galley and the adjacent sitting area. The lighting was too bright and startled our sensitive eyes as they could not adjust fast enough to the artificial lighting. I touched the key pad and held my finger on it as I was delighted to find that the lights were on a dimmer. When the lighting was subdued to a more acceptable level, I removed my finger and began to explore the galley.

The interior of the ship was expansive and luxurious. The ceilings were a full 8 feet high. The walls were mirrored in the galley and wood elsewhere. The furnishings inside were high-class. Everything was clean, modern and appeared to be very expensive. Artwork adorned the walls and plush rugs were placed appropriately on the teak-wood flooring. Maruia began to explore the cabinetry in the galley.

"Wow, they have everything on here. I could cook for weeks in here. I don't even know what some of this stuff is." She said as she pulled out a blender.

I laughed as I explained the blender to her. I made my way over to the refrigerator and opened the wood-paneled doors that hid the machine and blended it into the rest of the custom cabinetry. "Not much to cook, but there is some beer and wine in here." I announced with excitement as I pulled two Hinano bottles out of the fridge. "It is not cold, but it will do. I guess they don't leave the fridge on to conserve power."

"Where does the power come from? How do the lights work?" Maruia asked.

"There is probably a long power cord that is underwater that plugs in over in the city somewhere." I sarcastically answered as Maruia shook her head and laughed at me. "No seriously, I think this ship probably has a diesel generator and also solar power as well. The power is probably stored in batteries. We will keep the lights down low to save power and we also don't want to attract attention to ourselves."

"It is also very romantic with the lights down low." Maruia said as she embraced me and hugged me.

"Yeah, I was thinking that too." I said as I took a swig of the warm beer and headed from the galley into the starboard berth.

The berth was large for a sailboat even of this size and it had a full-sized bed with a hideaway bunk bed over top of it. The berth had its own bathroom complete with a stand-up shower. The bath was tiled in marble and the fixtures were all high-end stuff. LED lighting on dimmers illuminated the berth and bath with just the right amount of light to accentuate the beauty of the craftsmanship that went into building this floating wonder. We made our way back down the hallway toward the front of the cabin – passing other berths along the way. There were both nautical themed art and contemporary art hanging on the beautiful wooden walls. The stained and heavily varnished teak-wood floors were smooth under our bare feet. We reached the end of the hallway and entered the front berth. It was absolutely huge. I hit the light pad on the wall and brought the lights to their full illumination. The sight took our breath away. There was a huge seating area that would easily accommodate 12 people on Italian leather couches, love seats and over-stuffed arm chairs. A glass coffee table with intertwined jumping dolphins as the base was the center piece of the sitting area. The walls in the sitting area were mirrored and the seams of the mirrors were hidden and blended with faux-half columns made of real wood. The ceiling was wood paneling with two large retractable sky-lights built in. The sleeping area boasted a king-sized 4-poster bed filled with pillows and a feather-down comforter. The walls surrounding the bed were mirrored and glassed and offered an unbelievable panoramic view of the port. Maruia climbed into the bed and sprawled out on her back.

"Wow, this is the most comfortable bed I've ever laid in."

"Yeah, it looks quite comfy." I said as I lifted the comforter and underlying sheets to expose a very thick memory-foam mattress. "The mattress alone is probably ten thousand dollars."

"It feels like a million dollars." Maruia said as she tried to pull me onto the bed and on top of her.

"One second. I'm not done exploring here." I said as I dismissed her advances and wandered around the room. I hit a button on the wall and a door slid open revealing the master bathroom. I almost fainted when I saw inside. There was a huge Jacuzzi tub surrounded by marble and glass. A stand up shower enclosed in glass, double-basin under-mount granite sinks and countertops, a custom vanity for a woman's makeup, infrared dryers were built into the ceiling panels and led lighting on dimmers. The toilet sat back in a separate catacomb. I called Maruia into the bath.

"Wow!" She said as she froze in her footsteps when she entered the bath. "I have never seen anything like this in my life. I could totally live here."

"And so we shall – at least tonight." I said as I coaxed her back into the bedroom.

"This was a great idea – much better than sleeping on the floor at Chet's small apartment. In fact, I think the ship is twice the size of Chet's place."

"I know, I have dreamt about this ship since our arrival."

"Really, what else do you dream about, Stan?" She said as she took the Hinano from me hand, sat it on the night stand and then pushed me backwards onto the bed.

"This whole trip seems like a dream." I said as I sighed and looked deep into her dark brown eyes which seemed confused by my statement. "I mean, everything I dreamed about for this trip came true up until "The Day." Seeing you and the tribe again, building the community center, surfing – everything fulfilled my dreams. Then there were unexpected things that made the dream even more profound – like Mata Utu and the story of Hoku, the tribal dance and fire handling. I feel like I have been living in a true dream. But now, after "The day," I feel like I have been awakened from a horrible nightmare. Now everything has crashed down on me like a harsh reality."

"Is there anything I can do to make your dream pleasant again – at least for the night?" She said as she began to kiss my neck and cheek.

Unfortunately there wasn't, but I let her continue her affectionate intimacy anyway as I turned my head to look out the window across the harbor at the lights of the city. My lack of interest in her romantic advances did not deter her from continuing as she proceeded to undress me and then herself.

"There has never been a time or situation more perfect than now for me to show you my love." Maruia said as she crawled on top of me and straddled my naked body with hers.

"I know, Maruia, but I'm just not in the mood." I said as I tried to control my arousal. My comment was a lie. I wanted Maruia as bad as she wanted me, but I would not let her know that right now. I absolutely wanted to have sex with her, but not under these circumstances. Not now. I had waited this long and I could wait longer. Maruia was perfect to me – a virgin in my mind. This was a departure from the norm for me and I liked it for some reason. I watched as she began to touch herself and indulge in her own pleasure. I fought off my arousal with every ounce of will power I had. I remained cool as she pleasured herself and reached climax from her own touches. She then became intent on pleasuring me, but I pulled her down onto the bed next to me. "Just lay here and curl up next to me. I want to enjoy the moment without sex." She did not say a word as she followed my command. She laid face to face with me and stared into my eyes as she kissed my lips. Her womanly scent wafted to my nose as I closed my eyes with my last sight of the day being her beautiful, naked body.

I awoke the next morning at daybreak with Maruia still by my side. I got up without hesitation and checked out the plumbing in the lavatory. The sunrise on the horizon illuminated the inside of the bathroom. It was a beautiful sight, but it still invoked thoughts of fire and destruction. I emerged from the bathroom and stopped to admire Maruia's beauty as she lay on the bed naked and half awake.

"We should probably head back into town. I'm sure the others are worried about us at this point since we didn't come home last night." I said.

"Are you sure you don't want to take full advantage of this amazing bed before we leave?" Maruia pleaded.

"There will be other opportunities – I'm sure." I hesitantly answered as I put on my board shorts and shirt. She got out of bed and I helped her get dressed in her Parea and tied the knot in it for her. Her hair fell back into place and looked as if she had just stepped out of the salon. Her natural beauty never ceased to amaze me.

We surveyed the room and the rest of the cabin on our way out – taking special care to leave the place exactly the way we found it. I even took the empty Hinano bottles and tossed them into the outrigger of the kayak so that I could dispose of them at the terminal. I didn't want to leave any tell-tale clues that we had been onboard. I locked up the cabin and stashed the key back in the exact location where I had found it. It had been a wonderful experience and a comfortable night's sleep, but it was time to go. We said goodbye and "Mareva" to the Mareva as we slid back down off of the back deck into the kayak.

The city lights just began to turn off as the darkness gave way to the light of day. We paddled and cut through the harbor with ease on our way back to the dock where the other three kayaks still remained. We tied up and walked the dock back up to the terminal entrance. All was quiet as the city had not yet awakened. We made our way down the street and found our way back to Chet's apartment building. Chet's door was unlocked and we walked right in. Everyone was present and already awake – except for Lance. He was nowhere to be seen.

"Oh, thank God." Puatea exclaimed when she saw us enter.

"We were about to send the search party out for you guys. We were so worried. Where were you?" Tania asked.

"We were fine." I answered. "Just out exploring Tahiti.

"Where did you sleep?" Chet asked.

Maruia and I looked at each other and smiled as I answered only "In each other's arms."

"Aw, so sweet." Tania said. "But seriously, where were you? You had us all worried."
Tane tried to ignore the conversation and seem uninterested, but I could tell that he was the most concerned out of the group. Hoanui and Arenui were stretching and fighting with each other over crowded floor space as they had not completely given up the notion of rest. I decided to change the subject. "Well, we are here now and well rested. Has anyone seen Lance?"

201

"Nah, we thought he was with you brah." Arenui answered.

"Nope, we haven't seen him since we left last night." I said.

"Maybe he is down at the terminal." Chet offered.

"Nope, didn't see him there either." I added.

"Well, I gotta go down there and check in for the day. I don't plan to work today though. I don't think they need me since the port police are in control of the terminal and nothing is coming or going. My plan is to take the pontoon back to Rahiti with you guys today." The Aussie said.

I was somewhat relieved to hear that news. I don't think anyone was looking forward to another 4 hour kayak ride. We had our fill of paddling yesterday – the boat ride would be nice. Now, we just had to find Lance before we could depart.

"I'll scope out the area and look for Lance while you guys get ready. Maruia, why don't you stay here. I want to look for my brother and be alone for a while. I will meet you guys at the pontoon boat in an hour or so." Maruia kissed me on the cheek as I left the crowded apartment.

Okay, if I was Lance, where would I go? I thought to myself. I wandered downstairs to the street and my instincts told me to take a right and walk around the block. Granted, I had not spent much time in Tahiti, but I knew it was quiet for the city even at this hour of the morning. Everyone had gone into hibernation and hiding – the question was where Lance was hiding. I walked by stores, cafes, bars and places that were all closed – no Lance. I went into several hotels and checked the lobbies, but no Lance. My hour had just about expired, so I went down to the terminal to meet Chet and the Rahitian posse. I was disappointed that I could not find him and I feared that we would be stuck here waiting for him to return. Now that we were no longer at Chet's place, I was afraid he would not know where to find us. He couldn't have wandered far – it wasn't his style. He always stayed close to home – even when we were kids. I figured he had to be somewhere close by.

I wound up at the gate of the terminal at exactly the same time as Chet and the others. They were equally disappointed to see that Lance was not with me.

"No luck, brah?" Arenui asked.

"No, none. I searched about a three block radius and didn't see any sign of him. I even checked some hotel lobbies."

"Where do you think he went?" Chet asked.

"Dunno, he couldn't go far. Plus, he doesn't have any money to buy anything. I imagine he must be pretty hungry and thirsty. The only place I didn't check yet is the terminal, but Maruia and I were here last night and didn't see him."

"Huh, well let's pack up the pontoon and bring it around to the kayaks and get them tied behind it so we will at least be ready to roll when he gets here." Chet suggested.

We followed Chet down to the far dock where the pontoon boat was moored out of the way of the rest of the terminal. As we approached the pontoon, I was relieved to see Lance sitting on the deck of the boat.

"Hey, there's your brah. Lance! Lance!" Arenui called out as he ran down the dock to the pontoon with excitement.

We all followed quickly down the dock to the boat. Lance did not greet us with the same excitement that we all had. He sat solemnly with a serious look on his face. He hardly acknowledged us as we climbed on board the boat. He looked as if he hadn't slept a wink all night.

"You okay, man?" I asked as I put my hand on his shoulder.

"No." He said as he cut his eyes up to me.

"Do you need some water or food or bathroom or something?" Tania offered.

"No." He said as he shook his head in accordance with his statement.

"What happened man? Did you spend the whole night here on the pontoon?" I asked.

"Yep." He answered as he took a deep breath. "The world is screwed." He added.

"Yeah, I know. Did you find out any information?" I asked.

"I listened to sailors talk last night. The world is on lockdown. Nobody wants to leave port for fear of pirates. There is turmoil everywhere. Stores are bare and those that aren't are scared to open for fear of looting and theft. There are millions of dollars worth of food and fuel on those ships out there, but the port authority won't let them into port for fear of terrorist threats." He said as he pointed out past the harbor at the ships anchored several miles offshore. "Terrorist threat in Tahiti – go figure. The world has gone mad. If the ships don't come into port, the island might starve and run out of resources. The government doesn't have the technology in place to search all of the containers. They have no plan – just paranoia and confusion. Fuel is on lockdown by the government too. They are conserving every drop for emergency situations. No one knows what to do so everyone is lying low and doing nothing right now. I just wanna get the hell out of here, Stan."

"Don't fret Mates, I've got enough gas in the boat to make a couple of trips to Rahiti. I've also got a personal stash of gas in those drums over there. Let's take it to Rahiti for safe keeping." Chet said as he pointed over to several 55 gallon drums on the other side of the dock.

The guys followed Chet over to the drums and wheeled three of them over to the boat with dollies. I stayed on the boat with Lance and the girls. They quickly loaded the fuel onto the boat along with some supplies Chet had on the dock.

"They won't need me here today." Chet said as he fired up the pontoon boat and headed over to the kayaks. The sound of the engine firing up got the attention of the port police on the other side of the dock. Chet waved to them and disregarded their motion for him to come over to their dock.

"Don't you think you should go talk to them?" I asked.

"Nah, they will get over it. I think we should leave the outriggers though and get out of the harbor." He said as he throttled the boat up and headed for open waters. The port police remained on the dock and did not make any attempt to pursue us. "I know them – they will be fine tomorrow when I return. What they gonna do – fire me? I have keys to everything." Chet said with a smile as we left the calm waters of the harbor.

The breeze blew through Maruia's hair and made it dance in my face as we cruised through the water. The smell of the fuel permeated the seals of the barrels and filled our nose with the unpleasant odor. It was worth it I thought – to have the fuel onboard. It may turn out to be a priceless commodity – at least it would be enough to get Chet home and make multiple trips back and forth from Rahiti to Tahiti. That could prove to be invaluable to him if Papeete ran out of food and supplies. We cruised over the teal blue waters in the direction of Rahiti. We were all grateful that we didn't have to row the kayaks home.

We arrived back home quickly in comparison to the kayak trip, beached the pontoon boat and unloaded the fuel. Hoanui and the others filled the tribe in on our trip and the situation in Papeete while I gave Chet a tour of the Stan-dunk. Lance wandered off by himself. Chet was very impressed with the construction of the community center and the introduction of the water collection system. He couldn't believe that we had accomplished so much in so little time. He found it amazing that we converted the contents of Connie into such an awesome structure. I explained the construction process and how everyone had contributed. He admired the hand-crafted furnishings that now occupied the inside of the center. To add to his enthusiasm I cranked up some music on the sound system and explained how the entire center was powered by solar power.

"To be honest, I thought you lost your friggin mind when you shipped almost two hundred thousand bucks worth of supplies over here. I had no idea what you were thinking or hoping to accomplish here. I must say that I am amazed and very proud of you." He said in his Aussie tone.

"Thanks man. I take that as a huge compliment. Take pride in the fact that you were an integral part of it all. Had it not been for you helping us at the port and giving Connie a home for over a month as well as hooking us up with the pontoon boat, this would have never happened. I can't even begin to imagine how impossible it would have been to transport Connie's contents by outrigger canoe." I said as I laughed out loud.

"No way that would have happened Mate. One bag of concrete would have sank an outrigger!"

"Yeah, right." I agreed. "Hey you wanna hit a surf session for a bit?"

"Yeah, it's been a mighty long while since I rode a stick. I moved to Tahiti to surf every day, but work has gotten the best of me lately and I rarely find time to go." He regretfully stated.

He followed me around the Stan-dunk as we grabbed two boards and then headed across the village and down the path to the beach. I was not surprised to find Lance out surfing there on his usual break.

"There is your brah, Mate."

"Yeah, that's pretty much where you can always find him. Surfing is his life."

"I'm sure it is a great release for him in this stressful time."

"Well, even before "The Day" he was still out surfing pretty much all day, every day." I said as Chet and I waxed the deck of our boards.

"Race ya out to the break." I challenged as we strapped our leashes on.

"I think you gotta unfair advantage." Chet hollered as I took off and left him in the dust.

I dove thru the shorebreak, duck-dived a couple of inside rollers and then paddled swiftly out to the break as Lance dropped in on a nice overhead tube to my right. He gave me a head nod as he blew by me and snapped the lip to pull a fins-out floater. When I reached the break, I turned back to check on Chet who was struggling to power through the impact zone. I remembered how it felt to paddle out here my first time and sympathized with Chet. He is a great surfer, just a little out of practice. I caught the next wave and put on a little show for Chet as I gave him a shower with the spray from my board as I cut through the wave that he was duck-diving. I pulled a round-house cutback and then bailed over the backside and paddled up next to Chet.

"Nice ride, Mate." Chet said as he labored to breathe.

"You glad to be in the water?"

"You betcha, just a little out of shape. You guys are hardcore." He commented as we watched Lance take off on another wave.

"We made surfing a daily ritual. In fact, we have a secret we may share with you."

"Really, do tell my brother."

I smiled and we paddled out to the break as Lance finished his ride and met us back on the outside.

"Mah-tah" I called out to Lance.

"Ooo-too" Lance hollered back.

"Maaaaaah-taaaaaah" I repeated.

"Oooooooo-toooooo" Lance replied with an exaggeration in his tone. I'm glad we still haven't lost that connection I thought to myself.

"Lance, should I tell Chet?"

"About Mata?" He asked as Chet's intrigue grew.

"No, about you being gay – of course about Mata bro." I sarcastically replied.

"I assumed you already had." Lance responded as he turned to paddle into another wave.

"Crikey, what's this Mata?"

"Catch a wave dude and then I'll fill you in."

"I will if you guys will let one pass without taking it."

"Next one is you." I said pointing to the horizon as a wave built in front of us.

Chet turned and paddled hard, but missed it. He thrashed his arms in the water in disgust. "Shit, I'm out of shape and practice." He said as he shook the water from his long blond hair.
"Dude, relax and go with the flow. You are surfing, not doing brain surgery." My commentary relaxed Chet as he seemed a little stressed and nervous. I'm sure the situation in Tahiti and the rest of the world was bothering him as well and surfing with us may have been a little intimidating since it was his first time surfing Rahiti or even surfing at all for a while. He chilled out, found his energy and dropped in on the next wave and rode it well. He paddled back out thru the impact zone with more ease this time and a big smile on his face.

"Got it now, brah." He said smiling.

I proceeded to tell him the entire Mata Utu story in between rides. I told him the history of the island, Hoku and the Matain curse. I told him about our daily kayak, hike, surf ritual. I told him about my reef incident and showed him my nasty scars. He hung on my every word especially when I told him that he had to get Matahi's blessing to even visit the island.

"Dude, I'm stoked. It sounds like just the escape I need. When can we go?" He asked in jubilant excitement.

"We will consult with Matahi tonight and then take you tomorrow morning if he agrees." I answered.

We surfed for a couple of hours and tried to joke, have fun and forget about the situation in the world. Lance remained distant to our conversation as he caught wave after wave. Chet commented multiple times about how hardcore Lance was in his surfing. We wrapped up our session when Arenui paddled out to tell us that the girls had prepared a special lunch. Lance declined the offer and opted to stay out and surf longer. Chet and I paddled in and Arenui stayed out with Lance for a few waves before he paddled back in to join us.

Chet was amazed at the spread of fresh fruits, veggies and fish that was served on the deck at the Standunk. We had everything from mangoes, guava, cherry tomatoes, spinach, pineapple, coconut, strawberries, blueberries to fresh grouper and flounder.

"I swear this is the best meal I've ever eaten!" Chet complimented. "You guys eat like this every day?"

"Yep, at least 3 times per day. Just like this. For thousands of years." Hoanui answered.

"That's why you guys are so healthy and in such good shape. A few meals like this and some surf sessions and my little belly might look like a washboard like you guys!"

"Hey Hoa, Chet wants to visit Mata with us tomorrow. Can we ask Matahi for his blessing?" I inquired.

Hoanui turned to the head of the table and conversed with Matahi in Rahitian for a moment. "Matahi wants to know how you guys feel about a tribal dance tonight. He knows that it is not the best time to party in light of what has happened, but he thought it may help to change the mood and at least take everyone's mind off of the situation. He will give his blessing to Chet then." Hoanui said as he relayed the words of the elder.

"I'm fine with a tribal dance. I could use the distraction." I quickly answered. Chet also concurred. Maruia smiled and rubbed my arm as she must have been pleased by the agreement to dance.

We wrapped up lunch and Chet and I excused ourselves. I spent the afternoon walking the island with Chet and talking about the state of the world. He was very knowledgeable about the happenings in the world as he worked at the port terminal and caught all of the news from the sailors as they came and went. He told me that there had been rumors for a couple of weeks that the US military had captured Bin Laden in Pakistan and were holding him prisoner in an undisclosed military base. No US officials would confirm the rumors though. Apparently the US feared the exact retaliation that actually happened. How ironic. We both contemplated how the world would be and what would happen now. We both agreed on one thing – that the world would never be the same again. We also agreed that the South Pacific was far removed from the destruction and was probably the safest place to be.

The girls worked hard during the day to prepare for the tribal event of the evening. They even fabricated a tribal outfit for Chet just as they had done for Lance and me. Chet wore it proudly without hesitation. The tribal ceremony began with a feast for dinner and then evolved into a similar affair that they had thrown for Lance and I. The only problem was that Lance was not present at this party, nor was he to be found anywhere. I tried not to let his absence taint the event, but of course it bothered me and worried the rest of the tribe as well. I walked the island at dusk in search of him, but came up with nothing before I decided to rejoin the festivities.

Chet enjoyed the tribal dancing and the music, but declined to step into the fire during his dance. Hoanui and I wooed the crowd again with our fire dancing ability. We unanimously decided to forego the fire-handling ritual tonight though. My mind was not focused enough to handle that event. Instead, I was happy to focus my attention on another telling of the Mata Utu story by Matahi as translated and relayed by Hoanui. The story still had the same wonderment and mystique the second time around. I watched Chet as he sat in eager anticipation as the story unfolded by the fire light. Maruia sat on my other side and held my hand and caressed my arm in an affectionate attempt to take my mind off of Lance and the rest of the world. I engrossed myself in the story of Mata, the Matains and Hoku and looked forward to taking Chet to the island tomorrow – hopefully with Lance.

As the story concluded and the tribal festivities winded down, Arenui, Hoanui, Chet and I made plans to meet early in the morning for departure to Mata. I planned to get in a yoga session with the girls at first light before leaving. I hoped that Lance would magically appear in the morning. Maruia and Tania set Chet up with beddings in the Stan-dunk and we all said goodnight.

The night crept by slowly as I lay awake most of the night wondering where Lance was and how he was feeling. The aftermath of "The Day" was still fresh and would not leave my mind to a minute of peace. I tried to focus on the fun we would have at Mata tomorrow, but the absence of Lance took the excitement out of that for the moment. I got up out of my bed and sat on the deck of the Stan-dunk as the first twilight appeared on the horizon. I made my way down to the beach and watched as the sun rose on the horizon. The once beautiful sunrise just kept reminding me of a fire in the sky. I sat humbled by my helplessness and inability to do anything to help the rest of the world.

It wasn't long after sunrise before Maruia, Tania and Puatea joined me on the beach for yoga. Today, I needed it more than ever. We all practiced in complete silence, focusing on long, deep stress relieving breaths. The crisp, clean island air cleansed my lungs as I exhaled the stress and tension from my body. The ensuing salt-water bath cleansed the stress and toxic feeling from the rest of my body. I was invigorated and ready to eat, so we all dried off and headed up to the Stan-dunk for breakfast. Still no Lance in sight. I checked his hut on the way to breakfast, but he wasn't there. I woke up Chet who had slept like a baby. He commented on how peaceful and quiet the island and community center were. He was also blown away by the smorgasbord of fresh fruit the girls prepared for breakfast. Hoanui and Arenui joined us as we all feasted and prepared to depart for Mata Utu. I crossed my fingers and prayed that Lance would come to breakfast, but it didn't happen. I kissed Maruia goodbye and me and the guys headed down to the beach to fetch our surfboards and the kayaks.

Just as we were strapping the last board on the second outrigger, Lance appeared on the beach out of nowhere with his board in hand.

"Lance, good to see ya, brah." Arenui said as he welcomed him.

"You gonna join us, Mate?" Chet asked.

"You didn't think I'd miss a trip to Mata did ya'll?" Lance replied.

"Well, you did miss dinner, the tribal dance and breakfast. Where were you bro?" I asked.

"Don't worry about it. I didn't feel like eating or dancing. But I do feel like going to Mata." He responded with certainty.

This posed a very small dilemma as we had two kayaks ready to go and a fifth person with nowhere to sit and no one to pair up with.

"You want me to see if Tane or someone wants to go so you will have a paddle buddy?" Hoanui asked.

"Nah, I'm cool by myself." Lance said as he strapped his board on a third outrigger and began to drag it to the beach by himself. I jumped up to help him pull the kayak to the water, but he refused my help. "I've got it, bro." He said as he warded off my help.

"Ok, glad you are joining us at least." I graciously said.

The moment Lance's kayak cleared the beach he hopped in it and began paddling full speed without waiting for us. He made it clear that he wanted minimal interaction with anyone today. I respected that and thought it fortunate that he was at least coming. Chet and I paired up and rowed alongside Hoa and Are. I told Chet about how the dolphins would only follow us so close to Mata before disappearing. I told Chet of our previous experiences at Mata and confirmed the lack of animal life there. Chet's anticipation grew as Mata magically appeared on the horizon ahead of us. Lance would be there way before us as he left us in his wake. I had never seen him paddle so fast – especially by himself in the two-man outrigger. He was a man on a mission today.

Seeing the amazement and expression on Chet's face as we entered the lagoon at Mata thrilled me. For a moment I lost myself in the island's enchanted beauty again as if it were my first time there. For a moment, I forgot about the turmoil in the world. How can one place on earth be so beautiful and seemingly peaceful while several thousand miles away, violence and destruction now reigned the world? But even as peaceful as Mata seemed on the surface, the island also had its hidden secrets of past violence and ensuing curse which still plagued the island. I thought about how everywhere needed a cleansing process from time to time. In the bible there was Noah's story of the Arc and the cleansing flood that purified the earth and rid it of sins and sinners. Hoku cleansed the island of Mata Utu and rid it of the fierce cannibal tribe that inhabited it. It was forecasted and predicted by scholars and religious zealots that the earth would be "cleansed" and destroyed by fire instead of flood in "the second coming". Was this the end of the world and of mankind? It was certainly the end of the world as we had previously known it. Had it not been for the technology we brought to the island, would we have even known it or would we still be living in bliss? Was it coincidence or part of a larger life plan that put Lance and me in the islands and out of harm's way at this time? Would we be affected here? Would everyone flock to the safe haven of the South Pacific, Australia, New Zealand etc… and rape these lands of their natural resources? Rahiti and the "natural" islands could support their own – plus a few more maybe, but if the whole population of Papeete spread out to the other islands to seek food and water, it would certainly create a burden on the ecosystem of each island. Here sat this beautiful, yet cursed island of Mata – uninhabited and capable of supporting hundreds, if not thousands of people. Could the curse be broken? How many innocent wanderers would stumble into this paradise in search of a new home only to fall victim to the curse? And where the hell is my brother? He left us behind, beached his kayak and started the hike alone. Damn it and damn this situation. My mind started to reel back and forth between the natural beauty of the island and the turmoil in the world and my mind. I felt unstable. I felt like I was in la-la land. I felt like I was in a dream. I walked, board under my arm, through the jungle as if I were in a trance. I listened to Hoanui and Arenui telling Chet about all of the features of the island and prepping him for the massive, perfect wave he was about to surf. The words entered one ear and exited the other without fully registering. There was too much confusion in my head to process anything at the moment. I felt like I was having an outer body experience. I stayed quiet, followed along and tried to collect my thoughts and enjoy the day.

We surfed, celebrated Chet's first ride at Mata back on the spit with Lance and then paddled back to Rahiti. Neither Lance nor I hardly said a word the rest of the day. The reality of "The Day" really set in with both of us. Chet and everyone else sensed it and gave us our distance. Chet departed for Tahiti the next day with enough fruits, veggies, herbs and water on the pontoon boat to last him for a week or two. We said our goodbyes and he vowed to return very soon. I took a deep breath and a long, solo walk down the beach as the pontoon boat powered away from the shore.

I desperately wanted to rid my mind of the turmoil and lighten the load on my heavy heart. I wanted to do something to help the world. I wanted to know if everything and everyone was ok.

One Night in Mata

I really began to worry deeply about Lance. He was not handling his grief well. He was not eating at all that I was aware of. He would sit in solitude on the beach in a north easterly homeward facing direction while the village gathered for meals. The girls would take plates of food to him, but they were always discovered untouched where they were left. In a matter of two months he had lost over 40 pounds and was quickly wasting away to nothing. No matter how badly I grieved, it was difficult to pass up a delicious, organic Tahitian meal cooked up and served by Maruia, Tania and Puatea. Not only was Lance not eating, but he refrained from participating in any tribal activities or duties. The village understood and was more than willing to forgive him for not pulling his weight. On the contrary, I found that my best outlet for stress and fear was to pull double duty on my chores to take my mind off of "The Day." My double efforts more than made up for Lance's lack of work. I gladly did his part and never said a word about it. My new found appreciation and attitude carried me through the day without stress.

Lance had become more reserved in conversation and almost reclusive. No words could express his sorrow and longing for his wife and home. Although his mouth rarely spoke, his eyes told a million stories of sadness. I felt his pain and tried to impart sympathy sprinkled with positivity. By trying to cheer him up, I made myself feel even better. The village also tried to compensate and cheer him up. I became driven to help Lance through his tough times. He became the outlet for my positive emotions. Talking to Lance about his feelings helped me with mine. Although my talking seemed for naught, I stayed positive and kept the conversations going. Conversation was my release and listening in a meditative trance seemed to be his. The one common denominator that was the best outlet for both of us was surfing. Mata Utu's perfect right was perfectly right for escaping from reality. Our daily ritualistic trek to Mata was the one thing that had remained constant. We owed that wonderful release to Arenui, and even though he rarely went with us, he understood our fascination and the stress release that each daily surf session would bring. The long paddle, long hike and long barrel ride was the perfect daily attitude adjustment. Three hours of effort for three minutes of fun. However, the fun just didn't seem to be there for Lance anymore. It seemed like surfing Mata became something he had to do rather than something he wanted to do. So on a daily basis, I did yoga with the girls, finished morning chores and headed down to the beach to meet him at the canoes. But even in a completely depressed state, Lance got a little energy and glimmer in his eye when it was time to drag the canoe down and strap on the boards. "Mata" I would say and he would reply "Utu" and we would repeat and speed up the recitation until it became a chant. "Mata – Utu, Mata - Utu."

This morning, I finished my duties and walked down to the beach to find Lance standing at the edge of the water with the canoe already dragged down into the water and the boards already strapped on. I think if I had been a few minutes later he would have already been paddling and I would have had to swim after him to catch up. He must have been eager to go because dragging the canoe to the water was a task we both dreaded even when done together as a team. I was glad I didn't have to deal with it this morning. I wasted no time hopping in and casting off.

We rowed in the usual synchronized rhythm. Lance was up front. Before I could start into a story or song to pass the time, Lance turned his head to me with a big smile that I hadn't seen since before "The Day".

"It's gonna be a good one. I can feel it. Can you feel it?"

"Dude, it's always a good one at Mata. What makes today so special, Bro?"

"The wind is right, the sun is shining, the water is extra blue, it's coming up on low tide and the current is pulling us in the right direction. Mata Utu is calling my name."

"Doesn't Mata call our names every day Lance?" I chided at him in jest – "Lance, Lance come ride me! Come drop in and thrust your big stick deep into my barrels!"

Lance didn't find the humor and made an erratic splash with his oar which soaked me. I pulled my oar out of the water to splash him back and I quickly initiated a water fight. In our frolicking, we realized that we were still speeding along to Mata. The current was like a conveyor belt today just carrying us along in the perfect direction. We stopped rowing and let nature do the work.

"I'm glad you're in a good mood today, Bro. It's nice to have the old Lance back."

"I'm always in a good mood."

"No, offense but if you are always in a good mood, I would hate to meet the Grim Reaper!"

"Funny. I just don't have anything to be happy about."

"Sure you do, man. You've got me, surf, the beautiful nature and the villagers all love you. We are here for a reason. Let's make the best of it. There is no sense stressing and grieving over things out of our control."

"Easy for you to say - you didn't lose a wife."

"I know, but on the other side, I may never have a wife. At least you have great memories. At least you have those experiences that you can share with me."

"Whatever. Maruia is crazy about you. She would marry you tomorrow. I can never marry again. It just wouldn't be right."

"I like Maruia too, but I don't consider myself marriage material for her. So I guess the Duncan brothers will just have to be bachelors for life now." I didn't know what else to say, so I left it at that.

We coasted on the conveyor belt current and Mata grew nearer and nearer on the horizon. It was truly a beautiful island – from a distance and in person. The clouds had started their morning migration from the top of the volcano out to sea. It was like they left in the morning to make way for us. Then they returned to the volcano in the evening to lead those lost at sea back home. The weird thing is that no one ever came to this island to experience its beauty. I mean, the whole south pacific is beautiful, but Mata had a lure about it that we both loved. Strangely, no one had ever slept on Mata that the locals were aware of. It was rumored that any visitors (which were never seen by us) always left before sunset. Rumors of the Matain curse kept the island free for us. The ironic thing is that every surf session back in Virginia Beach was a competition to catch the few crappy waves that rolled through. Dozens of agro surfers would use cut-throat techniques to make sure they got every wave possible. God forbid someone dropped in on your wave – even behind you and out of the way. Here we had unlimited epic waves 50 times longer and four times taller and it was just the two of us. No competition whatsoever. In fact, we loved to both ride the same wave and share. A couple of sessions at Mata would chill out those agro fools back home.

The conveyor belt carried us on as we both sat in the canoe in silence. The morning sun glistened on the water. I could feel the enriching effects of the sun as my skin produced a sweet vitamin D smell. I didn't mind the sun on the canoe ride because I had my sunglasses on. However, I had to leave them in the canoe once we reached the island for fear of losing them while surfing. I was contemplating trying to surf with them on once, but I knew if I lost them I would be shit out of luck since there were no sunglass stores around and no mail order. Maybe I could weave a strap or something to hold them. My sunglass thought was interrupted as Lance broke the silence.

"Stan, I just don't care anymore."

"What?"

"I said, I just don't care anymore."

"Care about what?"

"Anything. I just don't give a shit about anything anymore. Nothing at all."

"Not even me bro?" There was a long silence. A very long silence. "Why?" I finally had to interject to end the awkwardness.

"I don't know. I lost my way. I lost my will. I really don't even care about surfing anymore."

"Now you're talking crazy talk, bro. You don't care about surfing anymore? I mean I can understand not eating, sleeping or talking, but surfing too – No way!" I was really trying to lighten up the moment by gently harassing him.

"Screw you."

"Dude, just stop now before you say something you can't take back. Let's just go surf together and forget about it all. Maybe catch a buzz afterward or something. Just chill man."

He didn't acknowledge me. He just sat there with his back to me, his oar resting in his lap and his arms folded across his chest. I really loved my brother but sometimes he could be a real asshole. He had never dealt with his emotions well. He was stubborn and grudge holding all of his life. I knew he was thinking this whole thing was my fault. If I hadn't convinced him to come on this trip, he would be home right now. If he was home right now, he could be dead, starving, sick or miserable – but at least he would be with his wife. He had to know that I hurt so badly too. He just didn't care about anyone's feelings except his own. We both lost everything from the past, but at least we still had each other and a new life in a tropical paradise. We had everything we ever needed right here – except for everything we had before. I often tried to imagine we had been born here and had never known anything different. I wondered what our mindset would be. I wondered how our lives would be different never having experienced the way of life in the USA. Would we even care about the crisis in the north? How would we perceive "The Day"? Of course "The Day" bothered the locals here, but was it only because they felt pain for us? If we were not here would they even care what happened in the USA and Europe? Hard to say. It was obvious that they could sustain themselves just fine without the rest of the world. Of all the places in the world to be in such a time, I was happy to be right here. Of all the people to be with, I was most fortunate to be with my brother. With that being said, I was more than willing to tolerate his bullshit and just appreciate the fact he was here. I held out for hope that his emotional pain would heal with time and my old bro would come back.

We reached the familiar outer reef at Mata and the water turned from deep blue to turquoise. I gently guided the canoe through the reef break and into the lagoon with a couple of short strokes of my paddle. The whole canoe ride had been effortless. I can't remember a day when the ride had been that easy. The current had literally conveyor belted us right to the beach. It wasn't uncommon for the current to carry us in the general direction of Mata, but we would always have to stroke at the end in one direction or the other to get off of the conveyor belt and into the reef break. Today, we literally glided through the reef, into the lagoon and right onto the beach. Lance hopped off first. I unstrapped the boards and tossed them onto the beach. Lance grabbed his and began to walk away – leaving me to pull the canoe up by myself.

"Hey, bro, can I get a hand here?" I asked.

He kept walking away as he hollered back "You get it, I pulled it down by myself earlier."
Okay, he did in fact do that, but not because I refused to help him. In fact, I was doing his chores in the village when he pulled it down by himself. Why was he being so damn rude all of a sudden today? It was a perfect day. I wish his attitude was the same.

I dragged the outrigger up onto the beach by myself and then took my time as I waxed my board on the beach. I figured I would let him go on ahead and he would wait up for me at the clearing or the point. I stretched in the sand a bit and took a few yoga poses and deep meditative breaths to calm my soul. I really didn't want my attitude to turn negative as well and spawn a fight with my brother. As I meditated, my mouth began to water for some fruit. I wandered down the trail and plucked a few pomello fruit and sat on a rock as I peeled them. The cool juice ran down both of my arms to my elbows. I often contemplated how the juice could remain so cool when the fruit basked in the hot sun all day. I enjoyed every last bite of the sweet fruit and even licked my fingers and arms. I was totally relaxed and comfortable. I really didn't want to make the hike today. I would be content just sitting on the beach at the lagoon waiting for Lance to return. I could go pick some herbs and be ready to fire them up when he got back to the spit. That would change his mood. Or it would piss him off if he sat on the point waiting for me and I didn't show up. How long would he wait before he took the plunge by himself? I didn't know.

I decided to go on and surf. I could hear the booming of the waves on the other side of the island and couldn't resist the temptation to go ride. I figured Lance was about 20 to 30 minutes ahead of me so I would pick up my pace a little bit so he wouldn't have to wait so long. I grabbed my board and made my way down the path. My pace was swift. I loved the feeling of the cool, moist, soft soil on my bare feet. My feet had become tough as leather since we arrived in the islands. I hated wearing shoes anyway. I felt more in touch with nature when I was barefooted. I had walked this path dozens of times and knew where every rock, root and other obstacle was. I felt like Hoku - I could probably make the trek with my eyes closed – at least until I got to the base of Mount Mata. That's where things got tricky. I ran through the lush forest as free as the wind. My longboard felt so natural under my arm that I didn't even know it was there. I loved the hike and the forest was my favorite part. It was so comfortable, cool and well shaded from the heat of the morning sun. Dew dripped from the leaves and dropped on me like giant raindrops. The raindrops made me thirsty. I diverted off the path for a moment and stopped to get a drink from the spring. I wondered how far ahead Lance was. I wondered if he had stopped to drink in the same spot. The hike just wasn't as enjoyable without him. Even when my leg was banged up from the reef incident, he had always waited for me and went at my pace. What had gotten into him today? Why the impatience and intolerable attitude? Why the increased need for solitude? What could I do to help him? I figured I would just be cool and go with the flow and not provoke him or make any demands of him. If he did something off the wall, I would let it go. If he said something hurtful, I would let it go in one ear and out the other without registering in my mind.

I kept on down the trail toward Mount Mata - I had a great pace going. I anticipated that I was gaining ground on Lance and would see him up ahead on the trail at any moment. If he walked our usual pace and I was running, I should catch up with him before the clearing at the base of Mount Mata. I figured he wouldn't pass that point without me. If there was a good waiting spot – that was it. Of course the point was the last waiting point, but it was a rocky, uncomfortable place to wait. I figured logic said I would either catch him or find him waiting at the clearing. I picked up my pace.

As I neared the clearing, I looked to the beach and didn't see him. I kept up my hustle and reached the clearing, but no Lance. I walked out to the beach and looked up to the trail on the hip of Mount Mata. I didn't see him on the mountain trail either. Surely his bright green 10' long longboard and his yellow board shorts would show up clearly against the black volcanic rock. I sat down on the beach and rested. I had run for nothing. I got a little exercise, but that was not my objective. Where had he gone? Did he stop to drink somewhere else? Did he stop to blaze one or drop a deuce? Had I run right by him? I was baffled. Should I wait here at the clearing or continue on to the point? My brother was not a runner. There is no way he could have out run me to the clearing – even with his 20 minute head start. Now I was in a quandary. What to do? Wait, proceed, or turn back. I decided to do none of the above. I sat right on the beach and watched the rights break and peel down the length of the beach. It was fascinating how the energy of the ocean traveled so far and was released right here on this perfect reef break. It was a perfect scenario that made the perfect wave. Even the slight curvature of the island elongated and accentuated the wave break. I had traveled to so many surf destinations in the world, but had never seen such an ideal wave. Not to mention how ideal the atmosphere was. If there was a place like this back in the states, it would be mobbed 24/7 by every kook under the sun. I wondered how many kooks would be deterred by the 2 hour round-trip canoe trip and then the hour long hike. I figured the pristine natural beauty of the island would be exploited and power boats and jet skis would tow surfer after surfer into the waves effortlessly. Sure, if we had a jet ski we could take turns towing each other into the break. We could ride dozens of waves each day instead of just one, but that would take away the challenge and fun and natural beauty of surfing one perfect wave just once a day.

The breaking of the waves mesmerized me. I watched the break begin at the point and then peel down the reef the length of the island and then taper off all the way at the spit on the opposite end of the island barely within sight. I counted in Mississippi's from the first formation of white water on the point to the close-out of the barrel and spray at the spit. I timed about 5 waves and came up with about 150 to 200 Mississippi's each time. Three minute barrels – one right after the other. After watching about 20 waves break with about eight second intervals between the start of each of them, I decided it was time to head to the point and catch one myself. As soon as I stood up, I saw a familiar sight - Lance's green board dropping in from the peak of the next breaking wave. It was a double overhead pitching break and he was right on it. I had watched him make the drop before while I stood on the point, but never from this vantage point. It was an awesome sight.

I dropped my board and ran parallel down the beach to keep him in my sight. He pumped hard down the line screaming at warp speed and then went vert and busted up to the lip carving out a big spray as he shot back down the face into a roundhouse cutback. He slalomed slightly and slowed his speed and pulled back into the tube. I lost sight of him as he was completely shacked by the rolling tube of water. I sprinted along the beach as fast as I could but was no match for the speed of the breaking wave. I stopped and watched the wave continue to break down the beach from over a couple hundred yards away. I couldn't see him emerge from the tube from my vantage point as the spray of the wave obscured my sight. It looked to be a perfect ride. I envisioned him launching over the lip at the end of the spit and going double overhead airborne. It was a cool thought and an awesome sight from the beach.

217

The one question in my mind was how he had beaten me to the point so fast. I was running full pace the whole trail. Lance was not that fast. Even if he had run at his full pace from the get-go, I still should have caught up to him before the hip. It was puzzling. Now I was left in a dilemma. Do I walk, surf or swim to the spit? I had already run about 20% back down the beach, but now had to go back to get my board. After watching that brilliant barrel ride, I decided it was a no brainer for me to do the same. I didn't care if Lance had to wait for me since he hadn't waited at the point. It was unusual for him to abandon me. He had been pissed off before, but Mata was something we always did together. I felt him distancing himself even more from me.

I took my time and hiked back to the clearing, grabbed my board and proceeded up the base of Mount Mata. As I hiked over the hip I could see Lance walking on the spit far below. I wondered if he would get impatient and leave me on the island. After all, he had dragged the outrigger down to the beach this morning by himself. It was a scary thought, but I quickly dismissed it. That would be the ultimate dick move. No way would he leave me on the island. Plus, the locals would surely miss me and question where I was. I put my paranoia aside and focused on the climb. I descended down the back of the hip and made my way to the point.

When I arrived at the point, I stood and watched the sets roll in. I already had the timing down from my observations on the beach. The break was always the same, only the size and timing changed. Today it was clockwork. The only thing that wasn't clockwork was my brother being here to take the plunge with me. I had a horrific thought for a moment that my brother was gone permanently. A tremendous emptiness came over me. I couldn't stand the thought of standing alone on the point. This was something we did together – our thing. From the day Arenui introduced us to Mata, we surfed this break together every time. I couldn't imagine Mata without Lance. I took solace in the fact that he would be waiting on the spit for me as I launched out of my barrel momentarily. I pictured him standing on the spit cheering. He would give me the high-five when I reached the beach just like good ol' times. He would be waiting with a spliff of Mata's finest already rolled and ready to spark. Just take the plunge, drop in, carve, barrel and launch – Lance will be waiting.

I stood on the point ready to plunge and a weird thought came over me. What if I missed the drop and went over the falls. There is nothing that Lance could do for me from the spit. He wouldn't even know. I could get dashed against the reef again and he would have no idea. How long would he wait before he came back to look for me? Why was I thinking like that? I had successfully made the drop dozens of times since my reef incident. Today there were perfect conditions. There was absolutely no reason why I would wipe out. Just do it, man. Surf, swim or walk. Surfing was my best option – no swimming today – no way.

I watched the sets roll in. I waited until I spotted my wave. The 6th one out was mine. It had my name all over it. The face was building and shaping up perfectly. I counted down from 40. As the fifth wave hit the point, I launched. I paddled, angled, arched my back and felt the wave welling up from behind me. It was on. Eight quick strokes and I was at pace with the wave. I was in perfect position. I popped up and dropped in. Every drop at Mata gave me just as much rush as the first time we were here. The sensation never got stale. The ritual never got old. Three minutes of pleasure made it all worthwhile. I pumped hard as if I were mad at the wave. My speed accelerated. I carved up the face vertically and then snapped the tail over the lip and dropped back down the face faster than any recent ride. I stayed low in the trough and walked up to the nose of the board. I hung 5 toes on my left foot over the nose and then brought my right foot into position. As I curled my right toes over the nose, I leaned back and slowed my momentum. I wanted the freight train behind me to catch up. I heard and felt the rumble fast approaching. I leaned my head back dangerously far, but still maintained my balance even in my back-bent position. It was such a beautiful sight as the barrel caught up to me. Seeing that wall of water thrusting and barreling over your head is such an amazing sight. The energy of the wave is evident in the sound, sight, speed, pressure, air turbulence – everything around you is pure energy – and there you are right in the middle of it. I dropped back far into the tube. I looked through the thick teal green wall of water as it distorted the sunlight that tried to penetrate its cloak. It was surreal as usual. The only thing missing was Lance next to me. I dismissed the thought and turned my focus back to the natural beauty around me. I was a good 5 or 6 board lengths into the tube as I felt the wave tapering down. I pumped hard and picked up momentum. I wanted to time my exit perfectly so I could give Lance a good show. I felt the spray increase as the tube was closing out more rapidly behind me. I pumped and pumped and emerged from the tube at the perfect point to launch over the lip. I know I had to have been airborne a good 15 to 20 feet for at least 4 or 5 seconds. I was sure Lance was applauding my perfect barrel ride and exit. I tucked and landed perfectly in the calm, teal water.

I surfaced and retrieved my board by reeling in the leash. I mounted the board and turned to the island to begin my short, leisurely paddle to the sandy spit. I was quite disappointed when I did not see Lance anywhere on the spit. "Shit, he didn't watch me" was my first thought. My second thought was – "shit, he left me!" My heart palpitated. What the hell is wrong with that guy today? We had certainly had our fights before, but I had no clue what had precipitated his attitude today. I didn't care as long as he and the canoe were still there. I coasted on into the spit on my board. I walked up onto the beach and saw him sitting at the lagoon facing the canoe. Thank God he was still here. I would not provoke him and ask why he didn't wait for me or how he beat me to the point so quickly or why he didn't watch my ride. I would just be cool and we would go on home in peace.

I walked up behind him, put my board down and sat down next to him in the sand.

"Hey man, I saw your ride from the beach. It was a different vantage point for me. It looked awesome. I had a good one too."

There was absolutely no response. No head nod, no emotion in his face, no acknowledgement of my presence. It was like he was in a trance. Lance was in a trance. I sat there in silence next to him staring at the lagoon and the canoe. "Dude, I'm gonna go find some buds. I think we could both use a toke." I walked down the trail into the jungle. I followed my nose to the most fragrant patch of herb. I picked a good sized, semi-dry bud about 6 inches long. I then walked over to the stash box and grabbed a couple of papers and the lighter. I returned to the lagoon with my bounty and got down to business. I rolled an extra large one today as I figured Lance needed all of the attitude adjustment he could get. I sparked it and got it going and quickly passed it off to Lance. He reluctantly took it, but quickly hit it. He took a couple of long, deep tokes and then passed it back to me. He didn't even look at me when he took it or passed it back. Why was he so pissed at me? What did I do? I figured it best to wait for the herbs to kick in before I tried to initiate another conversation. We sat and smoked in silence for the better part of an hour. His gaze never left the lagoon. He looked dejected and hollow. Something was weighing heavy on his mind. I knew he was depressed, but today was different. We finished the spliff. I put it out in the sand and turned to him. "You ready to roll man?"

He didn't answer. I stood up and extended my hand to him to help him up. "Come on, let's go, bro." He didn't look at me or even flinch.

I turned my back on him and grabbed my board and took it to the outrigger and strapped it on. I walked back to him and crouched down at his eye level. He cut his eyes to the side. "What's wrong bro? What can I do for you?" He didn't answer. I moved to the side where his eyes were cut to initiate eye contact. He immediately cut his eyes back to center to avoid me again. Ok, he wants to play childish games, huh? I remembered how our father used to play when we tried to be mad. He would say things like – "How long can you be serious like that?" or "Come on, you know you want to laugh. If you could see yourself now, you'd laugh your ass off. Ok, don't stay mad too long, your face will freeze like that!"

I tried every line I remembered. They all worked so well when we were kids and even as adults from time to time, but nothing worked today to break through to Lance. I sat down in front of him face to face. I stopped my jesting and got as serious as he was. I tried to mirror his emotions and feel his pain. I wanted to know what was on his mind. I sat there in silence for what seemed like hours trying to get through to him with my eyes and senses. His gaze was slightly above my head and to the left. I knew he wasn't looking at anything in particular, just not looking at me. His eyes were hollow and drowned in sadness. I knew he was broken beyond repair. My heart skipped multiple beats. I knew there was nothing I could say to him or do for him. His will to live was gone. Nothing brought him enjoyment anymore – not even surfing Mata with me. I wanted to say so many things, but I sat in silence with him.

As I stared into his eyes, I felt memories pouring out of his soul. I saw his wife Jasmine cooking for him back at their house in the very kitchen that I had renovated. I heard the dogs barking in the back yard. Out the window I saw Lance in the yard tending to the grass and the garden. A row of beach cruisers were propped next to the fence waiting for the next boardwalk ride. The smell of Jasmine's cooking permeated the house. Some Bob Marley played throughout the surround system in the house. Celebrity gossip magazines were strewn on the coffee table and a surf video played on the flat screen. Jasmine called from the kitchen window that dinner was ready. Lance entered the garage and washed his hands in the utility sink which was full of surf apparel. He walked into the kitchen and greeted her with a big hug and kiss. He grabbed a couple of dishes and carried them into the dining room and placed them on the glass table with care. She emerged from the kitchen with more food and soon the table was full of a delicious array of her creations. It was a big table that could accommodate 10, but they sat side by side at the same end of the table. It was a sight that I had the pleasure of witnessing dozens of times over the last decade. It was a scenario that I often wished I had in my life, but since I didn't I was more than happy to be married vicariously through them. They said a quick prayer and then broke bread. He always fed her the first forkful. It was a tradition that nauseated me at first but became cute and more acceptable with time. It was true love and a perfect marriage. He tended to the business and the yard, she tended to the family affairs and the home.

I felt his pain. I wished I could do something to make it go away. I knew how terrible the uncertainty was for him. Not knowing if she was alive or healthy. I think it was the not knowing part that really tore him apart the most. The helplessness of not being able to do anything about it was a burden on both of us. What to do? I extended both of my hands and grabbed his.

"I love you, bro and I am here for you." His only reaction was to pull his hands back from mine. "Come on, let's get out of here." He didn't move. I stood up and grabbed his board to take it to the canoe, but I realized his leash was still attached to his leg. I put the board down and walked over to him to take the leash off of his leg. I reached for the leash and he grabbed my hand.

"I'm not going back." He said with a serious tone in his voice.

"What? Don't be foolish, bro. Come on - let me strap your board on for you. It's time to go." I reached for the leash again and he smacked my hand away. "Seriously – It's time to go, let me help you."

"Fuck you, Stan."

"Ok, I'm trying to be cool and tolerate your attitude today, but please don't take your anger out on me. I feel your pain and I want to help, but I don't know what to do. I hurt also, but I don't want to hurt anyone else. "The Day" was not my fault – I'm suffering too. We have each other and a great situation here. Be thankful for that."

"If you want to help me, leave me alone." He said as he looked off in the distance with a scowl on his face.

"I can't do that and you know it. You can't stay here tonight. You're not staying and I'm not leaving without you."

"We have a big problem then because I'm not going anywhere. Leave me alone." He reiterated his point as he folded his arms across his chest.

I walked away and took a deep breath. I didn't know what to do. I could not leave my brother on Mata – for a number of reasons. The number one reason being that he was not stable enough to be left alone in any environment – let alone Mata. If I went back to the village without him, the locals would freak out and be pissed at me. We made a pact with them that we would be off of the island by dark. As many times as we had been here and as harmless as it seemed to stay the night - a promise is a promise. I didn't want to violate it. I didn't want to test the serenity of Mata and anger the Gods and arouse the past. I didn't personally subscribe to all of the rumors, yet I didn't want to test them either. I paced around the lagoon contemplating my next move. I am usually a very patient person, but this was testing every last ounce of patience I had in my body. I tried to put myself in his emotional state so that I could better reason with him, but I could not find that depth of emotion in myself. How do you deal rationally with someone who has lost all rationale? How do you confront someone who has absolutely no reason to want to live? I had a big dilemma on my hands. Should I honor my brother's wishes against my better judgment and leave him here? Should I break our pact with the villagers and leave him behind on the island overnight? Should I return without him and go get help? I decided after 30 minutes of pacing and thinking to give it one more try. I walked back over to him and with a strong sympathetic plea urged him to go with me.

"Lance, I am in an awkward position here. You are forcing me to make a very difficult decision. I want to respect you and honor your wish, but I have deep concerns about the ramifications of your actions. Staying here will not go over well back at the village. Staying here overnight alone may be detrimental to you as well. Please help me out."

His head hung low and his gaze was distant. I bent down to his level and put my hand on his shoulder. My gesture was met with angst as he jumped up from his seated position and proceeded to punch me square in the eye. Defenseless and unprepared for the assault, I staggered, fell and found myself lying on my back looking skyward. I stayed there for a few moments and composed myself while trying to comprehend what just happened. I then sprung up and turned to face him. We squared off for what seemed to be an eternity. I could sense that he meant business and was serious about staying and being left alone. My brother and I had fought dozens of times in our lives over ridiculous things. I usually prevailed; however, today I knew that would not be the case. He had feelings, desires, emotions and thoughts that I could not reconcile. Fighting him was not the solution. Maybe it was best to leave him alone.

I looked him in the eye with my one good eye and told him I loved him no matter what happened. I then turned and walked to the canoe. He stood there motionless and looked as if he was ready to hit me again. The tide was high so I had no problem pushing the outrigger into the lagoon from the beach. I washed my eye in the salt water and winced with pain from my contusion. I can't believe he clocked me square in the eye. I felt the swelling welling up in my face. The pain from the eye was nothing compared to the pain I felt in my heart. I hesitantly climbed into the canoe and began to paddle out of the lagoon.

I dreaded the solo paddle back against the current based on the swift direction of this morning's trip. I headed out of the safe harbor of the lagoon and back to Rahiti solo. I was pleased yet surprised to discover that miraculously the current had reversed in only a matter of a couple of hours and was now heading back to Rahiti just as swiftly as it had headed to Mata this morning. It was strange that the current was so swift, yet reversed so rapidly in such a short period of time. I didn't complain. Instead, I sat motionless and took the conveyor belt back home and contemplated what had transpired this morning.

Although I coasted effortlessly back to the beach at Rahiti, it was the longest canoe ride of my life. Upon my arrival, I found Puatea on the beach weaving some palm thatch basketry. She was quick to notice my solo arrival – and my swollen eye.

"Puatea, where is Hoanui? I have a big problem."

"It looks like it, Stan. Where is Lance and what happened?"

"Come with me to find Hoanui and I will explain."

Puatea took me by the hand and walked to the village community center. Maruia saw us walking hand in hand and rushed over to see what the problem was. She immediately gasped when she saw my eye. "Come on Maruia, we are going to find Hoanui."

We found Hoanui close by cutting foliage from some palm trees and undergrowth. He immediately stopped what he was doing and devoted all attention to me and my situation. I explained in great detail and with calm reserve what had transpired this morning. All three natives listened with careful attention. I could tell that they were just as baffled as I was about the situation. Hoanui immediately suggested that we had to tell Matahi about the situation and seek his wisdom. The four of us proceeded to his hut. Hoanui, with the help of the girls, relayed the story to him in Tahitian. I could tell by his facial expression and body language that he interpreted the situation as grave. After much deliberation and bantering back and forth between, Matahi extended his arms and embraced me in a hug.

"Stan, Matahi expresses deep sympathy and concern for your brother. Even his wisdom and experience is not enough to interpret the situation. He will consult the Gods and meditate. We will have a tribal meeting tonight after dinner and decide what to do."

Hoanui's words were no comfort to me. Dinner? How could I possibly even think about dinner and eating? It would be a long couple of hours to wait. I decided to part company with my friends and find meditation and solitude myself. I sat under a Banyan tree on the beach far from the villagers. I watched the sun trace over the sky as I counted down the hours to dinner and our subsequent meeting. I sat there in meditation as the palm tree shadows lengthened to the edge of the water indicating that the day was coming to an end. I soon heard the familiar conch shell bellow signaling dinner time. I composed myself and got on my feet and made the journey to the community center for dinner.

When I arrived at the center, it was evident that word had traveled fast. I could tell that the village didn't need to see my black eye to know something was wrong. I sat in my usual spot next to Lance's vacant seat. I was accustomed to his seat being vacant, but at least he was on the same island before. The girls served me up some food even at my refusal to accept it. I sat quietly and picked at my food while the others carried on mundane conversation. Dinner time passed slowly with little excitement and emotion. Even Tane walked by me and put his hand on my shoulder with a sense of calm understanding and sympathy.

Dinner wrapped up and everyone cleaned up. I stayed seated and did not help with my usual chores. I was ready to face the village and hear their consensus about a plan of action. Maruia excused herself from her duties and came and sat down next to me. She took my hand and lightly kissed me on my swollen cheek.

"It will be okay. Everything will work out. Your brother will be alright. You guys will find peace again soon." She said with a sympathetic and loving tone in her voice.

Her words were sweet, but hardly enough to put my mind at complete ease. Tania made her rounds through the center lighting the torches in anticipation of the meeting and upcoming darkness. The chores were abbreviated tonight and everyone quickly returned to the center and took their seats. Puatea came around and served some Kava Kava tea. I took a double helping. I needed all the calm I could get.

We all rose as Matahi entered the center in full tribal garb and took his seat at the head of the table. He made some chants and salutations and Nanihi blessed his head. As the tribal ceremonial meeting began, it was Hoanui who led the meeting and not Matahi. Hoanui focused his attention on me and started to speak.

"It is with great sadness and concern that we convene to discuss troubling issues with one of our brothers. Matahi has asked me to conduct this meeting as he feels I am better able to communicate with everyone on these matters. Does anyone object to me speaking on behalf of Matahi, the elder?"

No one responded. Their silence was their sign of acceptance. He continued.

"We have endured a great hardship in the world and, although far removed from the source of the tragedy, we feel the pain close to home through the pain and losses of our two brothers Stan and Lance. We can do nothing to change what happened in the rest of the world. We can only strive to coexist peacefully and productively here in our own environment. We are glad that our brothers were here with us and out of harm's way; however no distance can shelter them from the emotional pain of their losses back home. Stan has managed to find ways to cope with the trauma, but Lance has struggled since "The Day". Today was a sad day for both brothers as their rift became deeper. A fight at Mata occurred because Lance decided to break pact and stay on the island. Stan did everything he could possibly do at the time. Now we face decisions that must be made as a community. Lance's actions not only potentially endanger him, but could bring misfortune to all of us as well. Mata is sacred ground. Mata has welcomed the brothers daily for their surfing adventures over the last few months, but has not been tested on this level yet. Matahi spent the afternoon consulting with and praying to the Gods. He has asked forgiveness for Lance's actions. The God's responses were neither favorable nor objectionable – as if to say they were willing to look the other way in Lance's case. Matahi feels that in some unique way, Mata may hold the key to Lance's restlessness. After much thought, Matahi feels it best to leave Lance alone for the night. Maybe the mystique of the island will help him with the demons he is already facing. Lance will remain on Mata tonight. We will convene in the morning after breakfast. Stan, you and I along with Arenui and Tane will voyage to Mata in the morning to retrieve your brother. Tonight, let's all pray for Lance's safe return and for Mata's forgiveness. Rahitians, you are dismissed for the night."

Maruia was fast to volunteer to go to Mata as well. Hoanui agreed to allow it as a comfort to me. Everyone left the center except Maruia and I. We sat side by side in silence as she gently caressed my head, neck and back. The village was somber and quiet as if they were mourning the loss of someone prematurely.

"Lance will be okay, Stan. We will see in the morning. Mata will cure his distress. Everything will be okay. Come on, let's turn in for the night." Maruia took my hand and led me out of the dining area. We walked down to the moonlit beach. We sat in a hammock and gazed out over the moon's reflection on the ocean. I looked in the direction of Mata and wondered what Lance was doing right now. I wondered if he was looking up at the same stars and thinking of me. The sky was crystal clear, the moon shone bright and all the stars were evident. The eerie calm was suddenly interrupted by a wind gust that lasted much longer than the usual ocean breeze. I got chills on my spine. I couldn't tolerate the suspense. I just wanted to sleep through the night and wake up soon.

"Come on, Stan let's get you comfortable for the night." Maruia rubbed my leg and coaxed me out of the hammock. We walked in silence back to the center. I had no idea how I would sleep, but I wanted to badly. I just wanted to sleep through the night and wake up in the morning to discover that this whole drama had been a dream. Maruia lingered in my room and made her rounds lighting candles and straightening up loose articles. I sat on the edge of the mattress and breathed a deep sigh of exhaustion.

"Maruia, I appreciate your efforts, but you really don't have to do anything for me. You can go. There is no sense in you witnessing my depression right now."

"Nonsense – I am here for you. You have done so much for me and my community. The least I can do is to be here for you in your time of need. I want to be the one for you to lean on as you always do for others. I will stay here tonight."

"What? That's not necessary. I don't want to create any more drama. The last thing we need is Tane going crazy too. Or what will the others say?"

"I don't think anyone will question the fact that I am staying with you tonight. And, if they do, I really could care less. I am yours tonight and every other night you need me."

She made her way to me. Standing in front of me, her belly was at my head height as I sat on the edge of my bed. She placed both of her hands on my head and caressed me taking care not to touch my bruised eye. She pulled my head into her body and pressed it tight to her. The sweet smell of her skin filled my nose. The soft, soothing massage eased my mind. I reached around her waist out of both instinct and appreciation and squeezed her tight. The passionate embrace lasted just long enough to ease my mind and my nerves. When Maruia was with me, I knew everything was alright – at least at that moment. I loosened my grip around her waist and she instinctively backed away from me. The candlelight danced across the room and illuminated her beautiful figure. I admired her beauty with a somewhat stoic stare.

"I have something for you, Stan."

"What is that, my beautiful Polynesian Princess?"

"It's me." She replied with a look of seduction in her eyes.

She began a slight dance motion in her hips. Her body began to sway in the silence as if the Congo drums and banjo played a rhythmic melody. I had watched her dance dozens of times in the tribal gatherings, but never as sensuously as now. My eyes fixated on her every move. My heart skipped a few beats from passion instead of worry. She continued on with her seductive dance. She was trying her best to take my mind off of Lance – and it was working well. I began to feel her energy and rhythm. My seated body began to sway in unison with hers. I attempted to rise to my feet to join her in dance, but she gently pushed me back onto the thatched mattress on the floor. She stepped back farther and continued her dance. Her hip gyration and fluid body undulation was driving me to the brink of insanity. Just when I thought I couldn't get any more aroused, she proceeded to shed her parea wrap to reveal her naked beauty. Of course I had seen her nude countless times on the beach, but never in such an erotic nature. I lost control of my mind and my libido took over. It was exactly the medicine I needed. She approached me again in her undulating dance motion. Her natural scent wafted to my nose. It was the most pleasant aroma I had ever smelt. She put her hands on my shoulders and undulated her naked body inches from my face. I maintained composure against all instinct. I sat motionless and took in her energy. She gently pushed me backwards as to cue me to lie down. I didn't resist and fell backward into the bed. She removed my sandals and then made her way up to my waist and unfastened the waistband of my board shorts. She gently slid them down my legs revealing my erect member. She proceeded to kiss every inch of my naked body. She crawled on top of me and inserted me into her ready womb. Passionately she fulfilled me. It was my first sexual encounter since I left home. It may have been the most memorable sexual experience of my life despite the circumstances.

We embraced and spooned in our post-coital bliss. Slumber came quickly and easily. Lance spent the night in Mata and I spent the night in Maruia.

The Last Ride

The next morning I awoke at day break with Maruia nestled up next to me. Her beautiful face was illuminated by the red sunrise that shone through the window. I hated to wake her. She looked so peaceful and content. Her seduction had successfully brought me peace and slumber last night. It had been the culmination of months of attraction and anticipation. She was as wonderful as I had envisioned and fantasized she would be. I wanted to lie in bed with her forever, but there was business to tend to. The first order of business was to sneak her out of my place before the locals discovered the affair. The last thing I wanted was to create more drama at this juncture. I aroused her from her peaceful slumber by gently kissing her face and caressing her forehead. She awoke with a big smile on her face and her eyes locked with mine. She kissed my lips and said "Come on, let's go get your brother."

We rolled out of bed and dressed quickly. I had hoped that no one else was awake, but I sensed a presence outside and restlessness in the atmosphere. When I opened up the door to the Stan-dunk I was greeted by a strong gust of wind and a low flying bird. I walked out into the village and the first person I saw was Tane. Great – the last person I wanted to be awake was probably the only one who was. He was packing up the outside fixtures. He immediately spotted Maruia and I. He stopped what he was doing and approached us. I fully anticipated a confrontation. I didn't need another black eye. I knew that he realized Maruia spent the night with me. I didn't need any drama and I didn't want to give any explanations. We stopped and met him at the center of the complex. His eyes locked with mine and he said "There's a storm coming. It looks bad."

"What? How do you know?" Maruia clutched my arm as if to reinforce the fact that she was mine and that I would protect her from any storm.

"Look at the horizon – the sky is on fire. Red sunrise. Red sky at night, ships sail with flight. Red sky in the morning, ships sail with warning. Feel the wind gust and shift direction rapidly. Listen to the animals. The Gods are angry about something. Maybe your brother... Or maybe something else." He said as he cut his eyes over to Maruia.

I paid no mind to his gesture toward Maruia. He was right - the animals were all restless. Monkeys cried out, birds stirred, insects were out of sight. There was an intermittent and eerie calm in the air and a big ball of fire in the sky. I had never seen a sunrise like that. I had seen many red sunsets, but no red sunrises. Maybe it was because lately I rarely awoke in time to see the sunrise. Had it not been for my concern for my brother I would not have been awake this morning either. I could have slept through a typhoon with Maruia by my side. I told Tane that I would be down on the beach prepping the outriggers for the trek to Mata. We gave each other a head nod and I walked away arm in arm with Maruia. Tane cut his eyes and turned his head to enjoy a few last jealous stares at Maruia. We paid him no mind and headed down to the beach.

Down at the beach we discovered that Hoanui and some of the locals had already pulled three outriggers down to the water. My board was still strapped securely to the outrigger on my kayak. I almost unstrapped the board and left it behind, but my instincts told me to leave it on and take it along. I had absolutely no intention of surfing, but I followed my instincts and left it strapped. Maruia and I surveyed the beach, but saw no one. We sat down in the sand and commenced a morning yoga stretching session. The wind was picking up and sand blew in our faces. From a back-bend position I could see clouds racing overhead. A storm was definitely brewing. Larger than normal waves lapped on the usually tranquil Rahitian beach as we stretched and tried to prepare for the voyage ahead of us. I hoped that the storm would not impede our mission to retrieve my brother.

Maruia and I continued to stretch as we tried to relax. I needed some relaxation to quell the butterflies in my stomach. I was so nervous about my brother. I was eager to go get him and get back to this very beach safe and sound. As I bent into a "down-dog" position, I saw Arenui approaching from my upside down vantage point. I spun out of the position and sprung to my feet. He was eating a mango and with a mouthful of the juicy fruit he hollered out to me.

"Unstrap the board, dude. No need for that today. The seas are about to get ugly. Hoanui and Tane are on their way. We will head out soon."

"Yeah, I was about to do that, but I decided to leave it for some reason. I definitely don't plan to surf, but I felt like I should take it." I answered.

"Whatever, man. It's extra drag and you don't need that today. It's gonna be a tough paddle with the wind and the current. I say lose it brah." He insisted.

"Agreed." I responded.

I walked over and loosened the lines that held my board snugly to the outrigger on my kayak. When the tension was released, my board jumped off of the outrigger as a gust of wind grabbed it. The board danced on the beach momentarily until I was able to corral it and carry it up to shelter. On the way to stow the board, I passed Tane and Hoanui who were engaged in conversation as they walked toward the beach. I couldn't tell what they were talking about, but I assumed they were contemplating the voyage today in lieu of the new developments in the weather. I gave them a head nod as if to say I'll be back in a second.

Many of the tribe had gathered in the Stan-dunk, in the center of the village and also on the beach. They had all noticed the darkness on the horizon and the sudden, erratic winds as they shifted direction and came out of nowhere. It appeared to be a Typhoon on the horizon in the direction of Mata which looked to be heading right in our direction too. The red sky, the animals, the strong current and now the wind were all tell-tales. The locals began murmuring and saying that the younger brother had angered the Gods by staying on Mata and this storm was a sign. We had to get him off of that island immediately I thought.

When I returned to the beach, Arenui, Tane, Hoanui and Maruia were all engaged in a heated Tahitian conversation. Maruia was the first to break the Tahitian dialect and address me in English. "Hoanui and Tane don't want me to go to Mata today. I told them, no way. I am going. I can handle it." She pleaded to me.

Before I could interject any thoughts, Tane spoke authoritatively. "It's not smart for her to go. It's unnecessary. It's a dangerous paddle today – the seas will be rough. There is just no point in her going. In fact, I am pondering the point of any of us going right now. It's stupid. Damn Lance."

Tane made his point clear as he looked at me with disdain. I could read his mind. He was jealous and hating the fact that Maruia and I had shacked up last night. He was taking this opportunity to guard her and protect her from the storm – and from being with me. For the first time, I may actually agree with his jealous logic. The last thing I wanted to happen was to compromise Maruia's safety and well being. I absolutely wanted her to go along for support, but I didn't want to put her at risk. It was a dilemma for me –what to do? I really wanted her to go, and she obviously wanted to go, however; if anything happened to her I would never hear the end of it from Tane and everyone else for that matter. The Rahitian culture differed in that the man was supposed to speak up and protect the woman and make the best decisions for her where her experience may be lacking. Maruia was, in my mind, a more independent spirit and stronger soul than anyone else I knew – man or woman. I knew that she was more than capable of making any decision that needed to be made. My best option was obviously to support Maruia in whatever her decision was regardless of what Tane or anyone else thought. If she decided to row with me, I would make it my mission to get us back to this beach safe and sound. I would row and protect her like it was my job. Having her at my side was security and comfort for me. I never worried about her when she was with me because I felt in control and I knew what she was thinking, feeling and doing when she was with me.

Not knowing what to expect from Lance added to my desire for Maruia's company. She had a way of smoothing everything out when necessary. She could be the motivation, the mediator and the good luck charm all in one. I announced my decision to the group. "Maruia goes if she wants to go. It is her decision. She is capable of making a wise one and I support whatever she decides."

Maruia smiled and grasp my hand tightly in appreciation for my support. The others were not so happy about my comment and had no qualms about showing their disapproval. This decision may have been the first thing that I did against the will of any Rahitian, but I felt good about my decision to support Maruia. I would rather upset the entire Rahitian tribe than to disappoint my Maruia. So it was decided and done. Maruia and I pushed our outrigger into the sea and hopped in while the others reluctantly followed.

The paddle to Mata was the hardest that it had ever been that day. The current was flowing away from Mata and we all knew it would be a tough row. In fact, when we dragged the outriggers to the water, the current pushed them back onto the beach as if to say – "Stay home today. Don't go to Mata". We struggled through the surf just to get away from the Rahitian beach. The five of us paddled and fought against the current with all of our might. Our three kayaks were tossed and rocked violently by the wind and surf. Hoanui and Arenui took the lead and then Tane was solo in his kayak while Maruia and I brought up the rear. Tane could hardly see where he was going for turning around on just about every stroke to make eye contact with Maruia.

We struggled to time our oar strokes to hit the water due to the erratic nature of the seas today. We alternated strokes, but often came up with nothing but air as the passing waves lifted the kayak out of the water and then submerged the bow as we powered through the trough of the waves. Several times the bow completely submarined and the entire kayak became over-washed with surf. I think the Rahitian guys contemplated turning around on multiple occasions, but they continued on. I think they continued for two reasons: first, they knew that Maruia and I would continue without them and second, if we didn't get Lance off of Mata the wrath of the Gods and the Matain curse may wreak havoc on all of the islands – including Rahiti.

Determination and adrenaline kept me paddling. We braced ourselves in the kayak by pressing the outside of our thighs into the inside of the kayak walls. The ride was equivalent to that of a bucking rodeo bull, but we remained strong and paddled on. I was impressed with Maruia's strength and stamina and calmness under such danger and pressure.

The ominous storm loomed on the horizon and sent strong wind gusts in our direction as if to blow us back to Rahiti. We couldn't even talk to each other over the sound of the howling winds. My stomach churned, not from sea-sickness, but rather from nausea thinking about Lance's safety – or the repercussions of not getting him off of the island in time. I watched as Tane struggled to paddle his kayak solo and I hoped and prayed that Lance would be paddling back home in it with him.

Every few strokes we took seemed to be counteracted and undone by the current, the push of the waves and the strong wind gusts in our faces. I didn't care if I had to paddle all day – I wanted to get to Lance. Maruia and I paddled on and pulled ahead of the other two kayaks. Rahiti was out of sight behind us and Mata was not yet in our sights in front of us. We were somewhere in the middle between the two islands. The turbulence of the seas could have easily caused us to lose our bearings had it not been for the storm on the horizon which acted as our beacon toward Mata Utu. It was hard to tell where the storm clouds ended and the rough seas began on the horizon, but we remained focused as we paddled into the distant storm. Several lightning bolts flashed across the eastern sky and illuminated where the rising sun's rays were obscured by the clouds. In the sudden flash, I saw Mount Mata rise from the sea. The island blended into the storm clouds on the horizon, but for one eerie moment was illuminated against the backdrop of the pitch black clouds. The sight scared me, yet invigorated me to row faster. Maruia saw the same thing as she turned her head to give a slight nod and acknowledge that she had seen the same thing. I turned to check on Hoanui and the guys who were struggling to keep pace with us.

We all began to stroke harder and faster at a pace that I didn't think was possible. However, it seemed like the faster we paddled, the faster the wind blew in our faces. Maruia's hair danced violently in the breeze and the salty, foamy water smacked us in the face as we struggled to keep our balance and leg-hold in the kayaks. My arms were so pumped from the exertion that I thought my biceps would explode at any time. My back ached from the effort too. Just when I thought I couldn't paddle another stroke, there was another sudden and erratic shift in the wind and current direction. The same wind and current that we had been fighting the entire time just shifted in our favor. It was so odd that it was creepy. The wind swiftly pushed us from behind and the current turned on the conveyor belt and ushered us toward Mata. It was as if the storm was originally pushing us away and warning us not to go toward Mata and since we didn't heed the warning, it finally decided to let us in. I don't know whether that was a good thing or bad thing – the verdict is still out, but my back and arms were happy to get a rest for the moment.

We all took a much needed break from paddling and rested as the storm pushed and pulled us toward Mata. The horizon and sky were so dark with storm clouds that I could barely see Mata with the exception of when the lightning bolts briefly illuminated it. Although the wind and current were finally in our favor, we still struggled to keep afloat and stay aboard the kayaks in the heavy surf, but at least we didn't have to paddle for the moment.

We crept up on the eerie island as the storm lured us in. The approach to Mata was quite different this time than any other visit. It was a far departure from the normal, beautiful view of the island and the surrounding teal green waters. No dolphins were present today either. We rode the surf and hung onto the kayaks for dear life. Going overboard today would certainly mean death or at least a very difficult rescue. I was utterly amazed at Maruia's ability on the kayak. She constantly impressed me with her poise and stamina as she remained steadfast on our mission and undaunted by the perilous sea.

As we neared the island, Mount Mata rose high from the sea above us and seemed to almost connect with the storm clouds. To say that the sight was scary would be an understatement of mass proportion. Mata had shown us her beauty on every visit in the past, but today she was really pissed off and showing her bitch side at its finest. I couldn't wait to get Lance and get the hell off of the island and back to safety. I only hoped that we could survive the paddle back to Rahiti.

We entered the reef cut and steered the kayaks into the lagoon with our paddles. When we arrived at the lagoon, it was the same sheltered serenity that was usually found there. Even with a burgeoning typhoon on the horizon, Mount Mata sheltered the leeward side from the harsh winds. It was an eerie "calm before the storm" kind of feeling. The waves and angry surf subsided, the winds still howled, but only far overhead and to either side of the island. It was as if we had just rowed under and umbrella and wind shield. Lightning bolts still illuminated the sky, but somehow a little sunshine found a break in the clouds above the lagoon – just enough to illuminate the beach for us.

We didn't have to look far to find Lance. He was sitting on the beach at the lagoon in a calm, meditative state. A ray of sunlight shone down on him. It was weird to say the least. He stood and greeted us with calmness and lack of emotion as I quickly coasted and beached the outrigger on the sand in front of him. I was so happy to see him alive and well that I tossed my oar and bailed out of the kayak to run to him - leaving Maruia behind momentarily.

"Holy shit, bro. Thank God you are alive. We've gotta get the hell out of here. This situation is bad – this storm brewing – everyone thinks Mata is angry and it's your fault. Hop in the kayak with Tane and lets go, bro. NOW." I said with authority.

Lance looked me dead in the eye with a calm resolve and said the most fucked up shit I'd heard all day. "You didn't bring your board dude? Today is the biggest surf I've ever seen – and you're not gonna ride? What happened to your eye?"

I didn't know how to respond to his bullshit. He looked possessed or something. "Surf? Have you lost your freaking mind? We just surfed the outriggers here through the worst seas I've ever seen. We are all fortunate to still be alive. No one is surfing - not today." I tried to keep my cool and stay composed, but Lance was plucking my every last nerve. Hoanui and the others approached and stood by my side. "My eye – what happened to my eye? What's wrong with you, Lance? This is your fault - you hit me in the damn eye and now you are putting everyone in danger by being here. Why, bro?"

Arenui chimed in to back me up. "Yeah, brah – we risked our lives to come and save yours. Be smart dude. Surfing – no way, not today."

Lance stood there a second unfazed before turning his head and nodding it in the direction of the beach on the other side of the spit. "Shhhh." He said to quiet Arenui and silence Hoanui before he could even begin speaking. "Listen. You hear that? It's beautiful, precious – it's my melody. It's calling my name." He said as he stared off in the direction of the point on Mount Mata.

There were many sounds in the air at the time. The whistling of the wind far overhead and on either side of the sheltered cove rustled the palm leaves violently. The crack and boom of lightning and thunder rumbling in the distance was a constant reminder of the ominous storm looming not too far away. Rainfall could be heard hitting the leaves in the jungle as well. But nothing was more profound than the sound of the breaking waves as their thunderous booms could be heard for miles all over the island as the sound echoed off of Mount Mata from the point to the spit. It was this cadence that held Lance's attention. It was this hypnotic beat that kept his heart beating. Maybe it was the manifestation of the Matain curse and the Congo drum beat of the once mighty cannibals. I didn't know and I really didn't care. I was here to rescue my brother and I wanted to get off the island as soon as possible.

"Come and follow me." Lance said as he left his surfboard on its side at the base of a tall palm tree. He beckoned us to follow him as he walked up and over the sandy spit that separated the lagoon from the violent sea. We reluctantly followed as the wind intensity increased as we left the calm, protected lagoon.

The sight on the beach side was surreal. The storm was hanging in the sky just past Mount Mata. The red sun hung in the sky just above the storm and tried its best to cast rays of sunlight through the dense, dark clouds. I can't remember ever seeing a storm like this let alone a sight like this in my life. The sight was incredible. I wished I had my camera, but I quickly dismissed the thought as I snapped a mental picture of the sky-scape. Lance stood there staring in amazement as well, but not at the storm or the sky – in fact, I believe he was utterly oblivious to the sky. He was fixated on the wave that was breaking and peeling offshore and parallel to the beach.

"It's huge, bro." I said with both surprise and wonderment. "Too huge." I reinforced my disapproval of any attempt to surf.

"It's perfect." He said as he stood there motionless as he appeared to stare at the surf in a trance."

"What would be perfect is if we all made it back to Rahiti alive." Maruia quickly interjected. Lance didn't respond or acknowledge her comment.

"Lance, we must go. We cannot let you surf that wave and you cannot stay here any longer. You are putting all of us in great danger by being here. We have to leave now." Hoanui encouraged with authority.

Lance didn't budge or change his demeanor at all. He only quietly responded "I'm one with the island now. Mata is my mother now. I have a bond with her." He said as he continued his stare.

"Your fucking bond is about to unleash a devastating storm on us and the other islands as well. Lance, we have to go now." I said with firm resolve.

"Okay, let's go then." Lance finally conceded as we turned our backs to the wind and made our way back to the lagoon.

We passed Lance's surfboard as we walked across the backside of the spit. "Leave it – we will get it tomorrow – it's too rough to take it on the outrigger with us." I said to Lance as he followed slightly behind me. He didn't respond.

I was happy to be leaving, but was apprehensive about the paddle back to Rahiti. I said a quick prayer to myself in hopes that we would all be able to make the return trip safely. We got to the outriggers and prepared to board them as I helped Maruia into ours. Hoanui and Arenui pushed their kayak down the beach and into the water. Tane prepared to push his and turned to ask Lance for help. "Stan. Where did Lance go?" Tane hollered to me through the wind.

"Shit." I yelled back as I left the outrigger and ran back up onto the spit. Lance's board was gone and he was nowhere in sight. He must have split in a split second. He couldn't have gotten far as he was only missing for a few seconds. I took off running down the familiar trail that I had run dozens and dozens of times. Hoanui and Arenui followed and I assumed Tane and Maruia would eventually do the same. I had no time to waste. I couldn't let Lance go in the water – it would be suicide. Lance had saved my life after the reef incident and now it was my time to save his. I didn't care if I had to knock him out and drag him back to the kayak and tie his hands together. I wanted to save his life.

I ran like I had never run before - leaving the Rahitian guys in the dust. The wind blew hard in my face and huge raindrops began to pelt me. I expected to see Lance ahead of me on the trail at any time. I got déjà-vu from the last time he left me and went ahead. Last time he had a substantial head start of 20 minutes or so – this time not the case. Last time we were both running with surfboards – today my hands were free and he was encumbered with his board and also high winds to contend with. It should be easy to catch him this time. I ran full sprint. Lance was not a runner – only a surfer.

Every turn I made in the trail brought anticipation of seeing Lance around the corner. I ran barefooted through the muddy soil and trampled straight through water puddles with ease. The mud puddles in the trail invoked thoughts of Lance and Arenui's mud-wrestling episode a couple months prior. I would have laughed for a second, if only in my mind, had the current situation not been so grave.

Soon I was over halfway through the jungle trail and Lance was still not in sight in front of me and the Rahitians were not in sight behind me. It was not possible for me to pick up the pace because I was already running full speed. I had proven my running ability time and time again. I had run every morning back home in the States. I ran on the beach in Rahiti – beating Hoanui and the others in races several times. All of that had been practice for this moment – to catch Lance.

My mind reeled with the impossibility that Lance could outrun me – especially since he was carrying a surfboard. It just wasn't possible. But the impossibility became more of a possibility the closer I got to the clearing before Mount Mata. When we originally came on the trip, Lance couldn't run to the bathroom without getting winded. He never chose to run or workout with me. I just couldn't fathom the change. I knew I hadn't gotten any slower and it seemed impossible that Lance could have gotten that much faster in such a short period of time.

As I reached the clearing I finally saw Lance ahead of me as he was already climbing the rocky path up the side of Mount Mata toward the point. The unbelievable became a reality as he was about to beat me to the point. I kept running with him in my sites. My feet transitioned from the soft soil and hit the rocky ground and I grimaced with pain – not from my feet, but from the thought of Lance launching off of the point. I had to catch him. I breathed in deeply as the force from the misty, damp wind caused me to momentarily lose my balance now that I was in the open and out of the shelter of the jungle. I saw Lance strain to keep his board by his side as the wind played havoc on him as he climbed the hip of the volcano. I started to foot on him and close the distance between us. This was my last chance to catch him and I knew it. I climbed like a monkey as I steadily closed the gap between us. The wind and the rain made the climb treacherous. Lance descended the back side of the hip as I just reached its summit. I called out his name in a futile attempt to stop him. The attempt was in vain as the wind blew my words back in my face. It wouldn't have mattered anyway. He had no intention of stopping.

When I reached the summit of the hip, he was already well on his way to reaching the point. I jumped from ledge to ledge down the back side of the volcano. The point was obscured from my vision by the spray from the surf and the rain, but I could see Lance's bright green board less than one hundred feet ahead of me. I closed in on him quickly as he seemed to slow down on his approach to the point. He must have finally realized that it was not plausible to launch and surf from the point today. He must have had his own epiphany and changed his mind.

I finally caught him at the start of the point. Remarkably, I was out of breath and he was not. I could barely speak to him as he stood there, board under his arm, gazing out at the breaking waves on the point. The wind blew us both backwards with every gust. He held his surfboard tight to his body and leaned into the wind.

"Lance, please come to your senses. Don't do it." I tried to reason with him and talk him out of the suicidal ride. I tried to appeal to him by reminding him about all of the thousands of waves he would miss out on the rest of his life it he died today.

He wouldn't hear it. In fact, he said "If these are really my last moments, I am glad I am spending them with you. Let's not make this unpleasant or an argument. If I am going to die, this is how I want to go. My mind is made up. Surf, swim or walk, dude – see you at the boat."

"You don't have to die, man. Live to surf another day. Suicide is foolish." I urged and pleaded with him.

"It is totally my right to die if I choose. This is how I choose to go, bro." He said with resolve.

"Lance, please don't do this." I implored in between my labored breaths as he stood firm on his position – ready to fight if necessary.

He turned to me and locked eyes with me as he seemed to find momentary sanity in his crazed mental and physical state. "Stan, my brother, I love you. But I don't want to live anymore. I can't go on like this one more day. Surfing is my life and it will also be my death. Please let me go. It's what I want." He stood there staring at me with eyes that begged for forgiveness and understanding.

He put me in an awkward position. He was making me choose between fighting him to save his life or fighting myself to let him die. I could either do what I thought was right or give him what he thought was right. It was a tough decision, but I knew what the right one was. If I fought him, I may lose and he would still launch into the water and then my last memory of my brother would be another fight – I didn't want that nor did I want another black eye. If I won, I would have to hold him captive against his will and it would only be a matter of time before he found a way to end his life. It was the toughest thing I had ever done in my life, but I extended my arms and hugged him – board and all. Then I whispered in his ear. "I love you brother. Walk, surf or swim… I still love you man."

235

He hugged me back with his free arm and we embraced each other tightly for a few moments. Then I felt him release his grip as I did the same in return. I looked him in the eye one last time as he turned his head back in the direction of the point. His body and board followed suit and he took off running across the foam-covered rocky point and launched into the wind and off of the point in between two huge breaking waves. I strained to see him as he managed to make the launch and turn his back on the gigantic wave that was welling up behind him. He looked like a fly on a wall in comparison to the size of the wave, but his desire was larger than life. His desire propelled him down the face of the wave as he made the drop of all drops. I was able to keep him in my sight for a few moments as he dropped down the towering face and made his bottom turn. It was a glorious sight. Once again I wished I had my camera with me, but I snapped a mental video of what would certainly be his last ride. He dropped with perfect timing into a quadruple overhead pitching, thrusting barrel. I swear I could barely hear his scream of jubilation from the point as the wave rolled past. I watched from above in disbelief. The wave was by far the biggest, fastest, loudest wave I had ever seen. It was barreling and closing out 3 times faster than the typical right at Mata. Plus the face was bumpy due to the erratic winds and storm-driven surf. I knew he would have to have a more than perfect ride to pull out of the tube at the spit. I knew that the probability of survival was minimal and almost non-existent.

The wave was thick, meaty and hollow as the veil of water broke and pitched far ahead of the trough. Then suddenly the wall of water collapsed and sent a spray skyward that rained down on me as I stood on the point. The thunderous roar of the wave boomed loudly – I knew it was the sound of my brother and one hundred thousand tons of water crashing into the reef. I waited and looked intently as the gigantic wave broke and peeled down the reef sending a huge secondary wave past the reef and on to the beach beyond. That was it - close out time. The wave was too big for the reef below to handle. The wave was done – and most certainly, so was Lance. I stood there for a few moments waiting to see if Lance would emerge from the foamy, frothy surf. I waited to see his board floating in the impact zone. I knew even if I did see him, there was nothing I could do. Diving in after him would be pointless and suicidal. I breathed in deeply and prayed to God to free Lance from his turmoil and misery. Although I prayed for his survival, I knew that my prayer meant death. I just hoped it was quick and painless and liberating. The next wave then broke in the same spot – and then another, and another.

I remembered how painful my reef incident had been. I remembered how helpless I had felt caught in the impact zone. I remembered how Lance had come to my rescue and certainly saved my life. I remembered the size of the waves that day and knew they were only about a third of the size of the storm generated surf today. It was hopeless. It was over. My brother was gone. I didn't shed a tear because I knew he got what he wanted. Today would now be "The Day" – the day I lost my brother.

"Walk, surf or swim - Walk" I thought as I turned to walk back down the volcano. It was the longest walk of my life. Although I couldn't see that far due to the rainbow mist and spray in the air, I knew the Lance had not emerged at the spit. As I climbed down Mount Mata back to the clearing at the beach, the locals met me in solemn tone. They saw Lance's last ride too from the beach. They saw the entire barrel close out and spit just as he was getting into it. We expected to find his tattered body and shattered board at the spit. I knew the pain of getting tossed into the reef on a much smaller wave and prayed that if we did find Lance, he would be resting in peace – far from pain and agony – both physically and mentally. I looked at the scars on my leg and elbow from my reef wipeout. I knew that an impact from a wave that size into the reef was not survivable. I also knew my brother and his board may be buried in the reef permanently.

We all walked back down the beach toward the spit instead of through the jungle trail. We all hoped that Lance would turn up, but as we looked to the sea an odd thing happened. The storm that had been bearing down on the island all morning seemed to be dissipating and moving out to sea. The wind shifted and subsided. The surf seemed to calm down almost instantaneously. The booming of the waves and the thunder in the sky became more muted and distant. By the time we had reached the spit, the winds had almost completely calmed and the sun's rays began to shine down on the beach. The storm magically disappeared toward the horizon.

We lingered on the sandy spit for a while. No one said a word. We each just silently mourned and prayed in our own ways. There was no sign of Lance or his board anywhere. I didn't expect there to be. He was one with Mata now. This would be his permanent home.

Reluctantly, we all headed back to the kayaks as I took one last look at the surf from the spit. The sea on the lagoon side of the island had completely flattened out and calmed as if the storm had never happened. The teal water looked peaceful and inviting. We boarded the kayaks in silence and paddled across the lagoon. Once we reached the reef cut, we discovered that the current was swift and favorable in the direction to carry us away from Mata as if to say 'go home and do not return.'

As Maruia and I paddled back to Rahiti I had a long time to think about the moment that my brother launched off the point for the last time. I had the opportunity to fight him or stop him, but instead I gave him a hug and let him go. We both knew it would be his last wave. I felt I was fortunate to have the opportunity to hug him and say goodbye one last time. Some people never get the chance to say goodbye and have a last moment with a loved one – some die unexpectedly, some die far from their loved ones, some die in close proximity physically but estranged emotionally. I was glad Lance and I had made our final moment together peaceful and pleasant. Not many people get to choose how they will go as Lance did. I thought about everyone back home who perished on "The Day." They had no idea death was coming. They were walking down the street, driving their cars or sitting at their desks one minute and then incinerated in a nuclear blast a split second later. Is it better to know it is coming or not? Is it better to choose your own death or let fate handle it – or is it fate that lets you choose it? So many people do heroic acts as their final farewell - was Lance's heroic or idiotic? How could he justify taking his own life? He was clearly ready to die. His will to live was gone. I couldn't sympathize though – I loved life too much in spite of the radical changes I had experienced over the course of the trip. I still had too much life and drive left in me. I reasoned with myself that it would have been selfish to make my brother persevere and survive and continue to live in misery just for me. I found peace and resolution in my decision to let him go. I released him to the hands of God and the universe.

I decided to keep our last moment on the point together a secret between Lance and me. I wouldn't let anyone know that I had a chance to stop him. I didn't need to deal with anyone else's opinion on my decision. It was done and over – that was that. It would be my mental struggle and mine alone for the rest of my life. Rest in peace, Lance.

The Lost Brother

Lance's death catapulted me into a new state of mind. It was as if I had inherited his negative energy. The days after his last ride became the saddest days of my life. I tried to fight off my sorrow, but I found myself totally unable to eat, sleep, concentrate or function on any level. I became consumed with grief and loneliness. I still tried to appreciate the beauty of my surroundings, but I just couldn't find my positivity. I tried to find gratitude and appreciation again, but no amount of either could fill the void in my heart. I truly realized how much I cared about my brother and the role he had played in my life. He and I had balanced each other out perfectly somehow. He was the grief while I was the gratitude. He was reclusive while I was outgoing. He was negative and I was positive. Now I found myself burdened with both sides of the emotional spectrum. It was as if the universe had willed his energy to me. I wanted to continue to enjoy my surroundings and the people around me, but I just couldn't find inner or outer peace. I wanted to be happy for Lance that he had gotten his wish, died by his choosing and moved on to a better place to become one with the universe and reunite with Jasmin, but grief overcame my positive emotions.

I sat in the floor of the hut that was once ours and rummaged through the Rubbermaid container full of Lance's stuff. His size 40 board shorts were folded and stacked on one side of the container. They didn't fit him anymore anyway since he had lost so much weight. He had been wearing my 32's for the last couple of months. In fact, he was wearing one of my favorite pairs on his last ride. I didn't miss the shorts at all – I missed him immensely though. I perused through the container more and saw the wetsuit that Lance wore the night the hut flooded from the rain. I looked over in the corner of the hut where he sat huddled in misery that night. The memory was vivid - in fact so vivid that I swear for a second I saw him sitting there again. I shook off the delusion and returned my focus to the container. I picked up the satellite phone from inside the Rubbermaid and powered it up. The battery was half charged. I waited for a signal, but none came. I tossed the phone back into the container along with all hopes of talking to my family, friends or Lance again. I remembered the night when Lance found the gun - I wished that unpleasantness had never transpired. I wanted to erase all negative memories, but I just couldn't do it. I snapped the lid back on the container and put it in the corner of the hut.

Distance and uncertainty had provided a unique shield from the terrorist acts of the "The Day." My heart ached and was filled with sympathy for those back home in The States, but I was far removed from the situation and had found solace in the south Pacific – and the fact that my brother had been here with me. He was my one and only connection to my past life, and although I had decided to no longer live in the past, it was nice to have someone who could relate to it with me. Now that he was gone, the reality of everything came crashing down on me hard. All of the grief that I felt since "The Day" had been subdued and channeled into my effort to stay strong for Lance. Now he was gone and I not only lost my brother who I loved more than anything in the world, but I also lost my outlet for my emotions. I became grief-stricken and lonely. The Rahitians saw my shift and tried to comfort me in the same fashion that I had done for Lance. In spite of the locals' efforts to comfort me and be there for me, I felt helplessly alone. All hope of a happy and 'normal' island life seemed to have abandoned me. I knew things would never be the same here again for me.

Life in Rahiti changed dramatically. Everything I saw reminded me of Lance. I even had a difficult time looking at the ocean because every wave I saw reminded me of him. I couldn't bear the thought of never surfing with him again. Hell, I couldn't even bear the thought of surfing again. I tried to control my emotions, but was not able to handle the stress. The pain was unbearable. My thoughts were convoluted. My mind and body were ransacked with stress and lack of sleep. I couldn't do my chores or eat. I had become resistant to the locals – even Maruia. I didn't want any attention or anything from anyone. Solitude was my preference in spite of my loneliness. I was becoming what Lance had become and I didn't like it. We all grieved for Lance and the world in our own unique ways. My way became solitude and meditation.

I still continued to do my morning yoga sessions, but usually by myself on a secluded part of the island. The girls really missed the morning ritual, but seemed to understand that I needed to be alone. I still continued to run, but always alone. I still maintained my water intake and remained hydrated, but didn't eat much. Lance had been slightly overweight and his excess baggage enabled him to survive without eating. His weight melted off of his body and fueled him through his lack of appetite. I did not have that buffer. I had to force myself to eat to survive.

Kava Kava root became my best friend. I harvested basket loads of it and chewed it constantly. The earthy, succulent root was one of the only things I could find to calm my nerves and bring peace back to my body. I still continued to garden. I needed something to tend to and nourish and the garden was a good release for me. The bounty of fruits, veggies and herbs that the garden yielded was astounding. It seemed as if when one fruit was picked from the plant, two rapidly replaced it. I wished Lance could grow back and come to life again like a fruit.

The garden was now able to sustain the needs of the entire Rahitian tribe aside from all of the natural fruits and plants that were there prior to my arrival. It was an awesome thing to know that I had contributed that to the island. I appreciated the bounty the garden yielded, I just wished I had the desire to indulge and eat it myself. I would force myself to take a bite of fruit from time to time, but couldn't even finish a whole succulent mango. My nerves just wouldn't allow my mouth to enjoy food or my stomach to accept it.

My mind had shifted again and my focus changed to something else. I knew I had to get away for a while. I needed to find something else to occupy my time and energy. I wished for something different. And just as the wish left my mind, it was immediately granted.

I sat on the beach alone at mid day and watched the tide roll in as I saw something appear on the horizon. At first I thought my eyes were deceiving me, but soon the sight became more visible. Chet was motoring his way toward the beach on the pontoon boat. I sat and watched as the vessel powered its way through the calm sea. He approached the beach and powered up the engine so that he planed the nose of the boat up as the wake carried the pontoons high in the water and allowed them to glide onto the beach.

"G'day mate." Chet hollered as he jumped off of the bow of the boat and walked up the beach where I met him halfway. "How's life in Rahiti?" He asked in his Aussie accent.

I simply responded "It's changed a lot."

"Where's your bro? Not surfing today?" He asked.

I remained silent for a minute before telling him what had happened. He didn't ask twice. He consoled me and his cheerful demeanor quickly subsided as the news unfolded. He informed me that life in Tahiti was very different as well. Food was scarce in spite of the fact that the government had finally allowed the remaining cargo ships offshore to come into port. Once those ships came in and unloaded their cargo, commerce had ceased. Nothing else was coming or going. People were in seclusion and the attitude on the entire island was that of hopeless despair. His work at the port was minimal since no cargo was arriving or leaving. There was no transit anywhere as the fuel supply on the island had all but run out except for the emergency reserves that the government held. Communication was non-existent except for local air traffic. Tahiti was completely cut off from the rest of the world as well.

Chet was hungry and restless and sought an escape from his world. I was happy to take him to the village and share the bounty of food that we enjoyed. Chet fell in love with Rahiti and decided to stay for a while. He and Tania took a liking to each other and began to spend a lot of time together. Chet and Arenui surfed occasionally, but I didn't join them. The thought of surfing brought too many memories of Lance. So I gave Chet my surfboard and watched them instead. Chet took over many of the chores that I had once done. He became a welcomed guest on the island and brought something different to the tribe. Even hearing his Aussie accent was a fresh change.

Maruia, Tania, Chet and the others tried to lighten my spirit and re-interest me in life. I didn't openly show any negativity, but it was obvious that I had changed. I remained cordial to everyone, but withdrawn – spending most of my time alone walking, running, practicing yoga, gardening and meditating in seclusion. It was okay to pass the time, but I needed something different. I had an idea in mind, but kept it to myself temporarily.

Chet stayed in Rahiti for over a week before deciding to return to Tahiti. His burgeoning relationship with Tania and his life in Rahiti was a beautiful thing, but he needed to return to Tahiti momentarily if just to say goodbye to his former life. He informed the tribe that he would be leaving for a week or so, but returning soon to stay longer. He invited me to join him and I quickly accepted. Tahiti may not be pleasant either, but it certainly was a change. And that is exactly what I needed – a change!

Chet and I loaded up the pontoon boat with food and water and then fueled up for the trip to Tahiti. We took more than enough fruits and veggies to feed us for a couple of weeks and enough to share with some of Chet's friends. I filled dozens of my Fiji water bottles from the Stan-dunk sink and packed them too. Maruia helped us in our packing efforts and hinted multiple times that she wanted to go too. I had hoped that she would understand my needs at the moment – and my needs were to be alone. I had hoped that I wouldn't even have to tell her how I felt, but that wasn't the case. I didn't want to have an awkward conversation with her, but I also didn't want to leave my feelings untold – I learned my lesson about that from my regrets about not saying things I should have said to people back home. I realize that I may never have the chance to talk to them again and say the things I should have said. I didn't want that to be the case with Maruia. So I invited her to take a long walk with me before I left for Tahiti.

We walked along the beach together in Rahiti as the sun peaked in the sky. The day was beautiful and so was she. I had not only felt disconnected from the island and nature since Lance passed, but I also felt extremely estranged from Maruia – and that was my fault. I grabbed her hand as we walked and I tried to connect physically with her before I started a conversation. Her radiance was still there although I had not been receptive to it. I let my negative emotions go for a minute as her energy came flowing into my body. Just touching her brought a smile to my face. It had been a long time since I last smiled – it almost felt awkward to do so again. It had also been a long time since I spoke and shared my feelings with anyone.

"Maruia, I want you to know something." I said as we stopped walking and I turned to look into her eyes. She didn't say a word, but waited intently for me to continue. "Many things out of my control have changed since I arrived on this island, but the one thing that hasn't changed is my feelings for you. You are a brilliant and beautiful young lady with a kind heart and loving soul. You have brought joy into my life in so many ways and I appreciate that so much. Just thinking of you has brought me countless amounts of pleasure. I love you very much." My words flowed off of my tongue and into her ears and affected her emotions immediately.

She smiled, but remained silent as she pulled me close to her. Our eyes remained locked as we embraced in a passionate kiss. It was the first physical contact we had since the night before Lance's death. It was the first inkling of passion I had felt since that night – which ironically may have been one of the most passionate moments of my life. But my passion quickly subsided this time. It wasn't her, it was me. She was still the same – I was different.

"I don't know how to say what I'm feeling right now. I can't put it into words. But I feel I owe it to you to tell you how I feel." She silenced me by kissing me again. I curtailed the kiss and continued talking. "Look, I feel like I need you and want you in my life, but I feel like I need to be alone more than anything else right now. I don't know why. Maybe it's because everyone I loved has perished recently. Maybe I'm afraid the same will happen here and now to you – I don't know what my issue is. I just feel like I need to be alone for a while. I feel like I need a change. I feel like I lost my soul. I am going to go to Tahiti alone for a while, but I promise I will return."

She pulled me close to her, wrapped her arms around my body and hugged me as she whispered in my ear. "I know Stan. You do what you need to do right now. Don't worry about me – I'll be right here waiting for you. I love you too."

Her words almost brought tears to my eyes. Hearing those three words 'I love you' is so comforting and refreshing – especially when backed by the emotion and truth of someone as special as her. We held hands tightly and walked the remainder of the beach in silence and just enjoyed each other's company and the beauty of our surroundings.

When we returned to the pontoon boat, Tania and Chet were making final preparations for departure. Some villagers gathered to see us off. Tane was there as if to make sure that Maruia stayed behind on Rahiti. I think no one was happy about us leaving – except for him. Matahi himself blessed the pontoon boat and prayed for our safe return. Chet kissed Tania on the cheek and said goodbye for now. Chet promised to return safely to Rahiti soon. Without further ado, we shoved off from shore on the well-stocked boat. As we reversed off of the beach and backed into the sea, Maruia blew a kiss to me and smiled. I knew I would miss her for a bit, but I knew I would see her again soon. I promised myself that.

The Mareva

Chet and I motored across the sea to Tahiti and my mind began to wander and my spirit began to lift. Chet, however, seemed nervous and preoccupied with something. He was constantly scanning the water and looking over his shoulder. I sensed that he felt something was wrong, but I didn't know what.

"What's eating at you bro?" I asked in a tone and strong enough voice to overpower the wind and the roar of the outboard engine.

"Pirates." Was his one word response.

"Really? In these waters? Here?" I asked in disbelief.

"Probably everywhere right now, mate. The world is in turmoil and people are desperate. Who's gonna protect you out here, huh? A starving pirate or desperate passer-by would cut our throats just for the food we have onboard, let alone the boat and the fuel in it. I don't like feeling vulnerable, but the reality is that we are. This 'ol pontoon's not outrunning anything and we are defenseless if attacked by anyone carrying firearms or even a knife. So the best thing we can do is to stay alert." He explained at the top of his lungs.

I dismissed the fear of pirates. It was pointless to worry about a situation that I had no control over. Even being alert and seeing them coming was of no help to us as we had no defense and no ability to outrun them. I decided to focus my attention on things that I could control – like my thoughts and attitude. I took this trip from Rahiti to Tahiti as a starting over point for now – a way to wipe my slate clean for the time being – a way to escape reality and my current state – a way to forget about Lance. I ignored Chet's paranoid antics and let my mind wander into the future.

The boat ride from Rahiti turned out to be safe and uneventful. Chet powered down the engine as the pontoons came off of their plane and coasted through calm waters as we entered the no-wake zone of the harbor in Papeete. Chet knew these waters like the back of his hand and his mind seemed to instantly be put at ease as he navigated the familiar harbor. My mind, on the other hand, came to life at the sight of something familiar. My plan for the future began to take shape right before my very eyes. My pulse quickened and my heart lifted as if I had fallen in love. Indeed I had fallen in love. I fell in love the last night I spent in Tahiti. I fell in love that night I spent with Maruia on the Mareva, but not with Maruia (I already loved her) – with the Mareva herself. I had envisioned the Mareva many times in my dreams and in my mind since that night. Something was attracting me to her and to the sea. I knew that is where I needed to be.

"Ah, you like the Thirty Millie, Mate?" Chet asked as he noticed my head turn to keep contact with the Mareva as we passed her. She was still anchored in the same spot in the harbor where she had been the night Maruia and I visited her.

"The what?" I asked Chet as I momentarily broke my attention to the beautiful vessel to engage Chet's question.

"The Thirty Millie." He repeated as he slowed the boat down more and turned her slightly in the direction of the Mareva. The puzzled look on my face must have been the tell-tale that I hadn't a clue what the hell he was talking about. "That's the nickname I gave her cause she's worth around thirty million or so. Her real name is the Mareva (Mah-ray-vah) though. She's a gem – my favorite vessel in port." Chet explained. "Would you like to meet her – up close and personal?"

"Absolutely." I quickly replied as I tried to subdue my excitement.

Chet spun the wheel on the pontoon boat and turned the boat around to bring us parallel to the Mareva. She was absolutely gorgeous – even more so than I remembered before. The tiny pontoon boat paled in size comparison to the huge yacht as we slowly approached the rear port side of her hull.

"Gotta watch out for her anchor line - I don't wanna rip the prop off of our dingy here by gettin all tangled up with her. Done that before." Chet said as he carefully approached. "Grab the starboard Hawser and cleat her good. We're gonna moor up to the back of her. Hey - belay it tight – don't wanna end up adrift."

Chet's nautical terminology left me in a bit of a quandary. I thought for a moment he may be speaking Greek until he realized I didn't comprehend him fully. He then explained in layman's or 'landlubber's' terms as he put it. "Okay, mate – ship board lesson number one. A Hawser is a line or rope used to tie up a vessel and secure it to something – usually a port, a buoy, or in this case another vessel. It's also called a painter when secured to the bow of a small boat such as ours. A cleat is that shiny metal T-shaped thing bolted to the deck right there". He explained as he pointed in the direction of the cleat. "Belay means to secure or "make fast" a line around a fitting, usually a cleat – like in this case. Mooring just means securing a vessel to something. Now belay without delay, mate. I wanna moor up on the first pass and I don't want to have to come about and approach her again. The less attention we draw to her and ourselves, the better."

His instructions made better sense now and I hustled to fulfill the orders as we glided through the water and came along side the Mareva's massive hull.

"We're gonna go starboard to port on her. Meaning our starboard (right side) is going to meet her on her port (left side) parallel. If I wanted to go port to port, I'd loop around and "69 her" by pointing my bow to her stern. Got it?" Chet asked as he smiled.

"Aye, aye captain. Got it." I responded in my best sailor voice impersonation.

The massive yacht not only blocked out the sun and cast a shadow into the teal green water around us, but she also blocked out the windward breeze and provided shelter for our little dingy from the wind, current and wakes entering the harbor. I understood why Chet chose her port side before he even had to explain.

"She's got a hell of a freeboard, so we are gonna tie up and enter from her rear platform." Chet announced.

"Freeboard?" I asked. I knew what freeboarding was back home - I'd done it many times on my own little runabout boat as we towed a surfboard behind the boat and rode it as a water skier would do. I knew the term did not apply here and must have another meaning.

"Yeah, freeboard is the height of a ship's hull above the waterline. It's the vertical distance from the current waterline to the lowest point on the highest continuous watertight deck. This usually varies from one part of the ship to another. So the rear deck is the lowest freeboard and the easiest point of entry." Chet explained the sailor's term in his Aussie accent as he worked the wheel on the pontoon boat.

"Got it." I said as I readied the Hawser to moor up to her. "I didn't know you were such a seaman." I stated in a complimentary tone to Chet.

"I spent most of my life on the water dude. What do you expect?"

"Right. Of course." I answered.

"Get ready with that line, mate and keep me from bumping hulls. Grab that bumper over there too." He commanded as he eased the pontoon boat up to the yacht.

I leaned slightly over the side of the pontoon boat and extended my arm to touch the Mareva's massive steel hull and to keep distance between her and the pontoon. I didn't want to put a single scratch on the beautiful yacht. I slung the bumper over the side of the pontoon and then stepped from the pontoon onto the rear lower deck of the Mareva. It felt so good stepping onto her again. I found a cleat on her rear deck and began to tie off the Hawser to the pontoon boat.

"Make her fast." Chet instructed. "That means tight and secure – not speed or going without eating!" He continued sarcastically.

"Got it!" I assured him as I twisted the rope in a figure 8 around the Mareva's cleat.

Once I had secured the two vessels to each other, Chet grabbed two papaya from the stash on the pontoon. He tossed me one as he stepped up onto the Mareva's deck.

"Ahhh, my sweet Mareva – my thirty millie. I missed you, baby." He said as he kissed the side of the hull. I guess I wasn't the only one who loved this yacht.

"How long has it been since you visited her?" I asked.

"A couple of months, but I keep a close watch on her." Chet explained as we made our way up the back deck and into the cockpit. "She's a beauty. I've sailed on her many times."

"Really?" I asked.

"Oh yeah, brah. I know the owners– the Yancey's – from LA. I was just thinking about them the other day in Rahiti." He said as his mind seemed to wander a bit. "They were a cool couple in their early forties who visited twice a year and took long sailing voyages through the South Pacific - even to Australia once. We got along great and they always invited me on board when they were in town." He said as he reflected back on the past. "Depending on how you translated "Mareva" it could mean either gift or departure. It was their departure from reality and the world back home." He said as took a deep breath and sighed. He seemed to be very disturbed by the fact that he realized he may never see his American friends again.

Chet was very familiar with the ship as he made his way around the cockpit and reached up under the stowage bin. I knew exactly what he was going for because I had grabbed the very same key myself a couple of weeks prior. I watched and smiled.

"Yeah, so I don't think the Yancey's will mind if we take a tour. In fact, I don't think the Yancey's will be commin' back, mate. I'm gonna miss those blokes. They were about as cool as a couple could be in my book." He said as he fetched the key and directed me to the door leading below deck. He put the key in the lock and turned it causing the door to slide open. "Watch your step on the coaming." He warned as he pointed down at the raised threshold under the door slider.

I stepped up, over and then down the ladder-like stairs into the galley below. The smell of wood and rich furnishings filled my nose. The smell invoked thoughts of the night I spent here with Maruia. I debated whether or not to tell Chet about it. I kept the secret for now.

"So this is the galley and lounge area. There is an awesome bar over there." Chet said as he began the tour below deck. "This vessel can easily sleep a dozen or so guests in first-class style and about a half-dozen crew. She's got 5 berths and 6 heads (or baths) total." He continued as we made our way down the wood-paneled hallway. I admired the ship, its art and fixtures as if I had never seen them before. Even the second time around I was awestruck. Chet noticed my appreciation for the art as he explained some of it to me. "The Yanceys have sailed this boat all over – from Japan to Thailand to Hawaii to LA – and I even accompanied them to Australia and New Zealand once. They collected this art and the furnishings onboard from everywhere they went. I actually took this picture at sunrise from the deck when we were in Dunedin." Chet said as he pointed to a gorgeous 11x14" picture.

We made our way down the hallway and stopped to look in each of the berths along the way as we headed toward the forward berth.

"Notice the height of the deckhead. By the way – deckhead is the ceiling throughout the cabin – not a girl performing fellatio on the ship!" He slapped me on the shoulder in jest as he pointed up to the ceiling. "Even for tall guys like us, it doesn't seem like we are in the cabin of a boat. It's even higher than your typical ceiling height. I love everything on this ship – especially this." He said with excitement as he opened the doors to the front berth.

When the door flung open, I already knew what to expect, but it still took my breath away. The four poster bed that I had slept in with Maruia was perfectly made and there was no sign we had been there or anyone had been in it since. The mirrored walls with half-columns, the Italian leather couches, the glass coffee table with the leaping dolphins all invoked memories of that great night with Maruia. Chet began to explain all of the fixtures to me and how the retractable skylights in the ceilings had been installed as an afterthought in order to get the massive bed and other furniture pieces into the room. The hallway and door openings just weren't big enough. Plus, the Yancey's wanted to lay in bed at night and look at the stars. Chet hit the switch on the wall and the tinted skylights retracted to let sunshine pour in.

"Wow!" I said as if I hadn't seen it before. "What a sight. And it just sits here unused?"

"Yep, unbelievable – hey, mate?"

Chet and I sat down on the leather furniture in the sitting area and looked out through the massive portholes across the harbor. We just soaked in the view for a bit without saying a word. My dreams, thoughts, plans, ideas all came flooding into my brain. I knew what I wanted to do, but kept those thoughts to myself. I had to let something else out though.

"I have a confession to make, Chet."

"What's that Mate?"

"This is not the first time I have been on this yacht – or in this room." I said with a grin on my face.

"You devil – whataya mean?" He asked in his curious Aussie tone as he cocked his head to the side.

"Well, the night I came to Tahiti with..." I started to say Lance, but caught myself. "...Maruia and the Rahitians. After "The Day" – well, we went out walking late. Everyone else was crashed at your place. We knew it would be crowded there, but you were such a good host." I kissed his ass a little and felt him out as to how he felt about my previous uninvited visit on the ship. "We came down to the dock and sat for a bit and I noticed the yachts anchored out here. In fact, I noticed them the first time we were at the port on the day of our arrival. I couldn't get this ship out of my mind. I also couldn't resist the temptation to row the outrigger out here and check it out."

"Aye, did anyone see ya, mate?" Chet asked.

"Nope, we were very careful to remain incognito."

"Good. The less attention the better. I'm not worried about you guys – but there are a lot of people I wouldn't want near her."

"Right – I figured that. So, anyway we secretly rowed out here that night. Port security and everyone else were more worried about the safety of the port and its cargo after "The Day" than a couple of people rowing an outrigger in the harbor." I assured him. He nodded his head in agreement as his tilted head returned to vertical. "So we tied up and boarded in the same fashion that we did today. A hunch told me where the key was hidden – and in a moment or so we were in the cabin. We slept in this very bed. We were very respectful and left everything in perfect order as we found it."

"Indeed you did, you Rascal!" Chet said as he extended his palm in the air to hi-five me. "Believe it or not, I've never even slept in this bed and I've been onboard dozens of times. Man, you are incredible." He said smiling and shaking his head.

"I hope you're not mad. I know you're in charge of all the vessels in port and all... and I didn't want to tell you and risk undermining your peace of mind and security."

"Actually, you just confirmed what I had been thinking all along. She's too vulnerable out here – especially now. I'm damn lucky she's still here. It's only a matter of time before she's looted or stolen." He said with a serious tone. "The world has gone mad. People are in survival mode. Even the most honest of people turn into thieves when their life depends on it. I want to check something." Chet said as he eased up from the leather couch and made his way out of the master suite and back down the hall. I followed him down the hall, through the galley and lounge and up the stairs to the cockpit. Chet took position at the wheel on the helm in the cockpit. He put the key into the console and its insertion freed the wheel from its locked position and brought the console controls to life. He surveyed the instrument panel for a second or two.

"About a quarter tank of petrol." He said referring to the indication on the fuel gauge. "Not enough to get too far, but certainly valuable enough to steal. Pirates would siphon her dry if given the chance. Petrol is like gold right now." He said with concern.

"The fuel seems like the last thing anyone would steal off of this boat – I mean the furniture, art, the ship itself..." I said.

"Yeah, but fuel is for survival. Food and water are for survival – everything else is frivolous and doesn't matter to people right now." Chet explained.

"Hmmm." I said as I shook my head in agreement. Thoughts came rushing into my mind, but I kept them under my hat for now. Who needs fuel when you have the wind and sails?

Chet busied himself in the cockpit checking instruments and equipment. I hopped up onto the upper deck and took a stroll on the beautiful teak-wood deck toward the bow. I stood there on the bow towering above the water as I surveyed the harbor. I felt on top of the world. This was my domain and I loved it. I had become restless on Rahiti. I felt trapped and cramped there – 'island fever' had set in I guess. This was different. The ship was massive, but obviously small in comparison to the island of Rahiti; however, it was the mobility, the motion, a vehicle to the world that intrigued me. I loved the notion of being in motion. Even the slightest rocking of the ship as the tide rolled in was good for my soul.

"Quite a view, ey Mate?" Chet hollered as he walked up the deck toward me. "It's quite astounding every time I see it."

His commentary interrupted my wonderful daydream. "Yeah, it's awesome." I said as I remained focused on the teal green waters of the harbor and the smaller ships surrounding us."

Chet took his place next to me on the bow as we both leaned slightly over the life-line to get a perspective on the height of the ship. I could just picture myself diving off of the bow and into the placid water below. It seemed so refreshing. "Whataya say we take a plunge dude?" Chet asked as he must have been reading my mind.

"Brilliant!" I said as we kicked off our sandals and peeled off our shirts.

We slid under the steel life-line on the bow and curled our toes around the edge of the deck. Chet counted down. "Three, two, one…" And we dove off of the bow. It was an invigorating feeling. The free-fall was only a couple of seconds, but the feeling was liberating and lasted for much longer in my mind. I splashed down into the crystal clear teal green water and my momentum carried me deep below the surface. My ears popped as they adjusted to the pressure. When my descent slowed, I righted my body in the water and held my head back to see the sunlight sparkling on the surface of the water. I kicked my legs together to propel myself back up to the surface as my air supply had nearly run out. Chet and I broke the surface of the water at the same time and let out a "whoop" as we splashed each other like school boys.

"It's cool to swim 'unleashed' in this situation, but if we were out at sea we would be tethered to the ship with a lanyard or long cable. The last thing you ever want is for a sailboat to get away from ya – try out swimming the wind." He said in a serious tone before becoming more playful. "Swim ya under the boat?" Chet asked as he dove below the surface of the water. I followed him as we descended under the hull of the ship and into the shadow it cast below the water. The ship was even more massive from below. The keel of the hull was directly in the middle of the ship and appeared to extend about six feet or so below the hull. The ship above was amazing, but the clear water below it revealed a crystal clear view all the way to the bottom of the harbor maybe 20 or more feet below. We easily swam under the ship and surfaced on the other side. We both floated on our backs and stared up at the sky for a while. It was a very relaxing feeling to just float and enjoy the water. We then made our way back to the rear platform of the ship where Chet pulled down and extended a hidden ladder. We climbed back onto the rear deck and shook the water from our heads and bodies. The sun and light sea breeze started to dry the sea water and leave its salty residue on our skin. I loved the sensation and I loved this boat. I stood there behind the cockpit and stared the length of the ship toward the bow.

"She's about one hundred twenty seven feet stem to stern and the beam is around thirty feet at its widest point." Chet explained. "She was commissioned to be built in 2006 by the Yancey's and she was finished in early 2008. The Mareva is one of the most technologically advanced sailboats I have ever had the pleasure of seeing."

"Wow." I commented as I glanced at all of the instrumentation at the helm.

"You know, just a few years ago it would have taken a crew of at least half a dozen to sail this vessel. Decades ago it would have taken even more sailors to handle her. Now, with the help of technology it is possible for one person to sail this giant ship. It's truly unbelievable."

"How is that possible?" I asked as I stood behind the wheel and stroked the brass and mahogany.

"Lots of automation and perfect technology – millions of dollars of it in fact. That compass alone –" Chet said as he pointed to the glass and brass enclosed instrument on the control panel. "That compass probably costs twice what my pontoon boat does. It is a true magnetic compass, but has a GPS corrector to account for the false magnetic reading of the large steel hull - basically making it dead-on-balls accurate. And that's important when you are in the middle of the sea – a degree or two can mean missing a favorable current and your destination all together."

"What happens if the GPS goes down? Like now – all of the satellites and communications have failed right?"

"Well, let's fire them up and see." Chet answered as he turned the key and brought the console to life. A large, crystal clear navigation screen illuminated and showed our global position and exact latitude and longitude coordinates. Chet keyed in some info and waited a second or two. "Yep, GPS works. Satellite communication link is down. Internet is down."

"How is it possible the GPS still works?" I asked.

"Dunno. Different satellites? Maybe the boat is programmed on its own in case of communication failure." Chet said as he perused the rest of the display. "Wind speed is 3 knots NW. Water temp is 82. Air temp is 84. Barometric pressure is…" Chet continued to read the instrumentation as my attention returned to the beautiful vessel. Chet could tell I was more interested in the rest of the ship rather than the instrumentation. "Good to see ya smiling, Stan." He said as he patted me on the back. "Come on, I'll show you around some more." He offered as he put his arm around my shoulders.

We walked the upper deck and Chet began to explain all of the workings and fixtures of the ship.

"The big pole there in the middle of the ship – that's the mast, mate."

"I knew that much, bro." I responded back with sarcasm.

"Okay, then you know something else? The mast should always point upright. If it doesn't, you might be sinking or in trouble!" He said with a chuckle.

"That makes sense." I replied with a roll of the eyes.

"Ok, these steel cables coming off of the mast and extending to the rear of the deck – they are called backstays. The ones going to the sides of the ship are called shrouds. This big steel horizontal bar – it's called a boom. Do you know why it's called a boom?" Chet asked as he reached up to touch the large steel beam.

"No."

"Boom is the sound it makes when it hits you in the head – so always be careful when midship and make sure your head is clear of the boom. The ship can automatically decide to gybe or rather change from one tack to the other away from the wind. A gybe will turn the stern of the vessel through the wind and swing the boom from one side of the ship to the other. When sailing manually, the skipper or helmsman would holler "ready to gybe", and then the crew would each call "ready!", and as the turn is made the helmsman calls "Gybe oh!". When the Mareva gybes, she does it so quickly and smoothly that you better be out of the way of the boom – especially since you are tall. If you get "boomed" hard enough it's liable to knock you off deck and send you adrift – that's not good." Chet said as he shook his head in accordance with his instruction.

"Where's the sail?" I asked.

"The sail is on a furler inside the boom, hence the thickness of the massive boom. The lines or halyards coming out of the boom are attached to the sail on one end and an electric winch on the other end. Without the electric winches, it would be necessary to "jump the lines" meaning that you would have to put all the muscle you got into grabbing high and pulling low on the lines to raise the massive mainsail sheet. Then someone else would have to work the winch and 'tail' the line so that you didn't end up with a massive pile of tangled rope on the deck with no way to secure or pull taught on the sail. This line here is the downhaul and keeps tension on the sail. These lines are the travelers and automatically adjust the trim on the mainsheet. The "Jennie" or the genoa is also known as the jib – it is the foresail and it is also on a furler. The blocks or pulleys guide the lines or change their direction and add leverage before the line enters the winch. The Mareva does all of the work for you – rarely with fault or incident. The engineers who designed this vessel and its riggings thought of everything. Check out the baggywrinkles." Chet said as he pointed to a soft covering on the mast where the lines protruded. "Smooth as silk and designed to prevent chafing on the lines. Chafing – it's kinda the same as having sand in your boardshorts to rub your willie raw."

"Yeah, I know what chafing is." I answered with a laugh.

"It's important that the lines always run smoothly and freely with little or no friction. Hey, you ever heard the term 'know the ropes'?"

"Uh, yeah – of course."

"Did ya know it was a sailing term? A sailor who 'knows the ropes' is familiar with the miles of cordage and ropes involved in running a ship properly. A good sailor also knows how to tie a good knot in a rope. That's a bowline knot here – one of the most common knots used in sailing. Ok, do you know what a sheet bend is like?" I shook my head no in response. "No? Okay, good - I'll teach you the ropes more later as well as the art of knot tying."

"I'm ready to learn." I stated.

"Great, are you ready to set adrift, get underway and take a little cruise?"

"Really? Of course I am!"

"Alright then, let's unload the pontoon boat. Then we can free the moorings and anchor it." Chet said as we made our way to the stern. Chet handed up all of the food and water as well as our bags and Rubbermaid containers to me on the lower deck. My dream and plan was coming true. I smiled for the first time in a while.

When the pontoon boat was free from the Mareva and anchored fast on her own, Chet swam back to the Mareva and climbed the ladder to the rear deck. We stowed all of the food in the galley and put our belongings below deck in the den for now. The refrigerator in the galley was huge, but was not functional at the moment. Chet explained that we had to charge up the batteries with the solar panels or fire up the generator to get some power going. We decided to wait to fire up the generator until we were out of the harbor. He also wanted to conserve as much fuel as possible. Chet made his way around the deck and checked all of the lines and winches to make sure everything was ready to go.

"Let's see if we've got enough juice to lift the anchor." He said as he stood at the helm behind the wheel. He looked like a natural sailor. I aspired to be the same. He made some instrument checks and then with the push of a few buttons and the turn of a dial, I heard a noise from the bow of the ship indicating that the anchors were lifting. "We are about to be adrift." Chet said as I felt the ship turn slightly in the breeze. "Ordinarily, I would save the engine and leave harbor under sail, but I think we would draw less attention to ourselves if we kept the sails down and cruised out quietly." He said as he commanded the engine to life.

"You know best, Captain Chet." I said with a wink.

I was so excited to be sailing that I couldn't stand it. I had a momentary thought of Mr. Brooks and wanted to tell him about the Mareva. I wondered how it compared to his sail boat in the Hamptons. I dismissed the thought as it invoked a bit of sorrow and I turned my attention to the bow of the Mareva as Chet turned the wheel and the massive ship followed suit and pointed toward the inlet at the mouth of the harbor.

"Ok, mate – navigational lesson. Listen up. Aids to Navigation or ATONS (ATON) are external devices or signs intended to assist navigators in determining their position or safe course, or to warn them of dangers or obstructions to navigation. See those over there?" Chet pointed to some signs as he explained. "These day beacons are unlighted fixed structures on which there are dayboards or essentially street signs. They are numbered, lettered and different shapes and colors – all used to indicate direction, location and water depth. I'll explain more to you later, but the important thing is that when leaving port, the green signs will always be on your starboard or right side. When returning to port, the red signs will be on your starboard – just remember, 'red, right, returning' – easy hey?"

"Easy since you are driving." I said, but I was eager to learn because I had a feeling I would get some helm time soon.

"Thank God for radar and sonar too. That keeps me honest and keeps the ship from running aground on a bar. And I'm not talking about the kind of bar where you order a drink and meet ladies. I'm talking about all of the random sandbars that form, shift and migrate with the currents and tides. A bar will usually form at the mouth of an inlet or river. They make navigation treacherous at times, but ironically offer up shelter from large waves inside the harbor. Bars are bad, but they are more forgiving than a reef. A bar may hold us aground until the tide comes in, but a reef can rip a hole in a steel hull – even one as strong as the Mareva's. There are no shortages of bars or reefs in the South Pacific, bro – especially in these waters. I've gotta be diligent for a bit, so excuse my concentration until we get in open waters."

"Ok, is there anything you need me to do?"

"Nah, just sit tight and enjoy the ride."

I was happy to oblige his command. I took a seat on top of the upper deck and felt the breeze blow in my hair as we slowly turned toward the sea. We were the only vessel in motion in the harbor. The harbor was beautiful, but the quiet calm of the usually busy port was eerie in some way. I couldn't wait to leave the harbor and get out to sea.

The Mareva cut through the water and glided out of the harbor with ease. When we reached the mouth of the harbor, Chet hollered to me "We're outward bound now – meaning we are leaving the safety of port and heading for the open ocean. But first we gotta navigate the overfalls." He said as he pointed to break waters on the shoals. "Those overfalls are dangerously steep, breaking seas. They are caused by opposing currents and wind in a shallow area or by strong currents over a shallow rocky bottom. Either way, we don't want to go overfalls today or any other day." Chet stood at attention and alternated his eyes from the radar and nav screen to the water ahead. I watched intently as the Mareva stayed dead center through the channel and cleared the shoals and reef. "Technology makes this so easy." Chet said as he pointed to the nav screen. "Radar and sonar are lifesavers. Do you know what radar stands for?"

"Nope." I answered.

"It's an acronym for RAdio Detection And Ranging. Radar is an electronic system designed to transmit radio signals and receive reflected images of those signals from an object in order to determine the bearing and distance to the object." Chet explained. "See that thing up on our mast that is spinning?" He asked as he pointed to the top of the mast.

"Yeah." I said as I looked skyward into the sun.

"Well, that's our radar. It's our eyes and ears – in fact it's as good as all five senses to the ship. It shows me depth and anything and everything in it's radius around us."

"What's its range?" I asked.

"Range depends on the setting. Right now I've got it zoomed in for detail and our range is about 20 miles. Once we get out to sea, I can zoom out and have a range well over 100 miles or so."

"Interesting." I thought out loud.

"You know what else is interesting?" Chet asked as he continued to steer the ship.

"What?" I said with curiosity.

"Some other sailing terms I know bro. Do you know where the term 'the cat's out of the bag' comes from?" I shook my head no. "Well, back in the old days of sailing... A short, nine-tailed whip was kept by the bosun's mate and it was used to flog sailors when they misbehaved. When not in use, the 'cat' was kept in a baize bag. When the sailors saw 'the cat come out of the bag' they knew someone was about to get a beating - hence the term ' the cat's out of the bag'. The cat was also called the "Captains daughter" – and, trust me, no one wanted a date with the captain's daughter. Albeit, a date with the Captain's daughter was always better than a walk down the plank though." Chet amused me with his animated explanation of the sailing terminology. I was amused, but more interested in the notion that I was sailing.

"So we are traveling at 6 knots under power right now. Do you know where the nautical term "knots" comes from?" I shook my head no and he continued to explain. "Well, a knot is a unit of speed at sea. 1 nautical mile is 1.8520 kilometers or 1.1508 miles. Originally speed was measured by feeding out a line from the stern of a moving boat. The line had a knot tied approximately every 47 feet, and the number of knots passed out in 30 seconds gave the speed through the water in nautical miles per hour." Chet explained.

"Very interesting." I had heard the term all of my life, but had no idea what it meant.

"A league is a unit of length and is three nautical miles. A fathom is a measure of depth and is six feet. More lessons to come later. Let's get under sail." Chet said as he killed the engines and clicked away at the instrument panel. We were clear of the reef surrounding Tahiti and were drifting smoothly into the wind.

"Right now we are heading windward – meaning we are heading into the wind. The harbor would be leeward meaning that it is in the direction that the wind is headed. The reef and shoals we just cleared are considered a lee shore and a likely target if we are blown down wind. The term for that would be drift – or the lee movement of a ship when not under power." Chet explained as he played with the instruments.

"So how is it possible to sail into the direction of the wind? Wouldn't we get blown backwards?" I asked.

"Not at all. 'Head to wind' is the term used when the bow is turned into the wind. Proper sail placement and adjustment will create wind shear and lift to propel the boat forward in spite of the head wind. 'Hauling wind' is sailing directly into the wind – it has no correlation to the term 'hauling ass' as it is usually not the fastest tack to sail on. 'Running' is the term used when sailing the opposite - downwind. 'Beating' is sailing closer than 60 degrees to the wind. Sailing on a port tack is sailing with the wind coming from the port side, with the boom on the starboard side. Of course a starboard tack would be the opposite of that." Chet said as he pointed in appropriate direction to illustrate his words. "'Fall off' is when you change the direction of sail so as to point in a direction that is more down wind - also bear away, bear off or head down. It's the opposite of heading up, but definitely not what you want to do on the deck – fall off - of it! Ironically it's 'heads up' that keeps you from falling off!" Chet explained in jest. "Sailing 'by the lee' is sailing with the wind behind and slightly to the side that the sails are on. 'Hard alee' is the command given by the captain or helmsman to inform the crew that the helm is being turned quickly to leeward thus turning the boat windward and changing tack and boom direction. Usually the captain would give a head's up warning first by hollering 'ready about'."

Chet turned his head and smiled as he said "ready about".

I heard a 'whizz' and hum and in an instant three sails magically rose from hiding in the furlers and climbed the mast quickly. The light wind caught the sails instantly and filled them with air causing the ship to lean slightly to one side. Chet smiled even wider "We are under sail and under way, mate."

There was something so invigorating and natural about being under the power of the wind. Even the slight breeze had profound effects on the perfectly aligned sails as it propelled the enormous ship through the water. The hull seemed to slice through the sea like a knife through butter. The ship was built for cruising – smoothly and efficiently.

The wind in my hair, the sun in my face, and the rocking of the boat all soothed my mind and body. I felt as if I had just found my calling and my new home. I soaked in the moment in every way possible. Chet realized my mood had changed dramatically as soon as I stepped foot on the Mareva. I had gotten my wish and my plan was coming together nicely – and the best part was that I didn't even have to ask for it. I had purely manifested the situation in its entirety. My thoughts had become things.

"Hard alee!" Chet hollered as the boat abruptly turned 30 degrees as Chet turned the wheel and the boom and sails shifted positions to catch the wind from the new angle. "Right now we are sailing into the wind close-hauled which means our sail are in tight in a position to sail as close to the wind as possible. If we were on a close reach, we'd be doing the same, but the sails would be configured differently."

I loved hearing Chet teach me about sailing. The lingo was cool – especially when rendered in Aussie oration.

"You're a cool dude, Chet." I said to him in a complimentary tone as he stood tall behind the wheel with the breeze blowing through his blond hair. He winked his eye and his well-tanned crows-feet bearing face amplified the expression. "I think this is exactly what I needed. I had no idea you were such a sailor, but right now I'm so glad."

"Everything for a reason, mate." He said as he winked again.

That reason was clear to me. The whole reason I knew Chet – the culmination of it all – every conversation we had, every interaction – it all added up to me and him on a sailboat.

"Hey, dude – wanna know how to always have smooth sailing with the wind at your back and the sun in your face?" Chet asked.

"Yeah, how?"

"Me too – lemme know when you find out how." Chet chided back as he made some adjustments on the controls. "I just programmed our bearing and put her on auto pilot. The Mareva is the designated driver for now." Chet said as he relaxed and took a seat in the captain's chair.

"Hey bro – thanks for this, man. It's just what I needed. I've been dreaming about sailing for a very long time." I said.

"Really, why didn't you say something? We could have been going out long before now."

"I realize that now, but I didn't know then that you were such a sailor. You never told me and I didn't put two and two together bro." I said as I shrugged and quietly thanked my lucky stars that it had been revealed now.

Chet and I spent the next four days straight sailing. We hit Tetioria, Bora Bora, and Moorea where we stopped to spend a couple of nights in Opanahu bay.

"So, this is where the story 'Mutiny on the Bounty' took place." Chet said as we sat on deck in the placid waters of the bay in Moorea. We were almost completely surrounded by land on all sides as the walls of the volcano towered up from the sea around us. At some point in time one side of the volcano wall had collapsed and disappeared into the sea allowing the sea to flood in to fill the chasm and create a perfectly serene bay. I could totally understand why the crew aboard the Bounty wanted to overthrow Captain Cook and stay in this spot. I loved the spot too, but I had and urge – a calling to leave and go elsewhere. We stayed two nights and on the second night we had a long talk on the deck.

"Whataya thinking, mate?" Chet asked as we ate a bowl of fruit on the deck at sunset.

"Curiosity is killing me man. I need to know, Chet. I need to go."

"I know bro. I can tell. I know you have been thinking about going back to the States. I understand, but I hate the thought of you going."

"Why?"

"It's not safe - sailing the open waters by yourself. It's treacherous even for an experienced sailor, let alone a newby like yourself with no open water experience. Plus, factor in the pirates, the weather and the uncertainty of the condition of the world up north… why risk it? You know you are safe here. You know you are loved here. You have everything you need to survive here. Rahiti is totally self sufficient – why would you want to leave such a situation at such a time? I mean, look at me – I live in Tahiti, but can't survive there right now. You have helped me tremendously and I appreciate it. Because of that and our friendship, I want to help you out. I can only imagine your suffering, grief and internal hardships. Whatever I can do for you – I'm here. Whether it means making you more comfortable here by entertaining or helping you out or whether it means me helping you leave – I'm here for you mate."

Chet's words were comforting and inspiring – exactly what I wanted to hear.

While we were sailing I watched intently as Chet worked the computer that controlled the navigation system and all of the workings of the Mareva. It was amazing – he could even control the refrigerator temperature from the helm's control panel. The Mareva was very agile for such a large sailing vessel. We were able to sail around the reefs, bars and shoals with ease as we circumnavigated the islands. Chet seemed to know the channels and currents like the back of his hand, but he seemed to be most concerned about any other vessels on the move so he stayed glued to the radar screen. He truly was concerned about piracy and our safety. He took time to teach me the radar, sonar, GPS, buoys, markings and navigation systems so that I could take turns on watch. I happened to be exploring the controls on the Mareva's navigation system when I discovered that I could program an alarm to sound if there was movement within a certain radius around us – pretty cool. I also discovered some other awesome features including the sound system on board. I soaked in every bit of information I could. I even took the helm at times when the ship was on auto-pilot. I paid attention to anything and everything. I wanted to learn to sail as quickly and efficiently as possible. I knew I had a great teacher and the perfect vessel to learn on. It was on.

We finally returned to the port in Papeete on the fifth day. We found the pontoon boat still anchored in the same spot and every other vessel was also located in the exact same place as when we left. It was as if the entire island was sleeping. Speaking of sleeping, one of my favorite things became sleeping on the upper deck at night. I let Chet sleep in the master suite while I preferred the deck. I loved to lay on deck in the darkness that engulfed the world around me – it was as if I was connected with space and the heavens – I was on top of the world – or at least the highest point in the water for as far as the eyes could see. As I lay on the deck looking out across the harbor in Papeete, I saw all of the sailboats around me. Each had a single white light on top of the mainsail mast. There must have been over 100 boats there resting in the harbor waiting for their owners to return. The mast lights looked like fallen stars. They looked tangible and touchable celestial bodies hovering directly over the harbor as if heaven had descended onto earth. They appeared to be my beacon and my calling. It was my sign and signal that this was my mission - this was my way back home.

Chet announced that he would like to return to his apartment for a few days and then return to Rahiti for a while. He told me that I was more than welcome to stay on the Mareva as long as I wanted. He felt comfortable knowing that someone was looking out for her and protecting her, but he cautioned me not to draw attention to myself and to keep a vigilant watch out for would-be pirates. I dismissed the notion of pirates for now even though he seemed to repetitively dwell on the topic. We divvied up the rest of the food between us and loaded Chet's stuff on the pontoon boat for him to take home. I gave him a majority of the food so that he could share it with his friends in need. I knew that replenishment was just as easy as a one hour boat ride back to Rahiti. Chet said a temporary goodbye and promised to return in a matter of a few days so that we could return to Rahiti.

I made the Mareva my new home. I lived on the giant vessel all alone for the next few days. I fell in love - she was my new epiphany. She was my new life. I felt a calling to return to the US. I knew The Mareva was my answer to my calling.

Leaving Paradise

I spent several days alone on the Mareva anchored in the harbor while Chet tended to business in Papeete. I didn't leave the ship because I didn't have to - nor did I want to. Everything I needed to survive was onboard. I rationed out my food and water supply – not knowing when Chet would return and when I could replenish my supply in Rahiti. Although I wasn't very hungry, I appreciated every life-giving, energy-boosting bite of fruit and veggies I consumed. I was grateful for every drop of water I drank as it quenched my thirst in the heat of the South Pacific sun.

I spent a lot of time exploring every nook and cranny onboard the Mareva. I was like a kid in a candy store. The bar was fully stocked with wine and alcohol although I did not partake of any. I didn't want to – I wanted to keep my mind and thoughts clear. I didn't want to escape reality through the false illusion of drunkenness. I wanted to escape it a different way.

I found some interesting items on board the Mareva that I couldn't wait to ask Chet about. Everything from tools to foul weather gear to some kind of magnetic hand clamps. I pulled out everything from the stowage bins and cabinets to examine it and then put it back in the exact same fashion in the exact same place. It appeared that the Yanceys were just as OCD about organization and cleanliness as me. The ship was perfectly organized just as I would have done it myself if the Mareva were mine. I didn't change a thing.

When I finished exploring inside the ship, I sat on the deck in the harbor watching nothing happen. About the only real movement to focus on was the motion of the sun and clouds across the sky. It was so odd that activity had just ceased in the port and the city. People were just not out doing anything. How long would this continue? How long could I sit still here on the ship? I yearned to get sailing again, but didn't dare attempt it yet without Chet. When would he return?

No sooner did the thought of Chet's return enter my mind than did the sight of him rowing one of the outriggers we left in the harbor last visit enter into my vision. I was overjoyed at the sight of him heading my way as I waited on the rear deck to greet him.

"G'day mate." He said as he drifted up to the Mareva. "Can you toss me a line so I can moor up?"

"Of course, dude. Do you need a bumper too?"

"Nah, the wooden kayak is not going to even scratch the steel hull. Don't worry about it. How was your stay on the Mareva?" He asked.

"It was paradise – heaven on earth if you ask me. How was Tahiti, your friends and your apartment?"

"It was as I expected. I doled out all of my food and water to friends and now I need to go refresh the supplies. How are you holding out?"

"I've still got a few bottles of water and some pomello, mango, papaya, tomato and bananas left. Help yourself."

"I will gladly – I'm parched and starving. How do you have so much left? I hardly left you anything. Did you eat?"

"Yeah, I ate enough. I wasn't sure how long you would be gone so I went into rationing mode. The fridge kept everything cool."

"Ah, you got the fridge cooling?"

"Yep, I figured out how to charge the electrical system on solar power. We've had some strong sun, so I think we are fully charged."

"Look at you – taking initiative – good job mate. What else did you do?"

"Well, I inventoried everything on the ship as I did some exploring. I found some pretty cool stuff, but there are a couple of things I didn't understand. Check these out." I said as I went into the cockpit and retrieved the hand devices.

"Ah, they are magnetic hands!"

"I know they are magnetic, but what do they do?"

"Check this out." Chet said as he slid his hands under the adjustable strap on the back of the device. He then walked to the rear platform and stepped to the edge of the side of the deck. He extended his left hand to the outer hull and with a "clump" sound his hand was drawn and attached to the hull. "When the device is turned this way, the magnet is active. When you rotate it 90 degrees, the magnet disengages. They are used for "climbing the hull" – for cleaning, inspecting and repairing the hull if needed. Gotta have good arm and hand strength to use them though. Let me see what I've got in me. It's been a while." Chet said as he placed his right hand on the hull too. He then stepped off of the rear deck and hung over the water suspended by his hands as they were fixed to the hull. He then rotated his left wrist and his hand swung free from the hull. The weight of the magnetic hand caused his arm to fall and dangle as he freed it – leaving him hanging by only one arm. He mustered up some strength and swung his left arm back to the hull but further down the side. Once that hand was magnetized, he rotated his right one and freed that hand. He was more prepared for the result this time as the right arm did not drop or swing. He moved his hand over to meet his left and then engaged the magnet on the hull. He continued this spider man action a couple more times before becoming tired and disenchanted with the activity. He managed to crawl his way back to the rear deck having only gone a few feet down the hull. "Wanna try?" He said as he pulled the devices from his hands and handed them to me.

"Sure. It looks like fun." I said as I slipped them onto my hands.

"Fun, but a lot of work." Chet added.

I stepped on the edge of the rear deck and reached around to the outside of the hull in the same fashion that Chet had done. When brought into close proximity to the metal hull, the magnetic hands were drawn instantly to the hull and then held fast. I stepped off of the deck and suspended my body weight by my hands and arms. The grip on the magnets was unbelievably strong. My arms and hands flexed and strained as I turned my left wrist to free my grip. When the magnet released, my hand and arm dropped and my body dangled by one arm in the same fashion that Chet had done. It was surprisingly difficult. I swung my left arm back up to the hull and the magnet reattached, but not too far past the previous point. I then released the right hand and swung it over to the left. I was determined to do this. It would be a lot of fun and great exercise too – once I got the hang of it. I had been on many rock climbing walls, but this was entirely different. Chet watched me from above as I slowly crept around the port side of the hull. I knew every movement I made away from the rear would be one more movement I would have to make to get back – unless I did something else to get back up on deck. I kept going down the side of the hull about halfway down the length of the ship until my arms tired. Then I climbed vertical until I reached the edge of the deck where it met the hull. I realized it was going to be impossible to do what I wanted to do with the magnet still on my hand, so I slid my right hand out of the magnet and reached up to grasp the stanchion that held the life line around the deck. I pulled my body up with one hand and then slid my left hand out of the magnet as I grasp the life line with that hand. I then pulled my body up and over the edge of the deck and under the life line. I laid on the deck and reached down and turned the magnetic hands to release them from the hull – being careful not to drop them into the sea.

"Quite impressive, mate." Chet said as he walked down the deck to greet me at my point of entry. "It takes a lot of hand and arm strength to pull that off doesn't it?"

"Yeah, my hands and arms are pumped and feel like they're gonna explode." I answered as I wiggled my fingers and rotated my wrists to loosen them up. "These magnetic hands are quite 'handy'". I added.

"They are. Well, put them away in safe stowage and let's get out of harbor and on our way back to Rahiti. I'm sure Maruia and Tania will be happy to see us again. Plus, my stomach will be happy to get some of their cooking." Chet said as I followed him back to the stern.

Chet readied the Mareva to sail and made sure the outrigger was moored securely to the rear deck in a fashion that would allow it to be towed along for the ride without damage. I stashed the magnetic hands where I found them and grabbed some water and fruit for Chet. Within minutes, the engine was running and we were on our way back out of port. Chet beckoned me to the helm and allowed me to take the wheel. He stood sentry at the helm next to me and guided me out of the port as he ate his fruit. It was an awesome feeling to be in control of such a large ship. Even the slightest motion of the wheel would command the ship to go in any direction I chose her to go. I hoped I didn't have to sneeze while navigating the shoals at the mouth of the inlet.

"She's easy to steer when she's under power." Chet stated. "When under sail, you are not the only one controlling her – she will go with the wind first and the rudder second then."

I couldn't wait to learn how to control her under sail as well. I wanted to harness the power of the wind and save what little fuel she had in her for later. As soon as we cleared the shoals and were a safe distance from them, Chet killed the engines and we raised the sails. I paid careful attention to everything Chet did. I made mental notes of every control and setting that we used. It was a bit more breezy today than it had been the last time we were out, so when the sails filled with air the effects were more profound. Chet programmed our course and set our bearing for Rahiti which showed up on our radar screen.

"We will let the Mareva sail herself right now, but I want you to stand at the helm and pay careful attention to everything she does. Feel the wind and feel the movement of the ship. Watch the configuration of the sails and how they change according to wind direction. Feel the Mareva steer herself. Connect with her and the wind that moves her." Chet explained.

I couldn't think of anything I'd rather be doing than just that. I stood there at attention and took in everything that all of my senses could process at once. My eyes darted from the radar to the navigation screen to the sails to the wheel to the water and then they repeated the same sequence. I also noted the buoys and daymarks through the channel. I was sailing, or better yet, the Mareva was sailing and I was riding and learning.

The sail from Tahiti to Rahiti was swift due to the favorable wind and current. Rahiti came into our sight in a little under an hour of leaving the harbor and we had reached the outer reef at Rahiti within an hour and a half. Chet explained that there was no way the Mareva could navigate into the waters immediately surrounding Rahiti so we would have to anchor her a safe distance from the outer reef and ferry in to shore on the outrigger which was in tow. Initially, I didn't even really want to go ashore, but I realized that would not be the proper thing to do. I should go see Maruia and my Rahitian friends at least for a little while before returning to the Mareva.

Chet chose to approach Rahiti on her leeward side to minimize the chance of drift into the reef while she was anchored. He carefully studied the depth and shape of the bottom of the sea before choosing a spot to anchor. The spot he chose happened to be just outside of the outer break where we typically surfed anyway. That would make for a very easy kayak paddle to the beach that I was so familiar with.

As we lowered sails and dropped two anchors, we prepared the kayak for departure by loosening her lines that secured her to the Mareva. I couldn't help but think of Lance and how many times he and I had surfed the familiar break that we were about to paddle through. I remembered the day that I tossed my gun in the water at that very break to end our argument. My heart ached a bit at the thought, but I tried to subdue my sorrow and convert the thoughts to positive memories. It didn't work very well though. I wished so bad that Lance was on board the Mareva with Chet and I. He would love my future plans.

Chet and I stepped off of the rear deck and into the outrigger, taking care not to flip it over. We grabbed our oars and shoved off from the Mareva and started the short paddle to the beach in Rahiti. By the time we reached the beach, Maruia, Tania, Hoanui, Arenui and some of the tribe had gathered on the beach to greet us. They had seen the massive sail boat approaching and had become curious. They were all delighted to see Chet and I. Maruia ran to me and almost tackled me in the water as soon as I stepped out of the kayak. Chet got a similar greeting from Tania. The girls invited us up to the Stan-dunk for a delicious lunch. We ate and talked and we told them about the Mareva and happenings (or lack thereof) in Tahiti.

"Does Chet know about our visit to the Mareva last time in Tahiti?" Maruia whispered in my ear and then followed her question with an extended breath on my neck.

"He didn't at first, but I confessed and told him later. He didn't mind at all. In fact, I spent every night since I left Rahiti on board her. I didn't even go ashore in Tahiti with him." I answered.

"Really? Why?"

"I love that ship and feel so comfortable on her that I didn't want to leave it."

"Even to come see me?" She asked with a coy curiosity.

I resisted the pause that would have come naturally and answered immediately "Of course not, I've been thinking about you a lot and wishing you were on board with me too. That night we spent together on the ship was amazing. Lying in the bed under the open skylight gazing at the stars just isn't the same when you are alone."

"Well, can we go out for a ride later?"

"I'm sure we can. We need to stock up with some food and I'm sure Chet will want to take Tania too. Hoa, Are and anyone else who would like to join us is welcome to also." I answered, but not honestly. Not to be selfish, but I really didn't want anyone else on the Mareva – except for maybe a brief visit from Maruia. I had thoroughly enjoyed the last few days alone on the ship and I didn't want everyone to get too accustomed to her and want to stay on her too long – which was extremely easy to do. She was the perfect environment of solitude for me and I wanted to keep it that way.

After lunch, I took a walk by myself around the island. I resisted my urge to be reclusive and stopped to say hi to Matahi, Nanihi and many of the other locals that I hadn't seen in a while. They were all happy to see me, but I could tell that they hardly knew how to interact with me anymore. It was as if they all wanted to express their sympathy for me, but didn't know how to broach the subject. So they just left the subject alone. I spent most of my day wandering around alone, but met back up with Maruia before dinner time.

"We are having a tribal dance tonight after dinner. I am looking very forward to dancing for you tonight. I think it will make things a lot better. I remember how great our first tribal dance was. You mastered the dance and the fire walk immediately. You were great. Let yourself go and do it again tonight." Maruia said as we sat on the beach together looking out at the Mareva.

"I'll attend the tribal ceremony tonight, but I'm really not in the dancing mood to be honest with you." I said.

"I know, but maybe I can change that." She answered in a seductive tone as she began to kiss my neck and face. "I missed you so much while you were in Tahiti, but I miss my old Stan even more. Please come back to me baby." She continued as her passion unfolded. I didn't resist her advances, but I also didn't reciprocate as usual either. I still felt passionate toward her, but I couldn't express it the same.

We sat on the beach together for several hours until dinner time. Some of the tribe wandered down to the beach to check out the Mareva and to say hi to me. I made the Mareva the center of all of the conversation to take the awkwardness out of everything else. I promised (against my will) to take many of them out to the ship for a tour. I didn't think Chet would mind and I told myself to get over my own personal issues for now. I just couldn't be selfish and keep her to myself. I couldn't be selfish with my feelings and go into seclusion again – it wasn't fair to my Rahitian friends that truly cared about me.

I took a dip in the ocean to bathe and we left the beach and returned to the Stan-dunk just in time for dinner to begin. The dinner was a feast and included a lot of fresh fish that the tribe had caught that day. Several of the Rahitian fisherman told of how bountiful the fishing had been lately. In fact, they had to release many of the fish they 'accidentally' caught just to prevent them from being wasted since the entire tribe couldn't possibly eat all of the fish they hauled in before they spoiled. The girls also told of how 'fruitful' the garden had become and how it yielded so many fruits and veggies that they could hardly harvest them before they ripened too much on the vine. All of the Rahitians thanked me and appreciated the fact that I was responsible for the garden in its entirety. The tribe was grateful every time they ate from the garden and enjoyed their newfound taste and love of strawberries, tomatoes, cucumbers, lettuce, avocados – just to name a few of the new foods they were introduced to. Their appreciation temporarily brought mine back too and allowed me to enjoy the delicious dinner. In fact, I consumed more food in one sitting than I had in the previous two weeks combined. It felt great to have an appetite and a full belly again.

The wonderful dinner and the return of my appetite invigorated me to take more interest in the tribal dance that would ensue. I got a little excited as the time neared and dinner finished up. Maruia accompanied me back to my former hut where my tribal gear was safely stowed in the Rubbermaid containers. I fetched the container and withdrew the grass skirt, tunic and headpiece from within. Maruia brought the 'war paint' so that she could paint my body. I remembered the first tribal dance and the first time I put the tribal gear on. I remember how Lance had resisted it and how he ultimately gave in, but insisted on wearing his tighty-whitey underwear. I remembered the wedgie I gave him on the way back to the hut. I laughed for a moment, but then the urge to cry came over me. I caught myself and returned my thoughts to positive ones as Maruia painted away on my body.

"Hold still, honey." She said. "I'm making some special markings for you this time. Everything I am painting on your body has meaning."

"Interesting. What does it all mean?" I asked.

"My art tells your story. It tells of a kind hearted man who came from far away to a new land to share himself with a native tribe. It tells of love, courage, intelligence, and talent. It shows surfing, building, growing and also a few other things too." She explained as she made careful brush strokes on my naked body. I knew what the 'other things too' were, so I didn't ask. She continued her painting and the gentle brush strokes felt sensual as they gently tickled my skin. To add to the sensuality of the painting, she would blow lightly on the paint after each stroke to accelerate its drying. I let my mind wander as she painted me from head to toe. I couldn't wait to see the end result of her artistic effort. When she was done, I opened my eyes and surveyed the front of my body from my toes to my chest and arms. The absence of a mirror prevented me from seeing my face although I knew she had spent quite some time on it. The whole painting process had taken well over an hour of her careful attention. I felt honored and privileged to bear the art from her hand. She stepped back and took a long, hard look at my naked painted body. She nodded her head in approval and then proceeded to dress me in my tribal garb. She wrapped the grass skirt around my waist and tied it securely. Then she slid the necklace-like tunic shirt over my head and arranged its beads properly on my chest. Then she placed my headpiece on taking special care not to smudge her paint job on my face. She stepped back again and looked me up and down from head to toe before smiling and nodding her head in approval. "Ok, Stan you look totally tribal and very manly. You are ready now. I'm going to leave you and go get ready myself." She said as she turned and walked out of the hut.

"Can I help you with anything?" I asked out of respect for the time she spent prepping me.

"You can just relax and be you. Meet me at the fire in twenty." She said as she spun around and pranced across the clearing in the direction of her hut. Her hair swung from side to side in accordance with her body motion. She was truly beautiful in every sense of the word – physically, emotionally and spiritually. I loved her so much and I knew I was going to have a major dilemma and a huge decision to make very soon. I felt my heart skip a few beats as I pondered the situation.

I decided to kill twenty minutes by taking a stroll down to the beach. The first person I passed on my way out of the hut was Tane. He stopped dead in his tracks and did a double – even triple take as he saw me. "What?" I asked in as pleasant a tone as I could muster up for him. He did not respond, but based on his eye contact up and down my body, I could tell that my art was the source of his attention. I'm sure he knew Maruia did it and I'm sure he was well aware of how much time must have gone into it. It was one more thing for him to be jealous of.

I shrugged off my encounter with Tane and continued on my stroll. I couldn't help but think of Lance in his tribal gear. I laughed for a moment and then my heart sank the very next moment. I missed him so terribly much. My thoughts were interrupted as I passed Chet and Tania who were heading back from a stroll on the beach.

"Holy shit, mate. You are painted from head to toe. Look at you. Wow. That is some awesome artwork." Chet complimented. Tania concurred with a head nod as they both looked me from head to toe paying special attention to my face. They turned my body around and checked out my back too. Tania began to translate the art and tribal symbols for Chet and me.

"Stan, everyone on the island knows that Maruia loves you. It is no secret. But this really illustrates just how much she cares for you and appreciates you. How long did it take her to do this?" Tania asked.

"I guess about an hour or so." I answered.

"Wow, it would take me a whole day to do the same. I have never seen her display such talent. You are a very lucky man." Tania added.

"I know." I said as I nodded my head to concur.

I parted company with Tania and Chet and continued on to the beach. I took a seat in the sand, but took special care to not mess up any of the artwork on my body. The sun began to set and the sky filled with red and violet hues. I looked out to sea to see the Mareva anchored exactly where we left her. She looked so close, yet so distant. I wanted to be on her right now – alone. I really didn't want any interaction with anyone right now, but I knew the tribal dance would be a special event that I should not miss. Plus, I knew it may be the last tribal dance that I would attend for a while. I convinced myself to enjoy the festivities tonight and worry about the Mareva later.

I heard the drum beats from the start of the tribal dance echo across the island to the beach. That was my signal that it was time to leave the beach and head up to the village. I stood up and lightly dusted the sand from my legs as I began to walk. I turned to look at the Mareva one more time and prayed that she would be safe until I returned.

I reached the clearing and took my place next to Maruia who was already seated in the circle. The drum beats continued and a shout came from off in the distance that was answered with more intense drum beats. Then another cry rang out closer this time and was answered and repeated by the tribe in unison. A moment later Matahi and Nanihi appeared and entered the circle hand in hand. Matahi summoned the drummers to stop and they did instantly on command. Matahi tossed a handful of powder into the fire in the middle of the circle and sparks and flames rose high into the night sky. Matahi then began to pray as all of the Rahitians bowed their bodies and repeated each verse of his prayer in concert with each other.

"We are praying for your brother." Maruia whispered to me in between verses.

"I know. Thank you." I replied quietly.

The prayer continued on for several minutes before Matahi finished and signaled for the drums to start again. Although they prayed for Lance, no one drew attention to that fact toward me – and I appreciated it. The drums quickened and intensified as the tribesmen stood up from the circle and began to head to the center of it to gather around the fire. I preferred to sit this dance out and chill with Maruia, but I knew that it would be odd for me to not participate especially since I had performed so well the last time I did it. I decided I would do the dance, but skip the fire. So I stood up and made my way inside the circle around the fire. Arenui raked coals out of the fire and formed the pit for the dancing circle. The men began to chant "Hola-wola-wola-hi, hola-wola-wola-hi" as the drum beats intensified. My heart rate intensified as well. I just wasn't feeling like dancing, but my leg motion started anyway. We all got in our circle around the fire inside of the outer circle of women. The chanting got louder. "Hola-wola-wola-hi, hola-wola-wola-hi" as the dance began. I ended up on the opposite side of the circle from the fire pit so I had plenty of time to contemplate the fire dance. I decided not to do it, but everyone before me did it for at least a few seconds. It was remarkable that no one – not one man stepped to the rear of the fire pit and wimped out. Last time I did the fire dance it seemed like at least half of the men didn't do it. Now, I felt very awkward not doing it, even though my gut instinct told me to sit this one out. My turn neared as the circle rotated. I prayed that at least one other man would skip the fire, but that would not be the case. Each man did his dance for a few seconds or more then hollered "Hiiiiiieeee" and the circle rotated. My legs kept the rhythm of the drums and I moved my arms from side to side. I hadn't forgotten the dance at all. My motion seemed flawless and in accordance with what everyone else was doing. The circle rotated again and I was now the next man up to jump in the fire. I took a deep breath as the fellow next to me danced for about ten seconds and then hollered "Hiiiiiieeeee." He jumped from the fire as I jumped in.

Right away pain seared through my feet and lower legs. I almost lost my balance and fell from the pain. I stayed in the fire no longer than two seconds before I jumped back, not sideways and exited the fire without hollering "Hiiiiiieeee." I stumbled around for a second and then took off running toward the beach. I felt as if my feet would burst into flames at any second. I knew I had been burned badly. I knew I shouldn't have done it. I ran through the clearing and down the trail to the beach. My feet hurt so badly that my eyes started to water. Damn it – why didn't I listen to my gut? Why did everyone before me have to do the damn dance in the fire this time. 'Shit' I thought to myself. I made a big mistake. I hoped my feet and legs would not suffer too badly.

I reached the beach and hobbled to the water where I stood knee deep. I swear I felt steam rising from my burning feet. I was afraid to move them because I knew they were burned badly. I hated the fact

269

that I didn't listen to my own gut instinct regardless of what everyone else did. My mind and everyone else's was in different places. My feet and their feet were different tonight. I was not in the right mental state to do a fire walk and I knew it – I just didn't listen to myself. I stood there in knee deep water beating myself up mentally for my own stupidity.

"Are you okay?" I heard Maruia's voice as she approached me from behind.

"I'll be fine. I wasn't ready to do the fire dance. My mind wasn't in the right place. I should have listened to my instinct. I have changed a lot – a lot has changed now."

"You are still the same Stan Duncan and I still love you. Let's go take care of your feet. I have something to put on them." She said as she coaxed me from the water back onto the beach.

When the air hit my feet it reinvigorated the searing pain that I previously felt. I shuttered to think what my poor feet must look like. I didn't even want to know. It was all I could do to walk. I wanted to drop to my knees and crawl like a baby. I wanted to swim out to the Mareva and prop my feet up in the refrigerator. I wanted to kick myself in the ass with my burned foot for being so ignorant as to not listen to myself. But I followed Maruia back to the Stan-dunk. I laid on the floor as soon as we walked into the building. Maruia turned on the lights and sat down to examine my feet.

"Wow." Was her only response when she saw my feet. She instructed me to stay put as she went to fetch the aloe lotion and special potion for them. I couldn't resist the urge to look at my feet as well since Maruia didn't elaborate on their condition. I bent my leg and brought my foot up into eyesight. 'Holy shit' I thought to myself. I had several massive blisters on each foot and on my toes too. There were several deep red burns in between the blisters and all of the hair was singed off of my toes and ankles. I burned myself really, really bad. The tribal paint had also washed off of my feet and lower legs too, but that was the least of my concerns.

Maruia returned promptly with some aloe and herbal potion for my feet. She popped my blisters with a bamboo shard and applied the ointment to the wounds. I watched intently as she cared for my burns. It absolutely blew my mind that I could get burned so badly so quickly – especially since I had danced in the fire for such an extended time before and held a burning coal in my hand for what seemed like an eternity without so much as a singed hair. It goes to show that the power of the mind is strong and when the mind is not in the right state, the body is vulnerable. When she finished tending to the wounds, she kissed my cheek and laid down next to me for a minute. I appreciated her nursing and her company, but I really wanted to be alone to process the whole situation in my mind.

"Maruia, sweetheart, thank you for everything, but I really want to be alone for a while. I'm sorry, but I need to work things out in my mind. Life is just so different for me right now. Being alone is what I feel I need right now." I said in a compassionate tone that I hoped she would understand and not take offense to.

"I understand totally. I'm here for you if you need me - whether I'm next to you or elsewhere." She said as she gathered her stuff, kissed me once more and left the Stan-dunk. She caught Tania and Chet on the way out as they were entering to check on me and told them to let me be alone. They obliged and left with her.

I laid there on my back and tried to go to sleep, but sleep would not come natural to me. I had too much to think about. Sustaining the burns was a major reality check to me. It told me that I had lost control of my mind/body connection. It confirmed that I was not the same person I was months ago. It was my wake up call that I needed to do something to change my state of mind. I could not take this lying down. I had to take some sort of action. I rose from my mattress and found a note pad and pen on the kitchen counter. I wrote a note and left it on the counter for everyone to see. "Gone to the Mareva to be alone for a while. Please don't worry about me – I'll be fine. I love you guys, Stan." I left the note and the Stan-dunk in the middle of the night and hobbled down to the beach. The sand stuck to my wounded feet and caused excessive pain in them. I struggled to push an outrigger kayak from the beach down into the water by myself. I washed the sand from my wounds in the salty sea water as I hopped into the kayak and started to stroke toward the Mareva. The tribal paint ran down my body as it got wet and dripped into the ocean – an hour of talent and work lost forever. The moonlight illuminated the Mareva and reflected off of the water enough so that I could see where I was going. The pain in my feet, heart and mind kept me alert and enabled me to paddle through the surf and outside break to the Mareva. I moored the kayak to the rear of the ship and climbed up onto the rear deck. The ladder was painful on my feet, but I felt much better as soon as I got back on the ship. Sleep was not in my plans. I sat up all night by moonlight and studied the instrumentation and navigation system at the helm. I played with the controls and checked out all the settings. I checked wind speed, current direction and speed, water depth etc. I kept the anchors down and the lights off, but raised the sails, changed their configurations manually and then lowered them multiple times. I got it – I connected with the Mareva. I knew she would take good care of me.

As the sun's rays began to illuminate the horizon at first light of sunrise, I raised the anchors, fired the engine and motored away from the outer reef of Rahiti. I hoped Chet wouldn't mind, but I convinced myself that he would understand. When I was a safe distance from the reef, I killed the engine and raised the sails. I programmed the navigation system and set course for Mata Utu.

I mustered up the courage to make another trip to Mata to honor my brother and to seek solitude. I had an uneasy feeling and nausea that suddenly came over me, but quickly subsided and blew away in the breeze. I remembered how many times Lance and I had made the voyage together by kayak. I longed to see him sitting on the bow of the kayak stroking left as I stroked right. It was hard to believe that it would never happen again. I closed my eyes and imagined that he was sitting next to me at the helm of the Mareva. I pictured his green long board sitting next to mine on the deck of the ship. Thoughts of our last paddle together entered my mind. I remembered our little water fight and our conversation that day. I tried to keep my thoughts positive, but the fight on the beach at Mata crept into my mind as well. My eye had healed nicely, but the emotional scar remained fresh in my head. I know he hadn't meant to hurt me. It wasn't the real Lance. I told myself that it was an accident fueled by helpless desperation and anger. It wasn't me. If I had it to do over again, I would have just left him alone without pushing him to go with me. It was what he really wanted – just to stay on Mata that night. How could I have known what to do? I did what I thought was right. Now my last memories of my brother are tainted with that physical altercation. He made his point and I left him alone against my better judgment. I had no choice. Thank God I got to see him one more time after the fight to find some resolve and peace before he departed the world on his last ride.

As I drew closer to Mata, I became nervous about my visit. I grew anxious in anticipation of whether or not I would even be able to navigate the Mareva into the lagoon at Mata. I knew the water was deep in the lagoon and I knew the reef around the lagoon was deeper than six feet. I checked the tide chart on the nav system to make sure it would be favorable. Nausea welled up from within and I dry heaved several times. My stomach wouldn't let me vomit, but I went through the motion anyway. I shook with fear and chills ran up and down my spine. I told myself there was nothing to be scared of. I tried to stop my worry, but it didn't work. I gave myself the option to turn around, but still proceeded ahead. I had to do this on my own. I wouldn't wreck the Mareva – she wouldn't let me do that. Mata would welcome me into the waters of her lagoon and offer me safe harbor there – knew that and I prayed for that. I couldn't decide whether it was my fear of wrecking the ship, the pain from my burned feet or my nervousness of visiting the island that claimed my brother's life that was making me so uneasy. I reluctantly sailed on toward Mata. Every bit of breeze guided me closer to the place which had once been my safe haven and source of happiness. Now I dreaded seeing the damn place again. I didn't know how I would handle it. I knew I just needed to go. Maybe I would stay the night there too. Or maybe I would never leave. I decided to let all fears go and move forward.

Mata was in my sights in no time. It was a fast sail with favorable winds and currents leading me straight to the mystical island. Mount Mata appeared on the horizon as it was backlit by the rising sun. A ring of clouds formed a halo around the top of the volcano. Dolphins appeared on my starboard side and played in the surf created by the wake of the Mareva as she cut through the teal green water. The dolphins seemed to recognize me in spite of the fact that I was in a huge sail boat instead of the small outrigger. They played and frolicked in the water as they entertained me with their antics. Their playfulness eased my mind as I let the breeze and the Mareva carry me closer to Mata. When the ship got close to Mata's outer reef, the dolphins left as usual. I took it as my sign to drop the sails and start the engine.

I slowly motored over the outer reef and into the calm waters on Mata's leeward side. I kept my eyes glued to the depth finder and the sonar devices on the nav screen. They both indicated that I had more than enough depth to enter into the lagoon. The Mareva glided into the lagoon at a snails pace and when I was comfortably close to the beach I dropped the anchors and she came to a halt. I sat there on the deck for a bit and took in the sight of the familiar lagoon and spit in front of me. I looked down at my feet and shook my head in disapproval at the damage I had done to them. I mustered up the will power to stand on them and climb down onto the rear deck. The outrigger kayak had made the journey in tow without damage. I decided to leave the kayak and jump into the water and swim over to the spit. I knew the salt water would be the best thing for my burns. The water was inviting and refreshing so I took my time swimming to the beach. The swim washed off all of my remaining body paint. I crawled up onto the sandy spit and took a seat at the edge of the water as I looked back at the Mareva. I did it – I sailed on my own and navigated into the lagoon. The accomplishment felt good and I felt safe – and alone. I liked it.

I laid down on my back on the beach, but let my feet remain in the water as it lapped up onto the beach. I was tired from not sleeping the night before, so I allowed myself to fall into slumber. I awoke some time later as the sun had crept higher in the sky and the heat of its rays awakened me. I sat upright and looked down at my feet. They were swollen and shriveled from being in the water so long, but the pain and redness had subsided. I decided to test them out and take a walk. I headed down the beach and entered the trail leading into the forest. I ventured down to the stream and water hole and took a long cool drink of water directly from the stream. I harvested some Kava Kava root as well as some herbs to calm my mind and body. I ate the herbs and chewed the root as I sat in the shade of the jungle. I felt much more relaxed, but I also felt a presence. I heard the booming waves in the distance and took it as my calling to head to the clearing. I stood up and began to walk down the trail to the clearing as I chewed on the Kava root. The presence grew stronger and I got the impression that I was not alone on the island. My heart palpitated at the feeling and it invigorated me to walk a little faster. The cool, moist soil felt great on my feet.

The hike took longer than usual as I took great care with every step to not cause further injury to my feet. I stopped and grabbed a mango on the walk and enjoyed the succulent fruit as I walked. The presence grew nearer the closer I got to the clearing. When I got to the clearing, I stepped out of the shade of the jungle and back into the sunlight as I made my way down to the beach. I sat down on the sand and looked to my right at Mount Mata and then traced the side of the volcano down to the point. The waves today were typical for Mata   clean, glassy, double overhead rights formed at the point and broke the length of the beach in front of me. The sight was beautiful as always, but I was no longer tempted to surf.

As soon as the thought of surfing crossed my mind, my focus on the waves in front of me changed. I couldn't believe my eyes as I looked to the point and saw a perfect right break forming. I shook my head and did a double take. I saw Lance on his green longboard making the drop on the wave. He dropped down the face and busted a perfect bottom turn and then climbed the face to duck into the tube as it broke over his head. I hollered with joy. I jumped from my seated position and ran to the edge of the water. I could see him in the barrel riding the wave. I forgot all about the pain in my feet as I ran down the beach parallel to the breaking wave. I tried to keep pace with the wave, but couldn't. I lost sight of Lance as the break accelerated faster than I could run. I lost him in the veil of water that covered him. I ran and ran down the beach as fast as I could. I wanted to see him launch over the lip and exit the wave at the spit. I kept my eyes focused on the wave for that moment, but I couldn't see it. I picked up my pace to a full sprint down the beach. I ran and ran, but could not see Lance exit the wave as it had already closed out. I ran as fast as I could all the way down the beach to the spit and changed my focus on the beach there to see Lance as he paddled to the spit from the water, but I didn't see him. Certainly I would see him coming out of the water any second. But did he see me on the beach? I doubted it – he was too far into the tube and I was too far away. I reached the spit out of breath and exhausted. I stood on my burning feet and surveyed the scene – no Lance. He was nowhere to be found. I dropped to my knees and prayed for him to appear again. I closed my eyes and then reopened them, but no Lance. Had I imagined seeing him? No way. The image was too vivid – too real. Where did he go? I had no explanation.

My feet seared with pain again from running on the sand. I crawled up onto the spit and expected to see Lance sitting on the beach at the lagoon wondering where the sailboat came from. But I did not see him there. Was I hallucinating? My head felt great from the herbal intake, but my senses were still sharp. What the hell? Had it not been for the presence I felt on my walk, I could have more easily dismissed the sight as an illusion, but it was just too real for me. I sat on top of the spit in disillusion and wept. I had no expectation to see Lance again, but for a brief moment I had the best feeling in the world. And just as fast as the sight appeared and the good feeling came, it also left and sadness came crashing down on me.

I crawled across the spit to the lagoon and soaked my feet in the water. I laid there and daydreamed for a while. I pretended Lance was sitting next to me.

"That was a good ride, bro. Nice drop and turn. Perfect barrel. I couldn't see you launch off the backside at the end, but I'm sure you caught some good air." I said to myself and the wind. "Want some Kava Kava root?" I asked as I took the root from my mouth and extended my arm to offer it to him. "No, yeah, it's already chewed on. Sorry. I'll get you a fresh one." I continued. "Hey, you want to go check out the Mareva? Let's take a swim." I crawled into the water and began to swim back to the ship as if Lance were next to me. "I picked her up in Tahiti. She is a gift from the Yanceys." I explained as I swam on my side. "She's a beauty. I can't wait to show you the inside." When we reached the ladder on the rear deck, I let Lance go first. When I thought he had ascended the ladder onto the deck, I extended my hand. "Can you give a brother some help here? I burned my feet dancing on the hot coals last night. No, I know it serves me right for showing off the dance again. What was I thinking? I can make it up on my own. Thanks anyway." I said as I helped myself up the ladder. "So check this out…" I explained as I gave a fictitious tour of the entire vessel to my brother.

Halfway through the tour, I realized I was coming unglued. The pain in my feet became unbearable and I fell to the floor in the hallway outside of the master suite. I laid on my back staring up at the deckhead as tears began to well up in my eyes again. "Keep it together, Stan. Keep it together man." I thought as I passed out in the floor.

I woke up later in the afternoon and my head was still spinning from the illusion. I knew I had to occupy my mind. I stumbled over to the stowage bin near the cockpit and fetched the snorkeling gear from inside it. I knew being in the salt water would be great for my feet and I also knew snorkeling may take my mind off of Lance for a while. It was one thing we had not done together and it was the first time I had the gear and the opportunity to do so. I donned the mask and snorkel and jumped off of the back of the ship. I floated for hours on my stomach as I breathed thru the tube and gently paddled my hands.

The water was crystal clear. The coral and sand bottom of the lagoon was beautiful, but completely devoid of fish and sea life. At least I didn't have to worry about sharks I thought.

The sun began its descent in the sky signifying that sunset was approaching and it was time to get back on board the ship. My feet felt better while in the water, but climbing the ladder was painful. Why the hell did I have to go running down the beach? Why the hell did I have to burn them in the first place? I dismissed the thoughts and focused my attention on another matter. Should I leave Mata tonight? Would the curse apply to me if I stayed on the Mareva in the lagoon? Did the curse only apply if you were actually on land? Would the Mareva offer safety and would the lagoon offer a safe haven? I didn't know, so I decided to pray on the issue for a while.

"Dear Mata, please allow me to stay here for a while. Please offer me safety and refuge. Please exempt me from your curse. Please forgive me for trespassing. I love you, Mata. Please care for Lance too and let him surf here eternally. I won't stay here long – just until I get myself straight. Please help me do that. Please help Stan get back to himself again. Please, please – I pray this to you." I finished my prayer, but remained kneeling on the deck as the sun began to set. I felt a warm presence come over me again. I felt comfortable and safe. I felt like that was the answer to my prayer, so I made the decision to stay. The skies were clear and the winds were gentle – I hoped they would stay that way.

As the sun set to the west, a full moon rose over Mount Mata to the east. The moon seemed larger than life and brighter than ever and I felt the presence again. I took that as another sign of asylum here. I stretched on the deck and did some yoga in a seated position to give my feet a chance to rest. I chewed on my Kava root and focused on my breathing. At some point I passed out on the upper deck. I slept restfully through the night and awoke to a beautiful sunrise in the exact same spot where the moon had risen hours prior. The sky was also clear and no storm was brewing. I said another prayer and thanked Mata and God for the safety of the night.

I had no hunger or thirst in the morning – only the desire to sail. I checked the instrumentation on the nav system and lifted anchors. I fired the engine and turned the vessel out of the lagoon making sure not to damage the outrigger kayak that was still in tow. I coasted out of the lagoon and said goodbye for the moment. I eased out of the calm water and past the outer reef and then killed the engines and popped the sails. I wanted to practice sailing and this was the perfect place to do it. I decided to try to circumnavigate Mata. I wanted to attempt it on my own without the use of the Mareva's help. "Ready about." I called out to myself as if there was a crew there to listen. I turned the wheel hard to port and hit the controls to make the sails follow suit. The boom turned and the mainsail shifted as we began a starboard tack. I continued on that bearing until I was a few miles away from the island and then I turned ninety degrees to port again and sailed by the lee as the wind was at the stern. "Hard alee" I hollered as the boom shifted and the mainsail, and jib followed my direction and control at the helm. I adjusted the topping lift and downhaul to increase tension on the sails. I continued that course for a while until I turned to port again, but less of a ninety to bring the ship into a broad reach with the wind from behind, but not directly to the stern. The ship heeled slightly under a little gust of wind, but I adjusted the sails manually and turned more to port and more of a beam reach as the wind came broadside to the port side of the ship. I was on the other side of Mata now and was well beyond the outer reef break that Lance and I surfed. I could barely see the point on Mount Mata, but the breakwater made it evident to my eyes. I stayed pretty far offshore as I didn't want to test my luck with the current and end up in the break or the reef. I paralleled the beach on the windward side of the island on a port tack before heading to wind to make my final turn around the spit to bring me back into the lagoon. "Hard alee" I hollered again as I turned the wheel and the boom swung to the opposite side of the ship. The sails luffed momentarily before catching the wind from the opposite direction. I adjusted the controls and pulled the sail configuration into a more close-hauled setup. My confidence in my sailing ability grew as I rounded the spit and sailed back into the calm waters leading into the lagoon. I decided to be brave and enter the harbor under sail instead of under engine power. I cleared the reef and turned the wheel to direct me into the lagoon. I let the ship's momentum carry me into the lagoon. "Heave to." I hollered as I cranked the wheel hard and brought the rudder into opposition with the sails to stop the boat's forward progress and turn her around slightly. I dropped anchors and lowered sails with the push of a few buttons. The ship came to a complete halt and resumed her rest in the lagoon. In a matter of a few hours I had successfully circumnavigated the island manually. I had maintained distance and avoided danger and had brought the ship into the lagoon under sail and stopped her manually with the rudder and sails before dropping anchor. My confidence level grew tenfold.

I spent the next several days sailing around the island each day and then returning to the lagoon at night. Each night I said a prayer to Mata to offer me safe haven and asylum from her curse. My prayers were answered every morning as I awoke to clear skies and sunshine. I didn't eat for days – the fruit was plentiful on the island, but I chose not to eat it – instead I gathered it, filled my water bottles and returned to the ship to stow the food away for later. I didn't get hungry, but I told myself if I did, I would suffer through it and still not eat in spite of the tremendous stockpile of unripened fruit I had assembled onboard. I told myself that hunger was good - it's good to be hungry every once in a while. Hunger builds drive. It wells up from within and forces you into action. It increases your alertness, awareness and energy - that's survival mode kicking in. I knew that I would need to be able to summon this survival mode if I was going to accomplish my mission and goal.

I began fasting to build up tolerance and my ability to go long periods of time without food. My goal was to be able to go 40 days without food. I learned that hunger pains are fleeting and can be controlled mentally. Hunger is a mental struggle more than a physical one. I reminded myself that the body is designed to go long periods of time without food. I starved myself of food, but nourished my body with mineral rich water from Mata and sun and air from the sky. An enlightenment occurred in my mind and body. I went into "survival mode". Even with no caloric intake, I was still able to do strenuous physical activity daily as I practiced yoga on deck and incorporated push-ups, sit-ups and pull-ups from the boom. I even swam daily in the lagoon in circles around the ship. My body responded nicely as my body became even more lean and lithe. My muscle tone was profound in spite of my lack of protein and calories. I didn't crave food at all. I had absolutely no desire to eat and felt as if I could go indefinitely without eating in spite of all of the food I had onboard the ship. I knew my mind and body were in the state they needed to be in, so I left Mata and said goodbye for a while.

276

I had lost all concept of time during my stay in Mata. I really had no idea whether I had been gone for a couple of days, a week or even a month. I didn't count and I didn't care. I had sailed around Mata dozens of times – sometimes as much as three or four times a day. I had become very proficient at sailing – with or without the help of the Mareva's automation. I learned her inside and out. I sailed her solo with ease as I learned her controls and the feel of the boat and the wind in her sails. I learned the depths of the sea and the reef cuts. I sailed from island to island, but never too far. I ventured back to Mata at the end of every day to seek shelter in the safe haven of her lagoon. I was proud of myself for learning the ship and its navigation so quickly. I told myself that if I could navigate the treacherous waters around Mata that I could sail anywhere. With my newfound confidence and sailing ability, I set course back to Rahiti.

When I reached the outer reef at Rahiti, I dropped sail and dropped anchors in the same exact spot that Chet and I had done prior. I stood on the upper deck on my freshly healed feet. I looked toward the beach in Rahiti, but saw no one. I didn't want to go into shore yet – I had other plans. I grabbed the snorkel and mask and jumped off of the rear of the ship. I swam into the outside reef break and began to float and dive, float and dive. I continued snorkeling for a couple of hours before lifting my head to see two outriggers carrying Chet, Maruia, Hoanui and Arenui. I continued snorkeling until they reached me.

"What in the hell are you doing mate?" Chet asked. I could tell by the tone in his voice that he was pissed off and I didn't blame him. I took the Mareva and left indefinitely without his permission or even so much as giving him the courtesy of telling him where I was going or when I was coming back. I didn't answer him immediately, but righted myself in the water and pulled the mask and snorkel from my face as I treaded water.

Maruia was the next to speak. "Stan, thank God you are back. We were all worried sick. We got your note, but it has been almost two weeks since you left. Where did you go? And why for so long?" She pleaded.

I simply smiled and replied "I needed some time away. I'm cool now. Lets go onboard." I said as I swam over to the ship. The kayaks followed me and moored up next to the outrigger that was already there.

"Bro, how long has this kayak been in the water?" Hoanui asked.

"The whole time." I responded.

"Not good bro, it's gonna deteriorate in the water. There is a parasite that will eat the wood if you leave it in the water." Hoanui said as he inspected the inside of the hull of the kayak.

"Sorry man. I'll paddle it back into shore later and leave it there. I don't need it." The truth was that I didn't care about the damn kayak. It was the least of my worries.

"How are your feet?" Maruia asked as she looked down at them.

"They healed up nicely. Thanks for your concern and your nursing before I left. I didn't get to thank you properly."

Arenui and Hoanui turned their attention to the Mareva and gazed in wonderment at the ship.

"Come on mates, I'll give you a tour." Chet said as he began to show the guys the ship - leaving Maruia and I alone on the rear deck to talk.

"I'm sorry I left you like that for so long, but I had to."

"I know, Stan, but it doesn't stop the fact that I love you and worry about you. I feared you were leaving permanently and that I would never see you again." She said with concern as she looked into my eyes. I remained silent and my eyes drifted from hers to the sea. "Well..." She said as she stood waiting for me to make a comment. I returned my eyes to contact hers, but I still remained silent and emotionless. "You are leaving, aren't you?" She said as she dropped her head and turned it to the side.

"Yes." I answered as I embraced her. For the first time ever, she did not reciprocate my hug immediately, instead she half heartedly placed her hands on my arms.

"Why? When?" She asked.

"I don't know. When I'm ready I guess."

"Take me with you." She urged as she squeezed my arms.

I remained silent for a few moments before answering. "I don't know."

She released my arms and stepped back from me. "What do you mean you don't know?" She asked with hurt in her voice.

"You are my only dilemma in my plan. Everything else is crystal clear to me."

"How can I be a dilemma? I just want to be with you – I don't care how or where. Why can't you understand that?" She pleaded.

"I do understand and most of me feels the same way..." I started to explain as Chet and the guys emerged from below deck and headed back in our direction. "We will finish this discussion later in private." She was not thrilled about ending the conversation now, but she nodded her head in agreement.

278

"Hey guys, there is plenty of food in the fridge. Help yourself if you want." I said.

"I saw that. You have quite a stockpile. Where did you get it all?" Chet asked.

"Mata Utu fruit." I answered.

"Huh, you have enough food in there to last a month. Are you planning on going somewhere?" Hoanui asked.

"Too bad the fruit won't keep that long before ripening and spoiling." I answered to dodge the other half of his question.

"Seriously, brah – you going somewhere?" Arenui asked.

I hesitated before inviting the group inside to have a seat on the comfortable leather furniture in the lounge. I wanted to make them as comfortable as possible for the uncomfortable conversation we were about to have. I grabbed some fruits and a couple of bottles of water and placed them on the glass coffee table in the center of the room. No one touched the fruit as they sat down and patiently waited for me to answer the question they were all eager to hear the answer to.

"Guys, I don't know what to say. Since "The Day," things have been different for all of us in some way. I feel that I was very fortunate to have been here during the catastrophe. Although I missed my friends and family terribly, I was content being here on the island and starting a new permanent life here; however, since Lance's death things have changed even more for me. I still feel comfortable here and I appreciate the people and environment around me and I am grateful for everything and everyone here in my life, but I am no longer content here. Curiosity is killing me. I have to know what is going on back in the States. I have to know if my friends and family are alive." I explained as I paced back in forth in the lounge as they sat in front of me. I finally took a seat next to Maruia and a calmer demeanor came over me. "Look, for all I know my family and friends may be waiting for me and hoping and praying that I return to help them in some capacity. What if I am supposed to be their savior and return to rescue them and bring them back here with me? I don't know if it is possible or if they are even alive. It's the not knowing part that is driving me crazy. I feel like this is something I have to do. I spent the last two weeks in solitude pondering this dilemma. I decided this is what I have to do. Chet, do you mind if I borrow the Mareva?"

Everyone sat there staring at me and waiting for Chet's response. "Stan, the Mareva is not mine to give away. I have been her keeper for the last couple of years for the Yanceys, but it is clear that the Yanceys may never return. I will turn a blind eye to whatever you want to do, but I don't think it is a good idea. Trying to sail back to the States solo would be suicide. Even with all of us helping you, it would still be a foolish venture. First of all, the waters are not safe these days – piracy is running rampant and there is no one to protect you. The Mareva would be a sitting duck for a powerboat with armed pirates. You would lose the ship, your food and water and possibly your life too. That is just one of my many concerns." He said as he paused. "Even as advanced as the Mareva is, she is no match for the forces of nature. There are so many factors – storms, rogue waves, changing currents, reefs... the list goes on. You are no match for that – I've been sailing for a long time and I am still apprehensive about my ability to do a trans-ocean trip alone." Chet paused again for a long moment. "I can't go with you, brother."

I interrupted him before he could finish. "No, I don't expect you or anyone else to go with me. This is something I have to do alone." My comment did not set well with Maruia and she made it known by her facial expression and her body language, but she remained silent.

"Mate, I would love to go with you and I would normally insist, but I have a different plan. I have an announcement to make." He said as he sat upright and paused momentarily. "I am planning to marry Tania. No one knows yet, but I am telling you guys now, in confidence, because it is relevant. I want to get it off of my chest." Chet said proudly in his Aussie accent.

"Congratulations. That's great!" I said as I was happy to hear the news as it took some of the heat off of me and my plan. The Rahitians were not too shocked, but also happy to hear the news. The mention of marriage prompted Maruia to direct her attention to me with wanting eyes. Damn, this brought a new element into the equation. I could read her mind immediately as I knew she was thinking that Chet and Tania had only known each other a very short time in comparison to the time that her and I knew each other. I knew that Maruia was thinking that if anyone should be getting married it should be her and I. I realized that, understood that and even thought the same for a moment myself.

The other Rahitians went through the motions of congratulating and embracing Chet for a while. I took the time while they were distracted with that topic to regroup my thoughts. When everyone was done talking about Chet's wedding plans, their attention turned back to me as I sat on the edge of the couch pondering my thoughts in expressionless silence. Maruia grabbed my hand.

"My brother, I would have to ask you to reconsider your decision. Why not stay here with us and start a new life? Everything and everyone you need is right here. Rahiti is such a beautiful place. Forget about the States. What if you do make it back there only to find everything destroyed and everyone gone? How is that going to feel? What would you do then? If the chaos is as bad as I anticipate, you will starve, thirst to death, freeze or die of radiation poisoning. Think about it. It's a huge risk – its certain suicide." Chet argued.

I took a deep, exaggerated breath before I answered him. "I appreciate the beauty of the environment, people and energy around me, but a mind-shift has occurred in me and I am now determined to return to the States. I feel like my life is purpose-driven. I feel like everything has happened for a reason – everything I have experienced in my life has made me who I am today. Everything I have encountered happened for a reason – being here during "The Day," Lance's death, discovering the Mareva – it all adds up to this for me. I am prepared to embark on this journey alone. I am prepared for what I may find when I get back to the US. I am willing to accept that. I am also willing to accept the end of my life if that is the end result. Everything worthwhile is usually on the other side of fear. You must usually overcome the obstacle of fear to accomplish the things in life that you desire. Fear is usually the first and last obstacle that grounds people and keeps them from starting or finishing a task. It is the locked door, the doubt in one's mind or the unknown. This ship is my key to unlocking the door to the mystery and curiosity that looms in my mind about the unknown situation back in the States. I refuse to let fear keep me from doing what I know I need to do." I took a long sip of water to refresh my dry mouth. "I have tied up all of my loose ends in Rahiti and completed the mission that I initially set out to do here. I do have unfinished business at home and that has taught me a lesson. I have learned that I will never leave loose ends anywhere again. I hope I have the opportunity to finish my business in the States - to say goodbye to everyone or to say the things I never said to those who were close to me. I never meant to leave things unspoken. I realize now that I may never get another chance to say or to do the things that I should have said or done. But I must at least try." I paused as I collected my composure. I turned my attention to Maruia as I grabbed her hands and looked into her eyes. "Maruia, I love you with all of my heart, but right now my heart is torn to pieces. If the situation were right, I could see myself marrying you and having a wonderful life together. Right now, that is not possible. If I'm not happy with myself and my own life, how can I possibly make you happy and start a relationship on the right track?" Maruia tried to interject, but I silenced her and continued. "I know you want to be there for me. I know you think that you can help fix things for me, but that's just not the case. I need something else – something that you just can't give me. This is a one man mission – this is something I have to do for myself, by myself. Look at it this way, if I can do what I need to do on my own then I will be much stronger than I am now and I will be satisfied and ready to move on with you. I cannot guarantee anything to you, but I can promise one thing – if I don't do this, then my life will not be complete and I will be filled with regret and that 'what if' question will be in my mind. Please understand."

Tears welled up in Maruia's eyes as she struggled to reply. The others sat in silence and waited to see what she would say. She finally broke her tearful silence and with the sweetest, most humble tone in her voice asked "Please reconsider Stan. I want to spend the rest of my life with you – even if it means an early end to it. Please take me with you." She burst into tears as she got up and ran out of the cabin of the ship and onto the rear deck. I followed her out and stood on the rear deck and watched her hop into my outrigger kayak, untie it and began to stroke toward to beach. "I love you Stan – please." She said through her tears as she paddled away.

I jumped to the top deck and watched her stroke toward shore. My heart was torn in half. I hated to see Maruia cry. She was always so strong. She was never one to beg or plead. I had always supported her decisions and given in to her wants and needs. This time was different. She was as determined to be with me as I was determined to be alone. It was a damn awkward situation. I didn't want to go back inside the ship and face the others yet, so I grabbed the snorkeling gear off of the deck and jumped in the water.

I swam a little ways away from the ship back to the reef where I had been diving before. I focused on my breathing and collected myself as I began to dive down into the clear water. I pushed myself to submerge deep. I explored the reef below and ran my fingers through the powdery sand on the bottom. I held my breath as long as I could - exhaling slowly to send air bubbles skyward. My ears popped as they tried to adjust to the depth. I stayed down as long as I could while still leaving myself enough air to surface. I estimated the depth to be around 15 to 20 feet deep. I surfaced only long enough to clear my snorkel and get a full breath of air and then I dove right back down again. I dove a couple of dozens times as I moved down the reef away from the ship. I lost track of my position relative to the ship as all of my attention was directed on the bottom of the ocean. I was on a mission and I was also trying to put Maruia out of my mind for a little while. I just wanted to be alone for a bit before returning to face the guys on the ship again. Just as the thought of facing the guys crossed my mind, an outrigger kayak cast a shadow on the bottom of the sea as I swam along the reef. I looked up to the surface and saw two oars paddling and hovering above me. Damn, I would have to surface for air and confront them. I took my time surfacing as the kayak hovered above.

I broke the surface of the water to discover Hoanui and Arenui in a single kayak waiting for me to come up. I pulled the mask from my face and the snorkel from my mouth as I stroked over to the kayak. I hung on the outrigger and asked "What's up guys?"

"Stan, we know what you are doing over here." Hoanui said.

"What's that?"

"C'mon, brah – don't play stupid man. We know you're looking for the gun that you tossed out here months ago." Arenui said with an aggravated tone in his voice.

"Yeah, you are right my friend. I am looking for my gun."

"Why, brah? What good is that gonna do?" Arenui asked as Hoanui shook his head.

"Well, dunno. I just feel like I may need it. Something told me to bring it here to the islands in the first place. I tossed it because of Lance, but now he is gone and now something is telling me I need it again."

"Why do you think you need it? You know the odds of finding it out here are pretty incredibly slim." Hoanui said.

"I don't know why I need it, I just do. I know the odds are slim, but I like snorkeling and swimming anyway and I've got nothing but time right now to do it. I'm making it a game of hide and seek – right now the Glock is hiding."

"Well, have fun, brah." Arenui said as he put his paddle in the water with frustration as I sensed he was ready to paddle in to shore.

"You know you are welcome home here anytime, dude." Hoanui said as I released my grip on the outrigger as they began to paddle away.

I looked toward the Mareva and saw that one kayak remained. I also assumed that Chet also remained on the ship as well. I decided to go ahead and swim over and confront him while we were alone. I swam back to the ship and climbed onboard. Chet was chilling out in the lounge below deck eating a giant pommello fruit. I shook the water from my body and hair before entering the cabin.

"Hey, dude. That is some good fruit isn't it?" I asked to make a light conversation and break the awkwardness of the previous one.

"Yep, juicy, sweet – and huge!" He said as he lapped up the juice as it ran down the back of his hand and arm. "Look, Stan I want to help you, but I can't go with you. I totally understand where you are coming from and why you want to leave. I just had a similar shift in my mind and decided to leave everything in Tahiti behind to live in Rahiti permanently. I fell in love with Tania and out of love with my life in Tahiti. Things out of my control happened on both sides of the equation. I know that you cannot control your heart sometimes. I know your heart is still in the States in spite of your feelings for Maruia, the Rahitians, me and the islands. I bless you and condone the trip. I will be happy to see the Mareva put to good use. I will pray for your safety and return every day. I want to help you make a plan to ensure your success."

"I'm all ears man."

"Good. Then let's get started, hey?"

Chet and I began to talk in great detail about all the possible scenarios I could run into at sea. He instructed me on many navigational points including sharing some astrological charts and water current charts with me in case the Mareva's systems failed me. He warned me of the effects of extended solitude on the mind, but decided that I was prepared for that. He tried to figure out how I was going to survive on the food I had stockpiled. He explained that I would be okay for the first couple of weeks or so, but that the food would ripen, spoil and rot – even in the fridge. I told him that I had been practicing fasting and was sure that I could go weeks without eating if necessary. I also told him that I planned to fish while at sea. I was also going to freeze some food in the freezer as emergency reserve. Chet was concerned that the power reserves on the ship may be depleted if I went through extended periods of cloudiness or nuclear winter in the northern hemisphere. Chet also stressed the importance of using a lanyard to secure myself to the ship if I went in the water in the open ocean – even when anchored. He told me how easily a ship can drift faster than you can swim. But most importantly Chet was overly concerned about piracy. He didn't really think there was much I could do to prepare or defend myself in the event of an attack. He told me to stay vigilant and watch the radar and keep my sails in the wind and the ship away from other vessels. I told him that I had discovered a few 'bells and whistles' (literally) on the Mareva as I had explored her nav system and controls. I had learned a great deal about the radar and had found that it had a proximity alarm setting that would alert me if anyone came into a certain radius of the ship. He was shocked that I had discovered technology on the vessel that he didn't even know about. I think that really drove the point home to him that I was ready to go. I also added that I was searching for my gun at the bottom of the sea and that I would not leave until I found it. I told him the story of how I had tossed it in the water to appease Lance while we were surfing. He laughed at the notion that I would ever find it and commented that I may never leave. I had more optimistic plans.

Chet said goodbye to me and told me that he wanted to return to Tania and the island. He knew I wanted to be alone on the ship and in spite of its massive size and ability to comfortably accommodate many, he preferred to be on the island with Tania and the tribe. I wished him luck with Tania and the future wedding plans. It made both of us happier when he left in the last outrigger.

I immediately went back to diving for a few more hours until the sun began to set and visibility became difficult under water. Back at the helm, I zoomed the radar and GPS system in on the Mareva to vividly display the immediate area around and under the ship. I didn't expect to find the gun on the radar screen, rather I planned to map out the areas that I had already searched so that I didn't backtrack, swim in circles or search the same spot repeatedly. I devised a system for my diving and implemented it into my daily routine.

My daily routine consisted of morning yoga at sunrise on the deck of the ship followed by instrumentation and weather checks followed by equipment checks of the ship followed by food and water supply checks followed by repeating the cycle over and over again. My OCD side kicked in and kept me busy and focused. The food supply held out nicely because I wasn't eating it, but the water supply was running low because I was constantly drinking it. I knew I would have to go in to shore soon to fill my water bottles again. I rationed the water as long as I could, but after almost a week alone with no rain or replenishment, I planned to swim into shore to get more. I put on the snorkel and mask and prepared for the semi-long swim through the reef break and into shore. It shouldn't be difficult as I had gotten into excellent shape with all of the diving and snorkeling I had been doing lately. I spit into my mask to keep it from fogging up, put it on and dove off of the back of the Mareva into the blue/green water. I circled the Mareva once and checked the anchors and the hull before beginning to stroke in toward shore.

I timed my swim through the break in between sets to keep from getting pounded by the waves. I timed it perfectly and began to stroke hard with my face in the water and the snorkel in my mouth. It was easy to swim freestyle with the snorkel and mask as I didn't have to break momentum to turn my head to breathe or even think about breathing. The only thought on my mind was confronting Maruia again when I got ashore. I was considering how to handle my inevitable interaction with her and I was not paying any attention to the reef or the bottom of the sea; however, something caught my eye. I couldn't believe my eyes as I stopped swimming to focus my eyes and let the turbulence in the water around me subside. I was directly over top of what appeared to be my gun. It was lying on the sandy bottom just inside a steep part of the reef. Had it been on the dark reef just a couple of feet away, it surely would have blended in and I would have missed it, but there it lay as obvious as day – a black gun on the white sand. I took a deep breath and submerged head first to dive to retrieve it. It was pretty deep – in fact, much deeper than I had been diving previously. My ears whistled and popped from the pressure. The natural buoyancy of my body resisted the depth and wanted to stop and return to the surface, but I pushed on down – kicking and stroking to the bottom. I got a severe headache and a bit dizzy from the depth. The air in my lungs wanted to be exhaled from the increased pressure on my chest. I let a little out, but held the rest in tight for the ascent back to the surface. I pushed myself hard to reach the bottom. When my fingers actually touched the gun, a feeling of relief came over my body. I grasped it tight and then pushed off of the bottom of the sea with my legs and propelled myself to the surface. I busted through the top of the water and took a deep, gasping breath of air. It had been my deepest dive yet, but definitely the most worthwhile. I brandished the weapon as I treaded water. I said a quick prayer and thanked God and the universe for returning the gun to me. I kissed it, rolled onto my back and kicked my way to the Mareva instead of in to shore. I cocked the gun as I floated on my back and pulled the trigger. She fired instantly and didn't jamb even after months in the salt water and sand. The recoil from the shot forced me back in the water and the deafening blast from the gun rang my ears. I went back to the ship briefly to stash the gun before swimming back in to shore. I was glad I found it and that it worked flawlessly. My plan was unfolding nicely.

When I reached the beach, I was happy to find no one was there. I really didn't want any additional interaction at the moment. I was here to grab some supplies and return to the ship as quickly as I could. I made my way up the trail to my hut. I passed a few of the tribe, but no one spoke to me. I entered my hut and opened up a Rubbermaid container. I searched its contents and was delighted to find what I was looking for – bullets among other things. I knew I still had them, but was relieved to actually touch them. The infrared binocs, ropes and other supplies were also in the container. I knew it all may come in handy, so I snapped the lid closed and picked up the container to head out of the hut. Before I could reach the opening of the hut, Tane stepped into the hut.

"Stan, we need to talk." He said in a stern voice.

He was really the last person I wanted to talk to, but I sat the container down and listened to what he had to say.

"Look, Maruia is heartbroken about your decision to leave. I must admit that I am somewhat sorry to see you go too. You have done a lot here for us, my family, the tribe – everyone. You will be missed, but I understand your departure. What I fear is that you will change your mind and take Maruia with you. She is determined to be with you. And, although I truly want to see her happy, I do not want to see her leave. It is not right to take her away from her life here. This is all she's known. She is loved here. She is needed here – by everyone. I'm not speaking to you out of jealousy or want for her affection. I know she loves you and not me. I know that I can never have her like that, I just want her to be safe, happy and with those that love her. Please consider this." Tane begged as he extended his hand for a handshake.

I was blown away by his honesty and sincerity. I shook his hand, and for once, I agreed with him. "I know what you are saying Tane. My mind is made up. I will sail alone. Maruia will be hurt for a while and I will miss her tremendously also, but I want her to stay and be safe in Rahiti with her family and life long friends. You have my word I will not take her." I affirmed the pact with a long handshake and hug.

"Thank you and bless you." Tane said as he exited my hut.

I grabbed my container and followed him out of the hut. I made my way down to the beach and put the container inside of the hull of a kayak on the beach. I then went to the Stan-dunk and grabbed two empty containers and stuffed them full of as many plastic water bottles as I could. I still had a few dozen Fiji water bottles that were unopened, so I grabbed them and put them in the container first. I didn't want to take the time to fill the empty bottles in the sink – I just wanted to get out of there as quickly as possible as to avoid any contact with anyone. That was not destined to happen. Maruia entered the center and caught me packing the bottles.

"Let me help you honey." She said.

"Okay." I answered.

"You are leaving very soon aren't you?"

"Yes, soon." I answered.

"I sensed that. I want you to know that I will miss you and I will wait for you to return." She said as she looked up at me with her beautiful eyes. "I love you." She added. Her attitude had completely changed in the last few days since she paddled away from the Mareva.

"I love you too. And I promise you that I will return one day." I said as I took a break from packing the water bottles to stroke her hair.

"Let me help you pack. I will row a second kayak out to the ship for you. You need to take as many of these bottles as you can. I will fill them for you." She insisted.

"They will be heavy if we fill them now. I also didn't want to deplete the water supply here – it hasn't rained in a while. I have another plan to fill the bottles." I admitted.

"Okay, then." She said as we carried the containers to the beach and put them in the outriggers.

She and I shoved the kayaks into the water and began to paddle back out to the Mareva. I estimated I had gathered over 100 bottles – about twenty or so were still full of Fiji water (enough to last me until I could fill the others). The rest would be filled with Mata water. We reached the Mareva and Maruia helped me unload the bottles and the containers onto the ship's deck. When the unloading process was done, there was an awkward moment when neither of us knew what to do or say. Maruia finally broke the silence.

"If you are leaving me, I at least want one more night alone with you." She said with a wink and a somewhat forced smile.

"That would be very nice. Why don't you stay here tonight with me?"

I didn't need to say anymore. She accepted the invitation. We spent the rest of the afternoon sitting in the sun on the deck reminiscing about the good times we had since my arrival. All mention of anything negative was totally omitted. We laughed, flirted and embraced each other passionately. It was as if we had both decided to make our last night memorable and positive. We sat on the deck hand in hand and watched the sun set together. We watched the moon rise on the opposite horizon as the sun's rays subsided. We retired to the master suite and I opened the skylights to reveal the night skyscape. We both let passion overcome us as we made love to each other like it was the last time we would ever see each other. We passed out on the king sized bed under the stars in post coital bliss.

The Sail

The next morning Maruia and I awoke to a beautiful sunrise as the sun's first rays shined through the open skylights above the bed. The sunlight glistened on her jet black healthy hair and reflected in her eyes as she lay next to me. The beauty of the morning and the Rahitian beauty next to me fueled my desire for a morning passion session. We made love tirelessly and passionately all morning and took our time getting out of bed. I knew it would be nice to have her with me at sea every morning, but I knew it was the fact that she would not be going with me that made this morning's love making extra special. I wanted to appreciate every second of her presence with me as I knew that it would be a while before I would see her again. The thought of never seeing her again was subdued in my mind – I wouldn't let that happen. I made a promise to return to her and I planned on following through on it – just as I was following through on my promise to return back home to my family and friends in The States.

Maruia and I decided to practice one last session of naked yoga on the deck of the Mareva. I tried to focus on my breathing, poses and posture, but we ended up curtailing the yoga as we let our libidos take over and made love once more on the deck of the ship. Damn, I knew I was going to miss her badly and I wanted to enjoy it all right now. We had more sex in an eighteen hour period than we had the entire time I was in Rahiti. It was unbelievable – and amazing. I stopped myself before I started second guessing my decision not to take her with me.

After the love making was finally over, we fed each other fruit as we sat naked on the deck of the ship. It was one of the most romantic moments of my life. I didn't need a camera or a video recorder to capture these moments that I could replay mentally for an eternity. I knew I had to appreciate this moment. I was grateful for every second with her. I didn't think about leaving, but rather returning to her and this moment as soon as I could possibly get back.

"Do you really have to go Stan?" She asked as she held a piece of papaya to my lips.

"Yes, I really do."

"Why leave the comfort and safety of what you have here to venture off into the unknown?"

"Maruia, let me explain it to you like this. A ship is safest in the harbor, but that is not what it is built for. It is built to travel, to move, to experience rough seas and to go places. And, ironically, it is not smooth seas that make great sailors. Enduring storms and rough seas puts the ship to the test and gives the sailor experience and confidence which makes him better. I need that experience right now. I need this experience to make me better – to put my mind at ease and allow me to endure the storms in my life right now." She nodded intently as she listened to my explanation. "Do you know what I like best about sailing?" I asked.

"No, what?" She asked.

"I like sailing because although you can't change the wind, you can adjust your sails to take you anywhere you want to go. That is why I am choosing to 'sail through my life' right now. I feel like my life is this big open ocean and that the negative events that occurred since I've been here in the islands have been big storms that have tossed me to and fro. The storms have changed my beliefs and perceptions of things. They have changed my emotions – especially my appreciation of people and life. Now I feel like another big storm is brewing here in the islands that is blowing me in a different direction. This storm is causing me to be discontent and anxious. It is causing me to shun the very things that brought me peace and happiness for so long. I have curiosity, doubts, uncertainty and fears, but I have subdued them and I choose to follow my positive emotions of love, dedication and will power when it comes to making the decision to embark on this trip alone. I have always loved the water and the concept of sailing. I know I have felt this way for a reason – this trip is the culmination and what I am supposed to do. Now I have the Mareva and she makes the whole thing possible. So I'm going to raise her sails and regardless of the wind direction I am going to set my course for where I want to go. I will keep making adjustments to the sails and in my life until I end up where I need to be."

"I understand and I wish you all of the luck and love in the world." She said as she finished the last bite of mango and then kissed my lips.

She stood up and slowly wrapped her parea around her beautiful body to conceal her nakedness. I soaked in the sight and took a mental snapshot of her one last time.

"I wish I had something to leave with you as a memento, but all I came with is what I am wearing." She said with slight regret as she forced a smile out of her lips.

"Memories are the best and only memento I need from you. The memory of you will stay in my mind forever and help me endure any situation that comes my way. Thank you for that and thank you for making me the person I am today. I love you Maruia."

"I love you too." She said as she hugged me tightly and planted one last kiss on my lips. I loved every second of the kiss and wanted it to last forever. I took in the entire sensation – the touch of her hands on my back, the feeling of her lips on mine, the smell of her skin, the beauty of her face and body, the spirit radiating from her soul and the love in her eyes – all combined to form the most sensual moment of my life. I soaked the moment in for all that it was worth before she finally released her grip and hug on my back. She stepped back from me as our lips were the last thing to touch. She turned, and without another word hopped onto the lower rear deck and slid into the kayak moored to the back of the ship. She untied both kayaks from the ship and then strapped the two outriggers together. She looked up at me one more time to smile and blow me a kiss and then she turned and rowed the tandem of kayaks toward Rahiti. I stood at attention on the deck and watched her paddle through the outside reef break and into the calmer waters to the beach. Once I could not longer see her, I turned my attention to the Mareva.

Without further ado I raised the anchors, popped the sails up and set my course straight to Mata Utu. I had business to tend to there one last time. I configured the sails into a broad reach and sailed by the lee as the wind and current carried me straight to Mata. I kicked back at the helm with a Kava Kava root in my mouth and enjoyed the ride. The Mareva rode the conveyor belt and I didn't have to do anything at all except man the wheel through the reef cut and then drop anchor and sails in the lagoon.

I grabbed some netting and filled it up with empty water bottles and then tied it up like a sack. I tossed it into the lagoon and dove off of the ship behind it. The empty water bottles floated easily on the surface of the water as I dragged them into shore. When I reached the beach, I tossed the sack over my shoulder like Santa Claus as I hiked down the beach and into the trail leading into the forest. I went straight to the watering hole and spring that Hoku had poisoned long ago. I knelt in front of the pool of crystal clear water and drank from it like a dog. The water was cool, clean and delicious. After I fully hydrated myself, I began to fill each and every bottle with as much water as they would hold. I knew I would need every drop of this precious resource at sea. Every drop I took from the watering hole was instantly replaced by the spring feeding into it as if the universe were replacing what I was taking. Transporting the empty bottles to the spring was easy, but carrying them back to the ship was a challenge. Each trip I made back and forth from the ship to the spring was a blessing. I thanked Mata and God for the wonderful water that they shared with me. I didn't treat the job as work, but rather as a privilege to be transporting the best water in the world to my ship. I spent the majority of the day on the water project until every last bottle was filled to the brim and carefully stowed on the ship.

I then took the empty netting ashore with me. I began to shake palm trees to attempt to convince them to drop their best coconuts. When that didn't work, I put my climbing skills to work and scaled up the tree like a monkey. It was the first time I had climbed like that since my reef incident, but I picked it up again like riding a bicycle. I collected dozens and dozens of coconuts of varying ripeness and hauled them back to the ship. I returned with the net to collect mangos, papaya, oranges, pommel fruit, bananas, guava and anything else edible I could find as well. When the fridge and cabinets on the Mareva were packed as full as they could get, I called it quits and relaxed on deck for the night.

I slept peacefully on the deck under the stars as Mount Mata sheltered me and the lagoon from the windward breeze. I awoke to a beautiful sunrise that backlit the volcano that had sheltered me all night. Mount Mata was summoning me. I jumped off of the ship, swam to shore and hiked the familiar trail all the way to the point. I sat on the point for hours and felt the same presence return that was there on my last visit. I looked to the water, but did not see Lance this time. I wouldn't allow myself to hallucinate or to daydream. I couldn't afford to lose my mind and control of my emotions again. This time it was different. The presence was very comforting and it seemed to radiate from Mount Mata. The presence felt like a blessing of security. I looked to the point where Lance made his final launch and I realized that the point "pointed" to the sea. It was as if Mata was directing me to the sea. I had launched off of the point into the sea to surf dozens of times, but now the message was different. I got it. I said a prayer and final goodbye to Lance. "Walk, surf or swim dude – see you at the spit." I thought to myself as I chose to walk the trail one last time all the way back to the spit.

I stopped in the jungle to gather as much herb and kava kava root as I could carry. I took my board shorts off and wrapped the herbs and roots in the shorts and then walked naked back to the lagoon. I waded into the cool, clear water in the lagoon and then rolled onto my back and kicked with my legs so that I could keep my shorts out of the water with one hand to keep my herbal collection dry.

I prepped the ship and checked everything from top to bottom before raising sails and heading out of the lagoon. I turned back to look at Mata as I sailed away. The island looked so different, yet so familiar to me now. The once mysterious Mata Utu who had been home to the fiercest cannibals in the South Pacific was now all alone and void of all life. The same island that had cursed the lives of countless visitors had just blessed me and shared her bounty with me. I was grateful and appreciative as I thanked her one final time as I circled the island once before heading out to sea.

I sat down at the helm and plotted my course to California. I surveyed all of the instruments and took note that my fuel supply was almost gone – it didn't matter because I no longer needed it. A breeze, favorable currents and calm waters was all I needed for smooth sailing – and so far I had all three. The Mareva cut through the water like a knife. She was so smooth and so easy. It was almost too easy - everything was automated, everything was precise. Mechanically she needed nothing. She was a fine-tuned machine fully prepared to make the trans-Pacific voyage. My confidence level in her and my abilities was strong. There was no doubt in my mind that she would somehow get me to where I needed to go.

It was so nice finally being at sea. The wind was in my sails and in my hair. The sun was in my face and the salt air in my nose. There was something so relaxing about the sea and for the first time in my life, I felt comfortable being alone. I felt alone in more ways than one, but I was getting used to the feeling. The loss of my family and friends back home, the loss of Lance, and now leaving paradise and my Rahitian family and Maruia behind had trained me for this time. It was almost as if I was shedding "layers" of my life. Now I was at the core - it was just me left. I was headed into the uncertain and unknown, but I was prepared - both mentally and physically.

Days turned into weeks as I chose to disregard time altogether. I could have easily kept track of it by putting a notch in the wall or just writing it down - had I chosen to, but I chose not to. I chose to only focus on those things over which I had control – and time was not one of them. I chose to focus on controlling everything on the ship. My OCD nature and diligent planning and preparation kicked into overdrive as I got into a steady routine at sea. I followed my ritual every day and followed my self-imposed schedule to a "T" - even though I had nowhere to be.

I awoke at sunrise every morning and checked the instrumentation for weather and coordinates. I watched as the Mareva steered herself and adjusted the sails to the perfect configuration as the wind changed direction. I walked the deck around and round the ship to check out all of the lines, sails, winches, fittings etc... sometimes touching each one multiple times to make certain that it was in working order. My OCD nature wouldn't let my mind trust my eyes sometimes – I had to actually feel the 'whatever it was' as well. I realized this OCD nature was purpose driven to keep me alive at sea when care and preparation were the difference between survival and death. I practiced some drills in case of a sudden storm or an unexpected guest. I practiced changing a line or repairing a winch or pulley if necessary. Once I had appeased my OCD side and was certain that everything was in working order, I calmed my mind down more by practicing yoga on the deck of the ship. I stretched and posed as I rode the sea. I felt like I was on top of the world as I focused on my breathing and posture. The fresh, clean sea air delighted my nose and senses. It was an awesome feeling. There was also no shortage of meditation time alone at sea. I meditated on nothingness and calmed my mind, body and spirit. There were too many things out of my control to worry about – the weather, currents, pirates, running out of water and food – the list goes on and on. I decided to worry about nothing, but to remain cognoscente of everything as I diligently continued my routine day after day from sunrise to sunset.

I really enjoyed my solitude on the ship, but I occasionally longed for company. The ship was massive, but after walking and pacing around the deck countless times for countless days, the walls started to close in a little. When I started to feel claustrophobic on the giant ship, I would look out at the vastness of the sea. I realized the sea was the answer to my slight restlessness, so I got brave and decided to implement swimming into my daily routine.

I found a long, 100 foot extra cable on board that had a clip at each end. It would make the perfect lanyard or leash to secure me to the vessel for my swims. I looped and tied the cable around the stanchion holding the lifeline on the rear deck and then clipped the lanyard to the backstay cable for added security. Of course, I had to not only visually inspect it, but also touch it numerous times to satisfy my OCD that I would be securely attached to the ship. Once I had determined that the cable was safely secured to the ship, I secured the cable to my ankle and clipped it tight. I stood on the rear deck, spread my arms and sprung from my feet and dove off of the ship and into the deep blue sea. The water was refreshing and cool. It was my first time in the water for weeks since I left the lagoon in Mata. I swam against the direction of the ship until the slack in the cable was gone and the Mareva gently tugged on my leg to let me know she was there. I swam against the ship as she continued to sail with the wind and drag me backwards. It was a great release for me to be swimming in the sea. It made me feel free and connected with the world. I knew the same water that I was swimming in was connected to all of the water in the world – which was connected to the dock at the deepwater terminal back home in Richmond, Virginia. It was a cool thought.

The implementation of the swimming changed the dynamics of my days. If I wasn't doing my OCD checks, yoga on the deck or push-ups, pull-ups or sit-ups – I was probably swimming. I not only loved the physical exertion and exercise I was getting, but also the relaxation that ensued. I would swim against the ship as hard as I could for as long as I could and then I would roll onto my back and let the ship drag me along as I relaxed and let my mind drift into meditation. Then with my last bit of energy, I would use the lanyard to pull myself back up to the ship. I never thought about sharks because I couldn't control them – I just thought about my swimming, breathing and nothingness in meditation. It was a great combination for me.

My body loved being at sea and it reacted well to the workouts and to the intake of the fruits, herbs and water. I strictly rationed my food and water supply and inspected each piece of fruit for potential ripeness – removing them from the fridge in stages to ripen them in the sun on the deck for later consumption. I implemented this discipline and diet into my daily routine as well.

The Mareva offered something so common, but so unappreciated and so forgotten. Mirrors – lots of mirrors throughout – in the bathrooms, the walls, behind the bar – everywhere there seemed to be mirrors. I was able to visualize my appearance with my own eyes once again. I realized that I hadn't seen a mirror or my own face the entire time I was in Rahiti. I realized that the lack of mirrors made me look at my surroundings more and myself less. I had become more connected and paid attention to the people and things around me than I did myself. It was also interesting to think about how long man lived without the use of mirrors. The mirrors on the ship gave me the opportunity to fall in love with myself and be at peace with myself again. I even found myself talking to myself, posing, and even singing in front of the mirror. The mirror helped me see who I really was again and it was also great entertainment in the solitude; however, I often found myself longing for companionship.

In spite of my solitude, I consoled myself with the fact that it was very fulfilling to be totally self-sufficient. I didn't have to rely on anyone else and it was great to know that I only had to answer to myself. I also didn't have to rely on oil for fuel. All I needed was nature – the sun and wind provided all of the energy I needed. Nature had also provided the food and water that I sparingly enjoyed. The culture in Rahiti had been relying exclusively on nature for centuries. My time spent in Rahiti taught me that everything we need to survive is usually right before our eyes. Rahiti needed nothing from the rest of the world and had proven that they could survive despite what was going on in the rest of the world. I was inspired and motivated to prove that I could do the same.

There were times at sea when loneliness got the best of me and there were brief moments when I contemplated turning around and sailing back to Rahiti and Maruia. The loneliness I experienced was comparable to breaking up with a girlfriend or losing a loved one to death. But my curiosity and persistence kicked my motivation and drive into high gear and kept me sailing north east toward the USA. My love for my family and my desire to see them and my friends again kept me on course back home as well. My yoga, meditation, Kava Kava root and herbs kept my mind and body relaxed. My daily ritual of exercise and equipment checks kept me occupied and busy even when there was nothing to do. I tried to remain focused on my mission and goal to get back home to the States. I knew the end result could be worth all of the effort. I tracked my daily progress on the navigation system as I sailed on auto-pilot through the waters of the Pacific toward my homeland.

The Piracy

It was 7:48 am when the alarm sounded and pierced the peaceful silence of the morning. The chime of the alarm echoed from inside the cabin and was clearly audible from every area of the ship. I knew the sound well – it was the proximity alarm I had set up on the radar and GPS device aboard the Mareva. It was a sound that I had both anticipated and feared. My weeks of solitude at sea had brought hopes of encountering another vessel. Being alone for an extended period of time had made me yearn to see another human being. Although I desperately wanted companionship, I feared the looming danger of a visit from pirates. I hoped that I was finally in for a peaceful visit from an innocent passerby, but I knew the reality was that the world was in chaos and piracy was rampant in the seas. Therefore, I had prepared for this scenario countless times since the day I made the decision to embark on my journey on the Mareva. I had drilled dozens of times with my equipment and had formulated plans and procedures in the event of an attack. I felt prepared.

I silenced the alarm and took a long, hard look at the radar screen. Sure enough, there was a relatively small, fast moving vessel heading in my direction portside from about 25 miles out. I grabbed my binoculars and peered out of the portside window to scan the horizon. I couldn't see anything. That was good because if I couldn't' see them, it meant they still couldn't see me. I wondered if they had spotted me on radar as well. I wondered if they were on a path to intercept me or if it was pure happenchance that another ship was randomly heading straight in my direction. I didn't have the luxury to risk guesswork. I knew I had to treat the situation with worst case scenarios so I sprang to action. I strapped on my gun belt, snorkeling mask and dive vest. I grabbed the Mareva's oxygen tank and ventilator from their purposefully convenient stow-away cabinet. I pulled out the infrared binocs and activated them, pulling them over my head to let them hang around my neck for the time being. I emerged from the cabin onto the deck, but took care to stay low profile and keep out of sight. I knew the vessel would be entering eyeshot from a good set of binoculars soon.

My best advantage would be the element of surprise and the unknown. Whoever was making a bee line for me was coming onto my turf. The Mareva was my haven and if someone wanted to pay me a visit it was going to be on my terms.

I kept my eyes focused on the portside horizon as I quickly checked the deck for any signs of recent activity and life onboard my own vessel. I didn't want to leave any clues as to the occupancy of my ship. I stowed a couple of items in plain sight very quickly. I flipped the lid on the starboard stowaway in the aft of the steering well. I grabbed a retractable lanyard and the magnetic hands. I sat in the steering well at the helm and checked all of my equipment. I pulled the infrared binocs up to my eyes and gave a quick glance through them. I could see my own body heat radiating a glow in the lenses. I gave my vest a tug and pulled the straps tight for a sleek, snug fit. I checked the belt and pulled the Glock 23 from the snap tight grip on the holster. I pulled the clip from the Glock and verified it was full of 40 caliber hollow points. I slapped the clip back into the rubberized grip on the gun and returned it to its holster. It was amazing that the gun spent several months on the reef at the bottom of the Rahitian inlet without so much as a bit of rust forming on it. It was in perfect condition and good working order after its hide-and-seek in the sea. I hoped I wouldn't have to use it, but it was nice to have and to know that it was ready if I needed it.

I decided to leave the sails up and stay on my current course. If the approaching vessel was tracking me on radar I didn't want to let them know I saw them coming by making any sudden changes. I quickly surveyed the cabin as I clipped the magnetic grips and lanyard to my vest. Everything was as good as it was going to get onboard. I strapped the binoculars around my arm and rose my head up above the height of the deck to check the horizon again. I could see nothing with my naked eye. It was 7:56 am – eight minutes since the alarm had sounded. My preparation time was right on schedule as I had rehearsed so many times. It was time to go into defense mode. I pulled the binoculars to my eyes and looked to the horizon again. I focused in the area where the radar had last shown me the vessel. Sure enough, I saw an approaching boat. It looked to be a small speedboat about 30 to 40 feet in length. I knew the boat must be accompanied by a larger vessel somewhere not too far away. There was no way that a ship that size could be this far out in open water without having a mother ship to refuel and operate from. This was the scout or the cavalry and the headquarters was somewhere just outside of the range of my radar. I zoomed in close on the approaching ship with the binocs. It was about 10 to 15 miles out and traveling at a speed of what I estimated to be about 40 knots. I didn't have much time.

Although I could not yet make out the passengers onboard, I had a really bad feeling about the circumstances. I made sure that I stayed low and out of sight for now. I low crawled to the aft deck where I pulled my mask onto my face and strapped the grippers onto my hands. I then kissed the deck of the Mareva as if to say goodbye momentarily and then I slid into the water. I worked my way around the starboard side of the ship with the help of the grippers until I reached the bow. The gentle breeze was propelling my ship through the water at a manageable speed of about 8 knots. I had little difficulty clinging to the hull and maintaining my grip on my ship. I took a peek under the surface of the water and located the eyelet on the ridge of the bow slightly under the surface of the water. I clipped the end of the retractable lanyard to the eyelet and gave it a tug to ensure it was attached firmly. I wanted to make damn sure that I had a secure attachment to the ship so I didn't worry about losing the Mareva to the wind. Nothing was going to take her from me – neither pirates nor Mother nature. Once I was securely fastened, I released one gripper and slid my left hand free. I removed the mask and pulled the binocs to my eyes and peered around the bow from the starboard side back to the portside horizon. This time the approaching boat was in plain sight of the naked eye and was crystal clear in the cross-hairs of the binocs.

There were four men visible in the cockpit of the boat. One of them had an automatic weapon in his hands and a strap of ammo over his shoulder. Another guy was looking through binoculars as well – straight in my direction of course. I doubted they could see me at all from my vantage point. I was almost totally submerged in the water and in the shadow of the bow. Plus, I knew they would be looking on the deck of my ship for signs of activity rather than in the water. Still, I didn't take any chances and made a diligent effort to stay hidden as I continued to observe the approaching boat. I felt an adrenaline rush course through my body as I stared at the guy with the gun. The driver commanded the speed boat from a standing position at the wheel. There was no longer any doubt that I was about to be under attack from real life pirates. I was ready.

I put the binocs back on my arm, pulled the mask back down over my face and put the oxygen on my mouth. I slid down the hull and submerged my body underwater. When my ears submerged, I could hear the roar of the engine from the approaching speedboat. I breathed deeply into the ventilator and controlled my anxiety with calming breaths. The underwater view with the infrared mask was spectacularly clear. I reattached my left hand to the magnetic gripper and stuck it securely to the underside of my hull to keep a close grip on the ship. I heard the ship's engines roaring closer and closer and could hear the boat's hull smacking into the water with every wave it jumped. My heart slightly jumped as well with nervous anticipation. Bring it on pirates.

"Pirates, damn pirates!" I mumbled to myself. Pirates, loot, pillage and plunder - and kill. But what do pirates say? I believe there is a pirate slogan that goes something like "Dead men tell no tales." Well, I planned to live today to tell my tales. I planned to return home and tell of Lance, Mata Utu, Hoku and my Rahitian friends. I planned to learn the tale of the fate of everyone back home. I would survive to tell many more tales. I had no intention of dying at the hands of pirates today - or ever.

It didn't take long for my visitors to reach me. They made a big circle around the perimeter of the Mareva to check out all sides of the ship. I remained hidden well under the surface of the water as I clung to the hull. I could clearly see the underside of their hull and the two propellers from the twin outboards as they churned the teal green water into frothy foam around me. The boat tightened its circle and pulled portside aft to moor up to the Mareva. I heard one of the men shouting in a language I couldn't understand as if to summon any passengers on my ship to their attention. I remained silent and listened more. The shouting request continued. Although I couldn't understand the language, I interpreted the message as "get up on deck so we can shoot you and loot you" and, by the tone of his voice, he meant business.

From underwater, I held up the infrared binocs to my mask and they picked up the glow from the boat's engines. I could also make out the distinctive glow of body heat from all 4 men. Right now I was in the absolute best position I could be in to defend myself and the Mareva. It may not sound like hiding under my ship was a good defensive plan, but it allowed me to exercise my best weapon of surprise. I knew the pirates would board my vessel in a moment if they did not get a response. I knew based on the body motion of two of the men that they were tying up to the side of my ship. I had to be patient and wait for the right opportunity. I crossed my fingers and hoped that they would split up a little bit. I got my wish as three of the men climbed onboard my ship. They cautiously slid under the rail on the portside of the Mareva. I could tell by their posture and body motions that they had their guns drawn. They were ready to shoot and kill.

I watched in infrared as the three men boarded my vessel and walked down the deck to the cockpit. Had I not been awake and prepared, I would certainly be in big trouble right now as I would almost definitely be at gun point up on deck. Instead, I am hidden, well armed and well equipped. The element of surprise is in my favor. I can imagine the pirates must be wondering why no one is on board and who in their right mind would leave an expensive and exquisite vessel to drift at sea alone. I'm sure their life of piracy on the high seas has yielded some interesting scenarios and discoveries. I wanted this to be their last one. The fact that they are armed with automatic weapons tells me that they intend to shoot to kill. If you are going to loot someone and steal their boat, how can you possibly keep them alive? If you set them adrift at sea in a lifeboat, it is almost certainly a death sentence this far from land and with no means to call for help. If you take them prisoner with you, then you have to secure them, feed them and give them vital rations of water while you also constantly look over your shoulder to make sure they are not going to try to retaliate and kill you or steal their boat back and split. I wondered how many people they had killed already.

I surveyed the thermally illuminated scene above me. Two guys were descending into the cabin of the Mareva. One guy stood sentry on top of her deck. The fourth guy remained sitting in the speedboat. I formulated a plan. I convinced myself it was going to work flawlessly. I became focused. I knew what I had to do. I thought about the night I learned about Mata Utu and how Hoku had singlehandedly defeated the Matain cannibals. I imagined the courage, bravery and determination that he must have possessed while hiding out on Mata Utu and executing the Matains one by one. I imagined his fears or lack thereof. I imagined the bitter sweet feeling of avenging the death of his wife by killing the person that killed her and killing the cannibal tribe that ate her. Bastards! Now I had three bastards on my boat and one on the getaway threatening my life and my peace and tranquility. Forcing me to hide. Forcing me to take defensive actions. Forcing me to kill. I told myself it wasn't murder – it was self defense. Kill or be killed.

I checked my courage and focused my thoughts. I carefully and deliberately drew the Glock from its holster making sure not to drop it. A gun on the bottom of the ocean would do me no good right now. I let go of the hull, rolled onto my back and submerged deeper. I looked up at the hulls of the two vessels above me as they cast underwater shadows of the sunlight dancing through the surface of the water. It was calm and peaceful underwater. I took a couple of slow, powerful strokes backward to propel myself deep under the hull of the speedboat. I drew the gun and aligned the cross hair on the Glock with the chest of the driver who was seated in the speedboat. I could plainly see his body image through the infrared binocs and my mask. I contemplated whether to go for an easier hit in the chest or to go for the more difficult but instant kill in the head. I decided to risk missing and going for the head to minimize the possibility that my target would have the chance to let out a scream or to possibly have enough life left in him to shoot back. Firing the gun underwater should act as a silencer and keep my secrecy intact for the moment. I glanced over to the Mareva and noted the position of the guy on the opposite starboard side of the deck as well as the guys below in the front berth and in the galley. Aside from the gun, the mask and binocs were my best weapon. They gave me x-ray eyes and allowed me to pick the perfect time for action. As I floated on my back about 10 feet below the surface of the water, I realized that now was the time to make my move. The pirates were as separate as they could possibly be. I steadied myself, took a deep breath of tank oxygen and focused the barrel of the Glock on the head of the guy seated in the speedboat. He sat perfectly still. It was the first time I ever had someone in the sight of my gun – especially with the intent of killing them. Kill or be killed I told myself again. I pulled the trigger. The recoil from the gun was nominal and the noise was minimal and muted. But the reaction was immediate and profound as my target lurched forward, hunched over and then fell to the floor of the boat. I could see a large red splotch forming around him in infrared as the 98.6 degree blood flowed from his head onto the deck of the speedboat. I knew I had a direct hit. I also knew it would be only a matter of seconds or minutes before the lookout on the deck of the Mareva would notice.

I kicked my legs to propel myself back farther to clear the hull of both ships from my line of fire. I drew the gun up and brought the lookout into my sights. This time I aimed square at his chest as he was much higher up and farther away than the speedboat driver. I didn't want to risk a miss this time. I knew a direct hit to the chest would send him overboard if I got him while he was standing close to the edge. I waited patiently until he stood perfectly still. I breathed deep and pulled the trigger. I watched in infrared as the shock of the impact sent his body falling backwards over the rail and into the water. He splashed down into the water on the other side of the Mareva. I heard the splash and felt the impact of his fall even from my depth and distance in the water I knew I had to move quickly now. Certainly the pirates inside would have heard him fall overboard as well.

I grabbed the lanyard with my left hand and pulled myself back under the hull of the Mareva and over to the other side where the pirate landed. I saw him floating face down on the surface. He was staring at me. His eyes were wide open and the look of shock covered his face. A stream of blood poured from his chest and left a red trail in the water. "Shark bait" I thought. I wondered how long he would float there. I wondered if the weight of the automatic rifle and ammo strapped around his shoulder would pull him down quickly. I contemplated grabbing the gun off of his body, but thought it would be better to let it be and keep my hands free for the moment. I still had eleven bullets left. I was two for two. I returned my focus to the hull of the Mareva. I could see the two pirates rummaging through my stuff inside. I had them clear as day in the infrared focus of my mask. I could easily shoot them through the steel hull and they would never know what hit them. I hesitated to do that for fear of the damage that it may do to my own ship. I had tools and repair kits onboard and could probably easily patch a small bullet hole or two, but I had no idea how long it would take to get it done. I feared that a gunfight would break out from inside the ship. An automatic rifle could put a lot of holes in a ship's hull in a hurry. There was too much wiring, plumbing and delicate equipment inside the ship that could not be repaired at sea. I had to minimize the possibility of damage. A sinking ship would surely mean a death sentence to me aside from the pirates. I assessed the situation in my mind repeatedly. Two down, two to go. Advantage was to me as I still maintained the element of surprise.

Remarkably the two pirates inside the ship didn't seem alarmed as they apparently had not heard any of the underwater gunfire or the fall from the deck. They continued on pillaging the cabin of my ship. It pissed me off. I felt violated. The Mareva was mine. Granted, I had "inherited" her due to the apparent misfortune of her previous owner, but I got her fair and square in my mind. I pampered her, outfitted her and worked diligently to make her better for months. I appreciated the opportunity to sail and care for such a beautiful and luxurious vessel. I would never take anything from anyone at gunpoint. I would never go into someone's house, ship or sanctuary and take something by force that wasn't rightfully mine. These pirates had every intention of doing so. I am sure that now, in their eyes, they saw an abandoned ship and everything in it theirs for the taking. However, I am confident that, had the ship been occupied, they would have seen the occupants as obstacles and would have eliminated them in the same fashion as I just handled the two pirates. Kill or be killed I told myself again.

I watched the infrared images of the two remaining pirates from below through the hull of my ship. I was in a quandary as to what to do. I wanted to pull the trigger and drop them both while they were inside the ship, but I couldn't bring myself to shoot through the Mareva. My only other choice was to meet them on the deck and handle business there. The problem was that my element of surprise would be gone the moment they emerged onto the deck and found their lookout floating face down in the water and their getaway driver lying in a pool of blood in the speedboat. I had to maintain the element of surprise. I had to act fast – now. If they came up on deck, they would quickly figure out what happened and a flurry of gunfire from their automatic rifles would ensue. I seriously doubted they would be dumb enough to think the two pirates got into an argument and shot each other while they were pillaging below deck. Besides the fact they would have heard obvious and loud gunfire, the story probably wouldn't add up. Pirates killed and looted the innocent, not each other as far as I knew.

I decided it was best to risk two calculated 40 caliber holes put in the hull by me rather than hundreds of AK-47 rounds sprayed all over the ship by the pirates. The challenge was shooting through water and the solid steel hull of the ship. The last two targets were in open air and I had a clear, unobstructed shot from my underwater vantage point. The water has the ability to change the speed and trajectory of the bullet thus throwing off the accuracy of the gun, but I knew the gun was much more accurate going from the water to the air rather than shooting from the air into the water. I was glad I had listened and paid attention to my many conversations with my Navy Seal friends and military gurus that I knew back home. My concern with the current scenario was shooting through the water and the hull. The steel hull would most certainly flatten the tip of the hollow point rounds I was using. That would slow the bullet significantly and dramatically change its path and effectiveness. I could not risk a miss this time. A miss would mean disaster because the retaliation would be devastating to the safety of the ship.

I changed my mind and concocted another plan. I pulled myself to the bow with the help of the lanyard. I quietly surfaced from the water. I holstered the Glock and slipped the magnetic grippers onto my hands. I suctioned them to the side of the hull and then alternated releasing the suction with a slight twist of each hand as I climbed the side of the bow. I was cautious to stay clear of the view from the porthole as I made my way up to the starboard side rail. I wasn't too concerned with making slight noises as the pirates would certainly think that it was their lookout standing sentry on the deck. I still fixated on the infrared images inside. They were really taking their time going through my shit. They must have thought they hit the mother lode. I know the bastards were going through my equipment and I even saw the pirate in the galley drinking my precious Mata water and eating my fruit. I thought to myself "one last sip of the finest water in the world before you die asshole."

I released the magnetism from my right hand and slid my hand out of the gripper. I grasp the rail firmly with my right hand as I released my left hand from its gripper. This was the time when all of my pull-ups and workouts were going to pay off. I pulled myself up and over the rail and onto the deck with relative ease just as I had practiced so many times before. I imagined I was Hoku preying on the Matains – one against many. I quickly replaced that thought and substituted it with the image of a Navy Seal rescuing a hostage. Right now the Mareva was the hostage and I was her liberator. I took a second to kiss her deck before I planted my bare feet back onto the deck firmly and silently. I released the straps on my vest and oxygen tank and slid my arms out to free me from the semi-cumbersome load I carried on my back. I left the infrared binocs and mask on my face. I knew the deck of the ship like the back of my hand and could navigate it even in my infrared vision that was now impaired as I was in the heat of the sun and direct sunlight. Nonetheless, it enabled me to keep the pirates in my sight through the deck of the ship. I heard them talking from inside the ship. Their language was unrecognizable to me and I didn't care what they were saying anyway.

I made my way across the deck slowly and deliberately taking soft steps as to not alarm them below. I stopped in front of the cockpit above the stairwell to the cabin. I focused my infrared vision downward and back. The pirate in the galley was almost directly below me. His vision of me was blocked by the hatch over the stairs. I was in a great position now. I knew what I had to do. I was ready to make my move when I heard the galley pirate's voice directed up to the deck. I was sure he was talking to the lookout. He paused and waited a second before shouting something, possibly the lookout's name. Of course there was no response. Just as I was about to make my move, the galley pirate said something to the pirate up front in the berth. They conversed for a second and the pirate in the galley began climbing the stairs directly below me. I slid the infrared binocs and mask down my face and let it hang from my neck. I drew the Glock from the holster. I aimed the gun directly at the top stair. I knew this was going to be a close range shot that I couldn't miss. I crouched down just behind the hatch on the stairs where the pirate would emerge. I let his head fully emerge above deck and then pulled the trigger and blew a hole in the back of his head. From my crouched position I swiftly jumped over the hatch and into the stairwell. I landed on the dead pirate's bloody, limp body. I turned quickly, jumped up and charged through the galley and down the hall to the front berth where I met the last pirate face to face. He was so surprised to see me. The look on his face was priceless. His eyes darted over to confirm the hole in the back of his pirate friends head and then returned to meet the barrel of my gun pointed directly at his forehead. He froze and his eyes locked with mine. I was ready to shoot him with the slightest flinch or even if he blinked wrong. I realized the pirate was terrified as I saw a look of fear overcome his face. In a nanosecond I glanced into the berth and saw his automatic rifle lying on my bed. He was unarmed – or at least he didn't have his big gun handy. I assumed he may be carrying a sidearm or a blade so I kept my senses alert and maintained focus in his eyes. Three down and one of us would be the last man standing.

The look on his face changed something in me. The other three guys I had killed without seeing their faces. In fact, the first two I had killed from a distance in infrared vision and the third I shot in the back of the head, never seeing his face. The memory of the lookout's face floating face down in the water staring at me had not daunted me as much as the look on the face of the living guy in front of me. He remained silent, but his eyes pleaded for mercy. I thought from his point of view. A moment ago he was in seventh heaven. He and his three buddies had stumbled onto a multi-million dollar sailboat in the middle of the ocean. They entered, guns drawn, expecting to exact a hostile takeover of the vessel and rid it of its occupants. I'm sure they were surprised to find no one on board. They relished the thought of sailing back home on their new find and looting its contents. A moment ago they had no idea that I was here. A split second ago he was talking to his buddy who no longer has a face now compliments of the exit wound from the hollow point 40 caliber I shot through the back of his head at point blank range. Seeing his buddy lying there in a pool of his own blood and brains must have been a sobering sight. Now he was looking down the barrel of the same gun that had dealt the round to his friend's head. I'm sure he was shitting his pants right now. I'm sure this was the biggest surprise of this guy's life. I wanted him to take in the moment. I wanted him to be uncomfortable. I wanted him to realize that I had just defeated three of his pirate friends with three single shots – two of which went unheard and unnoticed. I wanted to see the fear of death in his face. I wanted him to feel it for the inconvenience and stress that he had caused me by paying me an unwanted visit.

I kept the gun inches from his face with my right hand as I gestured with my left hand for him to raise his hands and put them on his head. He slowly and deliberately obliged as to not make any sudden movements that may spook me. Once his hands were laced on top of his head, he quietly spoke something to me. I couldn't even figure out what language they were speaking or what nationality they were - and quite frankly I didn't care. I had not anticipated being face to face with the pirate. I had planned to shoot him at first sight, but I found myself suddenly incapable of shooting an unarmed man face to face in cold blood.

I motioned and pointed for the pirate to go up the stairs to the deck. I maintained a little distance between us to prevent a quick attack or attempt to grab my gun. He made his way from the berth through the den to the galley. He stepped over his dead friend's body and started up the steps looking down only momentarily at the bloody mess. I was prepared to shoot him with any wrong movement and he knew it. I tried to think from his point of view to anticipate what he may be thinking or planning in his head.

We reached the deck and he surveyed the scene. I'm sure at this point he was not shocked to find his lookout gone and his getaway driver dead in the speedboat. By my dripping wet appearance and the infrared binocs and mask on my neck, I'm sure he quickly started to figure out what happened. I'm sure it was a humbling realization to him that three heavily armed pirates had just been killed by one man with a handgun. I could tell by his demeanor and body language that he had accepted defeat. My feelings would be different had someone just killed three of my friends; however, I would have never been on the offensive in the situation. Pirates must know that when they enter someone's ship they are taking their lives into their own hands. I wondered how many ships they had looted and how many people they had killed. It must be an awakening to now be on the opposite end of the barrel of a gun.

I motioned him from the cockpit to the deck toward the mast. I grabbed a rope from the stowaway box next to the stern. I followed him from two steps behind with the gun held firmly in my right hand and the rope in my left, keeping him in my gun sight at all times. We reached the mast and I rounded him and came face to face. He cut his eyes down to the speedboat and saw his getaway lying in the floor of the boat with half of his head missing. He must be wondering where the lookout was, but I could tell he had little hope of a sudden appearance and rescue from his missing friend. I was at a critical point now. I would have to holster the gun and use both hands to tie him up. If there was a time for him to make a move it would be right now. I didn't get the sense that he was going to try anything. He seemed too dejected to try to fight. I wondered if he spoke English, so I asked. He responded quietly in his native tongue. Verbal communication between us was not going to work, so I motioned for him to turn around. I quickly clipped the gun into the holster and unfurled the rope. I was very cautious as I looped the nylon rope around his right elbow. I pulled his arm backward as I tugged the knot tight. I then grabbed his left arm with my left hand and pulled it back as well. He did not even try to resist as I looped the rope around his left elbow. I synched the slip knot tight and drew his arms together at the elbow behind his back and then square knotted it to keep tension. I reached to my belt and grabbed the buck knife from its pouch and cut the rope off. I then cut off a four foot section and bent down to tie his feet together. I was once again very cautious to stay clear of danger as I anticipated he may try to kick me in the face or pounce on me while I was crouched down. Once again he did not resist. Once his feet were secure, I rose and met him eye to eye. I motioned and pushed him backwards toward the mast. He shuffled his feet backwards and backed up to the mast. I spun around behind him, pulled his arms around the mast from behind and tied his hands together on the opposite side of the mast with my knot tying skills. He was now tied at the elbows between his back and the mast and then his hands were bound on the other side of the mast. It must have been a very uncomfortable position. I then tied the rope binding his feet together to the base of the mast. The probability of him escaping was next to impossible, but the chance of him losing blood to his hands and feet was highly probable.

I patted him down and searched his body for any type of weapon or blade. I found nothing. I guess the only weapon he brought to the party was the AK-47 automatic rifle that now lay on my bed in the front berth. I guess when you bring a weapon like that, you really don't think you would need anything else. For the first time since the alarm sounded, I could now relax. I looked at my watch – it was 9:02. This ordeal had lasted over an hour, but it felt like an eternity. Every second seems like an hour when you are in survival mode. I wondered how the pirate now felt about time. He must know that his time is very limited now. He has witnessed death and he knows that I have no qualms about blowing the head off of a pirate. I wondered what he was thinking. I wondered what he thought I would do next. I bet he regretted ever stepping foot on the Mareva.

I pulled the infrared binocs and mask from my neck and up over my head. I removed the belt and the rest of my equipment and got comfortable. I walked back to the cockpit and glanced around. The body of the faceless pirate was draped over the stairwell and covered in a bloody mess. It was a nauseating sight that was going to be an ordeal to clean up. Everything else on the deck was in order except for a couple of splotches of blood where the lookout once stood. I looked overboard for the lookout, but did not see him anywhere. I jumped back up on the main deck and made my way around the port side to the stern. I looked down between the two boats to see if the body may be lodged there, but it wasn't. I leaned over the bow and looked all around, but saw nothing floating. I assumed the body sank. His chance of survival was zero. I hit him directly in the chest before he plummeted into the water where he floated face down for minutes while leaking out blood. He must have sunk or a shark must have gotten him. I put any fears of the lookout surviving or coming back on board to rest. I did notice my captive curiously watching as I had been searching. I may have given him the brief glimmer of hope that his lookout was missing and alive. I addressed the captive pirate in plain, slow, enunciated English and asked "How does it feel now? How does it feel to be the captive?" He stared at me blankly and did not respond with his mouth, but his eyes answered with fear and uncertainty. I could tell he was thinking "why the hell did we have to mess with James Bond – of all the ships, we chose this one. Shit." He cut his eyes down to the deck and slouched slightly. He was accepting defeat.

Now I had a dilemma. I found myself in the same quandary that I assumed pirates were in when they took captives. I desperately sought some human contact after weeks of solitude, but there was no way I could trust this guy. He came to murder me and loot me and steal my ship. If I let him survive and stay onboard, I would have to live with the fear that he would cut my throat or shoot me while I slept in retaliation of the murder of his friends or just purely for the chance to steal again. I was also having difficulty grappling with the notion of killing an unarmed man in cold blood. The other three pirates had been easy, this guy was different.

For the first time, I really stepped back and checked out my captive. He was about 5'8" tall, dark complexion, black hair, brown eyes, medium build with a slight gut. His gut told me he must be a good pirate to be eating so well. He was wearing shorts, a tee shirt and no shoes. I guessed his age to be roughly about 25 years old. I wished he could talk to me. I had so many questions to ask him. I wanted to know where he came from and if others were on their way. I wanted to know where and how they fueled their boat and what the range on it was. Since I couldn't speak to him, I decided to do some investigation on my own. I also figured it would be nice to give him a taste of his own medicine by making him watch as I pillaged and plundered his boat.

I made my way to the port side of the Mareva where the speedboat was moored to her aft cleat. The speedboat was a 44' Scarab with twin inboard/outboards. The Mareva dwarfed it in size - making it look like a dingy or toy. The deck height of the scarab was several feet below the deck height of the Mareva. The scarab was, no doubt, a sexy, sleek boat. I couldn't wait to check it out closer. I slid under the rail and hopped down onto the bow of the pirates' vessel. It was a very nice boat and was painted purple and yellow and was as clean as a whistle on the outside. I wondered how long ago they had stolen it and who they had to kill to get it. I made my way aft and jumped over the console and into the cockpit next to the pirate lying in a pool of blood. I looked around the cockpit for a bit and then raised the lid on the engine compartment. I was amazed at the custom twin 454's that powered the vessel. They were decked out in chrome and braided hoses – someone put a lot of time and pride into building this boat. I glanced up from the engine compartment toward the Mareva's mast to check on my captive. He was still there and staring back intently at me as I looked about his boat. I had to hear it fire up. The boat had sounded beastly from underwater when they arrived - now I wanted to hear it from up close. I stepped back over the dead pirate and straddled the driver's seat. The key was still in the ignition. I turned the key and the engines rumbled to life. They sounded wicked. I goosed the throttle with it in neutral and the engines roared. What a machine! It was the perfect boat for speed to chase someone down, but not so practical for the open ocean. These twin engines must drink gallons of gas a minute. Even with additional gas tanks, the range on this boat was still probably less than 300 miles. The boat was probably capable of speeds in excess of 100 mph. My guess was that the pirates chose to cruise at around 40 knots as they had done when they approached me to conserve fuel. Fuel conservation was the last thing on my mind. I wanted to blast it out for a minute or two. I pushed the pirates' limp body away from the console and into the middle of the cockpit. I climbed on the rear deck and undid the moorings to the Mareva. I jumped back down into the captain's chair and perused the console to familiarize myself with the instrument panel and its gauges. I popped the throttle trigger and dropped her into gear. The beastly roar of the engines dropped in tone and began to lope and chop. This boat was ready to roll. I was also. I cut the wheel at a 90 and let the power of the engines at idle slide me away from the hull of my Mareva. I glanced back up at the pirate who was staring at me intently. I waved bye and nailed the throttle. The engines sprang to life and raised the bow out of the water and 45 degrees to the horizon. The scarab shot out of the water as if it had a rocket strapped to it. I hit 80 knots in seconds and put some distance between me and the Mareva in no time. I hunkered down into the captain's chair and spun the wheel hard to starboard. The ship turned on a dime and pulled some serious g's doing it. This was "getting it". She bounced and launched from wave to wave. The dead pirate on the deck bounced a foot or two off the floor with every launch and then slammed back down onto the deck – tossing from side to side like a ragdoll and bouncing him off the deck like a basketball. Blood was everywhere on the floor. I didn't care. I was having too much fun.

I aimed back 180 degrees in the direction of the Mareva. I laid into the throttle harder and closed in quick on the graceful Mareva dead ahead. I buzzed by her in an instant sending a huge wake to slap her hull and rock her like a baby in a cradle. The captive pirate spun his head around to keep watch on me as I whizzed by. I hollered at the top of my lungs out of joy. Whew – what a fun day! Kill three pirates, capture one, inherit some guns and then take a spin in the middle of the Pacific on a speedboat. I immediately started to think how I was going to keep my new toy.

I kept on the throttle hard as she launched and splashed into and out of the sea. Adrenaline rushed through my body. I love speed! I finally backed off the throttle when I hit 110. I glanced back as the Mareva got smaller and smaller in the rapidly increasing distance. My fun was momentarily spoiled when I got a sudden paranoid premonition that the pirate was scheming or escaping while I was out playing. I made one big wide circle as I wheeled the scarab back in the direction of the Mareva. I stayed in the throttle hard as the boat careened on its side and dug into the water. The damn thing handled like it was on rails. The dead pirate almost rolled clear out of the cockpit as the boat was angled so hard. I spun around full circle and then crossed my own wake and launched airborne as I nailed the wave. The engines roared loudly as they were momentarily relieved of the stress of turning the props in the water as I flew through the air. I braced myself and slammed down hard. Whoo! That was the most air I had caught in anything short of an airplane. I stayed full throttle until I was within a half mile of the Mareva again and then I pulled back hard and let the ship throttle down. The scarab quickly righted itself back down into a horizontal position and her forward progress slowed quickly. For a boat that moved so fast and nimble in the water at full throttle, she sure was a helpless pig without the horsepower propelling her. Kill the throttle and you get the same effect as throwing an anchor overboard – quite contrary to the Mareva's ability to glide and coast through the water even with little wind. I slowed all the way back down to a no-wake-zone speed and coasted back up to the Mareva on her port side aft. I wanted to take in the view of my beautiful vessel. I loved the quick exhilarating thrill ride in the scarab, but it was no substitute for the grace, beauty and natural efficiency of my sail boat. I wouldn't trade her for 1000 scarabs.

The pirate was still in full attention at the mast as he watched me approach. I could tell he was very curious as to what I was doing in his boat. I'm glad he was interested. I hope he felt as violated as I did when he was rummaging through my berth on my ship. I paralleled the scarab next to the port side aft of the Mareva and gently bumped her steel hull. I jumped up from the captain's chair and grabbed the mooring rope and tossed it around the cleat on the deck of the sailboat. I pulled the line tightly to secure the scarab to her hull. I didn't really care that the two hulls were rubbing together and slightly scuffing the paint. Who was gonna see it out here in the middle of the sea? Once the scarab was moored securely, I jumped onto her bow and then pulled myself up and over the rail onto the deck of the Mareva. I approached the pirate with a big smile on my face. "Wow, that was fun?! Are you having fun too – Mr. Pirate?" I sassed him, but he either didn't understand my sarcasm from the tone in my voice or he was too defeated to care. I made eye contact with him to attempt to connect with him mentally. He was blank – no expression or emotion remained in him whatsoever. I walked around the mast behind him and checked on the ropes that secured his hands and feet. The knots were still as tight and perfectly tied as when I left him. It didn't appear that he had struggled too much. The ropes were tight and slightly constricting the blood flow to his hands – I could tell by the redness in the skin on his wrists. I didn't care. If his hands fell off, he could replace them with hooks – after all, he was a pirate – right? I purposefully showed my lack of concern and went on about my business.

I returned portside and jumped down onto the deck of the scarab again. I checked out all of the gauges and instruments on the console. The speedboat was carrying what appeared to be over a half tank of gasoline which unfortunately was useless to me as the Mareva's engine ran on diesel fuel. I opened the hatch to her cabin and had a peek inside. It was definitely a pirate's berth. There was shit strewn everywhere, but I couldn't help but think that my quick jaunt around the block hadn't jarred a few things loose in the cabin. I pushed the dead pirate clear of the stairwell as I made my way down the ladder and into the cabin. The inside of the scarab reeked of stale cigarette smoke and booze – two smells I hadn't smelt in almost a year. The smell was repulsive, but familiar. The first cabinet I opened revealed the source of the booze smell. There was about a dozen or so bottles of booze and wine. Captain Morgan's spiced rum, Absolut vodka, Bacardi rum, Malibu and Goslings too – pirates really do prefer rum! I was also delighted to find two bottles of Australian shiraz. I guess the wine was for when the pirates were feeling "sophisticated". I pulled the liquor and wine from the cabinets and sat the bottles on the countertop. This would be a nice treat for later. I had earned some booze. Just to screw with the pirate, I let out a whoop and laughter to let him know I was having fun. Moments later, I emerged from the cabin of the scarab with a bottle of rum pressed to my lips and my head tilted back as if I were chugging it. I stumbled around the deck of the scarab as if I were drunk to amuse myself. I sang "ho-ho-hum, I gots me a bottle of rum. The open sea, it's good to be free – it's a pirate's life for me!" The pirate didn't find it funny and turned his head away to look in the opposite direction. I didn't let his lack of interest spoil my fun. I carried on my drunken stupor in jest to amuse myself. Thoughts of actually getting drunk later entered my mind. It had been one year since I smelt, touched, tasted or even saw a bottle of booze. Now I found myself with a liquor cabinet full of it. Party time – pirate style!

I put down the bottle and returned to the cabin of the scarab. I enjoyed rummaging through the pirate's shit in the same fashion that they had done to me. I pillaged and plundered through their mostly worthless belongings. I found a few other things of interest – some knives, additional ammo, cigars, a couple of playboy magazines and a wind breaker with rain poncho. I was also delighted to find a couple pairs of polarized sunglasses. I bundled up my findings in a pillow case and slung it over my shoulder like Santa Claus. I grabbed another pillow case and perused the galley. There were about a dozen or so gallon jugs of water, a couple cans of warm beer, and some packaged boxes and cans of food. The one thing that struck me as odd was the absence of any radar, radio or communication devices. It briefly made me question how the pirates had spotted me and tracked me down. It reinforced the fact that there was probably a mother ship somewhere not too far away. I grabbed everything of value and tossed it into the pillow case. I emerged again from the cabin of the scarab, but this time with a big smile on my face and yet a more serious demeanor. I tossed the stuffed pillow cases onto the deck of the Mareva and then hopped up on deck behind them. I proudly sat down on the warm teak wood deck of my own vessel and dumped out the contents of the pillow cases and looked over my bounty. I glanced up at the pirate who was pretending not to pay attention. "How does it feel Mr. Pirate? To have YOUR ship looted for a change?" He did not acknowledge me. "Ammo, food, knives, water and... what is this?" I grabbed one of the Playboys and walked over to the pirate. I opened it up and let the centerfold page drop out and fully extend. I held it up in front of him. "Nice, is this your girlfriend?" I asked. He looked away. "Oh, come on man, have some fun with me. You guys were having all the fun earlier, now it is my turn." His lack of response just motivated me to antagonize him more. I looked down at the deck of my ship and saw a rivulet of fluid running toward the side of the deck. I traced the liquid trail back to the mast where it appeared to originate from the pirate's feet. I then glanced up to his crotch and noticed it was wet. "Aw, did Mr. Pirate pee himself? Did I scare the piss out of you? I'm sorry, I meant to scare the shit out of you instead. Oh, well – the day is not over yet." I just couldn't resist taunting my captive. I didn't feel too bad about it considering that he couldn't understand me anyway in addition to the fact that he had come to kill me and steal from me. I was blessed to have the opportunity to taunt him. It could have easily been me lying on the deck in a pool of my own blood. Instead, I was me doing the looting. I inherited a total of three Ak-47 rifles with over a dozen fully loaded clips as well as several straps of additional ammo, knives, cigars, cigarettes, 14 gallons of water and some food as well as some good booze and wine. Plus I got to take a joyride at 100 mph in the scarab. Not a bad haul for one man in one day.

I put my newfound treasures back into the pillow cases and made my way back to the cockpit of my ship. Before tossing the stuff aside on the passenger seat in the cockpit, I stopped to look at the dead, faceless pirate who was still lying in the stairwell. I seemed surprised to see him there again even though it was obvious he wasn't going anywhere. I guess I had hoped that the mess was somehow going to magically disappear or clean itself up. Not the case. It was a gross situation that I knew had to be dealt with soon. Besides all of the blood that had spewed from his head and onto the deck below, there were also chunks of skull and brains splattered all over the place. I contemplated untying my captive and making him clean up the mess, but I didn't want to push my luck. For all I knew this guy could have been his brother. I didn't want to stir up any rage in the pirate, who up until now had remained calm and defeated. I would deal with the disposal and cleanup on my own in a little while. First, I wanted to rest and think the situation over.

I entered my berth and surveyed the scene of clutter thrown about by the pirates during their pillaging and looting. That bastard tied to my mast had trashed my room and had loaded my own pillow cases with some of my possessions. The faceless bastard in the stairs had drunk some of my precious water supply. Right now I had to put it out of my mind and relax for a bit. I fell onto my bed next to the pirate's AK-47. I grabbed the gun and ran my hands over the long, steel barrel and banana clip. This gun could have killed me! Wow – it was an interesting thought. My captive could have been my murderer – but he wasn't. Now I had a decision to make about him. Damn him for putting me in this position. Kill or be killed – right?

I wanted to sleep for a bit, but I was a little uneasy about the captive and more so the dead body in my galley stairs. That was going to be a bitch to clean up. I could deal with that later – he wasn't going anywhere. I also took comfort in my knot tying ability and the fact that the captive wasn't going anywhere either. My concern was that the pirate was probably losing circulation and precious blood from his hands and feet. If I didn't give a damn about his well being for a moment I could be at ease and think this scenario through clearly. I wanted an encounter and human contact and I had gotten it. Too bad there was a damn communication gap though! Plus the fact the pirate would have and probably would still kill me if he got the chance. What to do? Tired from my ordeal, I decided to rest a bit. A move I should have thought better of.

I closed my eyes and visions of Hoku and the Matains came into my head. I pictured Hoku showing no mercy and taking no captives as he methodically wiped out the cannibals. Kill or be killed – or be killed and eaten in his case! The Matains took no prisoners – they ate them - and that helped them maintain secrecy and power for so long. I had successfully maintained power and overcome the pirate attack, but had no interest in eating anyone. I did it – Hoku style. What would Hoku do now? Certainly the situation was different than what he dealt with, but the root of it all is life and death. I took three lives with little thought or effort, but now found myself having a hard time with the fourth. Maybe subconsciously I didn't want to have another bloody mess to clean up. Up until this point I had felt confident and comfortable with everything I had done. Now I was in a quandary.

I opened my eyes as I got a brilliant idea. I hopped up from the bed and dashed down the hall and into the galley. I paused as I went to step over the faceless pirate. I was tired of stepping over him. I bent down and grabbed the body under his lifeless armpits and dragged it up the stairwell and into the cockpit leaving a bloody smear behind. I hopped up on the top deck and pulled the body up behind me. The up close sight of the half-missing head and face nauseated me. I gagged several times as I tried not to look or think about it any longer. I wanted the mess cleaned up and gone as soon as possible. I grabbed the hands and dragged him across the teakwood leaving a blood trail on the wood. I brought him to the mast and dragged him just in front of the captive. I looked at the fear and remorse in the captive's eyes as he stared down at his comrade. His body remained motionless, but he cut his eyes up to me and I shook my head in disapproval. I then kneeled down and touched the back of the dead pirate. I stayed in my crouched position for a minute as if to show remorse and sympathy for the dead. Then I grabbed him by the pits and dragged him over to the rail right in front of the captive. Without further ado I muscled the body up and tossed him over the rail. He cart wheeled down the side of the Mareva and splashed into the water. The captive closed his eyes and tilted his head back as if to look to heaven. "Shark bait" I thought to myself. One mess was partially cleaned up and now to deal with my other situation.

I knew now what I had to do. Every man should control his own destiny. If I wanted to maintain control of mine, I needed to end this captivity. I would relieve myself of the burden and I would make the decision his. I approached the captive and stared directly into his eyes. We locked gazes for a few seconds until I shook my head in disapproval and he looked away. I pointed to him and said "You – You did this. You guys brought the weapons. You guys brought violent intention. You can't blame me. I did what I had to do. You have three deaths on your hands and now you will also bear the burden of the fourth death as well. It's your choice. You decide."

He stared at me intently, but blankly. I knew he didn't understand a word of what I said. I decided to illustrate my words. I raised my index finger to signify the number 1. I said "first choice." I then raised my right arm horizontally and let my hand hang slightly as I made scissor motions with my index and middle fingers to mimic a walking motion. I continued the finger walking for a moment or two and then made a diving motion with my hand as I pointed to the side of the ship. "Or option 2"… I raised two fingers with my left hand to signify his second option and then I made a gun with the thumb and index finger of my right hand as I raised it to my head and then squeezed my finger as if to pull the trigger to my head. "Your choice Mr. Pirate - take a plunge into the deep blue with no life vest, food, water or boat OR take a quick and easy bullet to the head. What will it be – number one or number two?" I gestured the options again and repeated "One or two?" as I held up my fingers accordingly. The pirate shook his head no on the first option and nodded yes slowly and hesitantly on the second. I asked "number two?" as I pointed my finger gun at his head. He nodded in solemn approval. "Okay, so be it." I turned and headed back to the cockpit to grab the Glock. I picked it up and unclipped it from the holster. I was three for three so far. I had tactfully and skillfully eliminated three targets with ease. I told myself to do it again one more time. Kill or be killed I told myself.

I wielded the Glock confidently and proudly. I cocked it for effect even though it was already loaded and I walked right up to the captive. I stood in front of him and pressed the barrel of the gun to his forehead as his head hung low. He mumbled a few words that I didn't comprehend. I stood there motionless with my finger on the trigger and the gun to his head. He closed his eyes and the weight of his eyelids pushed a tear out of the corner of both of his eyes. I watched as the tears traced down his cheeks and dropped onto the deck below next to the remnants of the urine stream. It was hard to have compassion for the pirate, but at this moment I felt sorry for him. Maybe this piracy wasn't his idea. Maybe the other three pirates were the ringleaders and had forced him to go along. Maybe he had to loot and steal to survive.

Maybe he had never killed anyone before. Maybe this was his first attempt as a pirate. He did seem like an amateur. He had left his gun lying on the bed amidst my surprise attack. I tried to anger myself over the events that had transpired. I tried to get up the guts to pull the trigger. My palm was sweaty and my hand shook slightly. The pirate held his breath and kept his eyes closed. I stood in silence and, other than my slightly shaking hand, was as still as a statue. Seconds turned into a minute or so. I couldn't believe my dilemma. I had shot and killed three pirates earlier with no hesitation. Two of them I shot from underwater at a distance and my hand didn't so much as even flinch even under the recoil of the gun. Now my hand and my mind were shaking like a leaf in a breeze. I pulled the gun away from the pirate's head with a quick jerk of disappointment in myself. The pirate exhaled and sighed heavily. More tears streamed from his closed eyes. He began to sob. I turned my back and walked away.

I decided to return to the stairwell and busy myself with cleaning up the remaining bloody mess below deck. Why couldn't I kill this guy? Why couldn't I go ahead and put him out of his misery and put my safety back on top of the priority list. I grabbed a bucket from the galley and returned to the aft deck. I filled the bucket with sea water and returned to the stairwell. I grabbed a sponge from the stow-away cabinet and began wiping down the walls. Bloody bits of brain and skull smeared the wall in the stairwell red. I scrubbed away diligently in hopes that not only would I clean up the mess quickly, but I also hoped that the sight of the blood would put me back into the mood to kill the captive. If I could clean up this nasty mess below deck, then I could easily clean up another one above deck. A couple of passes of the sponge on the walls and several dunks into the bucket turned the whole five gallon bucket of water crimson. I took the bucket aft and dumped the bloody mess into the ocean. I gagged a few times at the sight of the mess. I rinsed the bucket and filled it with fresh sea water. I scrubbed for an hour or two, and then dumped several buckets of sea water down the stairs and onto the deck of the cabin below. I had originally tried to contain the pool of blood on the cabin floor, but to no avail. I decided to just flush it down the drain in the center of the galley floor. I returned aft to fill the bucket again as I heard the bilge pump engage. I looked around the starboard side discharge as a stream of bloody red water spewed from the side of the hull. I had worked too hard to clean up this damn mess. I was happy to see the bilge pump ejecting the last of the bloody mess. I dumped several more bucket loads of sea water on the stairs and deck until the stream coming out of the bilge went from red to orange to clear. I then dumped a few buckets of salt water on the deck and hit it with a sponge to clean up the blood as well.

I was relieved that the bloody mess was finally clean with the exception of some remaining blood stains. The cleaning had inspired me to clean and organize the mess that the pirates had created during their pillage. I continued the cleaning process until the Mareva was back in the neat and tidy order she was in before the piracy ordeal. I put away all of my booty that I acquired from the pirate's vessel. I stowed and locked all of the guns and weapons with the exception of the Glock which went back into the holster and onto my hip. When the last items were stowed away, I laid down on my bed and took a deep breath. I was at peace with the exception of the quandary I was still in over what to do with my captive. It was going to take some motivation for me to kill him. I didn't want to be complacent and wait for him to escape or something before I did the deed, but I just couldn't bring myself to shoot an unarmed captive. As much as I tried to be angry at him, I couldn't help but feel a little sorry for him. I got up from the bed and went to the galley. I grabbed a gallon of the water that I had looted from the scarab and went up on the deck. The captive had begun to slouch and slide down the mast from his standing posture to more of a crouching position. The crouching position was putting more stress on his arms as they held the weight of his upper body against the mast. I knew he was getting tired and the heat of the morning was taking its toll on his body. I walked up to him with the water in hand. I unscrewed the lid of the jug and held it up to his mouth. He must have been relieved to see me approaching with water rather than a gun. He tilted his head back as I poured some water into his mouth. He drank quickly and swallowed as the jug emptied into his mouth. He was really thirsty – and so was I. We polished off the jug of water in a matter of minutes. I resisted the temptation to loosen the ropes on his arms and hands, but I could not resist the temptation of the newly acquired booze. I tossed the empty water jug down into the scarab and then grabbed the bottle of Captain Morgan's off of the deck. It had gotten slightly warm in the sunlight, but I didn't care about the temperature of the rum. I unscrewed the cap and put it to my lips. I took a big swig and swallowed it down. Its warmth and the heat of the spicy rum burned my mouth and throat all the way down to my stomach. Wow – I hadn't had that sensation in almost a year. I was cautious in my drinking as I knew the effects in the heat and with an empty stomach and low tolerance would be profound. I didn't need to get too drunk right now until I had resolved my quandary.

I sat down on the warm, smooth teak wood deck and looked off into the distance. I wondered if the pirates had reinforcements or a search party that would come after them if they were not back in a timely fashion. I waited patiently and looked and listened for any additional trouble that may be on the horizon. I was done fighting for the day and hoped to get some peace and quiet.

The sun was directly overhead and the sky was crystal clear. I swigged a few more shots of rum and reclined onto my back to look skyward. The sea was relatively calm and the small waves gently rocked the Mareva. The scarab gently rubbed the side of her hull with every passing wave. I was very thankful about how the events of the day had panned out. I looked to the heavens for an answer to my quandary. I had a scarab moored to the Mareva and a pirate tied to her mast. The scarab would be a perfect play toy and complement to the sailboat, but I knew that a few more runs like I put it through today and it would soon be out of gas and useless. I also came to the realization that leaving it moored to the side of the sailboat would not only impede my progress sailing, but would also potentially create a dangerous situation should the seas turn rough. Small waves would rub the scarab's fiberglass hull on the Mareva's steel hull and would only do minimal surface damage to the paint. Large waves could potentially pick up the scarab and launch it on top on the Mareva's deck – that would be catastrophic. I sat up and took another swig of rum as I looked down onto the scarab. I would also have to clean up another bloody pirate mess if I wanted to keep the scarab. I hit the rum again and laid back down on the deck and tried to forget about the dilemma and ultimate decision I would have to make.

Either the seas were getting a little more bumpy or the rum was kicking in. My head began to spin a little and the sun seemed to bounce in the sky like a giant yellow beach ball. I enjoyed the sensation. I had not experienced drunkenness in a long time. I hadn't really missed it, but it was a perfect time to experience it again. I closed my eyes and began to daydream. Maruia, Hoanui and images of Rahiti popped into my head. I wondered what they were doing. I wondered if they were thinking about me. I wondered why I had left. The pirate attack today was a reminder of the harsh reality of the state of the rest of the world today. Why had I left the safe haven in the tropical paradise? I knew the odds of making it back home were slim, but I reminded myself of the anxiety and curiosity that had motivated me to leave Rahiti and make the voyage. I had to know what happened back home. I had to remain focused and stay on course back to the USA. Today was a test of my determination – and I passed so far. When I embarked on my journey, I told myself that I would not let anything keep me from accomplishing my goal of returning home. So far I had done just that. My eyes remained closed and the daydream images of my friends and life in Rahiti faded into images of my family and friends back home. Thoughts of Lance entered my calm mind and brought both sorrow and happiness. I felt like he was still with me somehow, but I missed him tremendously. I breathed deeply and let my mind wander freely. My daydreams turned into dreams as I drifted off into slumber.

When I awoke from my nap on the deck, I immediately rolled over to check on the captive pirate. He was still there and looking pretty rough. He was hunched over and the weight of his body pulled his arms back straight on either side of the mast. His legs were bowed and his knees were slightly bent. I don't know why, but I felt some compassion for the guy. Maybe it was the peaceful thoughts and dreams that I had experienced during my slumber that put me in a better mood. I glanced up at the sun and located it at about 45 degrees above the western horizon indicating that it was probably about 4pm. The day had been long, interesting and productive.

I grabbed the bottle of rum and approached the pirate. I unscrewed the cap of the Captain Morgan bottle and extended it toward the pirate's face. He looked up at me with a surprised expression on his face. "Captain Stan would like to offer up some Captain Morgan to his Captive Pirate. Let's talk – or parley, if you may. Better yet, let's just drink." I knew he couldn't understand me, but conveying words to someone other than myself felt good – even if the words fell on deaf ears so to speak. My weeks of solitude were peaceful and relatively uneventful up until today. The pirates had given me some excitement and adventure – even though I didn't ask for it. The least I could do was ease the pirates pain a little bit with some rum. After all, he witnessed death and he himself had been an itchy trigger finger's pull away from death himself. He had pissed himself again and had been tied up in an uncomfortable position in the heat of the sun all day. He accepted my rum offer by opening his mouth and tilting his head back. I poured a shot into his mouth and he swallowed it down quickly. I kept the bottle to his lips and he sipped again. He flashed a brief smile and said one word to me that I couldn't comprehend, but decided that it meant "Thanks."

I thought to myself how ironic it was that during my weeks alone at sea I had hoped for a visitor or some human contact. Now I had a visitor that I couldn't communicate with due to a language barrier.

I paced back and forth on the deck for a while and sipped a little more rum myself. I was refreshed from my nap, but still had a little drunken sensation about me. I watched the pirate out of the corner of my eyes as he struggled to maintain posture on the mast. Fatigue was overcoming him and I could see that his hands and feet were becoming very red and purple from the strain of the ropes. I made the decision to give him a little slack. I figured that he would probably be too weak to put up a fight in lieu of the position that he had been tied up in. I approached him from behind the mast and cautiously bent down

311

and began to loosen the knot binding his hands together. I realized I really did a great job tying him up as I struggled to get some slack in the knot to loosen it. If there is one thing a sailor should do well its tie a knot – I guess I am officially a good sailor. I fought the knot for a while and the pirate remained perfectly still. Once I had his hands loose, I untied the knot that bound his feet to the mast. As soon as the tension was released, the pirate slid his back down the mast into a seated position. I pulled the knife from my belt and hesitated a moment as I cut the rope that was binding his arms together at the elbows. When the rope broke, the pirate let out a deep sigh. I knew it must have been a huge relief to him to be able to move his arms again. The binding was probably worse than being handcuffed – it was like being elbow cuffed and handcuffed. He bent forward and moved his arms around in a circular motion to get some blood flowing. I stayed close, but not close enough for him to try anything. "I'll give you a minute to stretch out, but the ropes are going back on again. I'll tie you up differently this time since you have behaved so far." He looked up at me as if he really wished he could understand me. I let him stretch a few minutes and then I motioned for him to turn around and face the mast. I untied the rope that was binding his feet together and I motioned for him to straddle the mast in a seated position. I then retied his hands and feet on the other side of the mast. This new position was not nearly as secure as the previous one, but it had to be a lot more comfortable for him. It made me feel less secure about the chance of him escaping, but made me feel more humane for ending what must have been an excruciatingly painful position. I hoped I wouldn't regret my kindness.

The pirate must have wondered what was going on. Just hours ago I made him choose between walking the plank and taking a bullet to the head. Now I was giving him rum and comfort. I guess I was just desperate for human contact. Not only was I desperate for some company, but the thought of the new food I had scored made my stomach growl in anticipation of eating soon. I was happy that I had scored some food from the scarab. Had I not, I may have been tempted to break my vegetarian fruit diet and eat the dead pirates as the Matain cannibals would have done. Instead, I had some canned foods - canned beans and several boxes of cereal and rice. I left the pirate in his new position and made my way back to the galley. Moments later I returned with a can of black beans, a can of pineapple, a can opener and two spoons. I sat down on the deck next to the pirate and shared some food together. It was the first meal I had eaten with another person in over a month. I felt a little weird spoon feeding my captive, but even as awkward as it was, I still felt better than untying him so he could feed himself. It didn't take long to polish off both cans of food. We washed the meal down with a few shots of rum. The pirate said a few words to me that I interpreted as a thank you.

I took advantage of the fact that I had a "captive audience" and I began to spill my guts and tell my tale. I didn't care that the pirate couldn't understand a word I said. I carried on an animated story of my trip. I illustrated the story with body language as I used my hands and facial expressions to make my words more understandable. Not that he had a choice, but the pirate sat and listened to every word I said. He seemed interested and eager to understand me as he maintained eye contact with me through my tale. The sun had begun to set. I pointed to the western horizon and said two words "Mata Utu." I missed that place. I told him about the lush paradise and the perfect wave. I told him how it was the resting place of my brother Lance. It felt great to talk. It felt great to share my tale with someone even if he couldn't understand it. I concluded my tale with daily sailing rituals. I then looked into the pirate's eyes and deep into his soul. "What am I going to do with you man?"

We both sat on the deck in silence as the last rays of sunlight illuminated the horizon in spectacular purple, red and orange hues. The pirate was weary and maybe even a little drunk. He leaned forward and rested his shoulder against the mast. His eyes looked heavy as he appeared to doze off a bit. I imagined he was exhausted and stressed, but thankful to still be alive. I picked up the empty cans of food, utensils and bottle of rum and made my way into the galley. I tossed the trash and stowed the utensils and then sat down at the command center. I looked at the blank radar screen and then checked my GPS coordinates. I wondered if I would get another visit during the night. I made sure the proximity alarm was set and operational. Surely if there were more pirates, they would be on their way by now. I tried to put the thought out of my mind. I needed rest in case they did come. I retired to my berth and dove onto my bed. Without the aid of the rum, it would have been difficult to fall asleep. Instead, I passed out within minutes of my head hitting the pillow. Subconsciously I slept with one eye open and my hand on the Glock.

I awoke the next morning to an unfamiliar sound. There was a slight banging sound on the hull of the ship. It was a sound that I had never heard before. Had I not realized that it was the scarab bumping into the Mareva, I may have dismissed the whole pirate ordeal from yesterday as a dream. I grabbed a bottle of Mata water from the galley and then climbed the steps onto the deck. I noticed that the pirate was still asleep. He was sitting upright, but slightly hunched over and hugging the mast. His head bobbed slightly with the motion of each passing wave. The seas had become slightly rougher since last night as was evident in the increased rocking motion and subsequent collisions of the two ships. I looked over into the scarab. The dead pirate was still there and his body rolled slightly from side to side as the waves rocked the scarab and then bumped it into the Mareva. I scanned the horizon 360 degrees. There was nothing in eyesight except for the burgeoning sun on the eastern horizon. I chugged a little water and then commenced to some stretching and yoga. I watched the pirate closely as I was curious as to when he would wake up. Twenty minutes or so passed and he remained in slumber. I quietly approached him and heard him snoring. A trail of drool ran from the corner of his mouth. The knots around his hands and feet were still intact. I decided to let him get some rest.

I took off my gun belt and stowed it in the cockpit stowaway. I clipped the lanyard to my ankle and quietly slid off of the aft deck and into the deep blue. The water felt refreshing – much more so than yesterday when I entered the water in full gear with survival mode in my mind. I took a little swim to wake me up and to get the blood flowing. I felt slightly hung over from the rum last night – a sensation that I hadn't felt in forever and hadn't missed one bit. I swam against the wind as the Mareva pulled me backwards by the lanyard. Each passing wave gave me a moment of slack before pulling me backward again. I swam for roughly thirty minutes or so before my body was ready for a break. I rolled onto my back and floated a bit. I breathed deep and relaxed. I felt at peace as I looked up at the bright blueness of the morning sky. Peace was what I wanted. Peace in the world would be great. Peace would have prevented the turmoil in the world that sent me on this crazy voyage. Peace would have prevented me

313

from killing three armed pirates yesterday. Peace would bring me home to my family and friends again. Peace would bring Lance back. It felt great to envision peace.

I rolled over and swam a few easy strokes over to the scarab. I unclipped my lanyard and climbed aboard the scarab instead of the Mareva. The dead pirate had started to bloat and turn purplish white. It would only be a matter of time before he started to stink. I contemplated tossing the body into the water, but I didn't want to get blood all over me again. I looked up at the captive whose head still nodded in slumber. It was time to start a new day and he needed a wakeup call. I climbed into the driver's seat and fired up the scarab. The roar of her engines startled the captive who immediately awoke and came to full attention. Hell, the scarab was loud enough that I feared her rumble may even awake the dead pirate on the floor. I goosed the engine in neutral just to hear the roar again. It was an awesome sound, but definitely not one of peace.

I left the scarab running and hopped back onto the Mareva. I reeled in the lanyard and tossed it on the deck as I made my way to the mast. "Good morning, pirate." He shook his head a little as if to clear his mind and vision. I wondered if he had hoped that the whole ordeal yesterday had been a dream. Well, I was about to make his dream a harsh reality. I grabbed a bottle of water off of the deck, took a big gulp and walked up to him. I extended the bottle to his mouth and he tilted his head back and took a mouthful. I screwed the lid back on it and made my way back to the cockpit. I grabbed the gun belt and strapped it back onto my waist and then returned to the mast. I did not say a word as I approached the captive. I drew my knife from the belt as I stood in front of my captive. A look of fear once again came over his face. I leaned down with my knife and cut the ropes binding his feet and hands. The look of fear was quickly replaced with a look of confusion. I extended my hand in a gesture to help him to his feet. He stood up with difficulty as his legs must have still been asleep. I gave him a second to compose himself and then I escorted him to the port side of the deck. I patted him on the back and then pointed down to the scarab. "Go." I said. He looked at me with confusion. I pointed to the scarab again and gestured with a head nod and repeated "Go." He broke eye contact with me and glanced down at the gun on my hip. He must have been afraid that I would shoot him in the back as he boarded the scarab. "Look man, get the hell out of here before I change my mind. Dead men tell no tales, right? Well, go tell your tale and tell your pirate friends to leave me alone. I want peace from now on." I followed up my words with the international gesture for peace and raised my index and middle finger. He got the gesture and returned it to me. We stood there in silence for a moment before he carefully climbed down onto the scarab which still rumbled with the sound of horsepower. He disregarded the dead pirate on the deck as he climbed over him and into the driver's seat. I untied the mooring line from the cleat on the Mareva and tossed the rope into the scarab.

The pirate looked up at me as he clicked the boat into gear. The engines dropped in tone and the scarab began to pull away from the Mareva. He smiled and nodded at me before he hit the throttle and launched the scarab off into the distance. I couldn't help but think that I either did the most humane act or made the stupidest move of my life. I felt good about it and hoped that it would be my last pirate encounter. I was now content to be alone at sea again and at peace in my own world. I looked at my watch – it was 7:48 am – the exact minute that the alarm had sounded 24 hours ago. Talk about

314

coincidental timing. It had been an interesting 24 hours. I had no idea where the pirates came from or where my captive pirate was going as long as I did not see him or his peers again. I was once again content being alone and at peace with the sea.

Peace

The days at sea following the pirate attack were calm and relatively uneventful. After the pirate was gone, I went from warrior mode to peaceful sailor mode. I returned back to my normal routine and once again became dedicated to my daily ritual. I slid back into the habit of my sunrise yoga sessions, swims, relaxing flotation, push-ups, pull-ups, sit-ups, cleaning, coordinate checks, deck checks and equipment checks - I had checklists for my checklists. I felt it was important to maintain my schedule and perform my tasks even when I didn't have to. I remained vigilant in my effort to stay safe and healthy. I learned that being prepared and practicing can make all the difference in the world when you are in a state of emergency or under attack by pirates. I also learned to be careful what I wished for. I had been lonely and bored and had wished for some action and companionship and I got more than I had bargained for. I asked and the universe granted. I now had my fill of company and was perfectly content being alone again. Being alone at sea was not a bad thing, rather an opportunity for me to really be in control and get in touch with myself. There was no one to please or to argue with. It was my time to do my best for myself. It was my time to be alone. It was my time to reflect on all of the things I would do differently if I got a second chance when I got back home.

I became very introspective and realized a lot of things about myself in the days and weeks that followed the pirate attack. One thing that really changed after the pirate attack was my appreciation of life. For the first time in my life, I had taken someone else's life. Blood stains on the deck and floor reminded me of the pirate attack and the blood that was spilled. I was responsible for the deaths of three pirates; however, I was also responsible for sparing the life of one pirate. Not killing the fourth pirate somehow made me feel better about killing the other three. I also consoled myself by reminding myself that by killing the three pirates, I essentially saved my own life. I could have easily been the one murdered by the pirates. It could be my blood on the Mareva's deck. I could be floating face down in the water right now as my body became shark bait. I could be held captive on my own ship awaiting death or an uncertain fate. The Mareva could be in the hands of pirates and all of my plans and dreams for the future could have ended. The story of Lance and our experiences in Rahiti would be lost – "Dead men tell no tales" I told myself. I was glad I was still alive to tell my tale. I regretted having to kill three men, but I appreciated the fact that I was still alive even more now. "Kill or be killed" I told myself to finalize my rationalization and to put the pirate incident out of my mind.

My appreciation level increased for the things that I had control over. I felt as though I had total control over my mind and body. I felt as though the daily routine, diet and workout regimens that I strictly followed kept me in peak health – both physically and mentally. I realized that I controlled my own health through the decisions that I made. I could choose to eat the healthy fruits and veggies from the islands or to not eat at all or to eat the junk food that the pirates had on their ship. I could choose to drink the booze in the bar on the Mareva or the bottles that I looted from the pirates – or keep a clear mind and clean body and not drink at all. I could smoke the cigars in the humidor on the Mareva or the cigarettes that were on the pirates' ship – or I could keep my lungs clean and enjoy breathing the fresh sea air around me. I could sit or lay on my ass all day and not work out or do anything physical at all – but I didn't. I chose to do the best that I could do with what I had to work with. I chose to take control of my attitude and focus on positives and things that I had control over. I chose to overcome depression, loss of loved ones, loneliness and fear by implementing discipline, routine, schedule and exercise. I knew that these principles had somehow been ingrained in me all of my life and were now manifesting themselves to help me get through one of the greatest challenges of my life. I began to look at this trans-Pacific cruise as just that – a challenge, not a death sentence or a hapless cause that would deliver me to destruction and death. It was just another chapter of my life – a chapter that I chose to read and live.

I found it ironic that I had always loved to be around people and it was my brother who had liked solitude, but here I was alone at sea and my brother was no longer. Being alone at sea gave me the chance to learn to be alone and to be one with myself. I spent a great deal of time meditating while alone at sea. Through my meditation, I learned that I was not alone. I discovered that the energy of the universe was with me and that I was connected to it. Not only was I connected to it, but it flowed through me and made me who I was. It was this connectivity that made me realize that Lance and my family and friends were right here with me. I even believed that Hoku was with me during the pirate attack. I was not a fighter, but had been able to single handedly defeat four pirates. Hoku was not a fighter either, but had single handedly defeated an entire tribe of the fiercest cannibals in the South Pacific – all by himself. Even if Hoku's energy wasn't with me, I was at least inspired by him in that I knew his story. Knowing his story translated into powerful knowledge and energy within me. The memories of my friends and family translated into powerful drive and determination within me.

Determination became a very important element in my mind. I became more determined to return home than anything I had ever done in my life before. This determination would not waiver regardless of whatever situation I faced. The pirate attack was proof of that. It was this determination that mentally and physically prepared me to walk coast to coast from California to Virginia If that is what it took to get back home. I wasn't going to let anything stand in my way. I was determined to see my family, friends and home again. I was determined to share my story. I was determined to do my part to help as many people as I could along the way.

Gratitude filled my heart, mind and soul again. I became grateful for everything I had experienced in my life. I became grateful for everything that I had around me – including my health - both physical and mental, the sun, the wind, the water, the Mareva, the food and water which nourished me, the navigation system on the ship that guided me, God and the universe around me and the intellect that I possessed and my experiences in life which made it possible for me to be grateful for everything. My gratitude increased every time I consumed any food or water because not only did the supply decrease due to consumption, but also due to spoilage. I had been very diligent in my rationing of food, but I had rationed too much and was not consuming food fast enough as it began to spoil and go to waste. I savored every bite – whether it was the ideal ripeness or not. I even ate moldy fruit and veggies. I laughed when I remembered how picky I used to be when shopping in the produce section of the grocery stores back home in the States. I would reject and discard produce if it had a soft spot – let

317

alone a brown spot. Here, that was not the case. I ate every last bite of everything regardless of how it looked or tasted. I appreciated it all and didn't waste anything as I was grateful to have it in my possession.

The food spoilage created a dilemma and forced me to break my rationing just to finish the food before it spoiled and rotted, but it disheartened me to watch the precious supply of fruits and veggies being depleted before my eyes. I mentally prepared myself for the fasting period that would ensue when my food ran out. I had practiced for the fasting when I was preparing to leave Rahiti. My grieving over Lance had also helped prepare me for not eating by taking my appetite away even long before I practiced fasting. I sat on the deck and took the last bite of the last remaining food – a Mata mango. I ate the fruit - skin and all right down to the inedible pit and sucked every drop of juice off of my fingers and hands. I enjoyed every last bite of that succulent fruit and knew that I would miss it – so I engrained the memory and sensation of eating it into my mind forever.

Days turned into weeks without food. I didn't keep track of time, but I knew it had been a long while since I had eaten. My hunger pains subsided after several days initially, but eventually the lack of nutrition began to take its toll on my mind and body. I found fishing gear on the Mareva, but unfortunately had nothing to bait the hook with. I sat on the rear deck of the ship with a knife in my hand and contemplated cutting off one of my own fingers or toes to use for bait on the hook. I gripped the knife tightly and let the blade press into the skin of my hand just enough to induce pain without breaking skin and drawing blood. I did this to prepare myself for the pain of losing a digit. I wondered if I should cut off a finger or a toe. I wondered which a fish would prefer – I wanted to choose the optimum bait if I was going to make a permanent sacrifice of my body. I sat on the rear deck and prayed on the situation. I prayed for the strength and courage to cut off and sacrifice part of my body in hopes that the sacrifice would bring results that would nourish the rest of my body. I prayed that my sacrifice would not be in vain and that my finger or toe would not fall off of the hook or be stolen by a fish who avoided being caught. I prayed and thought, prayed and thought. I decided after much deliberation that although I preferred to lose a toe instead of a finger, that a finger was the more logical choice. My pinky finger on my left hand would be the sacrifice. It was larger than any of my toes and would make better bait. It would also be easier to elevate my hand and control the bleeding and pain. I also realized that I needed to be able to walk, balance and navigate my body around the deck of the moving, rocking ship and that would be impossible to do with an injured foot. So it was decided that my left pinky finger would go. I stood up from the rear deck and made my way to the helm with my knife in my hand. I wanted to do it in a place where I could be more comfortable and a place where, if I passed out from the trauma, I would not drop the finger into the water or roll off of the deck. I grabbed a couple of towels and a piece of fishing line and tied a loop in it so that I could stop the bleeding once the finger was off. I admired my finger one last time and kissed it with my lips. I put the finger on the top of the metal control panel and put the blade of my knife on top of it. I planned to let my body weight push my right hand down on the blade to sever my finger. I took a deep breath as I prepared myself for the pain. A split second before I leaned forward into the knife, I heard a loud splash and a ruckus on the rear deck of the ship. I put down the knife, flexed my pinky finger and left the helm to inspect the rear deck to find the source of the commotion.

I could not believe my eyes when I looked onto the lower deck. At first sight, I was sure that I was hallucinating due to my hunger. But after a moment or two, I realized the sight was a reality. A large yellow fin tuna fish – probably around 50 or 60 pounds had jumped onto the rear deck of the ship. It was an unbelievable, timely and serendipitous thing that occurred a split second before I cut off my own finger. The tuna flopped around inside the confines of the rear lower deck as he gasped for oxygen in the unfamiliar air. The first thing I did was drop to my knees and pray in appreciation and thankfulness. The fish had jumped into the boat in the exact same spot where I had prayed in contemplation of sacrificing a finger or a toe so that I may be able to catch a fish. Wow – what a coincidental situation; however, what if there were no coincidences in life – what if everything happened for a reason - and happened when it happened for a reason? It reminded me of how Hoku was spared from starvation when a bird delivered a fish to him in the cave on Mount Mata. My mind reeled over the positive event as the fish suffered as he gasped for air. I retrieved the knife from the helm and jumped down to the lower deck. I knelt over the fish as he flailed wildly from the shock of suffocation. "Your suffering is over and so is mine". I said to him as I kissed the fish's face and then plunged the knife into his throat. I gutted and filleted the fish as quickly and as humanely as I could. I wasted nothing of the fish. I saved the entrails to be used as bait to catch more fish and baited the hooks and cast lines into the water as I savored the raw flesh of the fish. I ate sparingly and packed the rest of the meat into plastic bags to be stowed into the refrigerator. It was the first meat that I consumed in a very long time as I had been a strict vegetarian, but I didn't mind consuming flesh to save my own flesh at this point. As I cleaned up the mess from filleting the fish, I saw movement on two of the fishing poles I had baited and cast into the water. I spent the next couple of hours reeling in two more very large yellow fins that I caught using their friend as bait. By the end of the day, I had a fridge full of fresh fish meat. The fruits and veggies were gone, but conveniently replaced with "fruit from the sea". I was nourished and I was grateful.

With a full belly came a peaceful mind. With a peaceful mind came peaceful meditation. Peaceful meditation brought thoughts of world-wide peace. I pondered world peace and the tranquility and isolation in Rahiti in spite of the chaos in the rest of the world. The whole society in Rahiti was insulated from the rest of the world and remained self-sufficient in spite of the condition of the rest of the world. In fact, had I not taken the computer and technology with me to the island, they may have not learned of the chaos in the world for a very long time – if at all. I compared the isolation of the entire tribe in Rahiti to my own isolation on the Mareva. I didn't have a tribe here to keep me company, but my solo isolation had similarities to the island isolation. Rahiti was a peaceful island and the Rahitians were peaceful people who made up a tribe who helped, loved and supported one another. It was their love and respect for each other that kept them peaceful, productive and positive. It was a beautiful concept and a beautiful experience. I wished the rest of the world could embrace and engage in the same positive attitude. I knew the world would be more peaceful and that the events of "The Day" could have been avoided if everyone respected life and each other in the same manner that the Rahitians had taught me to do. I was now a one man tribe on my own mobile island at sea and was totally at peace with myself and the world. I discovered that heaven can really be a place on earth if you choose to make it that.

This peacefulness enlightened me and allowed me to discover what I believed to be the true meaning of life. I found that the true meaning of life is living it to its fullest and making the most of every moment of it. I found that the meaning of life was also to appreciate any and all positives despite any and all adversity and negatives – to be content and at peace with yourself, to appreciate everything even when you think you have nothing, to be productive and to help others, to become aware of things outside of your normal realm – your surroundings, the energy of the universe and your own spirit and soul within. I relished and cherished this enlightenment and my entire attitude about life and my purpose changed dramatically as I sailed through the calm waters on the deck of the Mareva.

I had been blessed thus far with smooth sailing, favorable winds and perfect weather and I appreciated every moment of it because I knew that those factors could change at any given time – and so they did. I watched a large storm forming on the radar screen which soon became evident on the horizon at sunset. I batten down the hatches, lowered the sails and prepared myself and the ship to endure our first night of what would surely be rough seas and unpleasant weather. The peaceful seas were about to become angry, but I focused on what I could control as I maintained my peaceful mindset despite the uncontrollable weather and seas.

The Swim

When you are alone at sea for an extended period of time, it becomes very easy to fall into a routine.

Having a routine had been my routine for most of my life. Life at sea was no exception for me - except for the fact that I was on my own and removed from society. Far from the turbulence of the rest of the world and the peace and tranquility of Rahiti, I had learned to easily adapt to life at sea somewhere in between. It was just me, my boat and a lot of water. Although marred by the world changing events that had taken place in my absence from the US, this was exactly the life changing experience that I had yearned for all of my life. I learned firsthand that sometimes there are calm waters and sometimes there are rough seas. I also discovered that sometimes when you think the seas are rough, they are really calm – because the rough can always get rougher. This whole trip, the storm last night and today's events would be testimony to that.

I hadn't slept worth a damn last night. A sudden thunderstorm with gale force winds had made the night quite unpleasant. I had to frantically batten down all the hatches and storm proofed the cabin and galley in a short period of time as a fierce storm has brewed up right on top of me last night. I literally tossed and turned all night and hoped that nothing would be damaged in the storm. I was both entertained and frightened by a brilliant lightning display I watched through the porthole by my bed. I had always been fascinated by the energy of a thunderstorm, but when you are the highest point on the sea with a big lightning rod mast on top of your sailboat, fears tend to well up inside you.

After a night of storms and angry seas, I was relieved to wake up to serenity, clear skies and a gentle breeze out of the west. The morning ritual was underway. I unfurled the sails but didn't yet hoist them, I secured and inspected all deck equipment, checked the navigational equipment, and my coordinates checked out as expected considering the strong winds from the storm. I stood on the bow drinking my morning water ration and thought that you have to have storms once in a while to appreciate the calm. I knew I must now appreciate every moment of calm for fear of what turmoil will lie ahead back at home.

The water looked enticing, refreshing and much more convenient than the shoe box sized shower below deck, however I didn't really feel up for a swim today after tossing and turning all night in the storm. What I really felt like was some good water relaxation. There was something so enticing about salt water on my hair and skin. Before I raised the sails I would definitely take a dip. But before I take a dip I should stretch.

My 20 minute morning Yoga ritual on deck made it easier to relax in the water and also limbered me up in case I did decide to stroke out a swim. So I commenced to stretching. The warmth of the morning sunrise on my face and a gentle breeze filled my lungs. I stretched and breathed – linking my motion to my breath. I felt appreciation for my breaths this morning as I had wondered several times last night during the storm whether or not I would make it to see morning. My deliberate breaths invoked a few yawns. My body couldn't decide whether they were "waking up yawns" or "still sleepy yawns". I didn't care – I felt strong and aware in spite of my meditative state. After about a dozen Vinyassa flow sun salutations, I pumped out a set of 40 push-ups and snapped my body into a more active state. Still slightly lethargic from lack of sleep, I decided that a quick dip would invigorate me.

After several dozen dips or so you finally get the routine down. I would strip down, and strap on the 100 foot lanyard around my ankle, making sure the line was secure and free from obstruction. Then I would go to the rear platform and lower the ladder. I didn't lower the ladder to enter the water, I lowered it out of habit to make my entry back onto the boat easier. There was only one way I entered the water – a swan dive right off of the deck. My only fear was getting eaten by a shark, however that was not enough to keep me from the inviting water each day. This morning the water seemed extra teal and extra clear. I would surely see a shark coming from 50 feet below. Maybe there was a layer of fresh water floating on top of the ocean after the downpours from the storm last night. I couldn't wait to dive in and find out. All I could think about as I clipped the lanyard around my ankle was floating on my back and staring up at the puffy white clouds. No chores yet – just pure relaxation for a bit.

I stripped down, clipped the lanyard on my ankle, crawled up onto the top life line and balanced in the breeze and stared down at the glassy water from my port side vantage. I could see my reflection in the teal glassy surface, but could see beyond it into the depths of the ocean. I had no fear of swan diving in head first – a contradiction to my water safety instructor training "feet-first" policy back home in the murky waters of the rivers and the Atlantic. Unlike the days of tubing and water skiing in the rivers back home, the probability of encountering any underwater obstacles was nil. So I sprung off the deck with the flex of my calves and dove gracefully arms spread as wide as the smile on my face. The rush of water down my body from head to toe was invigorating as I broke the surface of the water. I went deep until my ear drums popped which was sure to happen long before the 100' lanyard ran out of slack. I leveled off, turned vertical and looked up at the sun shine breaking through the surface high above. I slowly released air from my lungs into my mouth and traced the dancing bubbles rising to the surface. Then I snapped my arms to my side and flexed my legs pointing my toes and shot to the surface, outrunning some of the bubbles. I busted into air and took in a deep breath and thought this would be another good day to be on the water.

I laid on my back, arms outstretched, legs straight and toes pointed. I filled my lungs with a deep breath of south pacific air and felt my back arch as my chest rose out of the water. Over the years I had perfected the art of floating even though my lean body and muscle mass defied the physics of floating. The key was deep, long Yoga-like breaths – like the ones I practiced on deck every morning. As long as the lungs were full of air and the body was outstretched creating more surface area, it was possible to float for extended periods of time. These deep relaxing breaths also helped calm the soul and detox the body. Laying there floating and breathing was a deep meditation for me. It was the closest thing to nothingness, but so in touch with everything. My only focus was my breathing. I would take forty breaths and make each one of them last 30 seconds or more. Eight seconds on the deep inhalation, hold for ten and twelve seconds on the exhalation forty times would equal twenty minutes of serenity.

Seconds turn into minutes and minutes turn into hours. It could be so easy to lose track of all time out here. It is crazy how twenty minutes during a storm can seem like an eternity, but twenty minutes in this state can fly by in a few breaths.

The tranquility of floating was great. Floating naked with no motion also substantially cut down on your chances of getting attacked by a shark as I figured. No splashing, no shiny jewelry or watches to confuse the shark into thinking that you were dinner. These thoughts were subdued and forgotten during my usual 30 minute swim. When I swam, I would turn against the current and swim until all of the slack in my 100 foot lanyard was tense. I would then maximize my workout by attempting to swim against the current and also tow the weight of the ship. In only 30 minutes, I must burn the same calories as a 3 hour swim in the lap pool back home at the YMCA. My mind and body were unanimous today in their decision to relax and not swim. Just relax and enjoy the sea. Forget about how I got to this point and forget about the future that lies ahead. Just relax and enjoy life in this moment.

I was on my sixteenth breath when I broke my meditation with a thought. I found it odd that even in such calm water I had not felt the familiar tension of the lanyard on my ankle as the ship would usually drift and coax me along.

I raised my head and instinctively looked to the right. If I hadn't already done so this morning, I surely would have shit myself. I was looking at the stern of my ship, but from over 1000 feet away. I sprung upright in the water and reached for my ankle lanyard. It was there around my ankle, but unless it grew ten times longer, there was a problem. I frantically pulled it hand over hand as I treaded water with my feet. Then it hit me – right in the hand– the stainless steel clamp that always remained clipped to the port side stay next to the bottom life line. What the hell. Why was it unclipped? There was no way that I had even in my most careless moment undone it - even in preparation for the storm. I quickly came to my senses and felt a sense of urgency rise within me. It didn't matter how it came undone, the point is that I now had both ends of my life line on my body and a runaway sailboat quickly gaining distance on me thanks to a westerly breeze.

Adrenaline kicked in. I knew what had to happen. I had to swim like my life depended on it and catch up to the ship. If I didn't catch it, I would surely drown naked in the middle of the ocean with a lanyard around my ankle. So much for a relaxing dip and no swim this morning. This is not how I was going to go out after all I had been through. Right now I knew my mission was to swim. I broke into a freestyle stroke and quickly got up to speed. My breathing pattern had gone from calm to panic in a matter of seconds. I knew I had to calm down and get back to the meditative, yet active state that I had only seconds ago broken out of. I had to be fast and had to aim in the right direction. Every time I pulled my head up straight to get my bearings, my momentum would slow. Every stroke counted. I did not know how fast the ship was moving in the gentle breeze, but I could not afford to give up any more distance. It would be a monumental task to make up the estimated quarter mile swim I was facing right now. If the ship was moving at just two knots and I could swim at three with all of my effort, it would still take – hell, it couldn't think – it didn't matter – I had to catch the ship.

323

I paced myself on a six stroke breathing pattern keeping the ship in sight on my right. I reached far, dug deep, pulled hard and kicked with all of my might – all the while keeping my body stiff and svelte. I cut through the water with what I thought to be speed and grace. I wondered how long I could keep up this pace. I had not swum any significant distance since my beach lifeguarding days years ago. And I certainly never had to do it under this grave of a situation. I had rescued dozens of troubled swimmers during my 8 year tenure as a beach guard and now it was up to me to rescue myself. My daily swims at sea were intense workouts, but my only focus had to be breathing and rhythm with no regard for direction or speed. It's easy to swim until exhaustion in any direction and then pull yourself back to the ship with the lanyard. Right now I had to worry about everything – my life depended on it. Stay focused, take full advantage of every stroke and save as much energy as possible. It could be a real long swim. The only thing that would save me other than myself is if the breeze stopped completely or shifted direction 180 degrees. I knew this was highly unlikely as I was well within the reach of the western trade winds. Please God just don't let the wind pick up I thought. I also wished I had removed the lanyard from my ankle. I wondered how much the 100' of cable trailing behind me was slowing me down. I pondered if it was worth it to stop for a second and undo it – and if I did there would be no way to carry it. I would have to let it go. It didn't matter if I lost it at sea in my mind – as long as I wasn't lost at sea. I figured that I would be so happy to be back on deck that I may never swim again. If I had done my usual ritual and swam first and floated after, I would have realized immediately that the lanyard was undone. I would have swam 100' or so, not felt the tension and turned around and come straight back to the ship. Plus I would have already been in the mindset of swimming. But no – today I didn't want to swim.

Keep stroking dude. Catch the ship. Don't swallow any water. Keep your rhythm… and your bearings. 6 strokes to every breath, roughly one second to each stroke equaled 10 breaths per minute. I hadn't been counting breaths, only strokes. I estimated that I had taken over 100 breaths already which meant I had been swimming for ten minutes. I had no concept of time though. I was in the zone. I had to swim. Forget even thinking. I couldn't stop my brain though. Why hadn't I checked the lanyard? I had been swimming dozens of times before and always checked it. Why did I need to – it was secured with a grade-8 stainless steel clamp. How had it come undone? The clamp wasn't broken, just open. I was so OCD about my rituals – preparing for a storm, checking coordinates, adhering to my own self imposed food and water rations – why wasn't I more OCD about the lanyard? I had to soothe my mind to stave off panic and I tried to do so with thoughts of my morning before the swim and how great it would be to be back on the ship shortly. Then I replayed the swan dive several times in my mind and how I wished I could go back in time thirty minutes or so and not taken the dive and subsequent floating.

The fact is that I wasn't on the ship. I was lost at sea. I had to swim. I didn't have my goggles or sunglasses. I hadn't slept last night. I felt miserable and my life was in jeopardy. I dug deep and swam like I had never swum before. I pulled, rolled, breathed and extended while keeping my body lithe and limber. I tried to picture myself from above. I was stroking effortlessly and extending to my maximum reach on each stroke. I was propelling my body through the water with light speed and gaining on my ship with every stroke. I would be on the boat in minutes. I would get some water. I would stretch a bit. I would stand on the bow and watch the sunset tonight. One more sunset would be nice.

Then the burning reality of salt hit my nostrils and the back of my throat. I breathed before my head fully turned. I lost my focus and broke my breathing pattern. I tried to breathe in a split second before I rolled my body far enough to pull my head out of the water. I choked – bad. I tried to clear it with a quick cough and continue my stroke, but it was bad. I stopped and hacked so hard that I buked (burped and puked) at the same time. I felt the acid from my stomach hit the back of my throat and continue the burning that the sea salt had already started. Just as I had recovered from my buke, I felt a queasiness rise in me again as I looked to the ship. It had gained significant distance on me even during my diligent swim. I was screwed and I knew it. I reached down to my ankle and grabbed the freaking lanyard and unclipped the life line that may have cost me my life. I tossed that life line in disgust and I wiped my face with my forearm and was ready to swim again. I tried to regain my same rhythm, but it was impossible. I was severely fatigued. I had just puked and was tasting it bad and the little bit of salt I swallowed was making me more nauseous and dehydrated.

I collected my senses as best I could and started to stroke again. Pain seared through my arms with every stroke. I became disoriented and delirious. I knew I couldn't keep up any pace for long. The thought of dying at sea didn't bother me as much as the thought of defeat and surrender. I couldn't accept mental defeat and quit. If I died at sea, I would die swimming toward that damn ship. I changed up my stroke to a recovery stroke so that I could catch my breath and bearing. I knew that the recovery stroke was probably only half as fast as my previous pace which had only put me farther from the ship in the last ten minutes or so. Every stroke I took, the ship moved two strokes away. I didn't care – I had to keep stroking no matter what speed. I swam on my side. My recovery stroke was self taught, but inspired by watching the Navy Seals train up and down the coast of VA Beach while I lifeguarded. The stroke consisted of the top arm plunging and pulling like a freestyle stroke. The bottom arm worked in unison with the top arm, but did the side-stroke motion while the feet kicked the breast stroke or frog kick. I used to joke to my friends in lifeguard training that I could swim to Europe with that stroke – it just might take forever.

I began to pull the recovery stroke breathing every stroke. I kept the ship in sight with a constant glance on almost every stroke – some of which delirious. I stroked a count methodically and calculated every motion of my body. I made every breath count, but my efforts seemed futile. At every breath and subsequent glance, the ship seemed to move farther away. I stopped and stretched my arms upright on multiple occasions to get the muscles relaxed and the blood flowing and most importantly to get a gage on wind direction and speed. It became painfully evident that a prevailing westerly was blowing the ship east faster than I could swim. Any current was negligible in that it would push me in the same direction at relatively the same speed. Sharp pains continued to hit every inch of my body and my response was to smoothly roll onto my opposite side with a deep breath and sigh. "Please let me catch the boat and not let me get eaten by a shark in the process" was my focus and prayer. The thought of sharks entertained my mind versus the prospect of drowning. Thank God I had no jewelry or watch on to add to the attraction. Who cared what time it was – it was time to catch the boat. Screw the sharks.

The reality of death had eluded me on multiple occasions previously in my life, but had never been as tangible as now. The daring swim around the reef in the current swept waters in Tahiti was my closest brush with death until now. And the swim through the shark infested inlet in the Caribbean didn't daunt me like my current predicament. I could feel the eminence of death. The sense of urgency had kicked in. I tasted the adrenaline. I felt the helplessness. I saw the ship, but could do nothing to catch it. It was like a supreme force was taunting me. The ship was in sight, but not in reach.

For the first time in my life I truly felt death, the panic of death came over me and overwhelmed me. Every stroke I took burned and stung my arms, shoulders and back. My body writhed in pain. I felt that sense of urgency, but at the same time was bound by helplessness. There was nothing I could do. Every stroke I took the ship gained two on me. My ship was outrunning me by the second. I swam with determination and might, but watched the ship disappear in the distance. My nausea had momentarily subsided, but had now given way to breathlessness and dizziness. I knew I couldn't keep this up much longer. But somehow I kept my rhythm and I kept my count. I kept my stroke up, I kept rolling my head to the side to breathe. I timed my strokes with the waves so I would not take any more mouthfuls of water when I breathed. This went on for a while. I really have no idea how long.

As soon as I paused to think about the time, I lost all track of time. I lost my count, my rhythm and stroke. I was in trouble again. I was out of breath and delirious. I couldn't even count to two. I stopped for a break, but struggled to catch my breath. I've never had a panic attack in my life, but knew this may be one.

I tried to stay strong mentally. I told myself that there were much more horrific ways to die than drowning or being shark dinner. For instance, dying of cancer in a hospital bed was much more appalling than my current status. I had control – or at least I told myself that. Unfortunately, I had no control over the wind that was steadily pushing the ship farther from me.

When you are facing eminent death, the fear, the sense of urgency and the panic can quickly come in waves and then can subside just as quickly into a calm serenity of acceptance and mercy. It seems so easy to just give in and die. Just stop, just quit, just sink, just take one last breath. Peace awaits. Just die. It's so easy – no more struggle or fight required. But then that primal instinct kicks in and says "No, I will not die here today. I will not drown in this water. It is not my time to go. Not this way – not today." And then the fight kicks back in from within – stronger than before. And I stroked with all my might once again.

There came the point when the sun shone directly in my face from overhead indicating it was noon. A two hour ordeal has been the pinnacle of my existence. If I could swim for over two hours, then I could swim all day if that is what it took. "To hell with drowning or going out this way". The thought kept me stroking all day as I traced the sun over the sky. Every stroke I took – in my mind was a stroke closer to my ship and to home. I'd stroke all the way if I had to just out of curiosity and determination. I wondered if it had been done before. I once heard a story on the news about a woman who swam across the Atlantic Ocean, but she had a sailboat by her side. She could climb on board at night and eat and rest and then the next morning start out fresh again. I had a sailboat too, but I was chasing it across the open ocean. I wanted so badly to be on board and get a drink of water and some rest.

Where the hell were the dolphins who swam next to the outrigger kayak every day on the way to Mata? It would be nice to grab onto one of their fins and have them tow me to the ship. The thought of the dolphins invoked memories of the kayak trips to Mata Utu. I thought of Lance and wondered if he was here with me spiritually right now. I could use his help. He rescued me once from the clutches of the sea - one more favor would be nice. I remembered paddling for my life on the reef break at Mata while surfing with my brother. I treated each breath set as a wave welling up ready to pound me into the reef below. My arms were numb, but pumped. The cramps and pains became more tolerable as my adrenaline coursed through my body and my determination continued. My brother had saved my life that time, but I did not return the favor.

The thoughts of my brother caused different types of pain – emotional ones that brought thoughts of both determination and surrender. My brother had surrendered. He had gambled, and in my opinion, given his life up to certain death. But it was for something that he really loved. He went out in what he considered a blaze of glory on a triple overhead once a year wave. He seemed at peace and determined to surf even though we both knew his fate. I didn't try to dissuade him, nor did he try to persuade me to join him. "Surf, walk or swim – see you back at the boat, dude!" Those were his last words on the rocky reef point a Mata Utu. His last words replayed in my mind hundreds of times, but never had as much meaning as now. He never made it back to the boat and I believe he knew that he wouldn't. It was his time to go – and I let him. I walked that day. My long walk down the reef along the beach back to the boat that day will always stick in my mind. I imagined my brother's last wave. It must have been awesome for a few seconds before it closed out and ten thousand pounds of water buried him permanently in the reef. It was an easy decision for him to surf that ridiculous wave and his decision was followed by a quick, easy death. His decision was justified in the fact that, in his mind, he no longer had anything to live for other than surfing. I miss him terribly, but I respect his decision. I wished many times that he was on the ship with me, but never more than right now. I would have taught him to sail well. He would awake and find me absent from the ship. He would hoist the jib, make a couple of tacks, spin the wheel and turn the ship in my direction in a matter of minutes. My reality now was that I was all alone. I was not ready to die. Drowning was not on my "blaze of glory" ways to go out. "Walk, surf or swim – see you back at the boat!" I had surfed that break dozens of times and I did the walk that day without my brother, but today it seemed like swimming was my only option. I was not ready to surrender and join my brother yet.

I thought about my last moments with my brother on the point in Mata. There is a thousand things I wish I had said. There are so many things that I still wish I could tell him. At that moment, that day, there was nothing to say. I thought about my family back home and all of the things I wanted to tell them. I had a thousand questions that needed answering too. I remembered my last few emails and sat phone communications. I wished I had said I love you one more time to my mother before hanging up. I wish I had sent a couple more pictures in my last email. I wished I had one more opportunity to express some feelings to those I love. I had to carry on to do this.

The heat of the day and the sunshine began to subside. Was the day really over? All concept of time had been lost. It is amazing how a day at sea on a ship alone can seem like an eternity, but a day in the sea swimming after your ship can somehow melt into minutes and a million calories. As if I wasn't having enough difficulty keeping the ship in sight, the setting sun at my back didn't help a bit. Several times I caught myself swimming in the opposite direction from the ship. I knew I would have to stop stroking soon.

As sunset came on, I could barely make out the ship on the horizon. All concept of time had vanished, but clockwork earth kept it in check. My only link to time was the position of the sun in the sky and that too was about to leave me. It was time to stop stroking and recover. It was impossible to even know which way to go. Delirious and exhausted, I rolled onto my back and commenced the very breathing exercise that got me into this situation. How long could I stay afloat? I probably swam for 12 hours today stopping only briefly to stretch and gain my bearings and vomit several times. Could I float all night? What if I passed out from exhaustion – would I float? The big question in my mind was would I even see the ship in the morning. I swam all day and lost ground continuously. It was futile to even try to swim at night. I may waste my energy swimming in the wrong direction. No lights were on the ship and even if they were, I doubted I could see them from this distance.

I watched the sun set behind me and my beloved ship vanish into the dusk as I turned my head between breaths to look to the horizon. The sunset was mesmerizing and captivating. It was a natural and peaceful end to an unnatural and restless day. I felt entranced as I watched the sun kiss the earth's horizon. All day it had been impossible to determine where the horizon stopped and the sky started, but now the line was clear. In the daylight, embracing blues intertwined and sky and water melded into one. Now the horizon drew a line across the amber sun that backlit the earth. Intense rays of red, orange and yellow pierced the sky with intensity. Puffy white clouds became evident on the horizon in wake of the setting sunlight. I laughed to myself as I pretended the sun was plunging into the ocean and the clouds on either side were water splashing from the impact. I realized I was surrounded by the beauty of nature – and nothing else. It was a surreal feeling to know that it was me and a lot of nature. Of all the ways to die, this view was pretty good. Much better than a hospital bed or down the barrel of a murder's gun.

But I was not ready to drown or die here today.

East was the direction of flow and breeze. I would float all night and then stroke into the sunrise. As convicted of my goal as I was, I couldn't help but wonder if I could even swallow in the morning. My mouth was parched and my tongue was like a giant cotton ball in my mouth. What I wouldn't give for a sip of Fiji water. It didn't matter whether I could see the ship in the morning, my goal became surviving the night.

The last bit of the sun's purple, pink and orange hues subsided as the stars and a shroud of darkness set in. Rigor mortis also set in on my body. The sudden and abrupt extended rest coupled with dehydration tied my body into knots of cramps. A little yoga and meditation would do me good. My body hurt so bad. Pains and burning sensations radiated from my hands through my arms, shoulders and back. My legs also felt the same painful sensations. I rolled onto my back. I slowed my breathing into a long, controlled inhale and exhale rhythm. I floated easier than I had swum today. My fear was exhaustion. If I let sleep overpower me, I may sink. I was sure that if I took in one mouthful of water it would be enough to drown me at this point. I knew I had to stay awake and remain focused. I fixated on the stars. I tried to find the constellations and connect the dots. I wondered if my friends and family back in the States were looking up at the same stars right now wondering where I was. Or were they looking down at me from Heaven and the stars? I hoped they were still alive, but also pondered whether Heaven would be a better place for them now. I now felt like just letting go and sinking. Death had always been such a remote mystery that I never really pondered. Now I found myself wondering if it was so bad. I could be in the stars too in a minute. Or maybe I would be with my friends and family again. Maybe I had been to heaven and not realized it. Maybe Tahiti was heaven – or at least heaven on earth.

I think curiosity was the one driving force that kept me awake. The same curiosity about death and the afterlife, kept me avoiding it. I was too curious about what had transpired back home. I was curious about my own fate, but also curious how strong my will to survive could be. It became a fight within. How strong was my will to survive? I had always been driven and determined all of my life. However, there were still so many things that I had yet to experience. So many loose ends left untied back home. There were so many things I had meant to say to people but hadn't for whatever reason. I became determined to have one more chance to do those things. I appreciated life and my experiences too much. I couldn't give up. I wasn't ready to take a dive on a triple-overhead Mata Utu barrel as my brother had done. In fact, now I bore the burden of surviving for the both of us. I had to finish his legacy as well. I had to relay his story as well as mine. I had to care for his wife and his business if they were still there. I was disappointed that he had given up so easily, but I took solace in the fact that he had gone out the way he wanted to – surfing the big one.

So many childhood memories ran through my mind as I looked up at the stars. I remembered lying under these same stars with my brother when we were kids. We had so many dreams and aspirations. We accomplished so much, but never enough. I was proud of him. He had it made. Why did I take him away from it all? After all, it was my idea to take this damn trip. I twisted his arm and convinced him to come. If he had stayed home would he be alive now? Or would he have possibly died with his beloved wife? Or was it supposed to happen this way? Was he meant to die surfing – was that his destiny and the sole reason why he ended up going with me? At least I was there with him in his last minute of glory. I had silently protested, but supported his decision to launch off the point on his longboard for that one last ride. We both knew it was our last conversation. We both knew it was his last wave. We had a moment – an unspoken last goodbye that translated into "Walk, surf or swim – see you back at the boat, dude!". Now I found myself all alone in the middle of the same ocean he drowned in. It wasn't enough to think he was in this water with me. I needed a last moment – a goodbye with someone other than myself. It had to be my motivation to survive for now.

I breathed deeply – in and out in the same 8-10-12 fashion that started my day in the water. I could no longer feel my hands, arms, feet and legs. They hung loosely in the water as I lay floating on my back. The stars mesmerized me. An occasional shutter went through my body as if I was shivering from the

329

cold. I was pretty sure it wasn't cold, but I couldn't feel much sensation in my body. My limbs were cramped and numb from pain. A shark could bite my leg off and I doubt I would feel it. I had given 100% physical and mental effort today and now I had to give a different kind of effort to stay afloat all night. I had little energy, but a lot of will power. I now had a weak body, but a strong and determined mind. Sunrise would be around 6am. It would be a long ten hours of darkness. I knew if I could swim for 12 hours, I could float for 10 more. I wish I had slept during the storm the night before. I reckoned it had been about 40 hours since I had restful sleep. I was prepared to wait 40 more if that's what it took. I counted my breath in, hold and out. Stay awake man.

I traced the stars across the sky in their heavenly orbit. I was the highest point within sight. I was a mountain floating in a placid sea. I never had an outer body experience until this point in my life. First, I felt connected with space. I felt larger than life. I felt light and free. The stress of staying afloat subsided. It became easy. Everything became extremely easy and simple. I just wanted to turn my head or roll over and look down at myself. I knew I was floating, but it felt like on air instead of water. I felt like I was rising rather than sinking. I imagined myself lying on the water below and my soul levitating high above.

For the first time in my life I saw my soul crystal clear. All of my emotions came into sight. All of my motivations came to light. I felt enlighten and enriched. I grew ten times larger than life. I imagined turning upright and putting my feet down and touching the bottom of the ocean. I would be in chest deep water and I could walk back to the boat. No more swimming or floating. Solid something under my feet would make life so wonderful. My body lie there on its back floating in the glassy ocean water, legs dangled limp searching for the bottom, my mind pondered while my soul floated high above. I became very aware of my surroundings as I watched the stars rotate high in the sky above me. I was totally connected with nature and my body even though I couldn't feel my arms and legs. An awareness came over me and guided my focus and made me more determined to survive the night.

"Dead men tell no tales." I thought to myself. I had to survive to tell this tale. I also thought about all the unfinished business I had back home. By unfinished business I meant all of the things I wanted to say to my friends and family - if they were still alive. I wanted to tell my Mom "I love you" one more time. I wanted to tell Jasmin how Lance had mourned so deeply for her that he had to find a release. I wanted to kiss Claire and finally tell her how I really felt about her. I even wanted to tell Mr. Brooks that I had learned how to sail. I still wanted to do so much in life. I still wanted to know what happened back home. My disconnection and estrangement from home was too much for too long. Curiosity is driving me. I wanted to know if my loved ones are alive and well and thinking of me right now. I will be the knight in shining armor that will ride in on a white horse and save everyone. The only problem is that my 'white horse' just sailed away and left me. "I will survive" I thought. "I will live to tell this tale." I returned my focus to the stars and let my mind wander into space.

Thoughts of Hoku and the determination that he must have exuded when hiding out and fighting the Matains entered my mind. I imagined that he, like me, was on the brink of dehydration and starvation in that cave on Mount Mata. I recalled how rain clouds brought him water and a bird brought him food in

330

the gift of a fish. I remembered the importance of prayer and spirituality in his story of victory and decided to practice the same. I stared into the star-speckled ocean of black above me and began to pray.

"Lance, my dear brother. Please forgive me. I'm sorry that I could not save you in your time of need. I did what I thought best. I hope you are at peace and one with the sea that now engulfs me. Thank you for saving my life once and pulling me from the reef in Mata. I could really use another hand now. I promise to carry on our story. I promise to reach Jasmin and care for her if she is in need. I love you and miss you bro." I sighed as I exhaled deeply. I felt my chest sink as the air exited my lungs and then resurface with my next inhalation. I drew in a deeper breath as if to inhale the heaven and stars into me. I felt my chest rise up higher this time with the influx of breath. I wished I could breathe myself out of my body and float above in the sky. "Hoku - if you are listening please send me some determination. Your story inspired me. I believe in you like you believed in yourself. I too feel like you must have felt. I left the friendly paradise in Rahiti to travel into the unknown to free my family and friends from death and oppression. I have no idea what I will find when I return to my country much like you had no idea what to expect in Mata. You were alone in unfamiliar nature fighting an unfamiliar enemy. I am alone fighting for survival in nature. Please, God, please Hoku, please Lance send me the strength I need to survive this ordeal. Please help. Send me water, send me food, send me wings so that I may be able to fly out of here. Anything, please."

I drifted from prayer into a meditative state. I focused on my breathing. I would exhale and my chest and upper body would sink to the brink of submerging my face. Then when the salt water was about to enter my nose, I would inhale deeply until my chest rose skyward again. I counted the seconds between breaths and continued a rhythm through the night.

There are dreams and reality and sometimes the two intertwine. Such was the case when I caught first glimpse of sunrise. I am not sure whether I was sleeping, in a trance or even conscious, but to my utter amazement I "awoke" in a rhythmic and controlled state of breathing – and had survived. I had forgotten the last breath number I took and had absolutely no idea whether I had slept 5 seconds, 5 minutes or five hours. I felt paralyzed and could have been dead for all I knew. I wiggled my fingers and toes and much to my delight they all worked and had slight sensation, although distorted by cramps and pain. The pins and needle sensation of a limb "falling asleep" overwhelmed my whole body. Dehydrated and delirious, I leaned forward to achieve an upright position in the water. The blinding light of the rising sun was to my back. Oh what I wouldn't give for my pair of polarized sunglasses – the glare from the water was brutal on my blue eyes. I squinted and turned my body to face the burgeoning sun. My eyes adjusted to greet the sun in salutation and appreciation of survival of the night. The sunset was much more beautiful and tolerable. After being in the sun all day, your eyes are accustomed to the full spectrum of light. After being in the pitch dark of the night in the middle of the sea, it doesn't take much light to absolutely blind you. I squinted and winced. You never fully appreciate a great pair of sunglasses until you don't have them when you need them.

I squinted, my eyes were swollen from almost 24 hours in the salt water, but they started to adjust. I couldn't believe what my strained eyes saw. Surely I was hallucinating. Less than 100 feet away was the bow of the ship pointing directly at me. Adrenaline gushed up from within me. I tried to stroke, but couldn't lift my arms. I know there are mirages in the desert, but the ocean too? This couldn't be the ship. The odds of the ship ending up back at me had to be one in a million. Of all the directions and all of the water in the ocean… the ship was right here – about to run over me! The flag on the ship and the rising of the sun indicated an easterly wind. The prevailing westerly wind had shifted 180 degrees to the east. The wind that had taunted me and pushed the ship away all day yesterday had turned exactly in my favor and brought it right back to me. It was unbelievable. I told myself that I would not get my hopes up until I actually touched the hull of the ship and felt it for real. After all, I was delirious and probably hallucinating. I tried again to muster up the energy to pull a stroke or two, but could not. My arms would not function properly. I was paralyzed from the shoulders down. I rolled onto my back and began to kick gently, rolling my body from side to side to keep the ship in the corner of my eyes. I then felt an exhilaration run through me as the ship cast its shadow on me. Seconds later I turned over as the ship bumped into me at about 2 or 3 knots. My heart jumped a few beats and for the first time since my brother died, I cried.

I kissed the hull and slid my hands from the peak of the bow down the starboard side. I let my body press against the hull. I wanted to maintain as much contact as possible. I couldn't believe it was real. In my excitement, I realized I needed to accept the fact that it was real and quickly devise a plan to get on board and make use of my seemingly useless arms.

There was no way to enter the boat deck from the bow, so I slid down the hull as the ship gently glided by me. No sheets or guy lines were hanging in the water to grab and there was no way that my limp arms could extend to reach the life line, so my plan was to glide down the hull of the ship and then grab the ladder on the rear deck. As the ship glided by me, I stayed in contact with the hull until I came to the aft where I knew I would ultimately lose contact as the ship passed me. I attempted to reach out for the ladder which I had habitually and thankfully lowered before my dip yesterday morning, but I could not reach it. My arms would not come out of the water. A gentle side to side arm motion was all that I could muster up. I was about to miss a miracle opportunity as the ship passed me. I tried to press my hands on the bottom of the hull, but my wax job from months prior proved to still be in effect as the hull was too slick to gain any friction. As the ship passed, I made one last ditch effort and in an undulating fashion kicked my whole body porpoise style to give me enough momentum to tail the ship for a second. I reached deep on the rear of the stern and hooked my limp arm on the rudder just a foot or so under the water. The strain on my arm was painful, but touching something solid and no longer floating was a tremendous relief to the rest of my body.

I held onto the rudder with my right arm, but my arm had no strength. I leveraged my bent elbow to take the strain. The angle of my body forced my face close to the water. The wake of the ship sent water splashing into my face. I tried to time the wake and subsequent splashes with my breathing, but it was too random. How ironic that I had survived a 12 hour swim and 10 hour float, but now holding onto the very ship that I had been chasing was likely to drown me in its wake. Hooking my right arm through the rudder had turned my body to the left. The dangling ladder was visible in my peripheral vision about 5 feet to the right. I knew my body was 6'4" long, but I tried to figure how it would be possible to extend my body to the ladder without letting go of the rudder. My body was trailing the ship in its wake. Although the ship's movement was slow, any speed was faster than I could swim at this point. If I let go of the rudder even for a second, the ship would once again leave me alone in the water.

I wanted to rest and regain some strength and energy now that I had something solid to hold onto and no longer had to focus on floating. My plan may have worked, however, the constant wake in the face wouldn't allow me to catch my breath or relax. I had to do something soon, or I would be forced to let go – or drown. If only I still had the lanyard attached to my body. I could lasso it up to the life-line post or something and secure myself to the ship or at least clip it to the rudder. I didn't have that option. I tried to wiggle the fingers on my left hand, but they were extremely weak. I thought maybe I could let the rudder slide down my arm and grasp it with my hand to put a little more distance between my face and the water, but I doubted my hand was strong enough to grasp and hold it. My bent arm and locked elbow was barely doing the job. The ship hit a wave and sent a big wake under the hull and right into my face. I took a lot of water into my nose and mouth. I choked and wretched in pain and momentarily let my arm-lock loose. I almost lost my hold completely, but recovered at the last second. One more wake like that would certainly drown me.

I wasn't ready to drown yet. I hadn't fought hard for 24 hours and been given a miracle opportunity with the return of my ship only to drown now. If only I had swum one less stroke yesterday – would I have one more stroke in me today to propel me from the rudder to the ladder. I tried to curl my lower body up into a fetal position close to the rudder and then kick my legs out straight toward the ladder. I thought maybe I could hook my foot in the rung of the ladder. I was wrong. It was not physically possible. Multiple attempts proved to be futile. I felt the bow of the ship raise and momentum slow as the ship encountered another wave. I knew a wake and a face full of water was a second or so away.

In a split second decision, I let go of the rudder and pushed my body off in a twisting motion. I spun 180 degrees and lurched forward against the current. I kicked my legs in a porpoise fashion. A sudden burst of adrenaline and will power thrust my arms out straight overhead. I dove into the water in the direction of the ladder. I broke under the surface of the water just as the wake passed the aft of the ship. My momentum carried me back up to the surface past the wake, but well short of the ladder. I dove again and thrust my body hard with another porpoise kick and thrust my arms out overhead in a butterfly fashion. This time my hands hit the bottom rung on the ladder – hard, but I felt no pain. I locked my fingers around the rung with every ounce of energy in my body. I kicked hard and pulled my arms harder. I brought my body perpendicular to the ladder and forced my lifeless left arm to reach up to the third ladder rung. I extended the left side of my body and grabbed and pulled until I lifted myself out of the water and onto the ladder. 6 rungs and I crawled onto the rear deck. I had truly just spent the last remaining calories and adrenaline in my body. I convulsed and my body shuttered. My mind reeled in the reality that I was now back on the ship.

I wanted to shout out in joy, but my lips were swollen shut and my mouth was too dry. I wanted to cry tears of happiness, but my dehydrated body had no tears left in it. I needed water and rest. The need for both was immediate, but the rest was more overwhelming. I fought to keep consciousness as I lay on the deck. I tried to sit upright, but couldn't muster the strength.

Where was my water? I looked to the steering console less than 10 feet away, but did not see the familiar Fiji water bottle there. It was a long way to crawl to the cabin and I would have to navigate the steps down into the cabin if I wanted water. I knew I needed to drink immediately before I passed out from dehydration. I knew I also needed to get off of the back deck platform of the ship and into the safety of the main deck before I rolled off of the ship in another wake. I began to crawl onto the deck. I took a couple of baby crawl strokes and then took a break. I smiled with my pain.

I had somehow done it. I made it back to the ship. Now I just had to make it to some water and then get some sleep. Everything else could wait. I may sleep for days after this ordeal. I just had to get water before I slept. I managed to crawl up and over the aft life line and onto the main deck. A ten foot crawl had seemed like an eternity. I took a break and caught my breath. I tried to summon my legs to work, but they remained limp and lifeless. I knew I had to make it below deck to reach my water. I crawled through the cockpit to the stairwell leading below. I needed a drink of water and my bed. I pushed myself to continue down the steps. I crawled head first and used my weak arms to pull my heavy water-logged body into the stairwell. The sudden rush of blood to my head sent me into a state of vertigo as I fell down the stairs and crashed into the deck below.

The last thing I remember is seeing my precious bottle of Fiji water sitting on the table in the galley. I passed out in the floor less than 5 feet from the water from a combination of the impact from the fall, exhaustion and dehydration. That bottle of water is the last thing I remember seeing.

The Return

I awoke briefly in a semi-conscious state as I felt a hand on my forehead. My eyes stayed shut and I heard a muted sound in the distance. I felt nauseous and pain enveloped my body. My head was pounding and the noise in my ears contributed to the mental stress. I felt like I had a monkey with a tambourine constantly clanking in my head. I knew the fall and the dehydration had really taken its toll on me. I needed to get up and get some water. I needed to stretch somehow and relieve my limbs of the cramps that bound them. I needed to check my coordinates and find out exactly how far I had drifted. I needed to get into bed. My mind wanted to get up, but my body wanted to stay in its supine position on the floor. My mind and body continued the debate as I passed in and out of consciousness.

I felt a hand on my head again - this time it ran through my hair. I was hallucinating. It could have been my own hand for all I knew. I didn't have control over my limbs and the sensation in them was minimal. I wiggled the fingers on my right hand. Surprisingly, they responded. I pressed my palm against the deck to try to push myself upright into a seated position. My fingers sank into softness and my hand felt grass instead of wood decking. Perplexed, I rubbed a blade of grass between my thumb and index finger.

I felt a hand on my face for sure this time. Was I dead? Was Saint Peter himself caressing my face to comfort me as I passed into the afterlife? Was I lying on a grassy knoll in front of the gates of heaven waiting for access to be granted by the almighty?

I squinted my forehead to my cheeks as if to jump start my eyes open. I released the muscle tension in my scalp and forced my eyes open. Bright light seared into my eye sockets. I expected to see the familiar deck head ceiling and confines of the galley on the Mareva; however I was looking up at bright blue sky filled with puffy white clouds - and trees overhead. What the hell? If this was a dream, death would have been more realistic.

"Are you going to sleep all day, sleepyhead?" I heard a female voice say in close proximity. I opened my eyes fully and rolled onto my side and came face to face with - Claire!

I sprang upright into a seated position. "Claire?!" I exclaimed.

"Yes, honey - who were you expecting?" She replied coolly.

My head was truly spinning for multiple reasons at this point. "I...I..." I couldn't speak. I couldn't formulate a thought. I glanced around. I was at the terminal in Richmond. I was on the bank of the James River on my secret grassy spot. The noise that was ringing in my ears was the sound of Jims' crane operating close by on the dock. "Claire? I... what... happened?" I stammered as I asked.

"I think you were having a bad dream baby. You were tossing and turning all night. I tried to wake you several times, but you were sleeping like a log." She said as she caressed my arm.

I tried to stand up but vertigo got the best of me and I decided to remain seated for a moment. "What is today?" I asked.

"It's Sunday, silly." She replied as she rolled her eyes and shook her head at me in disbelief.

"Sunday? When Sunday?" I asked again.

"Ok, Stan you are freaking me out a little. It's the Sunday after your party - whatever day that was." Her face grimaced with concern over my question.

"How much did I drink?" Was the only thing I could think to ask to quell the situation.

"No more than me I would guess. We were pretty much one for one since I was fetching us both drinks most of the night - unless you snuck away with the guys and one-upped me." She quipped.

"How do you feel?" I asked her.

"I feel great - how about you?"

"Not so hot. I feel like I got hit by a bus." My words came out slightly slurred and I struggled to swallow. The truth was that my body swayed and felt as if it were being rocked by the ocean under a sailboat. My tongue stuck to the roof of my mouth and my mouth felt as dry as if it were full of cotton balls. "Do we have any water?" I asked.

"Not with us here. I'm sure you have a bottle or two in your truck as usual. I'd go get it for you, but I'm not quite sure how to get back up to the lot since you carried me down the trail in the dark. Are you okay honey?" She asked with growing concern.

"No." I answered as I tried to regain my composure. I got immediate tunnel vision and my ears starting throbbing as my head began to spin wildly. I passed out and my head landed in the soft grass. I could feel Claire shaking me in an attempt to revive me. I could hear her frantically calling my name, but I couldn't respond. Darkness filled my eyes and the ringing in my ears became more distant.

The next sensation I felt was water pouring over my face. My reaction was to gasp for air. I'm not sure if it was the mammalian diving reflex kicking in or if it was the sensation of floating on my back and breathing deep to stay afloat in the water all night. I didn't care what the source of the water was. My mouth was so dry that I could barely open it wide enough to allow the cool, refreshing liquid to enter it. I swallowed rapidly in spite of my mouth's inability to function properly. The water was refreshing and

336

momentarily revitalized me and brought me back to my senses. I felt someone lifting my shoulders from behind.

"Sit up and have a drink." A male voice said.

I didn't immediately recognize the voice, but I tried to comply with the instruction. I opened my eyes again to see Claire crouched in front of me with a Fiji Water bottle in one hand and the cap to it in the other hand. Both the water bottle and the sight of Claire were refreshing. She put the bottle to my lips and I drank like I had never drunk before. The water cut through the dryness in my mouth and brought hydration to my body. The sensation was heavenly. I told myself that I was truly in heaven. My prayers were answered. I had water - and Claire right in front of me. "Thank you Lance, thank you Hoku, thank you universe, thank you God." I thought to myself. I chugged the water until the bottle was empty. I turned my head slightly and saw a black hand on my shoulder.

"Are you okay Stan?" Clyde asked.

"I'm not sure guys. Give me a minute." I answered. I looked around at the familiar view from my secret spot. I looked to my left and could see Jim's crane operating in the distance. The huge cargo ship was also visible through the trees.

Clyde noticed I was looking over at the ship. "Connie has already been loaded onboard this morning. The ship leaves in an hour or two. I got the envelope containing the key and the bill of lading that you must have slid under my office door last night." Clyde said as he patted my back.

I didn't immediately respond. Either I had just experienced the most vivid dream of my life or I was experiencing death and reincarnation. Whatever the case may be, I was ecstatic to be here right now. I sat there smiling looking at Claire and the river in front of me.

"What happened to him last night? Did he finish off the rest of the beer by himself after I left the party last night?" Clyde asked Claire.

"No, not at all. We slid away from the party before it was totally finished. There were still a few people lingering and waiting for the limos to return to pick them up. We said our goodbyes to everyone who remained and thanked them for coming. Stan said he had something he wanted to show me. He picked me up on his back and carried me down to this spot." She answered.

"Did he fall or hit his head on a tree branch on the way down here?" Clyde asked.

"No, not that I am aware of. He was very alert and very fine. In fact we sat here and talked for quite some time and then we... well, never mind what we did then." She said as she blushed slightly.

"That must have been some really good... whatever you did!" Clyde exclaimed.

"We laid here and looked up at the stars and talked for a while afterward. Stan fell asleep before me. I awoke a couple of times because he was sleeping restlessly as if he were having a nightmare. I tried to wake him up to go home several times, but he was in deep sleep. I was comfortable in his arms and enjoyed being in nature, so I just let him sleep." She continued.

How could it be? I thought to myself. I looked down at my familiar party outfit that I was wearing. I scanned Claire from head to toe and recognized her knee-high autumn-colored party dress and high heels that she wore. Her hair looked as perfect as if she had just stepped out of the salon. I scratched my head and pondered the situation. I leaned forward and shifted my weight onto my heels. "Help me up, please." I requested of Clyde.

Clyde gripped me under the armpits and counted to three. With his help, I was standing in no time. My legs burned and tingled with pain as if they were 'asleep'. I felt like I had run a marathon - or swam for an entire day. I wobbled a little and almost fell forward onto Claire. "Easy now." Clyde said as he steadied me from behind. "Claire, you take his left arm and I will take the right." Clyde said as he put my right arm over his left shoulder. Claire did the same with my left arm and then they interlocked arms. We made our way up the bank and through the trail in the woods arm in arm. Each step was painful and laborious.

I had been hung over many times in my life, but had never experienced anything like this. "What time is it?" I asked.

"About 8 am." Clyde answered. "What time is the cleanup crew coming?" He asked.

I thought for a moment. "9 or so I believe." I answered. That was the time which I recalled I had arranged for everyone to meet here in the morning. The memories of the party, the terminal, Clyde and Claire were fresh in my mind although it seemed like this 'deja-vu' had happened an eternity ago. "Is anyone from the party still here?" I asked.

"Nope, not that I have seen. Look, why don't you and Claire go home and get some rest. I will handle things when the cleanup crew gets here in the morning." Clyde offered. I couldn't help but accept his offer.

"I will drive him home in his truck. Will my car be okay here for now?" Claire asked.

"Not a problem at all. Just leave me the keys in case I have to move it. I will be here all day so you can come back whenever to get it - even if it is tomorrow." Clyde said.

We made our way across the parking lot and my eyes wandered from the beer truck to the stage. I noticed that Connie was no longer behind the stage; however everything else still remained from the party.

"I'm sorry you are not feeling well this morning Stan. But that was one hell of a party last night - definitely the best party I have ever been to in my life. That Mista Beat guy was awesome!" Clyde said with an excited tone in his voice.

"I'm glad you liked it." I said as I struggled to walk. My truck was on the far side of the parking lot and every step felt like a mile. I couldn't wait to get there and sit down.

Clyde held me upright as Claire opened up the passenger door. I grabbed the handle on the A-pillar of the truck and pulled myself into the seat with a little help from Clyde. I reclined the seat slightly as Claire shut the door. Claire remained outside the truck and talked to Clyde for a bit. I heard her reassuring him that she could handle me and that everything would be fine. I reached into my pocket and dug out my cell phone. I looked at it to see if I had any messages or missed calls, but the screen was blank. I hit the power button, but the battery didn't have enough juice left to power the phone up. I leaned forward and plugged it into the car charger in the dash. I gave it a minute to charge. From my upright seated position I looked out across the cargo yard. I almost dropped a load when I saw the big blue container bearing the name 'Hamburg' in orange text. I opened the truck door and called Clyde back to the truck as he was about to walk away.

"Clyde, look man - this is going to sound strange, but when did that container come into port?" I asked as I pointed directly to the Hamburg box.

Clyde looked perplexed. "I believe it came in on the same cargo ship that Connie is leaving on. I think it was one of the last boxes that Jim unloaded this morning. Why do you ask?"

"So that box was definitely not there in that spot yesterday before the party?" I inquired.

"Nope, if it wasn't still on the ship, it wasn't there. Jim may have unloaded it yesterday or Friday, but it must have been relocated to that spot today. Why do you ask?" He repeated.

"I don't know. I want you to check the manifest for its origin. I want you to call the FBI and have them come inspect the contents of the box. Please just trust me - and please promise me you won't open the box before they get here." I urged of him.

"Stan, what has gotten into you man? Are you sure you didn't hit your head?"

"I'm really not sure what has gotten into me, Clyde. I just have a hunch. That's all. Have the FBI scan the box for radioactivity before they open the box. I believe there is a nuclear bomb inside that container." I whispered to him.

"You have lost your mind, Stan. Go get some rest." Clyde chuckled as he dismissed the request.

I grabbed him by the arm before he could shut the truck door. "Seriously, promise me that you will do it." I pleaded with him as I looked him square in the eyes.

"Ok, I will do it. I promise." He nodded with acceptance as he shut the truck door and walked back to his post.

Claire entered the driver side of the truck. "So what was that all about?" She asked.

"I'm really not sure." I responded. "I just had the craziest dream of my life. I want to be safer than sorry. I'm sure it's nothing, but it's worth checking out."

"Ok, whatever you say Stan." She said with frustration.

She started up the truck and as we pulled out of the parking lot I signaled with my hand for Clyde to make the call. He gave me the thumbs up. Speaking of calling, I powered up my cell phone and checked for messages. No new messages - that was odd. I dialed Lance's number. There were a million things I wanted to say to him, but the phone just rang and rang before going to voice mail. I left him a message. "Dude, call me immediately and let me know you made it home safe." I said on the message. "Damn, I wonder why he didn't answer." I said to Claire.

"Didn't he say he was going to paddle out for a damn patrol surf session this morning?" She asked.

"Yeah, that's right. He did." I recalled.

"Well, there you go. He is in the water right now. I'm sure everything is fine." She assured me. "What's gotten you so rattled this morning? You are not the calm, cool Stan I know."

"It's a long story, Claire. I'm not myself right now and don't want to talk about it. Just give me a bit." I said as I reached over and turned reggae music up.

My stomach had constant butterflies. My mind was reeling. My legs and arms were cramped in painful knots. What in the world was going on? By my best recollection a couple of hours ago I was in the water in the middle of the ocean struggling for survival. Less than an hour ago I was climbing aboard the Mareva desperately trying to get to my water. Suddenly I awake in Richmond and am riding home in my truck with Claire? Wow.

We got home in no time. Claire parked and instructed me to wait until she could come around to the passenger side to help me out of the truck. She opened my door and helped me slide out of the seat and plant my feet on the ground. She supported me as we walked to my home/office door. She handed me the keys and I fumbled through the key ring in search of the door key. "Shit, where is my damn key?" I said with frustration.

"Didn't you give it to your friends last night so that they could stay here?" She reminded me.

340

"Oh yeah." I said as if I remembered clearly.

"You really aren't yourself this morning. You need a hot bath, some water, food rest." She proclaimed.

"Agreed." I said.

"So how are we going to get inside?" She asked.

"Keypad on the garage door. The code is 'tikihut'." I said.

"Okay, can you make it or do you want to wait here while I go and open it?"

"I can make it." I put one arm around her shoulders and hobbled to the rear of the building. She entered the code and the door opened. We walked inside and found everything in perfect order as I had last remembered it with the exception of a thank you note from Ron on the kitchen counter. It read: "Thanks for the amazing party and your hospitality. Took the girls home this morning, but will hang around town for a while. Give us a holla if you wanna catch brunch. Ron." The key was lying on the note. I guess he figured I had a spare or could enter with the garage door opener.

"I will fill the hot tub for you and then make a snack." Claire said as she handed me a water bottle and helped me sit on the couch. She returned momentarily with a handful of crackers. "Eat these and take it easy for a bit. I'll check on the tub in a little while."

I sat there on the couch while the tub filled. Claire ran her fingers through my hair and rubbed my scalp. "I'm here for you - anything you need." She said in her comforting voice.

"Thanks, I'm so glad to be with you." I said as I focused my eyes on her beautiful face. Her beauty was the only thing that was certain to me at this point. She reminded me of Maruia in so many ways.

She helped me up and into the bathroom as the tub was done filling. "Do you need help getting in?" She asked.

"No, I actually prefer to be alone for a bit." I answered.

"Ok, call me if you need anything." She said as she rubbed my back and left me leaning on the bathroom sink.

I stood there looking at my face in the bathroom mirror. I had bags under my eyes and looked as if I hadn't slept in a week. I splashed some cool water on my face and then drank from the faucet. I looked over at the steam filled Jacuzzi tub and the bubbling water inside. I knew the bath was what I needed to relax me, but for some reason I had no desire to be in the water. I fought my resistance to bathe as I began to strip down. My hands shook as I unbuttoned my shirt. When the last button was undone, I let the shirt slide from my shoulders and fall to the floor revealing my well tanned upper body. I then unfastened my belt and unbuttoned and unzipped my pants letting them fall to the floor around my ankles. I held onto the sink top to steady myself as I stepped from the legs of my pants. I lifted each foot and kicked myself free of the pants. I turned to the tub and took a deep breath as I decided to take a dip. I bent my left leg and lifted it to step into the tub enclosure.

I am a firm believer that there are things in life that simply have no explanation. Such was the case when I looked down at my leg as it slid into the bubbling water. I recoiled my leg from the hot water in the tub and drew it back into a bent position and planted my foot firmly on the side of the Jacuzzi. It wasn't the heat of the tub that shocked my senses as much as the sight that my weary eyes beheld. I looked down in utter amazement at the scar above my left knee. I reached down and ran my finger over the divot in my thigh from the chunk that was missing from my leg. Images of the wipeout and the reef impact in Mata Utu came flooding into my mind. I shook my head in disbelief as I tried to make sense of the sight. I looked closer at the small alternating scars on either side of the divot. The scars could only be the result of an amateur Rahitian surgeon who had stitched the wound with love and a primitive needle and thread. Memories of Maruia as she held my hand and Lance and Hoanui as they restrained me during the surgery flashed through my mind. I was awestruck. My head began to spin and dizziness came over me. I tried to compose myself, but couldn't reconcile the situation. I panicked, but found resolve in a quote I found in my mind. "The only answer is that sometimes there are no answers. There are things in life we cannot and will not understand. The power of the mind can be one of them."

"Claire! Claire! Claaaaairrrrre!" I shouted with urgent desperation in my voice.

Within seconds the bathroom door flung open and Claire rushed in quickly. "Yes, honey? Are you okay?" She asked as she grabbed my arm.

I put my foot on the floor, turned and braced myself against the wall. I stood naked in front of Claire and quickly composed myself. "There is something I have to tell you." I said with seriousness in my shaking voice.

"Yes, what is it baby?" She urged as she looked into my eyes with great concern as she still grasp my arm firmly.

I gazed back into her beautiful green eyes and, for a moment, I felt like I was experiencing a second chance – even heaven on earth. I cleared my throat, took a deep breath and said "I love you."

Made in the USA
Charleston, SC
05 February 2013